WEAP

WEAPON OF FLESH TRILOGY II
BOOK 2

BY
CHRIS A. JACKSON
AND
ANNE L. MCMILLEN-JACKSON

ILLUSTRATIONS BY
NOAH STACEY

Dedication

For all our fans, friends, and family who have supported us in this series, we thank you. Without you, we would not be doing what we love most.

Acknowledgements

We would like to thank Noah Stacey once again for the wonderful cover art, and our readers for suggestions on plots and characters.

WEAPON OF PAIN
WEAPON OF FLESH TRILOGY II
BOOK 2

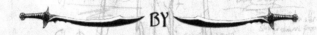

BY

CHRIS A. JACKSON
AND
ANNE L. MCMILLEN-JACKSON

ISBN-13 978-1-939837-15-8

JAXBOOKS.COM

PROLOGUE

I am in so much trouble...

Dee watched Mya slip from his bed, his hands already lonelier for the loss of her touch. His gaze lingered on the runic tattoos that danced on her sweat-slicked skin as she bent to pick up her robe.

"Would you like to touch them?" she had asked an hour earlier.

How could any sane man have said no?

"I need to be touched," she had said. "I need someone to make me feel...human."

Why did I ever say yes?

After years as her assistant, owing her his life, how could he deny her? Truth be told, he had often entertained fantasies of he and Mya together, but never dreamed that it could happen.

"I'm not in love with you, Dee."

Her words had been as cold and sharp as a sword's edge. No blade could have cut him deeper, but he had smiled through the pain, lost in the dream. Then he was touching her, tasting her, pouring himself into her like wine into a glass. And when he had no more to give, Mya had coaxed him into giving more. Dee had lost himself in her...and that was the problem.

Gods, I'm in trouble.

Mya donned her robe, leaving only the unmarked flesh of her face, hands, and feet visible. Wadding up the enchanted wrappings that she wore to conceal her tattoos, she turned to face him. "Thank you, Dee."

Dee's stomach clenched at the casual dismissal, the same tone she used when he drafted letters for her. *What does she see when she looks at me? A friend, a lover...or just an underling to be thanked for a job well done?*

A smile flicked across her lips, the only part of her he hadn't tasted. When he had tried, she'd turned away. Mya accepted his

1

passion, but nothing as personal as a kiss.

"Mya, you don't have to—"

"I do." She jerked tight the robe tie. "I just…want you to know that this meant something to me. I needed it. Thank you."

His heart ached at the thought that their intimacy had meant so much more to him than it had to her. Dee smiled through the pain, and his mouth moved without thought. "It was my pleasure." *Stupid…*

Her smile widened to a full-on grin. "I *thought* you were enjoying yourself. Well…I better grab a bath and sleep."

"Do you want me to watch over you?" He forced his languid muscles into action, reaching for his trousers as he swung his legs out of the bed and stood. "You shouldn't go alone."

"You're right, but…" She shook her head. "Forget it. I'll bathe in the morning."

"All right." He dropped back onto the bed, his knees quivering, his loins aching in testimony to his efforts to fulfill her every desire. "I'll help you with your gown for the coronation."

"Good." Mya reached for the door, but looked back again. "Thank you, Dee. I mean it. You've made me feel…human again."

Dee wanted to scream, "Stop *thanking* me! You're more than just human, Mya. You're beautiful and strong and brilliant and sensual, and I could fall in love with you in a heartbeat!" Of course, he couldn't say that, couldn't tell her how he really felt. This was *Mya*, after all—his boss, the Grandmaster of the Assassins Guild.

"Any time." Dee cursed himself as the words fell from his lips. *Like a man strapped to a rack taunting his inquisitor…*

"I may just take you up on that." Mya smiled again before opening the door and stepping through, quiet as a ghost. The latch closed with a click.

Dee collapsed back on the bed, closing his eyes to relive the last hour. Her scent redolent on his sheets and her taste sharp on his tongue, he imagined Mya still with him, his fingers still dancing across her smooth, tattooed skin.

"You're an idiot, Dee."

Dee knew he should sleep. Tomorrow was the coronation, and he had to help Mya with her gown and send her off. *Off to fight an archmage, maybe even to die…* And it had been *his* suggestion. It would have been easier to watch her walk into that peril tomorrow if she hadn't come to his room tonight, but what was done was done. *Who knows, maybe I just saved her life.* She needed to sleep and she certainly would now.

"Why did you do it, Dee?" He considered the question honestly, and the answer was simple. She'd needed him, truly *needed* him. Dee had been able to give her what no one else could—not Paxal, not her urchins, not even Lad. She was still in love with Lad, of that he had no doubt, but Dee owed Mya his life and loyalty. If all she needed from him was sex, that was fine. He could provide it unwaveringly.

She need never know what he truly felt for her.

CHAPTER I

Mya woke reluctantly, clinging to a dream of music, laughter, and dancing.

She smiled. Not a dream, but a memory. *I saved a crown prince's life yesterday and danced with a newly crowned emperor.* Before she could dwell on her triumph, the recollection of her subsequent failure crushed her spirit like a bug under a boot heel. The image of Lady T's blank, soulless eyes rose to mind, shadowed by a dark mist dissipating in the breeze.

Hoseph—gods damn him to the pits of the lowest hell!

The murdering priest had killed Lady T only moments after she'd acknowledged Mya as the Grandmaster of the Assassins Guild. The Tsing guildmaster had been the lynchpin she needed to secure control over the guild throughout the empire. Where Tsing led, all the outlying guilds would follow. Mya had worked for weeks to win Lady T's recognition at the cost of time, money, and innocent lives. She sobered as she pictured Tiny's shroud-covered body.

This is all Hoseph's fault! There was no doubt in Mya's mind that he was trying to turn the rest of the guild against her, even as she lay there in bed.

Over my dead body.

She had to take control of the Tsing guild, and she had to do it quickly.

So get to it!

As Mya flung off the sheet, a knock sounded at her door and Paxal's voice grated, "Breakfast, Miss Mya."

His usual preternatural timing... How often had the old innkeeper known what Mya wanted before she even asked for it?

"Down in a minute." Mya swung her feet to the floor and flashed a smile to her night watch.

Twigs sat cross legged against the wall beside the bed. Stretching out one foot, he prodded Gimp, who lay asleep. The little girl's eyes popped open and she struggled to sit up, her crooked leg sticking out at an awkward angle.

"Morning, Miss Mya." They grinned at her as they rose, hefting crossbows nearly as big as they were.

"Did you two get any sleep?"

"We took turns," Twigs declared proudly.

"And no whispering," Gimp promised. Though the urchins had been watching over her every night since she had enlisted their help, they sometimes talked too much and slept too little. Since Hoseph's first deadly attack, they had buckled down on their vigilance. "You?"

"Yes, thanks to you two." That wasn't exactly true, but her insomnia wasn't their fault.

Mya stretched and considered what to wear. Though she would have preferred to slip into trousers, a blouse, and a pair of soft boots, the constables had told her that someone would be by this morning to question her further about Lady T's murder.

As if they didn't ask enough questions last night. She sighed as she pushed aside one outfit after another. Avoiding the finery she had donned as Mrs. Addington when she and Lad had first arrived in Tsing, and the matronly clothes she had worn as Madame Bouchard the orphanage director, she settled on a simple dress, something that Moirin the bodyguard might wear. Finally ready, she motioned to the door. "Come on. I can smell the bacon from up here!"

"Don't have to tell *us* twice!" Twigs chirped with another grin.

They ventured out, Mya twisting and bending through the maze of taut catgut that webbed the hallway. The precaution had proven effective against Hoseph's ability to materialize out of thin air. The hallway still smelled of smoke from the priest's last ill-fated visit, the floor stained with fire and the blood of his mercenaries.

Another door opened, and Knock stepped out. The burly little crossbreed girl smiled, her single tusk jutting up from her crooked teeth. She smacked a hefty axe handle against the palm of her hand. "Knock!"

Nestor followed, gripping his crossbow tight in his small hands and bobbing his head at Mya. Then Dee…

Mya smiled as she met her assistant's eyes, shivering as she remembered their time together the night before the coronation.

5

With his help, she'd slept like the dead and woken refreshed. *Maybe I should have waylaid him last night, too.* Though it had been nearly midnight when the constables finally left, she had lain awake half the night worrying.

"Morning, Dee."

"Miss Mya." He matched her smile and followed her down the stairs. "More constables today?"

"Yes, and I'm trying to keep all my lies straight. I've used four pseudonyms in the past month, and it's getting hard to remember which name to answer to. Talk about a tangled web!" She plucked one of the taut strings and set a bell to chiming. To avoid setting off a panic in response to the tinkling alarm, she called out, "No worries, it's just me!"

"No doubt." Dee stepped over the last tripwire and followed her down the hall toward the back door and the kitchen. "The question is: what happens now?"

Mya opened her mouth to answer as she turned into the kitchen, but Paxal cut her off.

"No, the *question* is: will you two shut your yaps long enough to eat?" He hefted a huge skillet mounded with fried potatoes, onion, pepper, garlic, and thick bacon—enough to feed a small army—from the stove to the table, placing it next to the stack of plates and pile of forks. The smell was euphoric. "Now eat, or I'll hire the cook back and you'll be eating that slop of a porridge she makes for breakfast!" He started loading plates and handing them out.

"And I thought you couldn't cook." Mya accepted a plate and a thick slab of warm bread and sat down at the table, as did Dee, while the urchins took their plates and happily sat on the floor. The former inn also had a large dining room with plenty of seating, but it wasn't as informal—or as easy to defend—as the cozy kitchen. She poured blackbrew into a cup and lightened it with milk.

"This ain't proper cookin', but it'll do." Paxal scraped the last of the breakfast onto his own plate, then sat at the table and slathered butter onto a steaming slice of bread.

"It's proper enough for me," Dee mumbled around a mouthful. Swallowing, he took a gulp of blackbrew, then looked at Mya and repeated his question. "So, what happens now? With the masters, I mean. You *know* Hoseph probably got to them all before your messengers did."

"Yes, I know." She'd thought about that long and hard last night and come to a simple conclusion. "We wait for their answers. I've got to deal with the constables this morning."

Dee's brow furrowed. "And if they answer with an all-out attack instead of a polite note?"

"Then they're dumber than I think they are." Mya wiggled her finger in the air, the ebony and gold Grandmaster's ring glinting in the light. "They can't touch me."

"Hoseph can."

"Yes, but he's got to assume we're expecting him. He should know better than to attack again with us wary. He's tried twice and both times nearly got himself killed. Although..." Mya cocked her head as she thought. "The attacks *didn't* seem particularly well planned. A well-trained assassin would at least have had a contingency plan."

"Hoseph's not a well-trained assassin..." Dee looked thoughtful. "In fact, he's not an assassin at all, at least, not a *guild* assassin. He was just the Grandmaster's messenger."

"The Right Hand of Death." Mya considered Hoseph's self-proclaimed title. The man certainly had an ego; she just had to figure out how to use it against him.

"Well, he *should* be wary, but never underestimate someone's capacity for stupidity." Though Dee's sarcasm was obvious, there was something to that old adage.

"Hoseph's not stupid, but he's certainly desperate, and I've earned his enmity." She shot Dee a sly grin. "As have *you*. I'm not the one who shot him in the ass."

Dee's mouth twisted wryly. "A little higher with that shot, and we wouldn't have to deal with him anymore."

"You did well to get a shot off at all. That magic of his..." Mya shuddered as she recalled the priest's magic dredging up every horrible event of her life as if they were all happening again at once.

"Knock!" Knock grinned up at Dee from beneath her heavy brow. Ever since his lucky shot had saved her life, the girl had been his most ardent admirer.

"So, we're back to the question: which of the masters will go with Hoseph and which will accept you as Grandmaster? We could end up with a guild war."

Mopping up the juices on her plate with a piece of bread, Mya popped it into her mouth, relishing the last smoky, greasy bite as her tension eased a trifle. If anyone knew how to conduct a guild war, it was Mya. She'd fought one against the masters of the Twailin Assassins Guild only months ago. *And they're all dead.* Pushing aside her empty plate, she refilled her blackbrew cup and leaned back in her chair, feeling ready to slay any dragon foolish enough to test her mettle.

"About the masters... I think I can depend on Clemson being on my side. Her Enforcers heard Lady T acknowledge me as Grandmaster, and she'll believe her own people. The others..." Mya shrugged. "...I don't know. As eager as they were to deny me until Lady T gave her approval, I don't see them accepting me on the word of another master's underlings."

"None of them have done anything directly against you yet," Dee pointed out.

"Because they can't." She waved her finger again. "But nothing prevents them from hiring more mercenaries. And Hoseph took Lady T's ring. Dangling that prize in front of them will certainly serve as incentive to be creative."

"Well, you know you can depend on Sereth and the Twailin guild."

Mya hoped Dee was right. Sereth *had* sent her money and promised more, and she had always gotten along well with the Blade, now Twailin's guildmaster. But Twailin was a thousand miles and weeks travel away. She had to rely on what she had here and now.

"What about the caps? They'll be here soon and we can't have them pokin' around here like cats after a rat." Paxal jerked a thumb toward the upper floors. "This is supposed to be an orphanage, but that spider web of cat gut will raise some eyebrows, and maybe some questions you don't want to answer."

"Good point." Mya sighed, wishing once again that the constables had completed their questioning last night; she had more important things to do today. "I don't want to dismantle all our defenses, so no caps go upstairs. If anyone sees them headed that way, just sing out so I can hear you and I'll deal with it. If they insist, I'll pull my I-just-saved-the-emperor's-life card. What's the use in being a hero if you can't throw your weight around a little?"

"Heroine," Dee corrected with a wry smile. "And you're not that heavy."

"Right. Now, another problem is that they might want to question you two." She nodded to Dee and Paxal. "So, here's the gist of the story I gave them. I'm a bodyguard, relatively new in town, hired to see after Lady T's safety. She only needed my services when she was out and about, so I wasn't staying in her home. Pax, you're an old acquaintance giving me room and board in this orphanage you recently started up."

"And I'm helpin' you out of the goodness of my heart? With all these kids to support?" Pax scowled as he took their plates to the wash basin. Two of the urchins hurried to help. "They're not gonna buy that."

Mya smiled. Pax sometimes seemed to know her better than she knew herself. *He should, considering he nearly raised me.* In Twailin, she had paid him well to let her use the *Golden Cockerel* as headquarters for her faction of Hunters, but she knew that, truly, he did it for her, not for the money. Why else would he have accompanied Dee all the way to Tsing to find her?

"Good point. I'm paying you."

"Who am I?" Dee asked. "Do I work for Pax or you?"

"Me." Mya wasn't about to let Dee out of her sight…for many reasons. The memory of his skillful touch sent a shiver up her spine. "You're my assistant."

"Why does a bodyguard need an assistant?"

Mya smirked. "I'm a highly trained bodyguard to nobility! I need someone to handle my contracts, keep track of the money, do my correspondence…basically, what you've always done for me. In fact, I'll probably need you to—"

A knock at the front door interrupted her.

"If that's caps, they're early risers." Paxal scowled and nodded to the eldest urchin. "Digger, go check, but don't open the door."

"Yes, Master Pax." Digger ran off.

Mya rose from her seat, downing the last of her blackbrew. "Whoever it is, I'll deal with it."

Dee got up just as Digger returned.

"Caps, all right." He looked down at his fingers, counting. "Six of 'em."

"All right." Mya nodded to Dee. "Let them in, Dee. I'll be right behind you."

"Yes, Miss Mya."

"Right!" Paxal picked out two urchins. "Twigs and Digger, stand watch on the stairs. The rest of you look busy, and no weapons on the first floor! Go."

The urchins scattered.

Mya followed Dee to the door, girding her nerves as he opened it to admit the constables. Her stomach clenched. She had expected maybe one or two, but uniforms crowded the doorway. As Dee greeted them pleasantly and waved them in, she stepped forward, extending a hand automatically.

"Good morning, Constables. I see that you're…" She hesitated as she recognized the two in the fore. *Damn! Of all the rotten luck!* They were the very two who had taken an interest in her as she crossed back and forth from the Dreggars Quarters to Midtown in the days after the emperor's assassination. "…up early this morning."

"Good morning, Miss…" The sergeant's eyes narrowed as he shook her hand, then widened. "I know you! From the Fivestone Bridge—"

"Ah, yes. I remember that we met on the bridge a few times." Mya smiled disarmingly and gestured them all into the common room. "Welcome, Sergeant…" She dredged up his name from her trained memory. "…Benj. And this is Corporal Jorren, isn't it?"

"It's Sergeant *Benjamin*, Miss, and Corporal Jorren *Arryx*." His eyes narrowed again.

Mya cursed silently. In trying to be amiable, she'd pricked his suspicion by using the names she had overheard at a distance too far for normal ears to eavesdrop. Waving a dismissive hand, she declared, "I'm always getting names wrong. And these are…"

"Privates Alli, Wanless, Tovi, and Kert."

"Please come in and have a seat. Can I offer you blackbrew or tea?" Mya perched on an upholstered chair, hopeful that the sergeant would overlook her gaffe and just get this questioning over with.

"Blackbrew'd be welcome, Miss *Moirin*." The sergeant eased into the chair opposite Mya. Corporal Arryx remained standing at his superior's shoulder, a small notebook in hand. The four privates also stood, looking around as if bored by such mundane duty. Benj looked at her, his shrewd, calculating eyes belying his disheveled appearance and ingenuous manner. "Pardon me, but I don't remember you giving the name Moirin when you crossed the bridge. Are we both mistakin' names today?"

Mya had enough lies to remember, so she decided to go with the truth about this, at least. "No, Sergeant, you remember correctly. I was using the name Ingrid Johens. You'll also find that I have, at times, assumed the name Bouchard, posing as head mistress of this orphanage. I apologize for the confusion, but I occasionally take on pseudonyms to maintain the anonymity of my clients." She shrugged as if unconcerned. "You understand the need for propriety when serving the upper classes, I'm sure. Lady T contracted for the services of a professional bodyguard with the utmost discretion. Oh, and I also posed as the Lady's niece in order to accompany her to the coronation."

The corporal raised his eyebrows, but scratched notes without saying a word.

Benj nodded slowly. "Well, what I need are the facts. Is your real name Moirin?"

"Yes," she lied with a straight face.

"And where are you from?"

"Twailin." *At least that's the truth.*

"And you came to Tsing to work for Baroness Monjhi?"

"No." Mya cringed at the mention of Lady T's new title. She'd been a baroness for less than six hours before she was murdered. "I came here to work, period. It's only good business to go where the money is, and no other city in the empire can hold a candle to Tsing when it comes to well-heeled folks who need protection." She paused as Paxal brought in a blackbrew service and poured for everyone. Why had she ever offered refreshment? It would only encourage them to take their time. She had more important things to do.

The caps jostled for cups, smiling and nodding gratefully, all save the corporal, who shook his head and kept scratching notes.

Benj sipped his blackbrew and rubbed his jaw, his callused hand rasping against the stubble like sandpaper. "So, you arrived before or after the emperor was assassinated?"

"Sergeant Benjamin, I answered all these questions for your colleague last night. I don't see why—"

"Yeah, well, we find that sometimes a night's sleep can refresh the memory, bring back details you didn't even realize you noticed. So please, Miss Moirin, bear with me. Did you arrive in the city before or after the emperor was assassinated?"

With a sigh, Mya capitulated. "Before. Dumb luck on my part, I suppose. With the unrest following the assassination, I had more offers for work than I could take. I settled on the then *Lady* T, and...well...that didn't work out very well."

"Not for Baroness Monjhi, but it sure turned out well for our new emperor, from what I hear."

Mya shrugged. "That was just being in the right place at the right time. I attended the coronation to protect Lady T. She ordered me to intervene in the assassination attempt, so I did."

"And saved the crown prince's life." Benj looked thoughtful, obviously not the dullard she had hoped him to be.

"Yes." Mya sighed, trying for a forlorn look. "And then failed my contract."

"Pardon me, Miss, but..." The tall corporal fixed her eyes, his pencil finally still. "...how exactly *did* you manage to save the crown prince's life, if you don't mind my asking? There are rumors, and they've no doubt grown in the telling, but they all agree that you...um...showed some *remarkable* abilities."

"I actually *do* mind you asking, Corporal." Mya gave him a tight smile. "My...abilities have no bearing on your investigation of Baroness Monjhi's murder. My livelihood depends on people underestimating me."

He looked surprised, his pencil scratching another note. "Well, everyone's glad you did, anyway. Save the prince, I mean."

"Not *everyone*, obviously," she countered. "My mistress is dead."

"Yeah, well, about that." The sergeant glanced at his corporal, then looked to Mya. "Do you know why this priest, Hoseph, would want to kill the baroness?"

"No, Sergeant. I was only told what to look for and what he was capable of." Mya frowned. "Neither of us knew he could pop right into a moving carriage."

"I see..." The sergeant rubbed his jaw, the corporal's pencil scratched, and the questions continued.

Arbuckle had given orders that the first full day of his reign, Emperor Tynean Tsing III would be allowed to sleep late. After the tumultuous events of the day before, he figured deserved it.

Surprisingly, he slept deeply and soundly until the morning light dappled his silk-encased pillow. Stretching and blinking, he took stock. Alive—*Surviving one's own coronation shouldn't be such a trial!*—and hale, but sorrowful that the woman who had risked her own safety to save his, the valiant Baroness Tara Monjhi, had been murdered for that selfless act.

Justice... I'll bring that loathsome Hoseph to justice.

Climbing out of bed, he rang the bell on his night table. Baris was through the bedroom door before the bell's tone died, a brilliant smile on his face and fresh clothes over his arm.

"Good *morning*, Your Majesty!"

"Your Majesty...I almost expect to turn around and find my father behind me." The new emperor chuckled. "It'll take some time to adjust to being Tynean Tsing III. I still feel like Arbuckle. No matter. Good morning to you, too, Baris. How are things about the palace?" Arbuckle stripped off his nightshirt, handed it to his valet, and accepted clean linens and breeks. "Has everyone settled down from the excitement?"

"Not hardly, Majesty." Baris grinned. "Half the guests have sent messages that they don't intend to leave their suites today, and the other half are already packing to leave."

"That sounds about right." Arbuckle allowed his valet to fuss over his appearance with his usual deft efficiency, finding it hard to stand still with the enticing scent of blackbrew in the air. "Is Tennison about?"

"Did Your Majesty expect anything less? He's been pacing since sun-up, ready to commence with the business of your new reign. I wouldn't let him disturb your rest."

"Thank you for that, Baris." Arbuckle found his secretary an indispensable, but harsh, taskmaster. *Well, I've tarried long enough.* Finally dressed to his valet's exacting standards, he braced his shoulders. "Into the breach then, I suppose."

"*We* suppose, Majesty."

"We... Right." Referring to himself with the royal 'We' would also take some getting used to. *Bother...* "*We* suppose."

"Yes, Your Majesty." Baris opened the bedchamber door.

As Arbuckle strode into the sitting room, Tennison immediately ceased pacing and bowed, his face alight with relief. The rest of the company in the crowded room—a full squad of Imperial Guards, Captain Ithross, a knight, two footmen, Master Keyfur, and the imperial scribe, Verul—also bowed low and voiced their good mornings.

"Good morning, everyone. Please pardon Our late rise. We found yesterday's events rather *taxing*." Arbuckle seated himself and nodded to the footman who held the blackbrew pot to fill his cup. With a blissful sigh, he sipped the hot, strong beverage; he didn't feel quite human until his first cup of blackbrew. From the corner of his eye, he caught a glimpse of Tennison fidgeting. Studiously, he turned to his breakfast, swallowing the guilt that pressed him to hurry with the first bite of a delicious omelet. Tennison had taught Arbuckle to never allow another to interrupt the emperor's daily schedule except in dire emergency. There was no emergency today. He would enjoy his breakfast, then attend to business.

Finally, after popping the last bite of sweet pastry into his mouth, Arbuckle relented and waved his secretary forward. "All right, Tennison, what's got your feathers all ruffled?"

"The documents we drafted prior to your coronation are ready to be ratified into law, Majesty." The man fairly leapt forward. "I thought that you would want to sign them first thing."

"Excellent!" *Finally, I can pass whatever laws I like without having to kowtow to anyone.*

Arbuckle still didn't understand why so many of his nobles were dead set against equal justice for commoners. If they had read any history at all, they'd understand that Tynean Tsing II's unjust laws would ultimately—and grievously—fail. A populace could only be oppressed for so long before they revolted. With a flourish, he signed the parchments splayed on the table before him. "Just the first of many. Did you record Our actions here, Verul?"

"With pleasure, Majesty." The scribe smiled as he scribbled in the big book atop his lap.

Tennison swept up the documents and consulted his ledger. "Your Majesty has a full docket this morning meeting with departing guests who wish to pay their respects before they go."

Arbuckle frowned, irked by the bothersome protocols of the imperial court. "Can We dispense with any of this, Tennison? We must speak to the dukes, of course, especially Mir and Nythes, but We greeted the minor lords during the coronation. If they're in such a hurry to leave…"

The secretary tapped his pen against his chin in thought. "We could arrange a dinner tonight honoring *all* of your guests, Majesty. That would shift the responsibility for maintaining protocol onto *their* heads, not yours. It would free up most of this morning and several hours this afternoon."

"Excellent. Do so." The emperor sipped his blackbrew happily. "We want to work on Our new edicts. There are many wrongs that need to be redressed beyond the few We just signed, and We'll have to make a public announcement soon. So…what next?" He looked at the others and decided his single remaining wizard took precedence. "Master Keyfur?"

Keyfur bowed amidst a swirl of colorful robes. "With Your Majesty's permission, I'll begin interviewing wizards and assembling a new Imperial Retinue."

"Do We truly *need* one?"

The wizard looked confused. "There's *always* been an Imperial Retinue of Wizards, Majesty."

"But why?" Arbuckle persisted. "For the prestige of having magical power at the emperor's beck and call? Archmage Duveau's attempt to assassinate Us demonstrates all too well how easily that power can turn against Us. What tasks *really* need a wizard's touch?"

Keyfur considered the question for a moment, then slowly nodded. "Maintenance, mostly, Majesty. Maintaining the palace wards against magical travel in and out, the enchantments to detect poison, other safeguards, things like that."

Arbuckle grinned. "So, Master Keyfur, are you up to the task?"

"*Me*, Your Majesty?" The wizard looked shocked. "My expertise doesn't cover all of the disciplines of magic required. I could acquire the necessary skills for specific enchantments after some study…"

"Then please begin immediately. We grant you complete access to the former possessions—magical or mundane—of the deceased members of the Imperial Retinue, including Duveau's."

"Your Majesty is too kind." The peacock feather tucked behind Keyfur's ear swept the floor with his low bow before the wizard stepped back, his face cracking into a wide grin.

Arbuckle grinned back, pleased at how well his morning was proceeding. "And Captain Ithross! To what do We owe your personal attendance today?"

"Palace security, Majesty."

Arbuckle looked around the room at the guards. "Do you not consider a squad of your finest imperial guards sufficient for Our protection?"

"In all honesty, no, Your Majesty," Ithross confessed, his face flushing red. "You need *better* protection. There's no reason to assume that because you've been crowned the attempts on your life will simply end. You mustn't forget that there's a conspiracy against you. Duveau was merely their tool."

Arbuckle sobered, the last gulp of blackbrew seeming to burn down his throat like acid.

The captain continued. "We lost too many good men and women of the guard yesterday, as well as several knights. Though our troops are the finest in the empire, they're trained to *augment* the protection provided by your personal body guards."

"The Blademasters of Koss Godslayer…" The gruesome mass suicide of the monks in response to their perceived failure to protect his father still haunted Arbuckle. "It will be a generation before a new cohort can be trained."

"There are other martial orders," Tennison suggested.

Ithross shook his head. "None with the intense training of the blademasters, or their Koss-blessed skills."

"Any ideas, other than keeping Us locked up in these rooms for the first twenty years of Our reign?" Arbuckle laughed shortly and without humor. Would the greatest effort of his reign merely be staying alive? The only reason his people were wishing their new emperor a good morning instead of standing around his grave was because of— "What about that young woman who saved my life yesterday?"

Ithross looked aghast. "Your pardon, Majesty, but we know nothing about her."

"Or what type of magic she wields," Keyfur added. "I owe her my life, Majesty, but she *does* wield magic. She was gravely wounded in the fight with Duveau and by all accounts healed instantly."

"Not to mention bounding around like she had springs in her legs!" Ithross agreed. "I was nervous enough allowing her in the royal presence during the reception, Majesty. We don't know enough to trust her with your *life*!"

Tynean remembered dancing with the remarkable young woman at the reception. *Moirin...*

"And don't forget that she failed in her duty last night by allowing Baroness Monjhi to be killed by High Priest Hoseph," reminded Tennison.

Verul's pen scratching across parchment was the only sound for a long moment.

Arbuckle considered his advisors' concerns, then made up his mind. "We wish to know more about her. She saved Our life yesterday, Ithross. If she wished Us harm, all she would have had to do was stay her hand."

"There is that, Majesty." Ithross pursed his lips, looking like he'd just swallowed a lemon. "The constables will be questioning her with regard to Baroness Monjhi's murder. I'll contact Chief Constable Dreyfus and ask him for a copy of the report."

"Good. That's a good start. That's all for now."

"Yes, Majesty."

Arbuckle motioned to the footman to refill his cup. While he sipped his blackbrew, he thought about the attempts on his life and the young woman who had saved him. Yes, he would definitely like to speak to her again.

Chapter II

Hoseph materialized from shadow, staggering as pain lanced through his head. *Blessed shadow of death, soothe me...* The mantra wouldn't banish the pain, but it helped calm his mind. It was getting worse, there was no denying it. The more he used Demia's talisman to travel through the Sphere of Shadow, the worse he felt. Leaning against one rough brick wall of the alley, he waited several minutes until the pounding eased, his reeling vision cleared, and his stance firmed. The pain was still there, but manageable.

Pushing himself upright, Hoseph opened his palm to stare down at the talisman—the small, silver skull gifted to him when he ascended to High Priest of Demia, Keeper of the Slain—and wondered once again why using it had begun to pain him so. A spark of fear singed the back of his mind. The talisman was the means by which he traveled, flicking from one place to another with just the whisper of a word. It also kept him alive in the Sphere of Shadow, that incorporeal realm of banished godlings and demons through which he passed. He couldn't be the Right Hand of Death without it. Well, there was nothing for it. He had too much to do and not enough time to plod like a peasant through the cobbled streets of the city.

Hoseph blinked to accustom his eyes to the early morning light stabbing into the narrow alley. Orienting himself, he emerged from between the close-set buildings and set off through the Dreggars Quarter toward the address that Master Enforcer Clemson had given him. After familiarizing himself with her new headquarters, he would be able to use the talisman to travel there directly.

This was his second round of visits to the Assassins Guild masters in as many days. Last night he had informed them of Lady T's treachery—actually *saving* the crown prince's life when the guild's future depended upon his death—and her subsequent execution at

18

his hands. None of them had protested his actions or questioned his motives, a refreshing change from working with the cantankerous Lady T for the past weeks. And when he showed them the guildmaster's ring, offering it as the prize for killing Mya, they'd shown pointed interest.

That meddlesome usurper! She thought that merely donning the Grandmaster's ring entitled her to control of the guild. She would learn otherwise. Hoseph hadn't achieved his position—the *real* power behind the Grandmaster—only to lose it to this power-hungry Master Hunter from Twailin.

Every one of the masters had, however, used the same argument against confronting Mya: blood contracts. Every assassin signed one, binding them to the guild for life and preventing them from lifting a finger against a superior. Hoseph had eliminated that problem last night by burning the blood contracts. Now every guild assassin had free rein to attack Mya.

Hoseph rounded a corner into the full glare of the sun, and his head throbbed anew. Pulling the cowl of his acolyte's robe low over his face shielded his eyes from the glare, and also maintained his anonymity. His likeness was plastered on every posterboard in the city, a hunted man. They'd never catch him, of course, as long as he could fade into mist and shadow at a whim.

In due time, he arrived at the address he sought. All the Masters had moved their headquarters last night to avoid Mya. This shop was Clemson's new abode. Lamps and candlesticks lined the shelves behind the barred windows. Unprepossessing, it would never be suspected as an assassin's lair.

Hoseph turned the door handle, but found it locked. He rapped loudly on the door. Clemson had had plenty of time to make the move. He'd already visited Master Inquisitor Lakshmi and Master Alchemist Kittal in their new quarters.

So where is she? Hoseph rapped again, louder this time. When that still yielded nothing, he pounded.

"Ay there! Stop that!"

Hoseph squinted up at a ruddy face glaring down at him from a second-floor window of the next shop over. "I'm looking for Clemson."

The man scrunched up his nose. "Don't know who that is, and don't care. That lot spent half the night bangin' and clatterin' about. Packed up everything and lit out. Now go away and let a poor old man sleep!" The shutter slammed closed.

"Gone?" Hoseph peered through the window at the shop's interior and gritted his teeth. The shelves and hooks were bare. The festooned windows only gave the semblance of a working shop. "That lying..."

Hoseph strode away, back into the cool shadows of a nearby alley. He considered materializing inside the shop—no problem since he had seen the interior—but he couldn't afford to be frivolous with the use of the talisman, not how it pained him. If it was indeed an honest mistake, he'd find out soon enough. Flicking the talisman into his hand, he spoke the word of invocation and dissolved into mist.

In the Sphere of Shadow, Hoseph's pain eased and his mind cleared, untroubled by the fatigue or discomfort of a material body. Though lingering here was tempting, if only for a respite, he could not delay. He pictured another narrow alley, also in the Dreggars Quarter, and close to the smithy where Master Blade Noncey was resettling. He invoked the talisman and re-entered reality.

"Mother of..." His knees came close to folding as he appeared in the alley. Every time seemed worse, especially when he transited the shadows many times in quick succession. Yesterday had been trying, and today was becoming even more so. When his legs steadied and his vision cleared, Hoseph stumbled onto the street and turned toward the ironmonger's front stoop, ducking beneath the roofed porch. The broad double doors were closed. A simple, hand-painted sign hung from the handle.

"Closed for *renovation*?" Hoseph rattled the iron handle—the doors were locked and nobody answered—then snarled in frustration. "Noncey, too?"

This didn't bode well at all. He might excuse one missing faction as an error, but not two. Hoseph didn't believe in coincidence; this smacked of *treason*. If both the Blades and Enforcers had defected, the primary physical might of the Assassins Guild now lay in Mya's hands. However, with the Inquisitors and Alchemists safely loyal, he still controlled the brains and magical might of the guild. There was only one more faction to check, one he needed desperately. Mya was a Hunter; he needed his own to match her skills in stealth and surveillance.

Staggering back to the alley, Hoseph flicked the talisman again into his hand. "Shahallariva," he snapped, louder than he intended, but there was no one around to hear. The mists took him.

This time when he materialized, his knees *did* fold, but the crack of his shins against the cobbles was nothing compared to the pain in his head. His sight edged in black, darkness pressing in. Nausea welled up and his stomach emptied, bile burning his throat. *Shadow of death...please...* After a prolonged, excruciating interval, the pounding in his head finally eased. He could see again, breathe, think. He spat out the vile taste in his mouth and raised his head.

Across the narrow alley huddled a rag-clad man clutching a brown bottle. He stared at the priest with rheumy half-lidded eyes, looking as if he might fall asleep at any moment. *A witness...* Normally, Hoseph would immediately kill anyone who observed his magical arrival, but who would ever believe this old sot? As he sneered in disgust, something warm tickled his upper lip. Wiping at it, he recoiled at the blood on his hand. His nose was bleeding.

"Got the shakes, huh?" the ragged man croaked, holding out the bottle with in a trembling hand. "Wanna li'l nip? It'll steady ya. Works fer me."

Hoseph ignored the loathsome creature and forced down the cold trickle of fear. Something was dreadfully wrong.

It doesn't matter. I've got work to do. I can rest...later.

He dragged himself up the moldy brick wall until he stood, then staggered into a street that was noticeably dirtier and narrower than those he had recently walked. Why Master Hunter Twist Umberlin had chosen to seek refuge here in the Downwind Quarter amongst the dregs of society, Hoseph had no idea. The stench alone would keep most civilized people away.

Hoseph rarely frequented this area and didn't know many places here. Consequently, he had quite a walk to find the Master Hunter's new headquarters. He finally located the tannery by the increasing stench. Turning into the foul yard, the priest wrinkled his nose.

Stinking pots bubbled over coal fires, tended by a shirtless woman. Rivulets of sweat dripped from her pendulous breasts as she stirred a pot with a wide paddle. Along the courtyard walls, hides hung on drying racks. Two men, also bare chested, were beating the hides into suppleness with long, flat clubs. None of the workers even looked up as Hoseph strode forward.

At least this place is operating, he conceded, hopeful that he might actually find Umberlin here.

"Who are you and what do you want?" A tall woman with a thick brow and a wrinkled, upturned nose stepped from the shade of a shed and glared at him.

Her attitude and tone galled the priest. When Emperor Tynean Tsing II still ruled the Assassins Guild, Hoseph had dealt exclusively with the guildmasters, commanding the instant recognition and respect appropriate to his position. *And I will again…soon.*

Swallowing his pride, he said, "I'm Hoseph. Twist is expecting me."

The woman's nose twitched. "This way." She turned and ducked into the shed.

He followed her through a door, down a dusty hall, and through another door into a much cleaner and better-smelling room. A breeze of relatively fresh air wafted in from a duct in the ceiling. *A wind catch*, he realized. Many of the city's buildings had small sails on their roofs to funnel the breeze down and provide fresh air to interior rooms. The woman led him through a clutter of boxes, crates, barrels, and trunks—testimony to the Master Hunter's recent relocation—and motioned the priest forward.

"Hoseph here to see you, Master Twist."

Twist Umberlin stood from behind a shabby desk in the room's corner. A loaded crossbow lay atop a litter of ledgers and papers, but the Master Hunter didn't even spare it a glance. The three other Hunters sitting about the room didn't look as benign, regarding Hoseph with wary eyes, their hands on their weapons.

"You don't look good." Umberlin squinted at Hoseph. Delving into a pocket, the thin man dredged up a questionably clean handkerchief. "There's blood on your lip."

"I'm fine." Hoseph ignored the handkerchief and wiped his face with his sleeve. "What have you heard from the other masters?"

"Nothing." Twist tucked his handkerchief away and sat back down. "Should I have?"

"Clemson and Noncey are *not* where they told me they would be. I can only assume that they've gone over to the enemy." Hoseph's statement raised eyebrows around the room.

The Master Hunter frowned. "That's not good."

"No, it's not, but Lakshmi and Kittal are with us. We must strike quickly, before Mya can organize against us."

"Strike who, exactly, and how?"

"*Mya*, of course. She's the cause of all of this! Kill her, and the guild will be whole again."

Twist slumped back into his chair and rolled his eyes. "That brings up the 'how' part. She wears the *Grandmaster's* ring, remember? Usurper or not, we can't touch her. The blood contracts don't—"

"You *can* touch her," Hoseph interrupted, smiling grimly. "I've seen to that."

"You've…" Umberlin's forehead furrowed, then his eyes widened and he shot up from his chair. "You did *not*!"

"I did. I realize it was a drastic measure, but it was—"

"Fool!" The Master Hunter's face contorted. "If what you say is true…" His eyes flicked to his subordinates. "Bev, come here."

A short woman in snug leathers rose from her seat and strode to her master's desk, sparing a glance at Hoseph on the way. Her eyes were the hue of ice, and every bit as warm.

Umberlin held out a hand, palm down. "I want you to cut me, Bev."

"Master?"

"Cut the back of my hand. Now!"

The woman drew a dagger and slashed, quick as a viper, across her master's hand. Twist didn't even flinch as his skin gaped and bled, dripping on his stacks of papers. His eyes, however, widened in horror. In fact, every eye in the room save Hoseph's widened. The journeyman should not have been able to attack her master. It was impossible…until now.

"You *idiot*!" Umberlin glared at Hoseph and jerked the soiled handkerchief from his pocket to wrap his hand. "You have no idea what you've done!"

"I know *exactly* what I've done," Hoseph retorted with a smug smile. "I've given you the ability to kill the usurper. When that's done, we'll forge new blood contracts and appoint a new guildmaster."

Twist's eyes narrowed. "And our new guildmaster will be…"

"Whoever brings me the usurper's head, Master Umberlin." Hoseph fixed him with a stern look. "Your faction represents the best chance we have of a quick victory. I'm counting on you to get the job done, so work out the details for yourself. I know where she's living. Strike as soon as you can before she moves. Enlist whatever help you need from the other factions if you must, but get it done!"

Twist Umberlin just stared at him for a long moment, then swallowed and sat down. "Fine. What's the address?"

Hoseph gave him the location. "Be wary inside the house; she's got trip wires strung everywhere upstairs. Also, she's using street urchins for cover. They look harmless, but they're armed."

"Kids?" Umberlin looked disgusted. "How many?"

"I don't know. Five or six at least. Don't underestimate them. Do whatever you have to do to get to Mya. You *are* an assassin, aren't you?"

Umberlin's lips thinned and his countenance hardened. "Fine. But when I hand you her head, the guildmaster ring's mine."

"Yes."

"Then get out of here and let me work," the Master Hunter snapped.

Hoseph didn't like his tone, but decided to let the impertinence go for now. Nodding, he flicked the little silver skull into his hand, invoked Demia's grace with a whisper, and faded into mist.

By mid-morning Mya's head spun with too much blackbrew and too many questions. To say that the sergeant and his corporal were being thorough was an understatement.

"How many ways do I have to say the same thing?" she asked in frustration. "Can't we please take a break?"

"We were told not to rest until we found Baroness Monjhi's killer, Miss. Don't worry, we just have a few more questions."

"That's what you said an hour ago," she muttered.

The knock on the door came as a welcome respite.

"Dee, can you get that, please?"

"Yes, Miss My—Moirin."

Mya tried to ignore the near slip of Dee's tongue. It wasn't the first time this morning he had stumbled over her assumed name. It had only taken one look at his ashen face to realize why; Moirin had been the name of his barmaid lover, who had killed herself in front of him when he caught her spying on Mya.

Why the hell did I choose that name? she wondered.

Dee returned and held out a letter. "Message for you, Miss Moirin."

"You'll pardon me, gentlemen, this could be important." She stood and examined the envelope, which was sealed with black wax and impressed with a stylized "C". *Clemson?*

"More important than investigating Baroness Monjhi's murder?" Benj rose to his feet, his eyes sharp.

"This could very well be the key to finding the person who did it, Sergeant."

"You're conductin' your *own* investigation?"

"Are you suggesting I *don't*? As you have so kindly pointed out several times, Lady T was *my* responsibility, and I failed her. I'm sure that, if we asked him, the *emperor* would appreciate any assistance in apprehending the killer of the woman who ordered me to save his life."

Benj looked as if Mya had suddenly laid out a winning hand of cards. "Of course not, but I'd like to know what you find out."

Pleased that her dropping of names had worked, she mollified the constable by promising, "Of course, Sergeant. As soon as I get solid information, I'll let you know. However, right now I have to read this. Excuse me."

"Let me freshen your cups, gentlemen and ladies," Dee said as she strode away. "And I'll rouse out something to eat for you as well. Paxal!"

Mya stepped into her office and pressed the Grandmaster's ring onto the wax seal. If it worked in the same manner as her master's ring, it would shock her if the seal was a forgery or a trap. Instead of a jolt, she felt a reassuring tingle up her arm. Cracking the seal, she read the brief message.

> 27 Elderberry, DQ
> ASAP
> C

Mya burned the note, then strode back out to the front room. "I'm sorry, Sergeant, but I have to go meet a friend. This could be the break I'm looking for."

"About the priest?" The sergeant stood, wiping cookie crumbs from his chin.

"Maybe a lead to where I can find him, yes. If so, you'll be the first to know." She started for the door. "I don't know when I'll be back, Dee. Sergeant, I think I've answered all your questions about three times now. If you think of anything else, please get in touch and we can speak some more."

"Oh, I've got more questions," the sergeant said.

"Do you want an escort, Miss Moirin?" Dee followed her to the door, his brow furrowed with worry. "Or a carriage?"

"I don't' think I'll ever set foot in a carriage again after what happened to Lady T, but thanks for the offer, Dee." She gripped his arm briefly and gave him a covert smile. "I'll be back before you know it."

"Yes, Miss Moirin."

Mya was halfway down the block before she heard the door close.

CHAPTER III

"A distillery?" Mya squinted up at the swaying sign: 'Westwind Distillery', a black flag with crossed cutlasses painted below the name. She should have guessed; the distinctive sweet-yeasty tang had drawn her from blocks away. Opening the gate to the wide courtyard, she cautiously looked inside.

The place was busy.

To the left, a towering heap of sugarcane mounded high against one wall. Like keepers placating a ravenous beast, workers grabbed armfuls of the cane and fed it into the chute of an enormous grinder at the courtyard's center. Four mules plodded in a wide circle around the machine, driving the huge gears that pulled the cane in, chewed it up, and spat the waste into a heap. A wooden vat beneath the grinder collected the juice, and well-muscled workers hefted buckets full of the sweet liquid, carrying them into the shade of a slanted roof.

Mya paused, analyzing every person in the courtyard. Despite the authenticity of the letter, this could, of course, be a trap. The workers were beefy enough to be Enforcers, but they didn't move like assassins, and not one spared her a glance. Besides, assassins couldn't attack her. Clemson could have recruited mercenaries, but these just looked to be laborers, their hands scarred by the cane, but no marks of combat on their sweat-streaked bodies.

"Help you, ma'am?" A squat dwarf strode forth, unruly red hair atop a curiously beardless face. Then Mya realized that the dwarf's nearly spherical frame included breasts. The dwarf woman scratched one of the muttonchops that framed her round cheeks and looked Mya up and down. "Yer not lookin' fer work, are ya?"

"No, I'm looking for Clemson." She raised her hand and flicked her ring finger, the movement obvious to the dwarf, inconspicuous to anyone merely glancing her way. "I'm Mya."

Recognition shone in the dwarf's eye, but not alarm or deceit. "Oh! Well, then, follow me!"

Mya tensed as the dwarf led her across the courtyard past the grinder. Toss someone into that chute, and they'd be pulped as flat as any sugar cane. She doubted that even her runes would save her from that. But her guide's rolling gait didn't slow as she led Mya beneath the sloped roof. Despite the shade, the heat was oppressive, and Mya quickly saw why. The bucket haulers dumped the cane juice into vast metal bowls—wide and shallow—set over roaring fires. The liquid bubbled thickly, looking more like sludge than rum.

They continued through a door into an open, warehouse-like building. Here, taller stone vats full of amber liquid also bubbled, though there were no fires beneath them. Peeking over the rim of one tub, Mya watched as a fat bubble amidst the foam popped, releasing a yeasty smell.

"It's fermentin'," the dwarf explained. "From here, it goes into those boilers. The steam condenses in that copper tubing, then gets piped here." She plinked a nail against a curved glass chamber half filled with clear liquid, a tube in the center. "This separates the rum from the wood alcohol, then its decanted inta oak barrels ta age."

Mya gazed about in wonder. *All this just to make rum?*

"Sorry." The dwarf grinned. "My pride and joy, this place." Continuing on, her guide finally stopped outside a door and opened it, motioning Mya through. "Go on down. Someone'll meet you at the bottom. Don't mind the funny light; the lamps burn wood alcohol, not oil."

"Thank you." Mya looked down the stone stairway, eerie in the blue-tinged light, and felt a twinge of worry. The deeper she went, the more difficult it would be to escape if this was a trap.

Too late to turn back now. She descended the stairs. The bottom T'd into a corridor protected by a man holding a crossbow leveled at her chest.

"You are…"

"Mya." She showed her ring again. "Here to see Clemson."

"Right." He nodded down the left-hand corridor. "End of the hall. Knock."

"Thank you." Mya strolled down the hallway, attempting to look relaxed and confident, despite her jangling nerves. She cocked an ear as she passed several closed doors, but detected no noises behind them, no whispers or clanks of weapons being readied. None burst open to disgorge murderous mercenaries. The place smelled of rum, oak, and mold. At the door at the end of the hall, she knocked.

A familiar figure filled the portal when it opened.

"Hello, Jolee. I'm here to see Clemson."

"Aye." The massive woman's lips twitched in a hint of a smile that exposed thick tusks, making the greeting seem more threatening than welcoming. Backing away from the door, she waved Mya in.

Mya stepped across the threshold and stopped.

The room was pleasantly cool, well-appointed, and crowded. Master Enforcer Clemson stood and stepped out from behind her desk, looking slim and almost child-like among her hulking Enforcers. Mya envied the woman's snug black trousers, blousy white shirt, and soft boots sporting sheathed daggers. She felt awkward and out of place in a dress, but she hadn't dared change her clothes with the constables in the house, and a dress was less conspicuous.

"Grandmaster." Clemson nodded respectfully. "Good of you to come."

Master Blade Noncey rose with the grace of a dancer from a chair beside the desk. He towered head and shoulders above Mya, with the broad shoulders and well-muscled frame of a trained fighter. His deferential nod was echoed by the rest of the Blades and Enforcers crowding the room.

"Good of you to acknowledge my position…finally." Mya stepped forward, the junior assassins jostling to make room for her. Clemson and Noncey were the only two masters here. She cocked an eyebrow. "The others?"

"They've sided with Hoseph." Noncey's lip curled, marring his handsome face.

Mya's stomach clenched. "Do you know for that for a *fact*?"

The Master Enforcer nodded. "We were all in communication after Lady T's…death, trying to reconcile the information coming from Hoseph and my Enforcers. I trust my people; they wouldn't lie about something like this. If they say that Lady T acknowledged you, that's good enough for me. Noncey agrees. The others didn't."

"They're fools." Noncey plucked a dagger from his sleeve and spun it in his palm before burying the tip in Clemson's desk. "That priest's crazy. He accused Lady T of treason, but she didn't betray the guild, just him."

Only two out of five factions on my side... Mya tasted blood and realized that she had bitten her lip. The lack of pain was sometimes startling and inconvenient. More importantly, Lad had warned her against the unconscious tells that revealed her moods. Deliberately unclenching her fists and taking a deep breath, Mya forced her mind to calm. She had to give her two loyal masters the image of a Grandmaster in control.

"Of the other three, who is most likely to come over to our side if offered the right incentive?"

The two masters looked to one another, then Noncey said, "Twist, probably."

Clemson nodded as she leaned back against one corner of the desk. "I agree. He's ambitious, but pragmatic. We can send a discreet inquiry to one of his businesses and hope it reaches him. The problem will be finding the right incentive. Hoseph offered up the guildmaster's ring."

"In exchange for your head," Noncey added as he leaned against the other corner of the desk.

Mya scoffed. "Hoseph must be getting desperate. He's tried to kill me twice now and failed miserably. I don't know what he thinks the masters can do except hire more mercenaries, since assassins can't touch me." She wiggled her ring-clad finger. "What about Lakshmi and Kittal?"

"Lakshmi is *very* ambitious, so the ring will be quite a draw for her. She and Kittal are thick as thieves. There's no budging one without the other." Clemson quirked a smile at Noncey.

"That's true." The Master Blade smiled back.

Mya pursed her lips as she examined the two masters. They looked for all the world like a pair of deadly bookends. Clemson, though dwarfed by her hulking Enforcers, appeared confident and dangerous. Noncey, now casually fingering the curious buckle of his belt—wrought in silver and resembling the misshapen branches of a tree, it could have been some exotic and deadly weapon for all Mya knew—looked fearless and eager for the coming conflict. Mya might only have two of the five guild factions, but the Enforcers and

Blades represented the bulk of the guild's fighting force. She could have done worse.

"So, what do we do?" Clemson's incongruously dark eyebrows arched above her pale eyes. "Are we at war with the other factions?"

"Let's first find out if *they're* at war with *us*. I don't want a divided guild." *I had enough of that I Twailin*, Mya thought, remembering the five years of opposing her fellow masters. "You know the situation as well as I do, and your fellow masters much better. Any suggestions?"

"Yes. Kill that mad motherfucker of a priest." Clemson's curse belied her even-tempered tone.

"I agree." Noncey nodded. "Cut the head off the snake, get the guildmaster's ring back, and you hold all the cards. The others will fall into line. You appoint a guildmaster, and we're done."

"Excellent plan. I agree." Mya gave them a wry smile, pleased to find Clemson and Noncey's assessments in line with her own. "So, no killing other guild members yet unless they start a fight. Indiscriminate killing now will only lead to bad blood later. Send a message to Twist; recruiting him is at least worth a try. Lastly, issue a standing order to kill Hoseph on sight. Don't ask permission, just put a crossbow bolt in his heart. Clear?"

"Perfectly clear, Grandmaster," Clemson said.

"Crystal," Noncey added.

"Good. Now how do we *find* the mad motherfucker to kill him?" Using Clemson's own epithet drew smiles from both of them. "He's hard to get a hand on, impossible to track, and lethal if he catches you unaware. He can cast magic that knocks your mind for a loop and kill with a touch."

"We'll warn our people." Clemson frowned. "The problem is, we're not Hunters."

"Exactly." Noncey nodded. "We don't have the contacts necessary to track someone down in the city, especially someone who can appear and disappear magically."

Mya started to pace as her mind settled into problem-solving mode. "No, but you can observe. Send a few spies to watch the businesses of the other factions. If we're lucky, we might find out where they've moved their headquarters to. That information could lead us to Hoseph; he's got to sleep *somewhere*! Of course, we have to assume that they'll also be watching your businesses, so assign the rest of your forces to guard duty. If they spot anyone spying, capture them, but don't kill them unless you have to."

"I'll see what kind of information we can get from the Blades I've hired out as bodyguards." Noncey smiled at Mya as she whipped around to squint at him. "The order to form a security company came from Lady T, but it was your idea, I take it? It's a good one. We charge top rates and already have ears in several mansions in the Heights."

"Do you have anyone in the houses of Chief Magistrate Graving, Duchess Ingstrom, or Duke Seoli?" Inside information on Hoseph's co-conspirators would be quite the coup. Her hopes flagged as Noncey shook his head. "No matter. There's no such thing as bad information. Are we done here?"

The two masters shared a glance, then nodded.

"Good. Noncey, where're your new headquarters?"

"I'm set up at the Flint and Steel Cutlery Shop on Greenbriar, but more often than not you'll find me here." He glanced at the Master Enforcer and one corner of his mouth twitched. "Master Clemson and I...work well together."

Clemson flushed ever so slightly.

Something suddenly clicked in Mya's mind—the casual familiarity with which the masters sat beside one another, joked, exchanged glances, nearly finished each other's sentences. *Ahhh...* Well, that was their business. Both masters were no-nonsense assassins, and as long as they did their jobs, she wasn't interested in what went on behind closed doors.

"Until further notice, I'll be staying at the orphanage."

"The other masters know that, too. Do you want protection?" Clemson waved over several hulking Enforcers.

"No. I've got my own defenses, and caps will be coming and going for a while yet. Besides, I don't want to give the other factions any way to track someone from my home back here. I took some unusual precautions coming here today." She smiled. "I don't want to risk my two loyal masters."

Noncey laughed. "You've got balls, I'll give you that."

Mya just smiled. "I'll be in touch. I'll send my assistant, Dee, around to meet you. So you'll know him, he's tall, slender, clean shaven, and dark haired."

The masters nodded, and Mya left. Before she walked out the gate, the distillery's proprietor pressed a bottle into her hand.

"Gotta look like ya was here for a reason," she said, waving as the Grandmaster walked down the street.

Mya strolled back through the Dreggars Quarter, vigilant as always, but content that she at least had some assassins on her side. A delectable aroma stopped her in her tracks, and she stared at the tempting display of pastries inside a bakery window. Her stomach rumbled, reminding her that she hadn't eaten since breakfast. It was now mid-afternoon, and she had a long walk back to Midtown.

As she munched on a sweet roll and sipped a cup of blackbrew, her back firmly against a wall in a corner booth, she thought long and hard about her opposition: *Hunters, Inquisitors, and Alchemists…a deadly trio.* Mya was a great believer in the adage, "Know thy enemy". As a Hunter, she felt competent matching wits with Umberlin. As for the other factions, she had schooled herself on the relative strengths and weaknesses of each during her struggle against the masters in Twailin. But even more than that, one thing gave her comfort. She fingered the Grandmaster's ring as she strolled back out onto the street.

"They can't touch me…"

Dee drummed his fingers on the kitchen table, ignoring Paxal's annoyed glances.

Where is she?

Mya had been gone for hours to who knew where. He'd checked her office, but found no trace of the letter she had received. Had she gone to meet the masters? Had they lured her into a trap? Had mercenaries intercepted her? Was she lying dead in some alley? He knew he was being foolish. If anyone could walk the streets of Tsing without fear, it was Mya. The only person of any real danger to her was Hoseph, and if he tried to kill her in broad daylight, Mya would likely kick his head right off his shoulders.

Maybe that was what she was hoping for. Dee shifted in his seat, scraping the chair legs across the floor and earning him another annoyed glance from Paxal.

Why am I so damned nervous? Over the years he'd seen Mya off on hundreds of dangerous missions. What was so different now? Of course, in Twailin she'd had Lad to protect her, but now Dee knew she was every bit as capable and deadly. A vision flashed into his mind—Mya in his bed, their bodies flesh to sweat-slicked flesh…

Oh, gods, I'm in so much trouble! He hadn't thought that one night of intimacy would change how he looked at her so drastically.

The back door latch clicked. Dee vaulted up from his seat, bolting for the hall. The sight of Mya ducking through the door was like a gasp of air to a drowning man. Dee ran his eyes over her, relieved to see no torn clothing, no blood, no sign of any violence. Not even a sweat stain marred the cloth, despite what must have been a long walk in the sweltering heat. She'd explained that the wrappings she wore were enchanted to keep her comfortable, but he wondered if anyone else noticed that she never sweated.

Safe…she's safe.

Her sour expression stifled his relief. "What's wrong?"

"I saw a cap on the front stoop." Her voice was low, and she glanced toward the front of the house before pushing him into the kitchen. "Tell me our guests aren't back already."

"They never left." Dee's worry eased. If it was the constables she was concerned with, then whatever she had been doing must have gone well. "Paxal tried to run them off by serving lunch, but—"

"Hey! I heard that, you little pipsqueak!"

Laughter exploded from the urchins loitering about the kitchen.

"Admit it, Paxal, those sandwiches you served were vile."

"The kids ate them!"

Dee rolled his eyes. "I rest my case. Unfortunately, the constables also have strong stomachs and ate them. I bought some cookies from that bakery down the block to make up for the sandwiches."

Mya's expression turned stern. "Why are you *feeding* them? They'll *never* leave!"

"Hospitality." Dee raised his hands defensively and lowered his voice to a bare whisper. "Remember, they're here to talk with Moirin, concerned bodyguard of the late Lady T, heroine of the coronation, not Mya, impatient Grandmaster of Assassins and stone-cold killer. You're the one who brought them into this."

"Well, nothing to do but answer their questions, I suppose." Mya sighed and shoved a bottle into his hands. "By the way, Clemson and Noncey are on our side. I'll fill you in later."

"Good." Dee eyed the bottle of rum curiously as he considered her information. *Only two out of five?* Well, that *any* of the masters had backed Mya was good news. He had been afraid none of them would, considering the cool reception they'd given her so far. "Blackbrew?"

"Or how about something stronger?" Paxal grinned as he stirred a huge bubbling pot on the stove. "I can mull some wine."

"Maybe later, Pax. After their questions, I'm going to *need* a drink. Blackbrew sounds good right now." Mya strode down the corridor and greeted the constables. "Sorry I took so long. Thank you for waiting."

Dee busied himself filling a blackbrew pot and arranging another plate of cookies. He carried the tray out to the common room, not really paying attention to the conversation. Mya could handle herself there. Her mind had always been her best weapon, even considering the physical enhancements of her tattoos. He filled cups and handed out the cookies, playing the dutiful assistant.

A heavy thump at the front door brought the conversation up short.

"Tovi?" Sergeant Benjamin called, putting down his cup.

No answer.

A chill ran up Dee's spine.

The sergeant seemed just as discomforted. He rose to his feet, his eyes as sharp as his clothes were slovenly. "Wanless, check the window. Jorren, the door.

Mya also stood. Shooting Dee a warning glance, she jerked her chin at the door, and he followed Corporal Arryx.

"I don't see anyone," Wanless said as she peered through the window.

Arryx opened the door and Private Tovi slumped into the room, a crossbow bolt buried in his chest.

"Tovi!" The corporal bent over his fallen comrade, and a crossbow bolt buzzed over his head.

Dee felt the breeze of its passage before it thunked into the far wall. He was in motion even before Mya shouted "Close the door!"

Dee dashed forward to slam the door shut as Corporal Arryx dragged Tovi inside. Before his outstretched hands hit the stout oak, however, a gleaming cylinder flew through the open portal to strike him painfully in the chest. Stumbling back, he caught the shiny rod reflexively. As long as his forearm, capped on both ends with brass, and hot enough to scorch his hands, he'd never seen anything like it. Inside, a green liquid bubbled ominously.

This isn't good...

"Dee! Throw it!"

Dee pitched the cylinder out the door and slammed the portal shut. As the gap closed, he caught a glimpse of figures running from the burned-out building across the street toward the orphanage. The heavy latch clicked an instant before an explosion rattled the door against Dee's hands and popped his ears. Glass and splintered wood blasted inward from the three front windows.

Dee threw the bolt and whirled. The constables seemed unharmed, flattened against the walls, steel drawn and ready. Mya stood at the center of the room, a dagger in each hand, glaring out at the street. Glass pocked her skin and blood ran in tracks down her face, but she paid her wounds no notice.

"Pax!" she called toward the kitchen. "Watch the back! Dee! Get crossbows for the constables, then help Pax! They'll come at us from both sides!"

A crossbow bolt zipped through one of the shattered windows, and Mya jerked aside to evade it.

Dee didn't want to leave, but knew she was right. He dashed to the bottom of the stairs and shouted, "Crossbows!"

"Gettin' 'em!" Digger called from above.

Dee glanced down the hallway. The back door was still closed, and there was no sign of Paxal. "Come on!" he muttered, listening to the kids pounding around upstairs to retrieve the weapons.

Suddenly the back door crashed open, and a man with a crossbow stepped through, the weapon aimed directly at Dee's heart from barely twenty feet away. Dee stared, empty handed, unable to move to save his life.

Paxal lunged through the kitchen doorway and flung a huge pot of boiling soup into the invader's face. The crossbow cracked, but the bolt flew wild, lodging in the ceiling. With a scream, the man dropped to his knees, clutching his blistered face. The empty soup pot rang like a bell off the man's head, silencing his screams and sending him to the floor. Pax backed into the kitchen as another crossbow bolt zipped through the open back door to clatter off the wall.

Twigs and Digger trundled down the stairs, their arms loaded with crossbows and quivers. Dee grabbed one and leveled it at the gaping back door. "Take the rest to the common room!"

Digger dropped a quiver of bolts, and the boys dashed off.

A short woman in leathers leapt through the back door, firing her crossbow before she cleared the stoop. Dee flinched at the hot sting of the bolt grazing his side as the assassin dropped her weapon and charged, daggers filling her hands.

Dee shot her square in the chest.

Her startled blue eyes blinked in surprise, and her daggers clattered to the floor. She fell to her knees, mouth agape. The bolt's fletching twitched with the last beats of her heart, and she fell forward.

Dee reached for another bolt. "Pax, are you okay?"

"Bastard ruined my *soup*!"

Dee reloaded his crossbow. "Well, that's *one* good—"

"*Down!*" Mya screamed from the front of the house.

Dee flung himself into the protection of the stairwell as an explosion shook the building.

Mya dodged yet another crossbow bolt, her eyes flicking between the three shattered windows and the bolted door. Outside, figures flitted from cover to cover as they approached the building. The ones firing crossbows were not her biggest worry. The ones carrying explosives were.

Kittal... The Master Alchemist was obviously behind these attacks. Such specialized bombs weren't readily available. *Lakshmi and Umberlin, too?* she wondered. Would the three masters cooperate to kill her, or compete with one another, each eager to gain the guildmaster's ring?

Twigs and Digger dashed into the room clutching armfuls of crossbows. Without taking her eyes off the street, Mya motioned toward the constables, who took the weapons gratefully and aimed them out the windows.

Another bolt buzzed through a window. Mya knocked the shaft aside before it struck her, but its course was true. Without her enhanced reaction time, it would have hit her square in the chest. *Mercenaries. Better ones than Hoseph hired, and a lot of them.*

Digger caught her eye and Mya waved him and Twigs back. "Out!" she ordered. "Get—"

The front door smashed open, and a man leaned through and fired a crossbow. Mya flung a dagger at him as she dodged, but the bolt flew wide and high. *A distraction!* she realized too late. A rod of gleaming brass and glass tumbled through one of the windows.

"Down!" Mya snatched up the two fleeing urchins and flung them to the floor, upturning the divan over them. The constables sprawled for cover as the cylinder smashed against the far wall.

The explosion slammed Mya across the room. She hit the wall hard enough to ring her ears, but was back on her feet in a heartbeat. The room didn't fare nearly as well. Furniture had been shredded and splintered, and crumbling plaster hazed the air. Tongues of flame consumed the curtains and licked up the walls, spreading fast. There was no hope to control the fire. The orphanage would burn.

"Out! Out the back!" ordered Sergeant Benjamin as he hauled the dazed Wanless to her feet. Together, they grabbed their less-fortunate comrades—Alli and Kert lay unconscious or dead—and Corporal Arryx heaved Tovi to his shoulder.

Mya didn't know if the back would be any better than the front. Well-trained mercenaries, which these surely were, wouldn't leave such an obvious avenue for escape. Nonetheless, Benj was right; they couldn't stay here. The room was in flames and more assailants sprinted across the street, weapons at the ready. They'd be coming through the door and windows in moments. Mya flipped the scorched divan upright, and the two urchins scooted out.

"Digger, lead everyone out the back. Tell Dee and Pax I'll be right there." The boys dashed off without question. *Good kids...*

"Miss Moirin, we can't leave you!" protested the sergeant. "You're our only witness to—"

"Out!" she ordered. "I'll cover you. I can take care of myself here, but I can't take care of you, too."

"Go!" Sergeant Benjamin shouted after the briefest hesitation. The uninjured constables carried and dragged their dead and wounded down the hall after Digger.

Mya took a heartbeat to listen carefully, trying to filter out the shouts from the back of the house, hoping that they signified a successful retreat. *They'll be fine*, she told herself. I'm *the target here. Come get me, you bastards.*

Feet scuffed outside the front door. A man ducked in to shoot at her, but Mya was ready this time and put a dagger between his eyes. She took a step back, trying to look everywhere at once.

Attackers swarmed through the door and windows in a coordinated assault, crossbows cracking. Mya evaded two bolts, caught a third and sent it flying back at the shooter, and wrenched a fourth out of her thigh. Her eyes darted from one attacker to the next, seeking the real danger. *There!*

Though the door, behind the crossbowmen, a short figure stepped into the open, twisting the brass caps of a glass cylinder. Mya plucked her last dagger from her dress and hurled it into the man's stomach. He folded forward, the bubbling explosive falling from his grasp to roll across the floor. His comrades stared at the cylinder in panic and dove for cover.

Mya whirled and dashed to her office, slamming the door behind her. *One more thing to do...* She ducked behind her heavy oak desk as the explosion trembled the building. Smoke billowed under the door, screams and shouts attesting to the carnage outside. She muttered a prayer that it came from the mercenaries, not Dee, Pax, and her urchins.

Reaching beneath the desk, she hauled out the saddlebags containing the gold that Sereth had sent with Dee. Slinging them over her shoulder, she went to the door and warily opened it a crack.

A wave of heat scorched her face.

"Shit!" She slammed the door against the inferno filling the hallway. Even with her tattoos to heal her, she didn't want to walk through that hell.

But the office had no window. She was trapped.

"Like hell!"

Mya dashed to the desk and shoved it back near the door. Leaping across the polished surface to the other end, she braced her feet against the burning door and *pushed*. Her legs churning for purchase and a scream ripping from her throat, Mya shoved the heavy desk across the floor. Plaster shattered and wood splintered as the makeshift battering ram smashed through the wall and tumbled into the narrow verge between the orphanage and the next building. Mya plunged out behind it, landing in a pile of splinters and dust. She rolled to her feet, scanning for any mercenaries, but they must have concentrated their forces at the front and back entrances.

"Mya!" The desperate cry came from the alley behind the orphanage.

"Here, Dee!" Dashing around the corner, she breathed a relieved sigh as she skidded to a halt.

Aside from the injured constables, the only bodies that littered the ground were dead mercenaries. Dee's crossbow pointed at the open back door while the constables aimed theirs up and down the alley. Pax stood with a cleaver and butcher knife at the ready, and the urchins were armed with their own motley weapons.

Mya did a quick head count. *All here.*

"Sergeant Benjamin, I'm sorry about this." She ignored the startled looks the constables gave her. "I didn't think Hoseph would come after me again so soon, but he's obviously hired some professionals. Can you take care of your people?"

"Don't worry, Miss, I can take care of everyone." The sergeant brought a whistle to his lips and blew a high-pitched shrill. "Dozens of caps'll be here in moments. We'll take everyone someplace safe."

Uh-oh... "Oh, no, that's not necessary," Mya insisted. "They were after me. My remaining with you only puts you in danger."

"But..."

While the sergeant stuttered an objection, she strode over to Paxal and whispered, "Take the kids and find someplace quiet. When you're settled, leave a note for me where we first met here in town."

The old innkeeper nodded briskly. "Right! Come on, you little rug rats!" The urchins grumbled, but followed him down the alley.

"Wait! Miss, I can't allow witnesses to—"

"Sergeant, Paxal and the children were just bystanders and of no use to your investigation. *I'm* the one you were questioning. *I'm* the one Hoseph is after."

"That's why you have to stay with us." Benjamin ordered. "We'll take you into protective custody, keep you safe."

"No, Sergeant. I can't find the bastard behind this by hiding. I'll be in touch."

"You'll *stay*!" Benjamin's expression brooked no argument.

I don't have time for this! Facing the constable squarely, Mya put her hands on her hips. "Are you arresting me?"

"If I have to!"

"No, Sergeant. You *don't* want to do that." With only two of the constables uninjured, she knew she could easily best them. She saw the same realization on the sergeant's grizzled face. "I have to go. Don't worry, I'll be in touch." She grabbed Dee's arm. "Come on, Dee. We need to find someplace to get squared away."

"Yes, Miss Moirin." Dee trotted to catch up as she strode down the alley.

The sergeant grumbled and swore, but there was no pursuit. Mya brushed the dust and splinters from her tattered dress. "Sorry about all this, Dee. I honestly didn't think they'd attack so soon."

"Neither did I. I'm sorry, too."

She looked at him quizzically. "Sorry for what? You saved our lives by catching that first explosive."

"That was more luck than skill." He glanced over his shoulder toward the constables and lowered his voice. "When I thought you were caught in the fire, I...called you Mya, not Moirin."

"Damn...I didn't even realize. Do you think they noticed?"

"I don't know, but they certainly noticed *you*." As they rounded the corner out of sight of the constables, Dee reached behind her. She felt a tug, and he showed her a bloody splinter as long as his finger that he'd pulled from her back. "Your dress is ruined, and I'm going to be picking shrapnel out of your back for hours."

"Great."

Another whistle shrieked from the alley, answered by several others from all directions.

"Caps are on the way."

41

They strode quickly from the neighborhood, ducking through several narrow alleys to avoid the patrols running toward the burning orphanage. The clanging bell of a water wagon passed a couple of blocks away, obviously heading for the tower of black smoke that pinpointed the blaze.

Mya tried to channel her fury into some kind of a plan, but her head felt full of cotton, and her shredded dress tugged at the splinters in her back. She was too keyed up. She needed to settle down and think.

"We'll stop here." She pointed to a seedy flop house with a sign advertising rooms by the hour. "It's perfect."

"Really?" Dee winced and looked over her scorched and tattered clothing. "You don't think…"

"Don't worry. Nobody asks questions in a place like this, and nobody will think to look for us here. We'll find a better place tomorrow."

"Fine, but I'm not sleeping in a bed in a place like that. I don't need fleas."

Chapter IV

Even though the day had only just passed to evening, the tannery yard was quiet. Hoseph took that as a good sign; the Hunters were busy elsewhere. He crossed the yard unopposed, his stride quick and firm, his mood lighter than it had been in weeks. Even the stench of the curing hides didn't bother him.

He'd slept much of the day and woken with only the mildest of headaches, nothing like the persistent pounding that had plagued him for weeks now. To forestall a recurrence, he'd decided to conserve the talisman for emergencies and walked all the way to the Downwind Quarter. There was no rush. He'd seen the fire in Midtown and later walked past the burned-out hulk of the building where the usurper had hidden behind children. Mya was dead, and the Grandmaster's ring was within his grasp.

The two Hunters standing at the door to Twist Umberlin's office straightened as he approached, casting wary glances between them. They showed no sign of moving out of his way.

Hoseph's good mood twitched. "Move."

"The master's busy," said one guard, unintimidated by the priest's stare.

The high priest repressed a murderous urge. He didn't recognize these guards, so they probably didn't know who he was. He'd forgive the slight…this time. "I'm Hoseph. Twist may not be expecting me, but he *will* see me."

After another shared glance between the guards, one of them knocked and opened the door.

"Who the hell—" Twist Umberlin surged up from his desk chair. "Hoseph!"

"Master Hunter Umberlin." Hoseph smiled and strode toward the desk, ignoring the two Hunters in the office who trained their loaded crossbows at his chest. "Where is it?"

"Where is what?"

"The ring." Hoseph's smile fell. "The *Grandmaster's* ring! You took it off Mya's dead finger today, did you not?"

"No, I did *not*." The Master Hunter's tone was defiant, and he met Hoseph's glare straight on. "The mission was unsuccessful."

The priest's heart skipped a beat, and his face flushed with rage. "*Unsuccessful?* You had the *perfect* opportunity and more than half the guild at your disposal! How could you *fail?*"

"Killing someone like Mya isn't *easy*!" Twist snatched up a crystal tumbler half full of amber liquid and quaffed a third of it. "She took the brunt of two alchemical explosions without going down. I lost eight of my best Hunters and one of Kittal's senior Alchemists. Also, you didn't *tell* me she was working with the caps!"

"Since when do assassins work openly with the constabulary?" Hoseph scoffed.

"Since this morning. There were caps inside the house and out. My people think they killed a couple of them, but Mya got away."

"And did *your people* manage to follow her? You are *Hunters*, after all."

"No."

"Why not?"

"Because she's a *Master* fucking Hunter and as deadly as a rutting *dragon*!" Twist downed the rest of his liquor and slammed the glass onto the desk. "Tracking a Master Hunter is difficult. Tracking *Mya* would be suicide. She'd have slaughtered my people like sheep. Besides, there were caps all over the place. My people did well enough to get out of there."

Hoseph spun, pacing to the door and back, biting back a curse at the Hunters' incompetence and their master's lame excuses. "So now Mya knows she's being hunted and has undoubtedly gone into hiding. If she recognized any of your people, she might even know the blood contracts were destroyed, which will put her even more on guard."

"She's got to come out sometime," Twist grumbled. "And if she is working with the caps, they'll know where she is, or she'll come to them. Lakshmi's got a few caps on her payroll. They can find out where she's hiding."

"Possibly." Hoseph's anger ebbed slightly. There was still hope.

44

All he needed was patience, time, and competent assassins on his side. The last of those three he could do something about. "Who was in charge of the attack?"

"Bev, my senior journeyman. She's dead."

"Well then, she's already paid for her failure." Hoseph paused, tapping his chin as if in consideration. "Who is your current senior journeyman?"

Twist nodded toward one of the two Hunters in the room with them. "Embree's now my senior. Don't worry, he's qualified to take over for Bev."

Hoseph regarded Embree. The assassin still held his crossbow at the ready, not quite aimed at Hoseph, but his finger next to the trigger. He met Hoseph's gaze confidently.

Twist lifted the decanter from the corner of his desk and tilted it to fill his glass. "Why do you care?"

"Because..." Hoseph snatched the glass from under the decanter, and liquor spilled onto the papers beneath.

"Hey!" Twist righted the decanter and reached for his glass, just as Hoseph had hoped he would. "What do you think—"

Hoseph's free hand closed on the Master Hunter's wrist. With the invocation of Demia's blessing, pearly light flared between his fingers. Twist Umberlin opened his mouth in surprise and fell dead to his desk, his soul released to burn in whichever Hell suited incompetents.

"I *think*..." Hoseph put the glass down atop the sodden papers smeared with running ink. Dispassionately, he wrenched the master's ring from the dead man's finger and turned toward the appalled Hunters. "...that the guild needs a new Master Hunter."

Two crossbows pointed at his heart. They could easily kill him before he could invoke the talisman and melt away, but neither had fired. Doubt filled their eyes. They feared him, unsure exactly what he was capable of.

Good... Tynean Tsing II had ruled both the guild and the empire under the simple premise that fear begat obedience. Hoseph couldn't agree more.

Hoseph proffered the still-warm ring. "Are you up for the job, Senior Journeyman Embree, or must I find someone *else* who wants this ring?"

"Bloody…" The assassin's hand twitched on the trigger of the crossbow, but his eyes flicked to the ring.

Hoseph didn't even bother to glance at the second assassin; she wouldn't do anything without an order from her superior. Embree was next in the chain of command, and if there was one thing that these assassins held sacred, it was the hierarchy of power.

Embree lowered his crossbow and took the ring. He frowned at the circle of obsidian for a moment before slipping it onto his finger.

"Excellent, Master Hunter Embree." Hoseph tugged his robes straight and strode for the door. "Find and kill the traitor, Mya, and you might even make guildmaster before you're done."

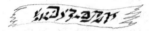

Arbuckle checked himself in the mirror and cringed. The crown on his head looked more ridiculous than regal, with its elaborate filigree and surfeit of gems and jewels. Whichever of his imperial ancestors had ordered its creation had possessed more conceit than taste.

He adjusted it and frowned. "Can't We wear something simpler, Baris? We feel like a fool."

"For your first formal dinner as emperor?" The valet looked as if he'd been asked to serve up his own firstborn as the main course. "Your Majesty dare not. It would be a grave insult to your guests."

"Fine." He shrugged his shoulders into the ridiculously flamboyant dress jacket that Baris held out for him, and sighed. "But we'll have to figure something out. We are *not* going to wear this heavy thing every day."

"You need only wear the formal crown for special occasions, Majesty." Baris tugged the jacket cuffs straight, then brushed non-existent lint from the emperor's shoulders. "There's a less-dressy one that's specifically for private audiences with ranking nobles, and a circlet will do for casual affairs and audiences with minor nobles or commoners."

"Wait!" A sudden thought widened Arbuckle's eyes. "What about the plaster crown We wore at the coronation? It looks amazingly real. No one will know the difference."

Baris shook his head. "I'm sorry, Majesty, but it was damaged during the...excitement. It will take some time to be repaired."

"Damn," Arbuckle muttered.

His secretary's suggestion that Arbuckle consolidate all his farewells at a dinner had seemed reasonable this morning and had saved him many appointments throughout the day, but the summons to bathe and dress for the evening had come when he was engrossed in the wording of the New Accords. Aside from having to dress like a peacock, he resented the need to appease the egos of those who had opposed his quest for equal justice for commoners and nobles alike. Some of those attending tonight's dinner had actually engaged in a conspiracy to assassinate him. *Politics!* There was no way around it. As emperor, he could pass whatever laws he liked, but the nobility was responsible for implementing those laws in the far reaches of the empire. If so inclined, they could thwart his will, and all his reforms would be for naught. As much as he despised most of them, he needed them.

"Is Your Majesty ready?" Baris reached for the door.

He adjusted the stupid crown again and sighed. "Yes."

"Your Majesty!" Tennison bowed low as Arbuckle stepped from the bedchamber. "I bear grave news."

Arbuckle knew that tone well; he had heard it too often lately. His stomach knotted, the tension highlighted by his bad mood. "What now?"

"There was an attack on Miss Moirin...the late Baroness Monjhi's bodyguard." Tennison informed him solemnly. "She survived, but several constables and bystanders were killed. The building she was staying in burned to the ground."

"Gods..." Arbuckle gritted his teeth. *Because of me...because she saved my life.* "That gods-be-damned priest, Hoseph! He's got to be behind this."

"The priest was not identified by the constables at the scene, Majesty, but there was no opportunity to question Miss Moirin. We don't know what she might have seen."

"Where is she? Is she safe?"

"She refused protection from the constabulary. She's gone into hiding, though she told the constable in charge of the investigation that she would be in touch. She didn't say when."

"Gone into hiding. And no wonder…" *The blademasters of Kos. Imperial guards and knights. Baroness Monjhi. Is everyone who helps me cursed to die by violence?*

"Should I order the constabulary to search for her?" Tennison asked.

Arbuckle waved a hand. 'No. If she felt the need to go into hiding, We'll respect her wish and hope that she's as good as her word. Leave a message for her with Chief Constable Dreyfus. We would *very* much like to meet with Miss Moirin at her earliest convenience." *If she's still alive…*

"Yes, Majesty."

Arbuckle strode toward the door, his cadre of imperial guards falling in around him. "And send for the high priest of the Temple of Demia. We need to speak to him about their homicidal cleric. We know We can't dictate to the churches, but We can *certainly* make requests."

"Yes, Majesty."

Arbuckle twisted his neck to loosen the muscles that seemed bunched up to his ears. Though the crown was a burdensome weight, it was a feather compared to the future of the empire resting on his shoulders. But he was emperor and must survive, despite the lives being spent to preserve his.

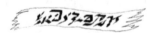

"You're sure this doesn't hurt?"

"No pain, just pressure." Mya felt a tug, and something clanked into the wash basin. "Was that more glass?"

"No. Porcelain." Dee sighed and pressed something against her back. "The explosion must have shattered the blackbrew service and sent pieces flying like sling bullets."

Mya clutched the pillow under her chin and wrinkled her nose at the strong smell of lye. At least it assured her that the linens were clean. The towels had been similarly laundered. Dee had inspected the lumpy mattress and pronounced it vermin free before he ordered her to strip and lie down. There was more pressure, then a tug and another clank.

"You've already healed over some of these shards. I don't know if I should try to cut them out or not. You've lost a lot of blood."

"Leave them. They don't hurt, and I never get fever from wounds. The runes prevent it."

"Handy things…" Dee's fingers rand down her back, stopped, and probed the flesh. "No, some are large. They've got to come out. Just because they don't hurt doesn't mean they won't do damage later."

He stood and strode two steps to the corner—the room was barely large enough for a bed and a rickety dresser—rifled through his things, and pulled out a dagger. It was the last one they had; all Mya's had been lost in the fight. Settling back on the edge of the bed, Dee bent over his task again, cutting, excising, swabbing.

After a long silence punctuated by several more clanks in the basin, he asked hesitantly, "How do they work? Do certain runes have certain functions, or is it all one big spell?"

"There are separate spells for each enhancement. The runemage used to chat while he…inscribed them. It took years." The memory of Vonlith's needles sent an unpleasant shiver down Mya's spine. "He said there's a lot of redundancy. If one rune is completely destroyed, there are others to keep the magic intact. As you see, they move around."

"Yes, I see…" Dee whispered.

Fingertips brushed her flank, and another shiver tingled her flesh, this one pleasant. Warm yearning spread through her, but she lay still as Dee dug yet another splinter out of her back. Not for the first time, Mya acknowledged the impulse that had compelled her to confess her secret to Dee. His admiration allowed her to once again see her tattoos as a benefit, not a burden. *Besides, there's no way I could have pulled all this shit out of my own back.*

Finally, Dee set aside the dagger and the wash basin. Dampening a clean towel with the ewer of water from the dresser, he wiped the blood from her back as gently as if bathing a child. "There. You're done." A drop of water trickled down her side. Dee wiped it off with a slow, warm finger.

Abruptly, he drew the sheet up over her and stood. "I should go out. Your dress is ruined, and we have nothing else for you to wear. You need some daggers, too. It's already late."

"And all the shops are closed," she reminded him, refusing to move. Maybe if she ignored the world it would go away. "Do it in the morning."

"All right. I'll put your wrappings to soak. You rest."

"Fine." Mya listened to him fuss at the dresser, rinsing his hands, dumping the bits of debris he'd dug out of her into the waste bin. It sounded as if the glass from all three windows had been lodged in her back.

Thoughts of the afternoon's attack raked her mind as wickedly as the shards of glass had pierced her flesh. Unlike Hoseph's previous attempts on her life, this one must have been guild-planned and guild-equipped. They had to have employed mercenaries for the actual attack, but such forces could be hired for the right price. A small investment considering the prize: the guildmaster's ring.

There'll be Inquisitors asking questions about me, Hunters tracking me, and Alchemists preparing more bombs. Mya clenched her hands beneath the pillow as her mind raced.

"Stop it."

Dee's command snapped Mya out of her obsessions. She looked over her shoulder at him. "Stop what?"

"You're tensing up like you're ready for a fight." Sighing, Dee sat beside her again and pulled the sheet down. His smooth hands ran down her back, deft fingers kneading taut muscles. "Relax. You're all in knots."

"I really should—oh!" Her shoulder muscle twitched as a knot crunched under his thumb, then eased as he applied pressure to the spot. "Ahhh."

"You need to *relax.*" His thumb dug in. "Breathe…"

Mya took a deep breath and let it out slowly as Dee pressed into the knotted muscle. His thumb made tiny circles that radiated outward from the center, working the knot into submission. Successful, he kneaded her shoulders until he found another knot. Mya concentrated on breathing as Dee's hands eased the tension from her muscles. Her mind, however, refused to give up its distressing train of thought.

"You're not relaxing," Dee complained.

"I can't stop thinking about the attack. I never *dreamt* it would come so soon, especially not with constables there." She heard a chirp, and realized she was grinding her teeth.

"Well, I can't massage your *mind*."

"No...but..." That sweet yearning returned. She twisted and rolled over. "You could distract me...please."

Dee paused, looking down at her with a curious expression on his face. For a moment, she thought he might refuse, but then he trailed his fingers down her belly, her legs...light and sure. His reply was low and husky. "I can do that."

"Do that..." Mya closed her eyes and smiled as his fingers brushed sensitive spots, a shiver chasing his fingertips. "Mmmm, yes...*that*."

Dee's fingers worked their magic, then his mouth, and finally all of him. Somewhere in that gentle, wonderful process, Mya forgot her worries.

CHAPTER V

Chief Magistrate Graving burst into his study bearing an armload of parchment and a scowl that would have curdled milk.

"Good morning, Chief Magistrate."

The portly man stopped cold, stifling a strangled gasp as the papers fluttered to the floor. His eyes widened, then narrowed at the robed figure seated behind his desk. "Hoseph!" He whirled and threw the bolt to his study door, then turned back to glare. "What in the names of all the Gods of Light are you *doing* here? Every constable in the city's looking for you!"

"I've come to salvage whatever I can from this debacle." Hoseph reclined in the thickly cushioned chair, his feet propped atop the polished wood of the desk top. "I hope you don't mind that I made myself comfortable. I didn't know how long I would have to wait."

"Mind?" Graving bent to scoop up the fallen documents. "Why should I mind a home invasion by the most-wanted felon in Tsing?" He flung the papers down on his desk and glared anew. "By all means, make yourself at home!"

Hoseph had, in fact, made himself quite at home. He'd arrived in the magistrate's study in the small hours of the morning to give himself time to recover from traveling through the Sphere of Shadow. Now the pain behind his eyes and the ringing in his ears had faded to a mild irritant, and he was able to maintain a mien of thoughtful assurance. He would need a clear head to deal with Graving.

"You've undoubtedly heard about Lady T's treachery and resultant demise." He paused to let the implication sink in fully. Graving already knew that betraying their conspiracy meant instant death, but the point bore repeating. Rising, he waved the chief magistrate toward the chair behind the desk, seating himself in one of the less-comfortable ones.

"Of course I heard. I've also seen new placards with your updated likeness on them." Graving squinted at Hoseph. "They're dangerously accurate."

Hoseph fumed. He'd seen them too. Mya had apparently described him anew to the constables, forcing him to abandon his acolyte disguise—*Forgive me, Demia*—in favor of a vagabond. He self-consciously rubbed the stubble on his head; it itched, but was growing fast. In a few days, he'd be unrecognizable. "We're talking about Lady T, not me."

"Why would she betray us?" Graving dropped into the chair with a grunt. "I thought she was part of your...secret constabulary."

"I don't know, though I have suspicions." Whether Mya had pressured Lady T into the betrayal or Tara had divulged their plot to her didn't matter at this point. "Suffice to say that she's been duly punished."

"But she *knew* us! What if she gave the emperor our names?"

Hoseph snorted dismissively. "If she had given your names to the emperor, you'd be in the palace dungeon. Now, I need you to get word to the conspiracy's remaining members to see what they—"

"Forget it!" Graving interrupted. His pudgy face puckered with displeasure, then slacked with apprehension when he caught sight of the thunderous expression on Hoseph's face. "Of course, *I'll* help you as well as I can, but the others... I doubt they'll be a part of any more subterfuge. The damage is done anyway." He gestured to the pile of parchments with disgust. "The emperor's *edicts* have been ratified into law. He's also drafting a formal document to rectify the inequities between the classes. He plans to give the commoners the justice he's promised, and now there's nothing to stop him."

Hoseph reined in his temper. These aristocratic fools had done little enough, and now they were just giving up. "Unless we do away with Arbuckle and place Duke Tessifus on the throne. What's been done can be undone."

"Not without risking open rebellion, I'm afraid." Graving shook his head sadly. "Denying the commoners equal consideration under the law is one thing. Granting it to them then trying to take it away is something else entirely. You saw the damage that rabble did during the Night of Flames, and that was when they were *celebrating*! Should they revolt, the only way to keep order would be to occupy the city with the entire standing army. Doing *that* would tempt our neighbors to the south. That border is far from stable, and the Morrgrey are likely to take advantage of any lapse in Tsing's defenses. We can't risk war."

"Why not?" Hoseph considered the prospect, a whole new scenario blooming in his mind as Graving gaped at him. "A war would certainly discredit the new emperor's dangerous policies, make him seem weak, and change the commoners' view of him."

"But…the loss of life! The destruction of property…" Graving swallowed, his chins quivering.

Hoseph waved away the man's concerns. "The lives of soldiers and the property of peasants are commodities to be spent when the need arises, Chief Magistrate. We wouldn't allow foreign armies to march on the capital, of course, but setting a few of the southern provinces afire would be a reminder that a *strong* emperor is the only thing keeping the empire safe. The last idealistic holdouts, like Duke Mir in Twailin, could *use* such a lesson. Now, about our disinclined colleagues … They tempt my wrath, Graving." Hoseph let slip some of his restrained anger. "Do I have to discipline them as I did Lady T?"

"Killing them will gain you nothing and risk much, Hoseph. They're all laying low, hiding behind well-armed bodyguards. You may be able to blink in and out of thin air, but you bleed. You're mortal. They'll have no compunction about setting their dogs on you. A trail of noble corpses would only compound the charges against you."

Hoseph fumed. Graving had a point, but not disciplining the reluctant conspirators would set a bad precedent. *And sending their wretched souls to Demia would be satisfying…*

"Besides…" Graving waved a hand at the piles of parchment. "…given time and enough of the emperor's new *laws*, they may come around."

"Time…" Hoseph gritted his teeth.

Was Graving being truthful, or simply deferring Hoseph's wrath? Granted, getting all the conspirators together would be problematic—using the talisman to transport so many people in so little time would tax Hoseph beyond endurance. Perhaps he should concentrate on finding and eliminating Mya first and worry about the new emperor later. Focusing his energy on one task seemed prudent. Tessifus' sons were still safely in Master Inquisitor Lakshmi's care, so their hold on the next in line to the throne was undiminished. And indeed, they needed time to condition the youngest boy to be the next Imperial Grandmaster. But Graving still might be able to help.

"What about the constabulary? Can you persuade them to ease their pursuit of me?" Hoseph could roam the streets of the Downwind District and Dreggars Quarter easily enough, but north of the river, the constables were looking closely at every priest and acolyte of every sect. The wanted posters hanging around the city now displayed his new guise all too accurately.

"Not likely." Graving interlaced his sausage-like fingers. "They've word directly from the emperor to spare no effort to hunt you down. Lady T's bodyguard is working with them. Murdering a noble has earned you the enmity of many powerful people, my friend."

Hoseph didn't for a moment consider Graving a friend, but took the advice for what it was worth. Graving had considerable pull with Chief Constable Dreyfus, but the chief magistrate wasn't about to stick his fat neck out to help Hoseph right now. There were, however, others who might help the priest...given the proper incentive.

"Very well." Hoseph stood, dissatisfied with the results of the meeting, but willing to adjust his strategy to suit the information the magistrate had provided. "I'll be in touch."

"Don't pop in here in the afternoon or evening. I often have people over."

Hoseph bristled at Graving laying down rules, but nodded in agreement. Grasping the silver skull, he invoked its power and faded away.

Dee clutched Mya's hand, relishing it while he could. It was just part of their ruse, of course, but that didn't matter; he'd enjoy it while it lasted. Surveying the tidy little flat in mock distain, he shook his head. "I don't know, Master Quince. It seems so…*small*."

Actually, he was quite pleased with the find. The apartment had a bedroom, kitchen, living area, and bath complete with—*thank the Gods of Light*—a hand pump to bring water from a cistern. On the border between Midtown and the Heights, it was far enough from the orphanage to confound searchers, yet close to many conveniences, not the least of which was a seamstress' shop just downstairs where they could have new clothing made to replace all they'd lost in the fire. They had seen no one on the stairs as they ascended, and the landlord lived elsewhere, so there were few eyes to see them coming and going. The place was exactly what they needed, but he wasn't about to let the prospective landlord see his delight.

He squeezed Mya's hand. "What do you think, my dear?"

"I think it'll have to do until we find a *proper* house." Mya pursed her lips in a moue. "You *did* promise me a proper house, Donally, and I mean to have one. My dowry won't buy us a mansion, but I'll not live as a pauper, even for you. If I need to ask Daddy for more money…"

"Not to worry, dear. We'll find your house, but these things take time." Dee nodded to Master Quince. "We'll take it for one month."

The landlord, whose eyes had lit up at the word 'dowry', now frowned. "I'm more interested in a long-term tenant. Two month minimum, and you leave at least two weeks before that's up to give me time to get another tenant."

Dee had a sudden vision of having to return to the flophouse if this deal fell through. They had decided for security reasons to stay in any one place no longer than a month. *But it's the principle of the matter…* "Your advertisement said *nothing* about a long-term requirement, and—"

"Sweet*heart*," Mya interrupted, a false smile on her face, "we can afford to pay that."

Dee tried not to wince at the pressure of her grip. They *could* afford it, but Sereth's money wasn't going to last forever. Granted, Mya could request more from Clemson and Noncey, but they couldn't expect an inexhaustible supply. A guild war was expensive, and who knew how long it might last? *But Mya's the boss…*

"I'll pay you for a month and a half, and we'll be out in one."

"Done." The landlord extended a hand and Dee shook it.

"Here's the key. Try to keep the noise down during the day. Mistress Gantry in the shop below has ears like a fox, and *complains*."

"We won't be noisy during the day." Mya smiled impishly up at Dee. "After *sunset*, however..."

"Dear, *please*." Dee blushed and looked mortified, hardly an act. "My apologies, Master Quince. New brides, you know..."

"All too well, my boy!" The man grinned, his hand still extended though Dee had released his grip. "The money, if you don't mind."

"Of course." Dee released Mya's hand and paid the man, who, with his pocket jingling, left the apartment with a smile.

Dee threw the bolt on the door, checked to make sure the windows were closed, and drew the drapes. The apartment occupied the southwest corner of the building, sporting a good view of two streets from the front room and bedroom, and a limited view of an alley out the bathroom window. He peered out, relieved to see nothing suspicious. Nonetheless, he pulled their disassembled crossbow and bolts out of one of their bags and started assembling the weapon on the table. "Well, nobody tried to kill us, so I think we may have made it."

Bringing Mya here in the middle of the day had been a huge risk, but there was no other option. He'd bought her an overly large dress, and they'd added padding to hide her shape. A hat with a veil disguised her hair and face.

"Don't count your eggs before they're in the basket," Mya warned, easily lifting the leather bags he had lugged up the stairs and heading for the bedroom. They didn't have much, but gold was heavy. "Put water on to heat. After two nights in that flophouse, I need a bath."

"Right." Dee doffed his jacket and draped it on a kitchen chair, then rolled up his sleeves before laboriously lighting the coal-fired stove. The heat would be oppressive, but a cold bath would be worse. Filling a huge copper kettle from the pump, he hefted it onto the stovetop. When the fire finally caught, he opened the damper. The iron stove clicked and popped with the rising heat.

Mya's raised voice reached him. "The bed linens are musty. They'll have to be laundered."

"Of course." Fishing a tattered page of parchment and a pencil from his waistcoat pocket, Dee added 'launder sheets' to his growing

57

list of things to do. "Are there towels in the bathroom?"

After a moment, a cupboard door slammed and Mya called out, "Just the one on the rack."

"What else?" he muttered as he prowled the kitchen, opening cabinets and drawers and jotting notes as needed. He added plates, bowls, and cups to his list—*Furnished apartment, my ass! No dishes?*—with a disgusted flourish.

"Put *food* on that list!"

Dee started at the unexpected voice and whirled to find Mya standing right behind him.

"Sorry, didn't meant to startle you," she said, an impish grin belying her claim.

"You'd think I'd be used to it after worked for Lad. He was quiet as a..." His voice trailed off when he realized that Mya was clad only in her wrappings, a single strip of black cloth snugged around her limbs and torso. Dee grew warm. "Shouldn't you be...wearing clothes?"

Mya waved off his question. "That dress was too uncomfortable. Besides, it's only you and me here."

That's the problem. Dee swallowed hard and tried to keep his eyes on his list.

"We've got a lot to do." Mya started to pace, as she always did when plotting strategy. "First off, I need to change the way I look again. Inquisitors and Hunters will be searching for me, but they've only seen me with dark hair." Mya ran her hand through her short locks, dyed black to hide her natural red hue.

"The blonde wig you wore to the coronation *really* changed your appearance."

"Yes, but a wig's too cumbersome. Pick up something to lighten my hair, and scissors for a trim. There's a cosmetic shop not far up the street, I think."

"Okay." He made a note. "What about clothing?"

"Definitely soft boots and dark pants and shirt for going out at night." She started ticking items off on her fingers. "A working woman's outfit. A decent dress for around town. And some boys' clothing. Let's say...something scruffy so I'd blend in with a crowd in the Dreggars Quarter. Oh, and maybe an outfit suitable for a well-bred young man on the town. I want all my options covered."

Dee's pencil scratched. "All right. Weapons?"

"I've got the daggers you bought, but can always use a couple more. Touch base with Noncey for those." Mya abruptly stopped pacing and picked up the crossbow from the table, looking at it, then at Dee. "You can't very well carry *this* around, but he might have something you can conceal. Something you can use better than a dagger."

Dee stiffened. His lack of skill with a blade had caused him no end of grief, and it still stung.

"I'm not *disparaging* you, Dee." Mya sighed. "You're lousy with a blade, so you gave it up. That was smart. Instead of becoming a mediocre fighter, you played to your strengths and became an *excellent* assistant. And now you work for the Grandmaster!"

Dee squelched the sarcastic remark he wanted to make. She was right. Had he continued to go the route of the rest of the apprentice Hunters, he'd probably be working as a bag-man on the streets of Twailin.

Mya resumed pacing. "The law against commoners carrying swords has forced Noncey to arm his people with some unusual weapons. He's got quite a collection, and I'm sure there'll be something to your liking. Ask him."

"Right." He made another note.

"Also check in with Sergeant Benjamin. Maybe they've made some headway in their search for Hoseph or gotten a lead in their investigation of the attack on the orphanage. If so, I want details."

"Will do."

"And check the *Prickly Pair* for a note from Pax."

"Got it."

"And we need *food*! I'm starved!"

"Already on the list." Dee waved his list at her. "Don't worry. This won't be nearly as complex as setting up Lad's household when he became guildmaster."

Mya stopped and grinned at him. "I'm glad you're here, Dee. I wouldn't know the first thing about setting up house. I'm too used to living in an inn with Pax to take care of me."

"You'd make a lousy housewife," Dee admitted with a smile.

"Actually," she cocked her head at him, "how do *you* know so much about it?"

"My mother was a housekeeper and seamstress at a minor noble's house." A long-lost memory stole into his mind, and he could almost smell his mother's flowery scent, feel her warm lips as she kissed his cheek. It had been a long time since Dee had thought of her, and guilt tweaked him.

"I never knew that. So, you had a happy childhood?"

"Yes," he admitted. "She'd take me with her while she did her chores and ran errands, which is why I know what's what around a house and about clothes. Nobles are finicky about their clothes. But she died when I was ten, and the master put me out on the street."

"Oh."

Mya was quiet for a moment, and Dee wondered about her own childhood. From what Paxal had told him, it must have been far from happy. He couldn't ask, of course. She started pacing again, biting a nail unconsciously before clenching her fists at her sides.

Dee watched her body slowly tense, like a watch spring wound too tight. He tapped his list. "All these errands will take several trips, and it's apt to take at least a day or two to get our clothing made. How about something to read to pass the time while I'm out and about?"

"Good idea. Pick something up for me. Anything. Sorry for making you do all the legwork, but too many assassins know what I look like. I don't dare go out until I've got good disguises. Although," she threw her hands up in frustration, "despite all my disguises, Hoseph was somehow able to follow me back to the orphanage, so it might be *useless* to try to fool him."

"No problem. The guild doesn't know what I look like."

"Hoseph does." She shot him a warning glance.

"Yes, but he's not *looking* for me, and Tsing is a big city." It was safer for Dee to go out than for Mya right now and they both knew it. Folding the list, he stuffed it into a pocket and rolled down his sleeves, then counted the money he was carrying to ensure it was enough for all the shopping.

"Be careful touching base with the constables. Don't tell them where we're living. The same goes for Noncey and Clemson. I told them to watch for you, but they might be twitchy." She turned and looked him in the eye, holding up two hands in a warding gesture. "And for the gods' sake, don't let *anyone* follow you back here."

"I've got it, Mya." Dee gave her a tolerant smile. "I *am* a Hunter, you know."

"I know."

The kettle whistled.

"Go get ready for your bath," he said. "I'll bring the hot water."

Mya flashed a final quick smile and trotted toward the bathroom.

Dee went to the kitchen and lifted the heavy kettle from the stove. As he approached the bathroom, he heard water sloshing into the big copper tub. Mya worked the pump handle with one hand and unwound her wrappings with the other, the long strip of enchanted cloth pooling at her feet. Dee poured the boiling water into the tub, trying not to look at the beautiful expanses of rune-etched skin and the lithe muscle rippling beneath.

The kettle empty, he turned away and hurried back to the kitchen to refill it. They'd need hot water for Mya's hair, too. "I'll dash out and pick up a few things while you bathe."

"Fine." The sound of the pump quieted.

Dee grabbed his jacket and turned for the door, but stopped short. Mya stood at the bathroom door with only a towel draped over one shoulder, casual in her nudity and oblivious to his body's spontaneous reaction.

A slow smile graced her lips, and she glanced down at his trousers, then back up to his face. "Sure you don't want to join me?"

Or maybe not so oblivious...

He stifled a surge of desire and tried for a wry smile. "If we start *that*, I'll *never* get the shopping done."

"Good point." She strode to the apartment door and threw open the bolt. "Hurry back, and be careful."

Dee stopped and looked her in the eye. If they had been in love, he would have kissed her and told her not to worry. *If we were in love...*

They weren't.

At least, Mya wasn't. Dee truly didn't know what his feelings were, beyond confused.

Gods, I'm in trouble...

"I should be back in less than an hour." He nodded to the kitchen. "Keep the water hot. I've got to do your hair."

"Right." She opened the door and let him out.

Chris A. Jackson and Anne L. McMillen-Jackson

It closed behind him and he heard the bolt clack into place. Hurrying down the steps, Dee tried to banish Mya from his mind. He had work to do and had to be vigilant. Mooning over someone who didn't love him—and never would—could get him killed.

As the footman cleared the breakfast dishes, Arbuckle sipped his morning blackbrew and examined the two pieces of paper lying on the white linen cloth. They were both lists of names, but that's where their resemblance ended.

The first was inked in Tennison's ornate hand on fine vellum and included many of the highest nobles and magistrates in Tsing. He and Tennison had compiled it after the first attempt on his life, a list of those who might benefit from Arbuckle's untimely death.

The second was written on poor-quality parchment, only eight names and a short note. This one had been delivered by the stealthy late-night visitor who had managed to invade his very sleeping chamber. Arbuckle shuddered and reminded himself that all the secret passages in the palace had been sealed. *Those that the dwarves know about, at least.* If the message was to be believed, these were the names of those who conspired to kill him. The note had saved his life, proving its validity.

Arbuckle drummed his fingers on the table. Nobody had tried to kill him since, but that didn't mean the conspirators had abandoned their plot. Now was the time to martial his forces and secure his safety against the eventuality of another attempt.

Absently holding out his cup for more blackbrew, the new emperor analyzed the lists. He'd examined them before, but so much had transpired lately that he'd had little time to really study them. Then a thought struck him, and his blackbrew cup clattered into its saucer.

"Verul, might We borrow your pen?"

"Certainly, Majesty." The ever-present scribe stepped forward and placed the beautiful object into the emperor's hand.

"Thank you." Arbuckle drew a careful line through the names on the longer list that were also on the shorter. When he was done,

62

the top name on the longer list remained unblemished. He handed the pen back and motioned his secretary over. "Tennison, what do you think of this?"

"Duke Tessifus remains the chief beneficiary of your death, Majesty." The secretary nodded. "As your nearest cousin, he is next in line to the throne until you produce an heir. Yet his name is not on the list of conspirators."

"Exactly! Which makes me wonder, if *these* people..." he tapped the list of conspirators, "...want Tessifus on the throne, why have they apparently not included the duke in their plot?"

Tennison's angular face became somber. "The duke *has* consistently spoken out against the changes Your Majesty is instituting. Perhaps they believe that he would revoke your new policies and return to your father's."

"But they couldn't be *sure* if he wasn't directly involved." Arbuckle shook his head dubiously. "They've worked very hard to have Us killed. We can't *imagine* what they offered Duveau to make the attempt. After all that effort, they can't just *hope* that an Emperor Tessifus would rule the empire to their liking." He tapped both lists. "There's something going on between them. We must find out what it is."

"The people Commander Ithross employed to discreetly watch them haven't reported anything unusual. Duke Tessifus meets with many nobles, but none more than any other. One of the conspirators," Tessifus pointed to a name on the short list, "Magistrate Ferrera, disappeared. She hasn't appeared in court, and her servants can't say where she is."

Arbuckle raised his eyebrows. "Perhaps her conscience got the better of her and she's dropped out of the conspiracy, fled the country. That may indicate their organization is falling apart."

"Commander Ithross would still like to have the rest detained and questioned."

"No, for two reasons." Arbuckle fixed Tennison with a resolute stare. "First, arresting them will tip my hand. Keeping them ignorant of what We know might give Us more than would an interrogation. Second, I will *not* imprison citizens without hard evidence and due process. This note is not sufficient evidence. But that brings us back to Our initial question: why does the conspiracy not include the person with the most obvious reason for wanting Us dead?"

"I don't know, Majesty."

"Well…We don't think any of the *conspirators* are likely to tell Us, but there is one person We *could* ask." Arbuckle downed the last of his blackbrew. "Arrange an audience with Duke Tessifus."

Tennison frowned. "That might tip your hand as well, Majesty, if he *is* involved."

"Perhaps, but We're tired of fumbling around in the dark." He tapped the list of conspirators again. "They *have* to have a plan for what happens after We're dead, and Tessifus has to be a part of that plan."

"It seems logical, Majesty."

"Yes." Arbuckle stood and frowned. "Tell Ithross and Keyfur that We plan to talk to the duke, and that We want security in place for the meeting. *Discreet* security."

"Yes, Majesty." Tennison scratched in his ledger.

"Good, now let's get to work. We've made a good start on the New Accords, but We want to get this right the first time. The stronger the case We make for instituting sweeping changes in the justice system, the less likely the next emperor will be to overthrow it."

"Of course, Majesty."

Tennison and Verul fell in line as the cadre of guards escorted the new emperor to his office.

CHAPTER VI

Oh, how the mighty hath fallen. Hoseph looked down at the noisome remnant of the former captain of the Imperial Guard. There wasn't much resemblance to the stiff-backed disciplinarian he had known from the palace. The grizzled and unkempt wreck lay on a rumpled bed that stank of alcohol, sweat, and cheap perfume.

It hadn't taken Embree's Hunters long to track Otar down to a gambling house in the Dreggars Quarter, where the former captain seemed intent upon squandering his not-inconsiderable pension on whiskey, trollops, and games of chance. Being dismissed from the highest post in the Imperial Guard had apparently destroyed his will to live. Hoseph wondered if there was enough left to be of use.

Hoseph closed the small room's door, banishing the noise of the raucous crowd in the gambling hall below. He had taken a chance coming here, but there was no way around it. He needed to talk with Otar in private.

"Captain Otar," Hoseph said quietly, less to ease the man's waking than to avoid irritating his own throbbing headache.

Otar didn't respond.

"Captain Otar!"

The sleeping man stirred, snorting and rolling his head away from his drool-stained pillow. One hand rose to wipe his face, but fell away, and he started to snore.

Hoseph's patience vanished. "Wake up!" He kicked the man's foot.

Otar jerked, two bloodshot orbs flung wide to stare at the man standing at the foot of his bed. "Who the bloody..." Annoyance evolved into recognition. "Gods!"

Otar lunged out of bed, but one foot tangled in the sheet and he sprawled naked on the floor. Scrabbling to the corner of the room, he snatched up the sword propped there and fumbled to draw it.

Finally, the scabbard clattered to the floor and the blade pointed at Hoseph, though it wavered unsteadily.

"What are you doing here? What do you want?"

"Lower your sword, Captain." Hoseph folded his hands, fingering his talisman should the man become unreasonable. "I'm here to make you an offer."

Otar blinked at him as if the words had not penetrated the fog of alcohol and fading sleep. "You...what?"

"I *said* I'm here to make you an *offer*. If you lower your blade and don some *clothing*,"—Hoseph gestured with thinly veiled disgust—"we can speak about it. However, if you're not interested in regaining your former position with the Imperial Guard, I'll simply leave and you can continue to slowly kill yourself with alcohol."

Otar stiffened as if he'd been knifed. The sword steadied, and his face firmed into a mask of indignation. Quicker than Hoseph would have thought the man could manage, the former captain buried the blade's tip in the floor, letting it stand within easy reach as he fumbled his pants on. After cinching the belt tight, Otar reached for a bottle on the night table and poured a measure of amber liquid into a dirty glass. He knocked the liquor back, then worked his neck and shoulders as if to relieve the kinks. After a moment he seemed to regain his composure and a faint semblance to the man he had once been.

"Start talking." Otar put down the glass and leaned against the wall, resting one hand on the pommel of his sword. "But stay where you are. If you try anything, I'll gut you like a codfish."

"I stand forewarned." Though Hoseph doubted the man's reflexes were as sharp as they had been, Otar could certainly use a sword. He folded his hands around the talisman and tried to look unthreatening. "I'm here because I need your help."

Otar cocked an eyebrow. "Oh, *really*? How the world has changed when a high priest of Demia deigns to consort with us lowly mortals."

Hoseph ignored the sarcasm. He'd never paid much attention to Otar; that the man resented him for his close association with the emperor didn't surprise him. Many had.

"Yes, the world *has* changed, Captain, and not for the better. When Tynean Tsing II was emperor, we were *both* powerful men, and the empire was well-ordered and prosperous. Now that Arbuckle is on the throne, gangs of peasants roam the streets with his blessing, while nobles cower inside their homes as their businesses burn. And we, loyal servants of the empire, are disparaged and cast aside."

"Miss the power, do you?" Otar snorted. "Don't glare at me, priest. I do, too. Get on with what you came here to say."

"As I said, I came here to make you an *offer*, Captain. You and I aren't so different. We have no place in this new world Arbuckle has forged. I wish to bring back the old world. How would you like to be reinstated as Captain of the Imperial Guard?"

"How are you going to manage *that*? Arbuckle won't—" Otar's words caught in his throat as his eyes widened. "Were *you* behind the assassination attempt at the coronation?"

"That is neither here nor there, Captain." The man was not so besotted that he hadn't heard the news, but Hoseph wasn't going to confess to him his crimes. "Suffice to say that there's a consortium of nobles and magistrates who feel as I do, who want to see someone more...amenable on the throne. Someone who recognizes that Tsing's glory lies in control and order, not some anarchist's paradigm of *equality*."

Otar seemed to consider this, one hand rubbing his stubbled jaw. "So what do you want me to do? I no longer have access to the palace and have no influence with the Imperial Guard."

"What would you say if I told you that a single person was responsible for both of our predicaments? Responsible, in fact, for *all* the upheaval and trouble. Responsible for murdering Tynean Tsing II and for thwarting attempts to rectify the situation." Hoseph actually believed that Lad had killed the emperor, but there was no sense in quibbling over extraneous details.

The captain's eyes gleamed and his nostrils flared. "I'd say point him out to me and I'll take his head."

Hoseph smiled. "A fine sentiment, Captain, but your role will be infinitely easier. I only need help finding this bothersome woman so that we can eliminate her."

"A woman who's thwarted your attempts to rectify the situation?" Otar poured another measure of liquor and swirled it in the glass, chuckled softly, and sipped. "Baroness Monjhi's bodyguard, I assume?"

Hoseph blinked in surprise. "I'm impressed, Captain. Your powers of deduction and attention to current events remain as sharp as your sword." The man might be a drunk, but nobody rose to Otar's rank by being stupid.

"And you can't find her?" Otar smiled wryly.

"Unfortunately, no. She's gone into hiding, and she's working with the constabulary now." It had been very sly of Mya to call in the constabulary; it not only absolved her of guilt in Lady T's murder, but put hundreds of more eyes on the street looking for Hoseph. It did, however, give him a place to start in locating her. Though it would have been easier to use guild resources—and far less annoying than dealing with the former Captain Otar—Lakshmi's contacts were all low-ranking street constables who weren't privy to details of the investigation.

Otar's eyes narrowed to reddened slits. "And you want me to do *what*, exactly?"

"I need you to talk with Chief Constable Dreyfus and find out— discreetly, of course—if they know where she is. If they don't, then how do they contact her? If she contacts them, then how and when?"

Otar sipped his drink and considered, finally nodding slowly. "I can probably do that. Dreyfus owes me dozens of favors."

"Excellent." Hoseph breathed a sigh of satisfaction.

"How do I contact you?"

"You don't. I contact you." He nodded to the room's single grimy window. "When you get the information, tie one drape open and leave the other hanging until you hear from me."

"All right." Otar rubbed his jaw again and knocked back the rest of his drink. "I'd best get cleaned up."

"Proceed with caution, Captain." Hoseph levied a humorless smile at the man. Otar showed no signs of deceit, but the priest wouldn't risk his life on it. He'd given the man enough information to tempt him into regaining his former position by delivering a wanted criminal to the new emperor. "If you tell anyone that you met with me, your life will be forfeit."

"I don't take kindly to threats, priest." Otar's hand rested on the pommel of his sword.

"I never threaten, Captain." Hoseph flicked the silver skull into his hand. "I simply state facts." With a murmured invocation, he dissolved into mist, enjoying the last glimpse of shock on the man's face before the Sphere of Shadow engulfed him.

Hoseph materialized in darkness, staggering with the familiar blinding pain and dizziness. It took so much longer to ease the pain now, and only one transition to bring it back. After resting a moment, he invoked Demia's blessing. Pearly light blossomed in his hand to reveal his surroundings. He regarded his safe haven with sly satisfaction. Who would guess that he once again resided under the very roof where he had devoted his life to the goddess of death? In the deepest archives of Demia's temple, where few ever ventured, Hoseph lay down upon a rumpled nest of cloaks and took his ease, the musty scent of aged parchment a comforting balm, and the cool stone easing his throbbing head.

Blessed shadow of death, sooth me... He banished his light and closed his eyes, content that his plans had been nudged into motion.

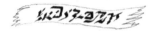

Dee felt like a cat walking into a kennel full of hounds as he strode into the central offices of the Tsing Constabulary. Since joining the Assassins Guild, he had regarded most constables as the enemy. The only good constable was one who could be bought. Never had he thought to work openly with them, but here he was.

He'd been dubious when Mya summoned the constables to investigate Lady T's death, but her strategy seemed to be working. They didn't appear to doubt her account of the murder or her reason for assuming multiple identities, and seemed sincere about finding Hoseph. Posters of the priest in his acolyte guise were plastered all over the city, advertising a hefty reward. Between the citizens and the constabulary, they might have a chance of locating Hoseph before he and the rest of the guild located Mya.

"You!" Sergeant Benjamin spilled blackbrew the color of tar down the front of his uniform. "Blast!"

Dee stiffened as every eye in the constabulary headquarters turned his way. So much for keeping his visit low-key.

The sergeant slammed the cup down on a desk and wiped

ineffectually at his stained uniform before striding forth and extending his hand in greeting. "Damn glad to see you, Master Dee. *Damned* glad!"

"Good to see you, too, Sergeant Benjamin." Dee shook the man's damp hand and forced an amiable smile; if their meeting looked casual, maybe some of those curious stares would go back to their own business. "How are your constables?"

The sergeant's smile fell. "You know Tovi was killed. Kert died before we could get him to a temple, but the others'll pull through. And your mistress? How is she?"

"Well enough. I've come to—"

The sergeant held up a forestalling hand. "Best let you save it for the chief." He led Dee through the maze of desks to a door with a brass name plate nailed to it. "He'll want to thank you for what you did."

"Just following my mistress' orders, Sergeant."

"Aye, just like I was following my chief's, but that don't change the facts." Benjamin lay a heavy, gnarled hand on Dee's shoulder. "Call me Benj. I'd be lookin' up at six feet of dirt if not for you, and I won't forget it."

"I appreciate that...Benj." How surreal to have a constable beholden to him for saving his life.

The sergeant knocked on the door and opened it, ushering Dee into the chief constable's office.

"Yes?" The man behind the desk looked up from a stack of papers two fingers thick.

Benj closed the door behind them. "Chief, this is Miss Moirin's assistant, Dee. He was with us when her home was attacked."

"Yes, I remember from your report." The chief constable stood, a stocky man of late middle age, slightly haggard, but still powerful. "Sergeant Benjamin says your quick reactions saved their lives, Master Dee. My thanks to you and your mistress for that." He peered beyond Dee and the sergeant. "Where *is* she?"

"In hiding, Chief Constable. She asked me to act as her liaison with the constabulary."

"Her *liaison*?" The chief constable's eyebrows shot up. "Who does she think she is? First she refuses protective custody, then sends a lackey."

Dee swallowed his apprehension at the man's flash of temper. "Captain, please understand, Miss Moirin went into hiding not only for her own protection, but to avoid danger to those around her. The presence of constables didn't prevent the last attack, and two of your people were killed. She refuses to put anyone else at risk for her sake, so she's found a place where she'll be safe for the time being."

Dreyfus sat back down and snatched up a pen and paper. "And where would that be? I'd like to send Sergeant Benjamin over to ask a few more questions."

"I'm sorry, Chief Constable, but I can't reveal where she's staying."

Dreyfus glared from beneath his bushy brows. "This is a serious case, Master Dee. The emperor himself has tasked the constabulary with solving it as quickly as possible."

Sudden inspiration struck Dee. "I understand that, sir. Miss Moirin is well acquainted with the emperor's vehement pursuit of justice. They spoke of it at length after the coronation."

The chief constable's glare remained undiminished. "If she refuses protection and won't cooperate with our investigation, she's *impeding* rather than helping us to apprehend the perpetrator."

Dee took a breath. "Rest assured, sir, Miss Moirin has every intention of remaining available to assist with the investigation and share any information we come by on our own."

"She better. And who gave her the okay to conduct her own investigation anyway?" Dreyfus shot a savage look at Sergeant Benjamin.

"No one, Chief Constable, but my mistress is no less interested than you in bringing Hoseph to justice." Dee shrugged helplessly.

"Well, while she's out conducting her *investigation*, tell her to come in anyway." Dreyfus opened a desk drawer and removed an ivory scroll tube embossed with an elaborate crest. "This came from the palace for her, and I was instructed to place it directly into Miss Moirin's hand."

"From the palace?" Dee blinked and swallowed. *What in the Nine Hells...* "Even so, she *won't* come in for it, I assure you. Please, Captain, let me to take it to her. You can trust that I'll put it into her hand myself."

"I'll vouch for him, Captain. I trust his word."

Dee glanced at Benj in surprise. The man was putting his career on the line for him. Constables, apparently, were much more trusting than assassins.

Dreyfus looked dubious, but finally nodded. "Very well, but it's on your head, Master Dee. I'll be sending a message to the palace stating that she refused to come in, and I was forced to hand this to you in order to get the message to her."

"Thank you. And I promise, Chief Constable, we *will* keep in touch."

"Set it up with Sergeant Benjamin. I've got enough on my plate." Dreyfus turned his eyes back to his desk as he gestured dismissively toward the door.

Outside the office, Dee navigated between desks and chairs beneath the curious stares of the constables, Benj at his heel. At the door to the street, he turned to the sergeant.

"I'll come by again in a couple of days," Dee promised. "I don't suppose—"

Benj's hand closed on Dee's elbow. "*Walk* with me, Master Dee." The sergeant opened the door and ushered him onto the street.

"What's wrong?" Dee hoped he'd hadn't gotten Benj in trouble with his captain.

"Nothin'. Just too many ears in there."

I wonder if he knows about Lakshmi's informants. "Do you think the constabulary's not *safe*?"

"Oh, it's *safe* enough, but caps gossip like fishwives." He released Dee's elbow. "Now, what were you sayin'?"

Dee had no way to know if the cagy sergeant was telling the truth or suspected a spy. He decided to play along. "I wondered if you'd picked up any information on Hoseph yet."

"Some uncorroborated sightings, but nothing definite." Benj looked disgusted. "There're more than a dozen religious sects in the city, and we can't very well stop every acolyte wandering the streets."

"I suppose not. We haven't found anything definite either." Dee stopped and extended a hand. "Thank you, Sergea—Benj."

"And thank *you* again." The sergeant shook his hand, then squeezed hard and glanced over his shoulder. "Next time we should meet someplace else. There's a blackbrew shop on the corner of

Archer and Wayland Avenue. Day after tomorrow work for you? Say, noon?"

"All right." That Benj wanted to meet in a café told Dee that he probably did suspect some of his constables were on the take.

"Tell your mistress she's smart to lay low. Word on the street is that money's being tossed around by people lookin' for her."

Dee had no doubt of that, but nodded in thanks. "I'll relay the message."

Benj clapped Dee on the shoulder and grinned, showing teeth stained by tobacco. "Watch your back."

"I *always* watch my back." Dee grinned back. "Working for Miss Moirin instills caution, if nothing else."

The creak of a stair snapped Mya's attention from her book, bringing her up off the divan like she'd been poked with a pin. *Lose yourself in a book, Mya, and you're apt to lose your head!* She dropped the slim volume onto the cushion and drew a dagger. She didn't know what had possessed Dee to buy her a book of poetry, but she found herself enjoying it. Too much, perhaps, if it was lulling her into complacency.

Mya flattened herself against the wall behind the door, listening as something metallic clicked into the lock. *Only Dee and the landlord have keys, but it could be a pick.* She knew her paranoia was piqued by two days sequestered in the apartment, but better paranoid than dead. She tensed and readied herself.

The lock clicked and the bolt knob turned. As the opening door stirred the air, Mya detected a familiar scent—male, sweat, with a hint of spice—and relaxed. Smiling, she put her dagger away, crossed her arms, and leaned casually against the wall.

Dee stepped in, his free arm draped with clothing. Scanning the room with a glance and finding nothing untoward, he turned to shut the door.

"Ah!" He started when he caught sight of her, barked a nervous laugh, and closed the door, relocking it. "Expecting trouble?"

"Always."

"Good." He looked her up and down. "You shouldn't lounge around in nothing but your wrappings. What if someone came to the door?"

"I'd just have to kill them." She scrunched her face in response to his sour look. "Nobody's going to drop in, and these are comfortable. Besides, I don't have anything but that uncomfortable dress. What did you bring me?"

"*Some* clothes, at least. The workwoman's dress will be done tomorrow, the fancy one the day after. Mistress Gantry is making a killing off of us." Dee draped two outfits over the back of the couch and pointed at first one, then the other. "Stealthy nighttime attire. Fancy young gentleman's outfit.; I said it was for our nephew."

"Wonderful!" Mya snatched up the casual clothes and hurriedly donned them. "Oh, Dee. This is beautiful!" She fingered the collar of the deep-crimson shirt, a soft, brushed silk that swallowed light like a bottomless well. The snug, black-suede pants fit like a glove. Slipping her feet into the supple leather boots, she strode back and forth. "Perfect!"

"Here." Dee unrolled a leather case to reveal four exquisite daggers. "From Noncey."

"Ahhh!" Mya pulled a blade from its sheath, turning it this way and that to examine the dusky variegated steel. "Damn, this is a beauty!" The light refused to reflect from the matte finish—better for stealth—and the edge shaved the hair off the back of her hand without resistance. She'd rarely seen such quality in Twailin, but here in Tsing, you could buy anything from anywhere…for a price. With a pleased grin, she slid this daggers into the custom-made sheaths in her boots and at her hips. "What did you think of them?"

Dee's brow furrowed. "The *daggers*?"

"No. Clemson and Noncey."

"I think you're lucky to have them," he said. "We might not have access to alchemical bombs or spies, but I'd bet on her Enforcers and his Blades over any squad of mercenaries the other side can hire. They seem sincerely loyal to you, and they're *certainly* loyal to each other." Dee hesitated a moment, arranging the other clothes on the couch before adding, "I was talking to one of their journeymen. It seems to be common knowledge that Clemson and Noncey sleep together, and no one thinks it's a big deal."

"I figured as much. But don't worry, Dee, *our* escapades will remain our little secret." She cast him a wicked smile and winked. She didn't want him to worry about coming to harm if anyone learned of their intimacy. "What about Pax?"

Dee fished a scrap of parchment from a pocket and handed it to her. "It's not much. Just an address down in the Wharf District."

"Good! It's about time." Mya had tried not to fret about the old innkeeper and the passel of urchins. They'd be safer away from her, out of the line of fire. Knowing that they had settled somewhere would ease her mind. Memorizing the address, she strode to the kitchen and tossed the note into the stove's fire box. "I'll check it out tonight. What did the constables have to say?"

"Mixed signals there. Chief Constable Dreyfus doesn't like the situation at all—me acting as your liaison and you conducting your own investigation—but he backed down. He delegated it all to Benj."

"Benj?" Mya's eyebrow rose and an amused smile played about her lips. "You're on a first name basis with the sergeant? Excellent work, Dee! We can use a source of information inside the constabulary."

"Yeah, well, it's not all good news. He said someone's spreading money around and asking questions about you. The guild, no doubt. They must know you're calling yourself Moirin."

"That wouldn't be hard to figure out, since that name is probably all over the poster boards in the news about my saving Prince Arbuckle's life at the coronation. Hell, some bard is probably already composing an ode to the *amazing* Miss Moirin." She smirked and made a rude noise, fingering the fine material of the trousers, shirt, waistcoat, and jacket draped over the divan. "I should try these on."

"Yes, you should, but I'm not done yet. Do you think we could deal with one thing at a time?"

"Sure, Dee." *What's he so testy about?* "What else?"

"Dreyfus gave me this." Dee withdrew an ornate scroll tube from the inside pocket of his jacket and handed it to her. "It's from the palace."

"The *palace?*" *Okay, that's enough to warrant a little testiness.* "Prince Arbuckle?"

"*Emperor* Tynean Tsing III, you mean."

"Right. Probably a bill for all the damage I did to the Great Hall while saving his life." She chuckled, though her heart fluttered nervously. *What could he want with me?* She could think of nothing, and her paranoia resurfaced. "Maybe you're not the only one with friends in the constabulary, and this is one of Master Kittal's alchemical explosives."

"I...hadn't thought of that." Dee's startled expression would have been amusing under different circumstances. "That would be..."

"Not a bad tactic, actually." Mya gripped the scroll tube in her left hand. The Grandmaster's ring would warn her of dangerous magic, but could it detect a simple explosive? She concentrated, but felt nothing untoward. "Maybe I'm just being paranoid, but I think I'll open this in the tub."

"The *tub*?" Dee cocked an eyebrow skeptically.

"Yes. If this explodes, the tub should contain the blast...to a certain degree, at least."

"I suppose, but it might still catch the ceiling on fire."

"But not *me*." She strode toward the bathroom. "If it explodes, get out of the apartment. I'll get myself out."

"Right." Dee had gone pale. "Be *careful*."

"Always." Mya flashed him an encouraging grin, wishing she felt as confident as she tried to look. She wouldn't put anything past the guild. Crouching low beside the heavy copper tub, she reached her left arm inside and popped the cap off the end of the scroll tube with her thumb.

No explosion.

Better paranoid and alive than careless and dead, she thought with relief. Standing, Mya pulled the rolled vellum from the tube and read the note.

Miss Moirin,

His Majesty, Emperor Tynean Tsing III, hopes you are in good health, and presents his condolences on the death of your employer, the most respected Baroness Tara Monjhi. You are hereby summoned for an audience with His Majesty. Please present yourself at the Imperial Palace at your earliest convenience.

With most respectful regards,

Tennison Umalshi, Imperial Secretary

It was signed with a flourish and embossed with the imperial seal. A foreboding chill tickled up Mya's spine.

"Are you all right?" Dee peeked around the corner into the bathroom.

"Yes, I...I'm fine." She handed him the note and sat down on the edge of the tub. "He wants to see me."

"He?" Dee scanned the letter and swallowed audibly. "Why in the Nine Hells does he want to see you?"

"I have no idea." Mya started to bite a nail and stopped herself. "But I can't afford to lose the emperor's good will. They'll be expecting me soon."

"You're *going*?" Dee sounded horrified.

"It's not an invitation, Dee, it's a *summons*. I don't think I can refuse, do you?"

"Not really." He threw up his hands. "Damn! There's no time!"

"Time? Time for what?"

He looked at her as if she were dimwitted. "To get your *dress* ready, of course! You can't attend an imperial audience wearing that!" He flung a hand out to indicate her comfortable pants and blouse.

Mya barked a laugh, trying to suppress a grin.

"What?" He looked at her with a perplexed expression.

"If what I'm going to *wear* is your biggest concern, we're on completely different pages here. I was thinking about how to get there without being *murdered*!"

"We could ask Clemson or Noncey to supply a carriage with one of their people as driver."

"No." Mya shook her head. "I'd like to go right from the apartment to the carriage, but I don't want to reveal our location to *anyone* yet."

"Well, I guess we'll just hire a hackney and make sure that you're disguised well enough not to be recognized on the sidewalk." He stepped over and fingered her short and now very blonde hair. "I'll put a rush on your dress, and we'll have to figure out what to do with your hair."

"You never cease to amaze me, Dee." Mya brushed his hand away, failing to suppress a grin. "What would I do without you?"

Chapter VII

"**D**emia cares not for the machinations of kings or empires, Your Majesty." The high priest of Demia's Temple, resplendent in his crimson robes, stared back with maddening tranquility. "The temple will not harbor a fugitive, but neither will we take overt action against one who has devoted his life to the Keeper of the Slain."

Arbuckle stared coldly at the priest. "This is...disappointing, High Priest Averen. We are not pleased."

"I am sorry that you are not pleased, Majesty, but I cannot excommunicate High Priest Hoseph without either enlightenment from Demia or evidence to corroborate his crimes." He spread his hands in a gesture of helplessness. "I am powerless."

"Very well." Signaling dismissal, Arbuckle rose and nodded politely. "When your recalcitrant priest's head falls into a basket, We daresay *Demia* will decide what is to be done about his behavior."

"Precisely, Majesty." Averen bowed formally, a serene smile on his sanctimonious lips.

The emperor turned on his heel and strode from the audience chamber, biting back the tirade that he knew would only buy him grief. Emperor though he may be, alienating high clergy was perilous. There was nothing he could do to force Averen to excommunicate Hoseph.

"Not that it would have done a fat lot of good anyway," he muttered.

"Majesty?" Verul asked, his pen poised. "I didn't catch that."

"Nothing. We were just talking to Ourself. Ourselves? *Whichever!* We're already *sick* of speaking in this manner."

"It's traditional," murmured Tennison.

"You and Baris with your traditions! Perhaps We should start Our *own* traditions, some that make more *sense.*"

The encircling squad of imperial guards and knights said

nothing, but he sensed an uncomfortable shifting in their ranks. He would have to learn to curb his tongue and be more…imperial.

"Is everything prepared for the audience with Duke Tessifus?"

"Yes, Majesty," Tennison replied, checking his ledger. "Master Keyfur is already in place."

"Good. Maybe We'll get to the bottom of this conspiracy." Arbuckle jerked his jacket straight and twisted his head from side to side in an attempt to relax the knotted muscles of his neck. Even the thin circlet he now wore had started to feel heavy. How naïve he had been to think that things would be easier once he was crowned emperor. Instead, the responsibilities smothered him like a pall.

They continued through the back passages of the palace, away from the larger, impersonal public chambers and toward the more intimate meeting rooms. Arbuckle breathed deep to calm his nerves, trying to put the unpleasant encounter with Demia's high priest behind him. He wanted to put the duke at ease. It wouldn't do to come on too strong or accusatory. Tessifus might simply clam up and claim ignorance. By law, the emperor could not compel a high noble to answer if they refused.

Captain Ithross met them at the door to the chamber, bowing stiffly. "Your Majesty, is there nothing I can do to persuade you not to go through with this? If, indeed, the duke is involved, this only provides them with the opportunity for another assassination attempt. There are safer ways to get information about this conspiracy. I can bring the alleged conspirators in for questioning—"

"No, Captain." Arbuckle held up a hand for silence. "Even if we had sufficient evidence, bringing them in will just tip our hand. We need to know why Duke Tessifus' name is not on that list."

"Yes, Majesty." Ithross bowed again, though his expression looked dubious.

Arbuckle looked around at his cadre. "Verul, Tennison, and Sir Draegen only. The rest of you stay here."

"Your *Majesty*, if I may—"

Arbuckle cut off Ithross' protest with a hearty laugh and a shake of his head. "Ithross, you're *killing* me here!"

"Majesty, I fail to see anything amusing in this situation." The captain looked a little stunned.

"What's *amusing* is that you're following Our orders by speaking out, and We find it ironic. Nobody would have spoken out to my father like you or even Tennison have, and that arrogance, if nothing else, is probably what killed him." He clapped the captain on his armored shoulder. "Thank you for your concern, but We'll be fine, Captain."

"Very well, Majesty." Ithross bowed and stepped away from the door, his face a mask of resignation.

Tennison opened the door and swept through, announcing, "His Majesty Tynean Tsing III."

"Your Majesty!" Duke Tessifus stood from an upholstered chair and bowed low. "My apologies for my delay in answering your summons, but I was out of the city attending to my estates."

"So We were told." Arbuckle casually surveyed the room, hoping everything was in place as he'd been assured. Save for two imperial guards at the other door, a single footman, the duke, and those who had just come in, it looked empty. *I hope Keyfur's actually here.* "Please be seated."

Arbuckle sat in the chair opposite the duke. To one side, on a low, highly polished table, sat a crystal decanter of amber liquid and two glasses. Waving the footman forward, he said, "Please, Tessifus, join Us in a spot of this fine brandy. We just spent two hours arguing with recalcitrant *clergy*, and feel the need for…fortification."

"My pleasure, Majesty."

The footman poured, and Arbuckle lifted and swirled his snifter. The heady aroma steadied his resolve.

"You haven't asked why We summoned you."

Tessifus shrugged as he swirled his own drink, then sipped it. "We are the two highest nobles in the empire, majesty. We have much to discuss with regard to our policy…disagreements. As you know, I oppose the changes you're putting forth. I believe they'll damage the empire's economy. If commoners can demand—"

The emperor raised a forestalling hand. "Please, good duke, We didn't summon you to discuss policy." He sipped his brandy, his eyes fixed on the man who would wear his crown should he die.

"Majesty?" Tessifus curled his lips in a faint smile that didn't reach his eyes. "Why then *did* you summon me?"

"The recent attempts on Our life have made Us acutely cognizant of the matter of succession. We are sure you're aware that, without heirs, if We should fall prey to an assassin, *you* will be the next Emperor of Tsing."

"Of course, Majesty." The duke lowered his glass, his expression now distinctly worried.

What do you know? Arbuckle was surprised at the disappointment he felt at the duke's reaction. Though they weren't close, they *were* cousins, and it pained him to consider the possibility of the man's treason. But then, that's what they were here to discover.

"We will speak plainly, Milord Duke. We have recently received a list of names purportedly responsible for the recent assassination attempts. We brought you here because your name is *not* on this list." Arbuckle withdrew the roll of parchment that the late-night intruder had given him and held it out.

Tessifus reached for the note as if it might sprout fangs. His eyes widened as he read it, though his expression remained uncertain. "I don't understand, Majesty. Why would these nobles and magistrates consort with Hoseph?" The duke's brandy rippled in his glass. "And why would the *lack* of my name on this list warrant a summons?"

"There's a conspiracy to *kill* Us, my good duke. We have no hard evidence to prove it, other than this note given to Us by an unknown benefactor. It did, however, prove accurate with regard to Archmage Duveau's involvement. If your name *was* on this list, We would not be confiding in you. We do, however, wish to know why these people would want *you* as their next emperor, yet not take you into their confidence?"

The glass in Tessifus' hand trembled, the brandy sloshing up the sides. He placed it carefully on the table and cleared his throat. His lower lip began to quake. "I...cannot say, Majesty."

"Cannot, or *will* not?" Arbuckle leaned forward. *What do you know?*

"*Cannot.* My..." He looked down, then flicked his gaze around the room like a cornered animal looking for escape. When he finally turned his eyes to Arbuckle, they glinted with tears. "My...*sons.*"

"Your sons?"

"They've taken my sons!" Tears rolled down the duke's cheeks. "They said...they would...return them in pieces if I don't do as they tell me."

"Good Gods of Light…" Arbuckle sagged back in his chair, his heart wrenching with sorrow. His own lack of children now seemed a blessing rather than a curse. *No one to love…no one to risk.* Then another realization surfaced: kidnapping and terror could not be allowed to influence the future of his empire. "We've *got* to find them!"

His musing turned to panic as Tessifus lunged from his seat. A chime with no notable source rang loud and clear, and a dozen imperial guards materialized around the duke, swords drawn. Master Keyfur appeared at the emperor's side, whispering words that evaporated before the emperor could comprehend. A scintillating shield of rainbow light snapped into being between the emperor and the duke. The door flew open, slamming against the wall as Ithross and the rest of the guards charged in.

But Tessifus didn't even notice the blades at his throat. He wasn't lunging to attack, but to prostrate himself before his emperor.

"*Please*, Majesty! We can't try to find them! No one can know! They'll be killed. *Worse* than killed! He…promised that my wife would receive packages with…pieces. That they would die *screaming*." The man pressed his face to the floor at the sovereign's feet, his shoulders wracked with sobs. "Please…"

"Guards, stand down. Keyfur, drop your spell." Arbuckle waved Captain Ithross and his men back. Keyfur snapped his fingers, and the rainbow shield vanished. The emperor knelt and placed a hand on the man's heaving shoulders. "*Who*, Tessifus? Who told you this? Who took them?"

"No one can know!" the duke said, looking around wildly as if only now seeing the guards.

"No one will," Arbuckle assured him. "Not one word will leave this room. You *must* trust Us."

It took a long moment, but eventually the duke got himself under control, though his face remained twisted with torment. "The…priest. Hoseph."

"That…" Arbuckle gritted his teeth against the curse, longing to call back Demia's high priest and threaten to tear down his temple brick by brick, but knowing he couldn't. If Tessifus was right and word got out that he'd learned of the boys' abduction, they were as good as dead. "Here. Let Us help you up." He put a hand under the man's arm and lifted.

Two guards were there in an instant to help. The duke wavered on shaky legs, looked dazed as they sat him back in his chair.

"Here." Arbuckle pressed a snifter of brandy into the duke's hand. "Drink that down. We need to talk."

"Majesty, I…" The snifter trembled.

"Uh-uh!" Arbuckle pointed to the glass. "Drink!"

Tessifus complied, coughed, then took another gulp.

As Arbuckle watched the man wipe his eyes and draw a shuddering breath, he motioned Captain Ithross over. "All is secure here, Captain. Please dismiss your guards and warn them to breathe not one word about this to *anyone*, not even amongst themselves. If you would please stay, We would have you hear what the duke has to say."

"Of course, Majesty." Ithross nodded to the lieutenant in charge of the detail, and the guards started to file out.

Arbuckle turned to Keyfur. "I'll need your help here, too, Keyfur."

The mage bowed without a word.

Arbuckle refilled the duke's glass and poured an additional splash into his own. "Milord Duke, We need to ask you some questions, and We must insist that Master Keyfur confirm that your answers are truthful. Will you agree to that?"

The duke nodded, his hands wrapped around his snifter so tightly that Arbuckle worried it might shatter. At a gesture from the emperor, Keyfur withdrew a feather and waved it over the duke's head. He nodded; the spell was cast.

"You said that Hoseph was the one who threatened you. Do you believe that he was working alone?"

Tessifus shut his eyes tight as if thinking, then answered. "No. He definitely said '*we* need your help'."

Arbuckle held out the parchment once again. "Did he mention any of these people?"

"No, no." The duke shook his head without even looking at the list. "I would remember if he named them. I'm acquainted with all of them."

Glancing at Master Keyfur, Arbuckle was relieved to see the wizard's nod of affirmation; the duke told the truth. "Have any of these people mentioned anything to you about a conspiracy?"

Another sullen shake of the head. "We've discussed politics, of course. That's all I have in common with most of them. But none have spoken outright of...treason."

Another nod from Keyfur, and Arbuckle sipped his brandy thoughtfully. They had answered the question of Duke Tessifus' loyalty, but in doing so, a dozen more questions had been raised. "Now let us speak of how we can deal with your...difficulty, Milord Duke."

"Deal with it?" Tessifus wiped his runny nose on the sleeve of his dress jacket and sniffed. "How *can* you, Majesty? Hoseph said if I told anyone, my sons would die. I've already killed them."

"No, you haven't. No one will know what you've told Us here, We *promise* you that. And We swear to you on Our oath as Emperor of Tsing, We will spare no effort to bring your sons home to you. We don't know *how* yet, but We will explore every possibility."

"I..." Tessifus swallowed hard and straightened his shoulders. "I believe you, Majesty. And I thank you. I'm sorry for—"

"You should not be sorry because you love your sons, cousin. You did not conspire to have Us murdered, and committed no act against Us."

"But...your policies. Your edicts... I opposed you at every turn."

"Fah!" Arbuckle quaffed his brandy and fixed the man with a firm stare. "That's just *politics*, man! Blood is thicker than water, they say, and let Us tell you one thing." He leaned forward and smiled coldly. "We will *not* be intimidated by acts of brutality and terror. If Hoseph and his cabal of assassins want blood, We are going to *give* them blood. They're going to *drown* in blood before We're through with them!"

Tessifus drew back from the emperor's vehemence. He blinked and looked down at the snifter in his hand, then downed the entire tot. Wiping his mouth, he clenched his jaw and met his sovereign's eyes. "Tell me what you wish me to do, Majesty, and I'll see it done."

"First, tell no one what we spoke of here, not even your lady wife." Arbuckle frowned. "If anyone wonders why I summoned you,

85

tell them that We wanted your support for Our New Accords, but you refused. Feel free to bandy my name about shamelessly and insult my policies; anything that will convince people that we're at odds. Meanwhile, We'll see what can be done to find your sons...*discreetly*." He stood and held out a hand to the duke.

"I'll do it, Majesty." Tessifus stood and they clasped hands. "I'll do anything you ask if it means getting my sons back. Thank you!"

Only after Tennison had shown the duke out did Arbuckle feel the impact of the duke's words. "I'll do anything you ask..." It was exactly the same pressure Hoseph was using to control the duke. Did it matter that he had offered to save the boys, whereas Hoseph threatened to harm them? Brandy-laced acid burned his throat, and he swallowed hard, quelling the urge to retch. He wouldn't manipulate anyone like that. He *couldn't*.

I just did.

Damn, it feels good to be out of that flat!

Mya breathed deep of the cool night air, the sea-breeze giving the waterfront a respite from the sweltering heat. The cool slate roof under her hands was dangerously slick with dew, and the air reeked of the river and shore, but neither kept her from reveling in her freedom. Being cooped up day and night had been driving her crazy. Even when she was only a Master Hunter, she'd insisted on going out daily into the city. She couldn't understand how any of the others managed their operations, only receiving intelligence gathered by others and sending out orders. Where was the fun in that?

The humid air carried a drunken sea chanty and laughter to her ears. The Wharf District never slept. Unfortunately, that meant more frequent patrols of constables to keep the revelry to a dull roar and violence to a bare minimum.

Mya shifted her stance and slid down the roof's slippery slope to the eaves. There, she gripped the edge and peered over. The alley two stories below, though not vacant, was dark enough to keep her hidden. Flipping her legs over the edge, she hung for a moment, and let go. She landed without a sound, confident that the couple in the midst of a vigorous exchange of gold for carnal favors wouldn't notice her. Their business transaction continued without pause as she slipped through the shadows toward the street.

Mya had used all of her tricks for the trip from the apartment to the Wharf District, shimmying up gutters, racing across rooftops, and leaping over alleys. Lad had taught her how to best use her magically enhanced skills to avoid detection. Though *he* might have been able to follow her, no one else could have.

Mya's heart panged with the memory of skulking through the city with Lad, his agile grace and quiet confidence making the most difficult task appear easy.

Forget it! She wrenched her thoughts back to the here and now. *Love is a weakness. Pay attention or you're dead!*

Stepping from the alley, Mya looked around to get her bearings, then headed down the street at a sedate pace, avoiding the light of streetlamps and pulling her knit cap low over her blonde hair.

Sailors of a dozen nations laughed and drank and sang as they traipsed or stumbled down the streets. Hawkers assailed passersby with inventive cries of, "Come in and see Sea Serpent Sally and her slithering dance!" or "Cold ale, hot steaks, and hotter barmaids!" On a second-floor balcony, a woman squealed with laughter as a man brazenly pawed at her drooping bodice.

"Take it inside, Doris!" called the leader of a squad of caps striding down the center of the street. "How many times have we got to tell you?"

"Don'cha worry, Corporal Penkin! You'll get yer turn!" Doris cackled and dragged the man inside.

Mya sighed. Wherever there were sailors ashore to spend their sea pay, there would be taverns and brothels to supply the commodities they sought. There was no doubt in her mind that the guild operated a number of these places, or at least got a cut of the profits. But she wondered at Pax's wisdom in seeking refuge amid such open debauchery. The urchins might have seen a lot in their short lives, but they were still children, and it chilled her to consider what might happen to them in such environs. There were undoubtedly slavers and worse lurking about who wouldn't balk at abducting a child.

Mya reached the corner and checked the street names painted on the buildings. *Mango Street and Sloop Avenue.* The streets here were named after fruits and the avenues after ships. She hadn't taken much time to learn the Wharf District, and tried to recall her map of the area. *Two blocks down and one south,* she decided.

The hubbub quieted as she crossed some imaginary line that separated the bawdier streets from the quieter ones. Though a few sedate drinking and gambling establishments could still be found, the signs above the shops mostly advertised chandleries, rope makers, and riggers. Ship supplies, bronze hardware, blocks, and cleats figured prominently in the dark, barred windows. She finally reached the address from Paxal's note and wrinkled her forehead in confusion.

"Tawny's Maritime Victuals?" she muttered. The street-level storefront sported no windows, just closed double doors below a sign picturing two barrels. Four chimneys thrust up from the roof, and a faint light glowed in one of the two windows on the second floor. "What the hell?"

Mya knew she hadn't misread the address, but had expected a boarding house or tenement. She considered climbing up to look in the window, but decided against it. Not only would she risk notice by some passerby, but Paxal and the urchins might have rigged traps as they had in the orphanage, and she didn't want to catch a crossbow bolt in the chest by accident. Not knowing what else to do, she walked up to the door and knocked loudly.

"Who's there?"

Mya immediately recognized the raspy voice from the window above. Stepping back from the door, she looked up. "Who else would be knocking on your door at this hour, Pax?"

Paxal stuck his head out and grinned. "Be right down."

She heard him bark orders, then small feet trundling down stairs. A light shone through the crack under the door just before a heavy wooden thump sounded from the other side, then three heavy clacks as bolts were thrown.

This has to be the most secure building on the street, she thought as she waited patiently.

Finally, the door opened and a grinning face leaned through. "Miss Mya!" Digger pulled the door wide and motioned her inside with a grin. A wave of heat blasted her in the face as she stepped through.

"Good to see you, Digger. Why is it so blessed hot in—" An assault of capering urchins quelled her question. They chattered so fast that she couldn't' understand a word. She found herself laughing at their antics as they hopped around and gesticulated wildly.

"Quiet, you little ruffians. Let her breathe!" Paxal came down the stairs, his smile belying his harsh commands. "Bolt the door, Digger, and let's get upstairs where *we* can breathe."

As Digger threw the three metal bolts and lifted a heavy oak bar to the brackets across the door, Mya looked around the sweltering room. The flour-dusted floor was crowded with long, low tables and rows of barrels stamped with the shop's name. Four large brick ovens dominated the back wall, heat still radiating from them.

"A *bakery?*"

"We make ship's biscuit!" Nails announced, picking up a small disk from one of the tables. "Hard as nails and tastes like chalk, but sailors eat 'em like bread."

"I see." She looked askance at Paxal. "Why…"

"Why not?" He shrugged and motioned for her to follow him upstairs. "The owner was lookin' for workers, and there's a loft above the place. Seemed like a win-win to me. The ruffians work the dough and pack the biscuits after they're baked. The baker's glad for the help, and we can stay upstairs." At the top, he opened a door and stepped through.

Mya followed, trailed by the urchins, who shut the door behind them. The upper floor was indeed cooler, the salty sea breeze wafting in though open windows, all of which, she noticed, were strung with catgut and bells. The only furnishings were a table surrounded by chairs and a barrel of water in the corner.

"The owner doesn't live here?"

"Cripes, no, nor the baker. There's only beds for the hired help, and when a gambling house down the street went up in flames, the previous crew of workers packed up and left." He opened another door and showed her a room outfitted with bunks. "Home sweet home."

"And all the biscuits we can eat!" Twigs chimed, pulling a rock-hard biscuit from a pocket and gnawing off a bite.

Mya repressed a grimace. Only a street urchin would consider hardtack a treat. "I see."

"You and Dee set up somewhere?" Pax asked.

"Yes. Everyone have a seat, and I'll fill you in."

It only took a few minutes to recount the events of the last few days and give them her new address. The urchins all went wide-eyed when she told of her summons from the emperor, but Pax frowned.

"Don't like *that* at all. You get all gussied up and prance around in front of half the nobles in the realm, that bugger of a priest'll find out for sure."

"That's a danger, but I can't refuse the summons. Not if I want to maintain my Moirin identity and have the constabulary on my side."

"Dunno why you want the help of a bunch of caps anyway," Digger said.

"Yeah, they're dumb as a bag of rocks!" Gimp declared.

"Knock!" Knock said in obvious agreement.

"Maybe, but they're useful," Mya said. "They patrol and have contacts all over the city. With any luck, they'll capture or kill Hoseph and save me the trouble."

"Not bloody likely," Digger scoffed.

"What about the guild? Why not use them to look for Hoseph?" Pax asked.

"I am, but Blades and Enforcers are even less subtle than caps." Mya raised a hand to forestall any more arguments. "Which brings up what I need from you. The masters have all abandoned their former residences, but the businesses they use as fronts are still open. I have some Blades watching them, but they're known by the other guild members and might be spotted. I'd like to have anonymous eyes watching. *Your* eyes." She pointed to the urchins.

"Watching for what?" Digger asked, looking intrigued.

"Anything suspicious. I'll give you descriptions of the masters and any of their people that I've seen. I want you to watch for people coming or going at regular intervals, even if they look like workers or customers. Assassins might be carrying weapons, or looking around to see if they're being followed. And of course, anyone who just looks like they don't belong there."

"And then you track them back to their master. Smart," Pax agreed.

"Yes. If I can find out where Lakshmi, Twist, or Kittal are holed up, I can lay a trap for Hoseph. Now, I don't want *any* of you following anyone. Just keep track of who comes and goes." She fixed her urchins with a grim stare. "I *mean* it. No ignoring my orders this time. These are *assassins*. They're after me with a vengeance and they know I've recruited you. If they spot you watching them, you're dead." Mya hated putting them in danger like this, but there are so many urchins roaming the streets, they probably wouldn't be noticed.

The children agreed with somber nods and pouts.

"What about Hoseph?" Nails asked. "What if we spot him?"

"Be doubly careful and don't let him see you. Just get word to me."

"About this trip to the palace." Paxal frowned again. "I still don't like it. You'll be alone, unarmed, and surrounded by a whole *company* of imperial guards."

"Don't worry, Pax." She gave him a disarming grin. "At least I won't be fighting an *archmage* this time."

"You *hope*." Pax's frown remained undaunted. He pointed to her ring of gold and obsidian. "And what if that new emperor sees that? It used to be on his own father's finger. Think he won't recognize it?"

"Dee's way ahead of you, there, Pax. I'll be wearing gloves." Mya tried to sound nonchalant, though her own thoughts were darker. *If the emperor ever recognizes this ring...I've got an even bigger problem.*

Chapter VIII

Dee adjusted the lace veil that partially obscured Mya's features and stepped back. Despite the cheery gown—a pastel blue with bright frills and ruffles—he had the disconcerting feeling that he'd just dressed her for a funeral.

Her own funeral. He looked into her eyes and knew he was being foolish. This meeting with the emperor couldn't be more perilous than the coronation. The trip to and from the palace would be the most dangerous part. *Stop it, Dee. You're being an idiot!*

"What's wrong?" Mya regarded herself in the small hand mirror he'd purchased for her, turning her head this way and that. "Do I look stupid?"

"No, you look...you look fine. You just don't look you very much like *you*, which was what we were trying for." Dee stepped forward and adjusted the high ruffled collar and the tilt of her hat. They'd chosen not to go with a wig; the bonnet covered most of her hair anyway.

"Good." She clenched and relaxed her gloved hands. "I feel naked without a dagger."

"You always say that. You know you can't take a dagger into a meeting with the emperor."

"I know, but that doesn't mean I don't *want* one."

"You're better off without one." Dee made one more minor adjustment to the lace frills of her bodice and stepped back again. "If all Nine Hells break loose, you should run, not fight."

"Right." Mya tried to take a deep breath, but the restrictive garment wouldn't allow it. She twisted and turned with a scowl. "Gods of Light and Darkness, why did anyone *ever* design clothes like this? I can't move at all!"

"Because they look good. Don't! You'll rip a seam." He stepped around her to check the lacings. "I'll loosen the stays a bit. Don't forget, this dress isn't like your other one. It won't fall apart if you try to rip it free; it'll just tear and trip you up."

"I won't forget." She twisted more carefully. "Just give me five minutes alone with whoever designed *corsets*."

Dee could tell by her banter that she was nervous. *Good, nerves might keep her alive.* He adjusted the stays and stepped back. "How's that?"

Mya heaved a deeper breath and smiled. "Better. Is the carriage here?"

"I'll check." Dee looked out the window to the street and saw the hackney he'd arranged stopped out front, the driver lounging in his seat as the horses shifted impatiently. He had a sudden urge to send it away, tell Mya to forgo the emperor's good will and stay here…out of danger…with him. But he couldn't. "It's here."

"Okay, time to play the dutiful husband and walk me down." Mya went to the door and waited, casting him an impatient glance.

"Don't look like you're in a hurry. Relax."

"I am relaxed." She took a breath and nodded to the door. "Now walk me down."

With a resigned sigh, Dee walked Mya down the stairs, casting a cautious glance up and down the street before stepping out in the open. At the carriage door, he held out his hand to help her board, longing to grab hold and not let go. *If this is some type of trap, I might never see her again.*

"Goodbye, darling. I'll be back soon," Mya said, playacting as the newlywed wife, as if they were in love.

If we were in love…

Without thinking, Dee reached out, lifted Mya's veil, and kissed her. Her lips were warm and soft, and he could have lost himself in them, in her. *Oh, gods, Mya!*

Dee pulled back, cringing at the wide-eyed shock on Mya's face. He resettled the veil with trembling hands and helped her into the carriage. "Sorry!" he whispered as he closed the door. Mya didn't say a word, her face set in stone behind her veil.

Whirling, Dee strode back toward their apartment. *Idiot! Why the hell did you do that? You know she doesn't love you!*

Movement caught his eye. Mistress Gantry stood in the doorway to her shop with a smile on her face.

"How sweet," she said with a wink and a cherubic smile.

His face burning with embarrassment, Dee took the steps two at a time, berating himself all the way up the steps. He closed the door and leaned against it, banging the back of his head against the wood.

Stupid!

Mya sat like a statue in the carriage, her mind spinning, her lips still tingling from the kiss. "Dee?"

He kissed me... I told him I didn't love him...wouldn't love him. So what the hell was that for?

Mya suppressed the urge to leap from the carriage, grab hold of her fleeing assistant, and demand what the hell was going on. Their relationship was physical, not emotional. It was just stress relief, just sex. He *knew* that!

Then she saw Mistress Gantry, her coy smile and wink, Dee's red face as he pounded up the stairs.

Of course! Mya relaxed back into the seat. Of course a new husband would kiss his bride goodbye. *Good for him, picking up on Mistress Gantry's presence.* Mya had been all caught up in her trip to the palace to notice. As always, he was watching out for her.

"Where to, ma'am?" asked the driver through the little hatch above her seat.

"The Imperial Palace."

"The...*palace*, ma'am?" The hackney driver looked down at her askance.

"Yes, the *palace*. It's the big white building on the bluff!" She'd expected this—Midtown residents probably weren't often invited to the palace—and had an appropriately haughty response prepared. "You *do* know how to get there, don't you?"

"Of course, ma'am, I just..." He swallowed and nodded, then closed the hatch. "Right away, ma'am."

With a crack of a whip, the hackney lurched into motion. Mya leaned back in the seat and tried to breathe in the close confines of the carriage, focus on her surroundings, stay vigilant. Lad had taught her to mistrust carriages—deathtraps, slow, noisy, confined, too little room to fight—and now she knew that Hoseph could pop into one at any moment. She recalled the swirling black mist dissipating around Lady T's soulless corpse and shuddered. If Hoseph appeared, Mya had to kill him before he could touch her. She was fast enough. She could do it. But she had to focus.

As if intent on distracting her, Mya's lips tingled with the sensation of Dee's kiss. It had taken her so off guard that she had felt like a mouse under the spell of a viper's gaze. The last man she kissed had been Lad—twice. The first had been a betrayal, a distraction that allowed him to slip the Grandmaster's ring on her finger. She had initiated the second, a kiss goodbye. That was the problem with kisses; they were too personal, always fraught with emotion.

"Stop it, Mya!" She clenched her hands into fists. "Pay attention or you're dead!"

Mya stared out the window, scanning the people on the street, watching for gray robes or black mists. She didn't really expect any trouble en route to the palace. If the guild knew where she lived, they would have sent more mercenaries already. She'd have to be more vigilant on the return trip. Several of the conspirators on her list had access to the palace. They might have a way to contact Hoseph quickly, and he could be lying in wait for her to leave.

As the carriage labored up the hill toward the east end of the bluff, her mind wandered again. The buildings they passed started out as merely affluent, evolved to breathtaking splendor, then climaxed to jaw-droppingly grandiose. If she survived this guild war, where might she live in this vast city? Who might she make herself out to be? As Moirin, she had the emperor's notice. If she lent Moirin's name to Noncey's security company, nobles would line up to hire his bodyguards without a clue that they were assassins. Her mind spun as she considered the intelligence they could gather with ears in the homes of the highest ranking nobility, not to mention the money they would rake in. She might even be able to afford one of these mansions.

Dee would love that. Mya smiled at the whimsical notion of Dee decorating and fussing to his heart's content. Musing, she imagined an enthusiastic romp with him on an elaborate four-post bed with lace coverlets and canopy. A deep warmth spread up Mya's neck and face despite her enchanted wrappings.

The carriage hit a misplaced cobble and jolted her out of her reverie.

"Stop it!" She blinked and tried to breathe. *You're going to see the godsdamned emperor, and you have half the Assassins Guild hunting you! You don't need to be thinking about...that!*

Mya shifted in her seat as the carriage rounded another corner and she recognized the broad avenue that led to the main palace gate. She fought to calm her tumultuous thoughts. She had to be at the top of her game here. When the carriage lurched to a stop, she fumbled with her ridiculously tiny handbag to withdraw the letter from the emperor's secretary.

An imperial guard strode up to the carriage and touched the rim of his helmet respectfully. "Do you have an appointment to visit the palace?"

"I have this." She handed over the note and lifted her veil. "It said at my earliest convenience."

He perused the letter and his brows rose. "Yes, Miss Moirin." The man looked at her with something new in his eyes—Recognition? Respect?—and handed the note back. "Driver, take Miss Moirin into the inner court."

"Yessir!" Stirring his horses, the man drove the hackney through the wide tunnel that led to the outer palace courtyard, then through the next tunnel that brought them to the vast inner courtyard Mya remembered from the coronation.

The courtyard looked very different without a thousand courtiers bustling about in a rainbow of colors, their excited voices rising to the parapets. Curiously, empty and quiet, it seemed more intimidating, foreboding even. Imperial guards stood at silent attention, their eyes riveted on her carriage, the only carriage in sight. She was alone. There was no crowd to hide in now.

The carriage stopped before the main entrance to the palace, and a squad of imperial guards marched down the stairs, halting with a clash of arms. An officer opened the carriage door and glanced inside, then extended her hand to help Mya down.

"Miss..." The officer blinked at Mya, and recognition gleamed in her eyes. "Miss Moirin! Very good to see you well. We'd been told to expect you at some time."

So much for my disguise, she thought discontentedly. But then, she had been a focus of attention at the coronation reception, accepting the thanks and handshakes of many of the Imperial Guard. To the officer's credit, a new dress and blonde hair hadn't impeded her identification. Hopefully, if Hoseph dared to try an infiltration, the officer would see through his disguise just as easily.

"Thank you." Mya stepped down. "Do you need to see my invitation?"

"No, miss." The officer signaled and four imperial guards hurried forth. "Escort Miss Moirin by the back way to the garden-view audience chamber and inform Master Tennison that she's arrived."

"Sir!" One young guard dashed off, while the other three formed a cordon around Mya. The corporal in charge gestured toward the palace doors. "This way, Miss."

Mya followed the guards into the palace, less awed by the surroundings than she had been during her first visit. They immediately turned left and entered a side passage—avoiding the vast foyer and the Great Hall, the scene of her battle with Archmage Duveau—proceeding through a labyrinth of hallways toward the back of the palace. Mya memorized their path—their very *long* path—just in case she had to find her own way out again. Of course, getting out with the entire imperial guard blocking her way would be nigh impossible.

You're in deep now, Mya…

Corridor after corridor they walked until, finally, her escort stopped at a white door ornamented with gold inlay. The corporal opened it and waved her through. The room beyond was small but elegant. A low dais stood off-center to her right, with a simple upholstered armchair atop it and a door behind. A divan, low table, and a few chairs lined the opposite wall, obviously for nobles awaiting an audience. Sunlight streamed through a bank of floor-to-ceiling windows that commanded a stunning view of the palace gardens.

The corporal bowed and waved toward the chairs. "Please make yourself comfortable, Miss. His Majesty's schedule is always full, but we've been told he'll make time for you. Can I send someone with refreshments?"

"No, thank you. I don't mind waiting."

"If you need anything, just knock on this door. There will be guards posted outside."

I bet there will be... "Thank you."

The door closed and she was alone. Mya sighed and paced before the windows. The gardens were lovely, and she recalled strolling through them the night of the coronation reception, a drink in hand, giddy with the adoration of all who witnessed her deed. The wide expanse of glass would have made her feel exposed anywhere else, but Lady T had told her the palace had wards against magical transport; Hoseph couldn't reach her here.

She jumped when the door behind the dais opened. She hadn't been listening closely or she'd have heard the boots of the four imperial guards and the clank of the knight in chainmail from beyond the door. Behind them strode the Emperor of Tsing.

"Your Majesty." Mya curtsied deeply and held the pose.

"Please rise, Miss Moirin."

Mya raised her eyes and found the room more crowded than it had been when she began her obeisance. She recognized Master Tennison, the emperor's secretary, whom she'd met after the coronation. The wizard, Keyfur, unmistakable in his flamboyant clothing, smiled at her and nodded. Three paces from the emperor stood a stern man in a highly decorated uniform of the Imperial Guard; *Captain Ithross*, she dredged up from her memory. A fourth man hovered inconspicuously in the background, one arm crooked around a heavy ledger, a pen poised over the page. *Ah, of course, the imperial scribe.* Four additional imperial guards followed and, hands on swords, took station at the doors and around the emperor.

Keyfur strode forward without preamble, grinning widely. "Wonderful to see you again, Miss Moirin!" He surprised her by bending to kiss her gloved hand. "As always, I'm forever in your debt for saving my life..." He held up his hands and wiggled his fingers. "...and my *hands.*"

"Pleased to see you again, Master Keyfur." Mya remembered the wizard in the red gown at the coronation, using magic to surreptitiously check all the guests for weapons. Had Keyfur just magically frisked her? *Probably.* She smiled at him nonetheless, grateful that she carried no dagger for him to discover.

As the wizard backed away, the emperor stepped forward, guards at his sides, and extended a hand. "May We formally offer Our condolences for Baroness Monjhi's death."

"Thank you, Your Majesty." Mya curtsied again as she lightly touched his fingers, acutely aware of the heavy gazes of the guards upon her. "Lady T was...one of a kind."

The emperor regarded her. "We are also glad to see you well. We heard of the attack on your home and feared for your safety."

"Thank you, Majesty. I never thought Hoseph would come after me like that, especially with constables there!" She smiled apologetically. "I hope you understand that's why I went into hiding, and why I didn't receive your summons sooner."

Tynean Tsing waved away her apology. "We know what it's like to fear for one's life, Miss Moirin. In fact, that's one reason We summoned you here. We both seem to be far more involved with assassins than is healthy."

Mya's mind stumbled at the inference. *What does he mean by that? Could he know I'm with the guild?* She considered potential avenues of escape. *Through the windows, across the lawn, up the wall. The damned dress will have to go...*

The emperor continued, obviously unaware of her mental panic. "You saved Our life under incredible circumstances, and, according to the report from the constabulary, you saved the lives of several constables and bystanders when your home was attacked. You're an amazingly capable bodyguard and a competent and honorable woman of action."

What? Mya's heart stopped pounding, though her confusion mounted. Was she here to be arrested or praised? *Stop gaping and go with it, Mya!* She dipped her head in a polite nod. "I like to think so, Majesty."

"Then We will come to the point." The emperor gestured for her to walk beside him as he strolled to the windows and gazed into the beautiful gardens beyond.

The guards now stood in a semicircle around the two of them, but none interposed between them. It was a deliberate show of trust, she realized, allowing her to stand so close, knowing firsthand what she was capable of. The guards seemed twitchy, but Tynean Tsing appeared to be entirely at ease.

"We are without Our customary blademaster bodyguards—We're sure you heard of their tragic end—and We fear for the wellbeing of empire should We fall. The changes We've instituted aren't...appreciated by all." He smiled wryly. "What my opponents don't realize is that reverting back to the inhumane laws of my father would devastate the empire. In the interest of preserving that which I hold most dear—the Empire of Tsing—We summoned you here to offer you the position of Our Imperial Bodyguard."

For once in her life, Mya was completely without words. Her jaw dropped open. "I...I..."

The emperor raised a hand as he faced her. "Please let Us make this offer clear before you respond. This would *not* be an easy duty. Your sole responsibility would be Our safety. Other than during the time We sleep, you would be at Our side. However, the position would not be without reward. Compensation would be generous. You would, of course, live in the palace with all its amenities, as well as its security." He gestured to the beautiful view out the window with one hand and to the imperial guards with the other.

I don't believe this! Mya struggled to prevent herself from bursting into laughter at the irony. *All the trouble Hoseph has gone to trying to establish Assassin Guild access to the throne, and the emperor has just invited me to live alongside him.* Granted, the position was as bodyguard, but close quarters day in and day out would breed familiarity, trust...and influence. *It wouldn't be the same as an Imperial Grandmaster, but a discreet word here or a suggestion there...*

To her own surprise, Mya carefully considered the offer. Living in the palace would indeed keep her safe from Hoseph and the traitorous factions of the Assassins Guild, an attractive prospect. Just as quickly, she rejected the notion. She couldn't fight a guild war or hunt Hoseph from the palace, and she'd have neither the time nor opportunity to be the kind of Grandmaster she needed to be.

But how do you say no to an emperor?

Mya looked into his expectant face and smiled ruefully. "You honor me with your trust, Majesty, but I must respectfully decline your offer. I feel personally responsible for Lady T's death, and I've vowed retribution against Hoseph. I can't...do what I must while sequestered in the palace. I'm sorry."

Tynean Tsing's hopeful smile faltered. "We're sorry, too, though We understand your reticence. A life of such singular purpose isn't easy."

Mya waited quietly as the emperor looked out the window, his face unreadable, her impatience tempered by relief. He didn't seem angry or even unduly disappointed. Arbuckle's temperament was a far cry from that of his father.

Finally, he seemed to make up his mind about something and turned back to her. "There's another service you could perform for the empire that may be more to your liking. Indeed, it coincides closely with your own stated goal."

He wants me to hunt Hoseph for him? Mya kept her face carefully neutral. She'd happily accept any help he was willing to provide, but she mustn't let him suspect that she knew far more about Hoseph's assassination attempts than had been made public. "And what would that be, Your Majesty?"

"Your Majesty?" Master Keyfur squeezed between two of the guards, a long feather gripped between his fingertips, his eyebrows arched with an unspoken question.

"Yes, of course." Tynean Tsing sighed and beckoned the wizard forward. "We apologize, Miss Moirin, for this seeming lack of trust"—he shot a sour look toward Tennison and Ithross—"but what We are about to tell you is vital to the security of the empire. *No one* outside this room must know what your task is. If word got back to Hoseph, innocent lives would be lost. Our advisors insist that your loyalty must be confirmed before We reveal any details. Master Keyfur will verify the truth of your oath."

Uh-oh. Surrounded by guards and only an arm's length from a wizard, Mya didn't stand a chance of escape. *At least, not without making myself the most wanted woman in the empire.* But to allow herself to be enspelled…dare she risk it? Her only other option was to refuse the task and hope the emperor would allow her to walk away, but the amity of an emperor was not something to be spurned lightly. She calculated the odds, balanced the pros against the cons, and threw the dice.

"Don't apologize, Majesty." She smiled disarmingly. "In my business, I understand the need for confidentiality, but I must be forthright. Despite whatever rumors might be spreading about me,

I'm not immortal, invincible, or omnipotent. I do what I do very well, but I can't do it alone. I share all details of my assignments with my assistant, whom I trust without question. I also have a few indispensable contacts who are helping me in my search for Hoseph. If you would prefer not to confide in me under these conditions, then I understand."

"We see." The emperor seemed to consider for a moment. He glanced to Tennison, Ithross, then Keyfur, all of whom remained expressionless, then looked back to Mya and nodded. "Master Keyfur, please proceed."

Without a word, the wizard waved a feather, then nodded to the emperor. "It's done, Majesty."

Good Gods of Light! Mya had at least expected some mumbo-jumbo or incantation to accompany the spell. *So simple…like the magical frisking. What's to prevent him from casting another spell on me without my knowing? Or has he already?* Hairs on the back of her neck tickled with trepidation.

"Good." Tynean Tsing nodded to Mya. "You must vow that everything We tell you today will be kept in the strictest confidence you can maintain in the performance of your duties to the empire, Miss Moirin."

Mya chose her words carefully. "I vow to keep what you tell me secret, except from those I deem utterly trustworthy and necessary to help me fulfill the task you assign me, Majesty." She glanced at the wizard, then the guards. "I also vow that I mean your majesty no harm whatsoever."

The emperor glanced at Keyfur, and the wizard nodded with a smile.

"Very good." Tynean Tsing looked into her eyes, and his expression darkened. "There exists within Our empire a secret guild of assassins, brutal killers who will stop at nothing to achieve their goals."

Mya's eyebrows shot up. *He knows about the guild?* She folded her hands in front of her, grateful that she wore gloves.

Misreading her surprise, the emperor said, "Yes, it seems preposterous, doesn't it, that such a wicked organization could exist here, in the heart of Tsing? Alas, it's worse than you could imagine." He frowned and waved dismissively. "But you needn't concern yourself with all the sordid details. What's past is past, and we need to look to the future. Suffice to say, Hoseph is deeply involved with this guild, and is also the mastermind behind a conspiracy to subvert the government. They want nothing less than to rule the empire from behind the scenes, controlling the emperor as a puppet-master controls his marionette."

Mya suppressed the urge to ask for details. *How did he learn of the guild? How much does he know?* She mustn't appear to know more than what any imperial citizen might have learned from the public posterboards. "And how do they propose to do that, Majesty, if you're aware of the plot?"

The emperor smiled grimly. "Assassinate me and put another on the throne. Someone they can manipulate. Someone who wouldn't *dare* refute their commands."

"I see," Mya acknowledged studiously. Now he was telling her something she didn't know; Hoseph's plans for control of the empire.

"Duke Tessifus is next in line to the throne. His three sons have been abducted by this guild." The emperor pursed his lips. "Our task to you is to recover them."

Whoa! Mya stared at the emperor in shock. She'd been quite sure that he would ask for her help in apprehending Hoseph. When the initial shock subsided, she thought, *But if the Assassin's guild took the duke's sons... Why didn't I know about this?* Why hadn't Clemson or Noncey told her? *Perhaps they didn't know,* she reasoned; kidnapping was as often tasked to the guild Hunters, and Twist Umberlin had sided with Hoseph. *That, or they're not as loyal as they say...*

The task—using her guildsmen to recover children abducted by Hoseph's guildsmen—appealed to Mya's sense of irony. Additionally, rescuing the boys would certainly thwart Hoseph's plot and might bring him out into the open. It was worth the risk...with some assurances.

"Your Majesty, I am willing to try, but I must warn you that it will not be easy—or safe—to attempt this. In fulfilling my task, innocent people may die, one or more of the boys may die, and members of this guild of assassins will most *certainly* die. If what you say about this assassins guild is true, they won't give the boys over without a fight, and might kill them rather than allow them to be taken. If I do this, I'll have to strike quickly and decisively. I *must* be allowed to perform my duty without fear of… repercussions."

"We understand." He nodded to his secretary. "Tennison, draft a document that gives Miss Moirin immunity from prosecution for any act she commits in the performance of this service to the empire." He turned back to her. "Will that suffice?"

"That will suffice nicely, Your Majesty." Mya curtsied again and smiled inwardly. *An assassin with immunity from prosecution… How perfect!* But the devil was in the details. "That immunity will also cover the death of High Priest Hoseph, of course."

Tynean Tsing must have glimpsed a telltale gleam in her eyes, for he frowned. "Deliberately killing him without the due process of a trial under the law would be murder, Miss Moirin."

"Murder is no less than what he delivered to Baroness Monjhi, Majesty, and apparently what he was attempting to do to *you*." Mya fixed the emperor's stern gaze with one of her own. "I'll get the duke's sons back, but only if the immunity you grant me extends to Hoseph's death, should it happen to occur during my performance of this task…or not."

The emperor's frown deepened. He glanced at his advisors, who remained mute and unreadable as far as Mya could tell, then finally nodded. "You are a shrewd negotiator, Miss Moirin." He extended his hand again. This time she shook it firmly. "You shall receive the assurances you request and *any* other assistance you need, be it from the constabulary, Our Imperial Guard, Master Keyfur, or the Imperial Treasury. You will not find the Emperor of Tsing ungrateful."

"Thank you, Your Majesty." Mya curtsied and released his hand. "I'm sorry I couldn't be your bodyguard. The offer *was* tempting."

"Not tempting enough, evidently, but We understand." A fleeting smile passed his lips as he looked around the gilded room. "A palace is little more than a prison, albeit an elegant one."

Mya rubbed the Grandmaster's ring on her finger. "I understand that better than you will ever know, Majesty."

CHAPTER IX

Hoseph trudged up the hill past shop after glittering shop. Prior to all this...trouble, he'd enjoyed the occasional walk through the Heights District, stretching his legs and enjoying the deference accorded to him by passersby. Those who hadn't been impressed by his close relationship with the emperor had usually respected his position as high priest of Demia.

Lately, however, he walked to avoid the debilitating effects of using the talisman, and his identity had to remain anonymous. His vagabond disguise proved useful in that regard. In the poorer districts, he passed unnoticed, one of a legion of unfortunates who wandered the city begging for alms. In the rich neighborhoods, the nobility actively avoided looking at him, as if, by not acknowledging him, they disallowed his existence.

Coming abreast of the shop he sought, he pretended to survey the wares in the window. Master Inquisitor Lakshmi's new abode was the olfactory antithesis of the Master Hunter's fetid tannery. The shop sold soaps and cosmetics, and myriad scents—floral and spice, citrus and musk, all clean and crisp—suffused the air even on the street outside. Inside, a threesome of well-dressed young women perused the shelves, sniffing bottles of bath oil and tissue-wrapped soaps, chatting and laughing.

Hoseph ground his teeth in annoyance. A vagabond entering such a shop would immediately be tossed out, and he couldn't afford to call attention to himself. He considered checking to see if there was an alley and back entrance, but these blocks were long, and his legs already ached from the uphill hike. Fortunately, the saleswoman was wrapping up the customers' purchases. They wouldn't be much longer. When they left, he could slip in.

Genteel laughter perked his ears, and he spied a pair of matrons approaching, their eyes on the soap shop. Cursing the need for this ridiculous disguise, Hoseph sat down on the ground directly next to the door and stuck out his hand.

"Alms," he croaked in a hoarse voice.

The women hissed in disgust and made a wide arc around him before continuing down the street.

As the younger women exited the shop, one exclaimed, "Oh, look out!"

They skipped around him and hurried away, their heads tilted together as they admired their acquisitions, the beggar on the stoop already forgotten.

With no one else approaching, Hoseph made his move. Lurching to his feet, he opened the shop door and entered. His worn boots clicked against the white marble floor as he strode past the tastefully arranged shelves. He walked straight up to the stunningly beautiful woman behind the counter and fixed her with a stern gaze. "I wish to see your mistress."

Recognition flicked into her startlingly blue eyes. "Of course." She nodded graciously and motioned him around the gleaming counter, turning the polished brass handle of the door there and pushing it open. "Just through here."

"Thank you." The door clicked closed behind him as he walked down a hall as bright and spotless as the shop. A man and a woman guarded the door at the far end, their faces as threatening as the previous woman's had been welcoming. He approached without fear. "I need to speak with Master Inquisitor Lakshmi."

"Of course." The man knocked upon the door.

"Yes?" The voice from the room beyond was faint and distracted.

The guard opened it just enough to lean through. "Hoseph here to see you, Mistress."

"Let him in."

The Master Inquisitor reclined on a divan, gracefully draped from shoulders to ankles in an orange embroidered sari, the nails of her bare feet painted a matching hue. Gold gleamed at her neck, wrists, and ankles. The rest of the room shone with equal opulence and luxury.

Decadence... Hoseph stifled his distaste. Demia cared nothing for luxuries; they were distractions, weaknesses, useless and pointless. "I require the use of some of your Inquisitors."

"Good afternoon to you, too, Hoseph." Without looking up, the Master Inquisitor continued reading a document on the small lap desk. Scrawling her signature, she handed the parchment over to her secretary and accepted another. When he refused to respond to her cordial banter, she sighed. "What do you need them for?"

"To gather information on a constable at Tsing headquarters. Sergeant Benjamin is in charge of Lady T's murder case. He's questioned Mya, and she's apparently agreed to keep in touch with him. I want to know if we can buy or coerce him into cooperating with us."

"And how did *you* come by this information?" she asked, signing her name and handing over the document.

"I have my sources." Hoseph had been pleased with how quickly Otar had carried out his commission; the man had a future yet. Once reinstalled as captain of the Imperial Guard, he'd provide valuable intelligence about the goings on in the palace, and he'd be able to watch over Tessifus personally. But Lakshmi didn't need to know who his source was; she just needed to do as he asked.

"Well, can your *source* get Mya's address?" Another document exchanged hands, and another signature scratched upon the parchment.

"No. She's gone into hiding, thanks to that fiasco of an attack on her home. She sent her lackey to the constabulary." Hoseph mused on the description of the lackey that Otar had provided: tall, dark-haired, and well spoken. It had to be Dee, Lad's former assistant whom Hoseph had met in Twailin, the same man who had shot him with a crossbow at Mya's home here in Tsing.

"All right, Hoseph." Lakshmi's nut brown features wrinkled in a frown. She waved away her secretary and put aside the lap desk, then swiveled and stood in a graceful motion that rippled the folds of her sari and belied her years. "It's time to get a few things straight. You have only yourself to blame for this *fiasco*, as you call it. *You* are not an assassin, so when it comes to killing, please allow *professionals* to decide how, where, and when. Twist's attack on Mya was rushed and ill timed. Had he consulted with Kittal and myself, I have no doubt that Mya would now be quite dead."

Hoseph couldn't believe his ears. *She's blaming Umberlin's failure on me?* "I didn't *decide* anything. Umberlin planned the attack. All I did was give him her address."

"No, you dangled the guildmaster's ring in front of him as a prize!" Her wizened lips pressed together in a wrinkled line. "You set this up like some kind of *competition*; bring in Mya's head and win the guildmaster's seat! That's not the way we *work*, Hoseph! If you'd bothered to notice, our factions are specialized. Each has its strengths and weaknesses. We work as a *team*."

"Kittal knew about the pending attack. Umberlin said he sent one of his Alchemists to help."

"Twist didn't consult Kittal *or* me! He just asked to borrow a senior Alchemist. Kittal complied because we *always* help one another!" Lakshmi threw up her hands, the tiny jewels on her elegantly manicured nails glinting in the lamplight. "Twist was a damn fine Hunter—he could track a flea through a crowd of beggars—but he didn't have the *talent* to be guildmaster. He didn't see the big picture. He knew that *winning* the ring from you would be the only way he'd ever get it!"

Hoseph sneered. "And *you*, I take it, *do* see the big picture?"

The Master Inquisitor smiled, a haunting expression on her inscrutable features. "Yes, I do. And the picture right now demands *cooperation*. In fact, Kittal and I are working together to exploit another opportunity."

"To kill Mya? What is it?"

Lakshmi rolled her eyes dramatically. "Of *course* to kill Mya. But it's an extremely sensitive operation, so the fewer who know about it, the better. I'll let you know how it works out."

"With all your talk of cooperation, I assume you've consulted Master Hunter Embree." Hoseph was sure he could get the neophyte master to tell him what was going on.

"Yes, of course. Now, about your request. In the interest of cooperation, I'll assign three of my Inquisitors to look into this Sergeant Benjamin. Trust me, we'll find *something* to exploit—everyone has their weaknesses—but they'll be reporting to *me*, not you."

Hoseph opened his mouth to protest, then thought better of it. He had gotten what he wanted, which was someone to look into turning the constable to their side. *Let her think she won.* "As you wish."

"Excellent." Lakshmi waved her hand at her secretary. "Joshi, have Noesha pick three Inquisitors who are well acquainted with the constabulary."

"Yes, Mistress." The secretary put aside her papers and hurried out.

Hoseph withdrew a small silver chime from a pocket of his robe. "And in the interest of *cooperation*, I'd like to give you this. Chime it at need and I'll come, but only if it's *important*. Demia's gifts are not to be used triflingly."

The Master Inquisitor took the chime, looked it over curiously before placing it gently on the small table beside the divan. "Very well."

"One other small matter," Hoseph said with a casual gesture. "You've had plenty of time to get the Tessifus boys resettled. I need to know where they are."

"Don't worry. They're well-hidden and well-protected. I have my most loyal people watching over them."

"Good, but your *people* can't whisk them away magically if danger threatens. *I* can." Hoseph was sick of being stonewalled. "Tell me where they are."

"No." Lakshmi sashayed over to an ornate table that held a silver blackbrew service and four narrow glass cups with silver bases.

"*What?*"

"I said, no." She poured liquid as black as tar from the silver pot into a cup. "Surely you're familiar with the word."

He ignored her sarcasm. "Why won't you tell me?"

"Because I don't wish to end up like Twist Umberlin." The Inquisitor spooned an inordinate amount of sugar into her blackbrew and stirred it. "I'm the only one who knows where they all are, and I've given orders that if I die, they die." She lifted the cup and turned to him, sipping daintily. "Then you have nothing."

What is it that makes Inquisitors so difficult? First Lady T, now Lakshmi. How he longed to reach out and send her soul to Demia, but he resisted the temptation. She was right; without Duke Tessifus' sons, he had no hold over the man who would be emperor.

Reining in his temper, Hoseph asked quietly, "Why must you contest my authority on every matter?"

"Hoseph," Lakshmi held up a forestalling hand, "I'm not *contesting* your authority, because you *have* no authority here. That said, you *are* a valuable asset to the guild, and one day will be a valuable asset to our future Grandmaster."

Hoseph fumed, but kept his expression neutral. "And how is our young future Grandmaster progressing?"

"Patience, Hoseph, patience." Lakshmi sipped the syrupy brew again, obviously savoring both the stimulating beverage and her control over Hoseph. "It's only been a few weeks. We have *years* before he'll need to assume the throne. We've earned his trust, and are now slowly turning him against his father and brothers. In time, we will train him in the techniques of inquisition. These things can't be rushed."

"He needs to become accustomed to *me*," Hoseph insisted. "I'll be his right hand, so he needs to know and trust me."

Lakshmi smiled. "In time."

Hoseph decided it was time to leave, before he did something rash. He smiled grimly at the Master Inquisitor as he flicked the silver skull into his hand. "Kill Mya and see to the safety of the Tessifus boys. If you fail, it's not *me* you'll have to answer to, but Demia."

Whispering the invocation, Hoseph dissolved into mist. The look of unease on Lakshmi's smug features was worth the pain he would endure.

Crack!

What in the Nine Hells? Mya froze halfway up the stairs to the flat. The trip back in the carriage already had her nerves singing like violin strings. The unfamiliar sound from the flat snapped her senses to a fever pitch. First checking the street below, she moved as quietly as her uncomfortable shoes would allow to the top of the stairs. Outside the apartment door, she rummaged through her tiny purse so any passersby who happened to see her would think she was searching for her key. In fact, she was listening.

Crack-thud.

The crack might be a whip or a slap of a palm against flesh, but the accompanying thud... *Almost like...* Mya stiffened with a remembrance: the crack of a crossbow and the sickening thud of the bolt plunging into the flesh of her leg. *Dee?*

Mya eased her key out of her handbag and slipped it silently into the lock. With a single motion, she turned the key, thrust open the door open, lunged into the apartment...and stopped. "Oh, for the gods' sake!"

Dee stood on one side of the living room, a startled look on his face and an odd little crossbow in one hand, aimed directly at her chest.

His startlement eased and the weapon lowered. "Oh, it's only you."

"Yes, it's only me. I thought you were being attacked in here." Mya closed the door, threw the bolt, and took off her hat, tossing it onto the divan. "What are you doing?"

"I'm practicing." Dee aimed and squeezed the trigger of his tiny weapon. *Crack-thud!* The short, black dart shot across the room to stick alongside several others in a blanket bound around the back of a kitchen chair.

"From Noncey?" she asked, peeling out of her gloves.

"Yes." He reached into his coat—long and full, one that Mya had never seen before—and drew out an odd device with a handle and two triggers. He squeezed one trigger and the small bow flipped out crossways, already cocked and loaded, tensioned by some type of spring mechanism. Now it looked just like the other crossbow. He aimed and squeezed the second trigger, sending another bolt thudding into the blanket.

Placing one of the little weapons on the kitchen table, Dee cocked and reloaded the other, then folded the spring-loaded bow back in line with the handle. Thus prepared, it nestled easily into a specialized holster inside his coat. He reloaded and stowed the second weapon.

"Ingenious." Mya contorted her arms behind her back to loosen the laces of her dress, but couldn't quite manage the knot. "You'd have to hit something vital with one of those to stop someone, though."

"He gave me a couple vials of poison as well. One's an anesthetic, the other's deadly." Dee drew and fired again. The bolt struck just slightly off center. "I'm not very fast yet, but I'm not missing the target by much."

"With poison you don't have to be as accurate." Mya struggled with the knot, annoyed that Dee didn't offer to assist with her gown. He was usually more attentive. "Can you help me with this thing? Your knots are impossible."

"Sure." Dee took the time to reload and holster the crossbow before stepping behind her.

Mya breathed a sigh of relief as the laces loosened. Before she could thank him, Dee strode to the chair, plucked the darts from the target, and tucked them into slots sewn into the lining of his coat. Tugging the jacket straight, he walked back to his firing position, drew, and fired. The tiny bolt popped into the target, dead center.

"That's pretty good for only a few hours of practice."

"Thanks." He drew the other crossbow and fired left handed. The bolt hit the target on the edge. "I'm not so good with the left, yet. Noncey said to learn to shoot before I work on speed. It's nothing like firing a regular crossbow."

Mya shrugged the dress off her shoulders and tugged the sleeves free, then stepped out of the garment. "Practice will get you there. How fast can you reload?"

"Faster than a regular crossbow, but with poisoned bolts I'll have to be more careful."

Mya unlaced her shoes and kicked them off, then stretched, stiff from hours in the restrictive clothing. Dee seemed to be ignoring her, though he could just be preoccupied with his new weapons as he reloaded, drew, and fired, time and again.

As Dee reloaded once more, he broke his silence. "Mya, about this morning...the kiss...I didn't—"

"Oh, that?" *Is that what's bugging him? Is he afraid I'll be mad?* Waving a dismissive hand, she said, "Don't worry about it. Quick thinking, actually, playing the loving husband in front of Mistress Gantry. I didn't even know she was watching us. Now, are you going to ask me how my talk with the emperor went or not?"

"How did your talk with the emperor go?" he asked obediently.

"He offered me—well, *Moirin*, actually—a job as his bodyguard." She twisted her stiff back sharply, eliciting a sharp crunch.

He gaped at her. "He did?"

"Yep. I turned him down, of course, but then he offered me *another* job."

"What job?" Dee turned back to his target, drew, and fired first one crossbow, then the other, in quick succession. Both bolts hit the target not far from center.

"He wants me to rescue some kidnapped kids. Duke Tessifus is next in line for the throne, and Hoseph had his three sons taken. I see his plan now: kill the emperor, then control the next one through his sons."

"That sounds about right. Can you?"

"Get them back?" She shrugged. "I don't know yet. There's also the question of whether Clemson and Noncey knew about this plan and, if they did, why they didn't tell me."

Crack-thud. Crack-thud.

"Maybe they defected before learning about it."

"Maybe. I'm certainly going to find out. But look at this!" Mya pulled the document signed by the emperor out of her tiny handbag and flourished it. "The emperor gave me free rein to do the job as I think best, and immunity from prosecution if I have to kill to do it, including killing Hoseph!"

"*Really?*" Dee turned to face her, eyes wide.

"Really. I'm going to go see Clemson and Noncey to see what kind of plan we can work out."

"Shall I come with you?"

"No, I can move faster on my own." Mya also didn't want Dee in the line of fire if the two masters didn't have the right answers to her questions, but she wasn't going to tell him that. There was no need to have him worry about her, which he seemed to be doing a lot lately.

He turned back to his target without a word, drew and fired both of the weapons at the same time. *Crack! Crack!* The darts thumped into the blanket dead center.

"Hey, two bull's eyes. You're getting good!" Mya strode into the bedroom, tossed her dress onto the bed, and donned her comfortable clothing and weapons to the steady cadence of Dee's target practice. He seemed unduly quiet, probably worried about her again. Well, she couldn't do anything about that. Peeking out from behind the drawn shade, she saw that dusk was already fading to night. *Perfect.*

"I don't know what time I'll be back," she said as she strode back out into the front room.

Dee didn't respond, painstakingly reloading and cocking his curious little crossbows.

Yep, he's worried...

Going to the front door, she listened carefully, but heard no one on the stairs.

Crack! Crack!

"Don't wait up for me," she said, turning the bolt and easing open the door.

"I won't."

She glanced back, but Dee's attention was on his target practice, so she ducked out.

Mya made her way down to the river, skulking through dark alleys and occasionally flitting across rooftops when constables crossed her path. Crossing the river and striding through the shabby streets of the Dreggars Quarter, her mood vacillated wildly.

If I rescue the duke's sons... Her mind whirled with ways to take advantage of the emperor's good will, then her stomach fluttered anxiously as she considered Clemson and Noncey. Were they betraying her, or simply ignorant of Hoseph's plan? There was only one way to find out.

Mya scrambled over the wall of the dark distillery and dropped lightly into the courtyard. She tensed as she approached the main structure. Two Enforcers stood at the door, crossbows trained on her as she advanced. Of course, they couldn't shoot her, but having weapons pointed at her still made her nervous. They lowered their crossbows as they recognized her.

"Are they both here?"

"Yes, ma'am."

"Good."

One of them opened the door for her and closed it behind.

Mya easily picked her way around the huge stone vats and

distillation equipment in the darkness. Listening, she heard nothing but the burble of the fermenting vats and the scratch of a rat somewhere among the machinery. The door to the stairs wasn't locked or guarded, so she opened it and started down.

The Enforcer at the bottom of the stairs whipped up his crossbow when he noticed her, then slowly lowered it as she descended into the light of the wall sconce behind him. "Grandmaster." He nodded respectfully, then looked pointedly at the door to Clemson's office. "I'd recommend knocking."

"I will."

At the end of the hall, Mya knocked, but opened the door to the Master Enforcer's office before anyone answered. Clemson and Noncey were alone, sitting close together on the leather-upholstered divan, sipping golden liquid from crystal tumblers, and thankfully not intimately engaged. She briefly admired the tableau—like a pair of leopards, perfectly matched, beautiful and deadly—then stepped casually into the room and shut the door.

"Grandmaster." They started to rise.

"Relax." Mya waved them down, sauntering over to sit in one of the comfortable chairs across from them. "Sorry about dropping in unannounced, but…something's come up."

"*Something?*" Noncey raised one eyebrow before knocking back the rest of his drink and standing.

"What kind of something?" Clemson handed over her glass.

Noncey took it and strode to the sideboard and refilled them. The Master Blade raised a third empty tumbler at Mya with another arched eyebrow.

"Please."

He poured a measure and returned, handing glasses to Mya and Clemson before he sat down once again.

"So…" Mya sipped, the smooth liquor burning a sweet course down her throat. "This something involves three boys that the guild abducted, the sons of Duke Tessifus. Did either of you know about that?" She watched their responses closely.

Noncey nodded without any sign of unease. "Yes, we knew. My Blades and Twist's Hunters abducted the boys under Lady T's orders. We delivered them to Lakshmi."

"Did you know Hoseph was behind the abduction?"

Noncey looked surprised then, and exchanged a glance with Clemson. "No, Grandmaster, I did *not* know that." He still didn't look worried.

"Do you know why they were taken?"

"No idea. Once we delivered them to Lakshmi, it was out of my hands," Noncey said. "Lady T didn't volunteer any additional information, and I didn't ask. I followed my orders."

"So…" Mya swirled her drink and breathed deep of the spicy fragrance, then sipped the smooth rum, "…why didn't you tell me?"

The two masters exchanged another glance, then looked back to her.

Clemson spread her hands. "It wasn't my operation."

Noncey shrugged. "And my end of it was done before Lady T was murdered. It didn't seem relevant to the current situation. What do three boys have to do with our guild war?"

Mya scrutinized the two masters, trying to guess what they were thinking beneath their placid façades. *Lad, where are you when I need you?* That man could read people like a book, picking up on seemingly trivial details—a slight catch of breath, a shift of posture, the unconscious flick of a finger—that signified feelings and intentions. Mya was not so apt, but the masters *seemed* guileless.

"It turns out that these particular three boys have quite a lot to do with our guild war. Hoseph intends to use them to pressure Duke Tessifus, who's next in line for the throne. If his attempts on the emperor's life had been successful, he'd already be holding the reins of the empire."

Clemson cocked her head. "Establishing the guild's control over the throne."

Mya shook her head. "Hoseph would run things for his own benefit, not the guild's." She voiced a question that had long been on her mind. "Did you *know* that the previous emperor was Grandmaster?"

The two masters both shook their heads, and Clemson said, "We suspected so after he died. Their simultaneous deaths were too coincidental."

"When Hoseph showed up after Lady T was killed, that pretty much confirmed it," Noncey added. "Why else would the emperor's spiritual advisor be involved with the guild?"

"Although," Clemson smiled slyly, "you seem to be cultivating your *own* relationship with our new emperor, saving his life at the coronation."

"I found out Hoseph was behind the attempt. That was the only reason I needed."

The masters smiled and nodded their agreement.

Mya made up her mind; the two seemed honest, and their stories made sense. *And they're all I've got.* Muscles she didn't even realize were tense suddenly relaxed, and she pushed ahead. "We have a new objective."

Noncey grinned. "Other than killing that lunatic priest, you mean?"

"Yes, but that could be a bonus."

"And this objective has to do with the boys?" Clemson asked.

"Yes." Mya sipped her rum. "We need to get them back. I don't suppose either of you knows where they're being held."

"No." Noncey frowned. "But if we're to get them back, we'll have to infiltrate Lakshmi's organization. That'd be hard enough if we *weren't* at war with her."

"I know." Mya swirled her glass and inhaled the heady aroma. "They're probably being held separately. At least, that's what *I'd* do; spread the risk if one's discovered. So, we need information on where the boys might be. Don't discount anything. There's no way to know what might be important."

"Of course." Clemson nodded.

"Well, I won't keep you." Mya tossed back the rest of her rum and stood. "I'll send Dee by regularly. You can tell him anything to pass along to me. Thanks for the drink."

"My pleasure, Grandmaster." Clemson stood and took Mya's empty glass, glancing sidelong at Noncey with a curious smile on her lips.

"Something funny?" Mya asked, flushing as she suspected a private joke at her expense.

"No, Grandmaster, but we were discussing earlier how unaccustomed we are to a Grandmaster, or even a *guildmaster*, for that matter, who plays such an active role in guild affairs. It's…refreshing."

"Get used to it. I'm the hands-on type." Mya started for the door, then turned back. "I'm also the type who appreciates being told when I've made a colossal blunder, so don't hesitate to tell me when I'm wrong. I'm still learning about the guild in Tsing, and I'm *not* your former Grandmaster."

"Very well," Clemson nodded respectfully, her action mirrored by Noncey. Yes, the two were a perfect pair.

"I'll be in touch."

Mya departed with her mood much lighter than when she arrived. Nodding to the guard stationed at the bottom of the stairs, she started up toward the distillery.

Crack!

Mya's first thought was of Dee and his little crossbows. *Dee's not here!* She leapt straight up, trying to evade as Lad had taught her. Unfortunately, her assailant was too close.

A finger-thick bolt punched into the middle of her back just below her shoulder blades, shattering bone. She felt no pain, of course, only the sudden and worrisome sensation of...*nothing* below her waist. Her legs were completely numb, useless. Mya wheeled her arms, trying to catch herself, but crashed facedown onto the stairs.

My spine! Her heart hammered in her chest, waves of nausea and weakness washing over her. *It will heal!* she reminded herself. But first she had to remove the bolt. Gripping a stair with one hand, she reached back with the other. From the corner of her eye, she saw the guard at the bottom of the stairs pulling out another bolt to reload his weapon.

Assassin? Mya's mind reeled. She'd recognized the guard from her previous visit, assumed he was guild-bound. *They can't touch me!*

The click of the crossbow being cocked jarred her out of her shock.

Figure it out later, Mya. He's going to kill you unless you do something... But what could she do? Her legs were useless, and she couldn't get a good grip on the bolt to pull it out. *Think, Mya!* She slowed her fumbling fingers, then went limp, holding her breath and praying to any god who would listen that the guard thought her dead. *Got to get him close enough...*

The brush of his boots on the stairs coincided with the click of a crossbow bolt sliding into place.

Now!

Mya put both hands on the stairs, cocked her elbows, and thrust with all her might. Up and back she flew, right into her assailant. The impact drove the bolt through her body until its bloody head protruded from her stomach an inch below her sternum. *Too close...*

The crossbow cracked and another bolt punched through her leg as she and her assailant tumbled down the stairs and crashed into the floor at the bottom. Thankfully, Mya landed on top. Air whooshed from his lungs, but he wasn't knocked senseless, as she'd hoped. A strong arm wrapped around her throat, and he shifted beneath her.

He's going for his dagger! Mya reached back and grabbed his wrist as the blade came down at her throat. Twisting it sharply, bones snapped beneath her fingers, and the dagger clattered to the floor. He screamed. Without a pause, she drove her elbow back as hard as she could. His ribs shattered, and the scream died to a soft wheeze. Still, the arm around her neck didn't loosen.

Tough bastard... She couldn't breathe and was weakening quickly from blood loss.

Mya gripped the bloody head of the crossbow bolt transfixing her torso and wrenched it out of her body. Gagging on the bile and blood that surged into her throat, she thrust the bloody bolt point first over her shoulder. Something crunched, and the arm around her throat went slack.

Mya dragged a breath into her lungs and flung herself off the man. She reached for a dagger, but it wasn't necessary. One of the guard's eyes had been pierced by the crossbow bolt, the other stared blankly at the ceiling.

"Olsen, what the hell's all the—" Clemson and Noncey stood in the doorway to her office, staring wide-eyed at the dead assassin and Mya each in turn.

Mya lurched up, her legs tingling as her severed spine knitted. Her knees wobbled, but she drew another dagger and put her back to the wall. Steadying herself, she swallowed blood and stared at the two masters. Had her trust been so misplaced? Not two minutes ago she would have sworn that they were on her side. As she watched them, however, her thoughts of treason and conspiracy faded; the shock in their eyes could not be feigned.

"Grandmaster, what..."

"Your man just shot me in the back, Master Clemson." She pushed off the wall and fought to remain upright. "Why hasn't he signed a blood contract?"

"*All* my people have signed blood contracts!" Clemson strode forward, Noncey at her heels wielding two curved daggers. Other doors along the hallway opened and sleepy-eyed assassins emerged.

"Then he must be an imposter." Mya slowly lowered her daggers, but kept her eyes on the rest of the assassins. She was in no condition to fight. "Maybe some kind of disguise or magic?"

Clemson knelt to inspect the dead assassin, then looked up to Mya. "No, this is Olsen. He's been a junior journeyman with me for more than a year."

"Then how the hell could he shoot me in the back?" Mya began to shake as the implications chilled her blood.

"Grandmaster, you're still wounded!" Noncey pointed to the crossbow bolt sticking out of Mya's thigh. "You need—"

Mya wrenched the bolt from her leg and flung it aside, her leg muscle twitching as the wound closed and healed. "What I *need* is to know how in the Nine Hells a member of this guild could shoot the Grandmaster in the back if he's signed a *blood contract!*"

Clemson stood and held out her hands, shaking her head helplessly. "Grandmaster, I don't *know*. *No* one gets in without a blood con—" The Master Enforcer's face paled and she glanced around at her assassins. "Jolee, come here!"

"Yes, Mistress." The hulking woman strode over.

"Slap me," Clemson ordered.

Jolee looked aghast, her long, lower canines jutting from between her lips as she frowned. "Mistress, I—"

"Do it!" the Master Enforcer snapped.

The Enforcer lashed out with one meaty hand, the open palm smacking Clemson's cheek hard enough to knock her back a step. The blow was certainly not as hard as Jolee could have made it, but even so, it left a red print on the Master's cheek.

"Impossible!" Noncey's incredulous tone mirrored the shock on everyone's faces.

"Obviously it *is* possible." Mya's legs threatened to collapse beneath her, due to blood loss or the shock of what she'd just witnessed, she didn't know. She might have believed someone destroyed one assassin's contract so he could kill her, but if Jolee could strike Clemson... *How many others?* she wondered. *All?*

Clemson seemed to be reading Mya's thoughts. "Alek, you, too. Slap me."

A young man, barely old enough to shave, stepped forward with wide eyes. Hesitantly, he reached out and also slapped his master's cheek.

"Jolee's been with me for years, Alex a couple of months. It doesn't seem to make a difference." The Master Enforcer shook her head.

Mya's mind whirled. "The attack on the orphanage! Those were Hunters and Alchemists, not mercenaries!" There was only one possible answer. "Someone's destroyed the blood contracts."

"Gods and devils preserve us." Clemson's oath drew Mya's ire like a magnet.

"We'd best see to preserving ourselves, Master Clemson." Mya fingered the bloody hole in her shirt. "If we don't, I doubt the gods will take up the slack. Where are the blood contracts kept? Who's in charge of them? In Twailin, all new contracts were given to the Grandmaster's collection agent."

Clemson shrugged. "We never knew where the repository was. All contracts went to Lady T, and from there..." She shrugged again.

To the Grandmaster? Mya wondered if that was how the Emperor knew about the Assassins Guild. But no, if the contracts had been discovered in the palace, Lady T would have been in the dungeon, not seated beside the new emperor at his coronation reception.

"Hoseph..." Noncey's face flushed red. "It *must* be! No *sane* assassin would destroy the contracts. It'd mean chaos. Every junior journeyman with a grudge against a superior would be free to seek revenge."

"The other factions must already know this since they staged an attack on me, so there'll be as much mayhem in their ranks as in ours." Mya gritted her teeth. "Hoseph's destroying the entire guild just because he wants me dead."

"He's neither sane *nor* an assassin." Clemson looked around at her Enforcers. "Jolee, get rid of Olsen's corpse and spread word of what's happened. There's no point in hiding it. The damage is done."

"Yes, Mistress."

Mya turned to the two masters. "This doesn't change our new mission, but it does mean that we have to be careful who knows what we're planning. The other factions have already infiltrated our side." She jerked her chin toward Olsen's body. "We can't afford for them to know our plans, so make damned sure that your people are loyal. And let it be known that *anyone* exploiting the destruction of the blood contracts by attacking a superior will be executed."

"Yes, Grandmaster," Clemson and Noncey said in unison.

"Do you want an escort home, Grandmaster?" Clemson asked, glancing around at her Enforcers.

"No." Mya shot the master a level stare. "I'm safer alone. Right now I don't know who I can trust."

Clemson reddened in embarrassment. "I understand, and I'm truly sorry that one of my people has let me down…let *us* down. It won't happen again."

"Make sure it doesn't." Mya swept her eyes over the junior assassins, noted the awe—and a little fear—in their eyes. Perhaps it was just as well that they saw her recover from the seemingly lethal wounds; it would make them think twice about crossing her. She started up the stairs. The tingling was gone, but her legs still felt weak. It was going to be a long walk home.

Who can I trust? she wondered, but realized that she already knew the answer to that question. She could trust no one.

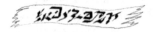

Dee flexed his aching hands. He'd fired bolts into the padded chair until fatigue worsened his aim more than practice improved it. Still, it hadn't been enough to keep his mind off Mya.

I sent her out without a word. Why didn't I say goodbye? In this business, surviving to meet again was never a sure thing. But his hurt feelings had sealed his lips until after she'd left. *Without me, because I'm apparently too slow.*

Dee sat back in his chair, his fingers drumming a sharp tattoo on the wood as he tried to think straight. When Mya was at the palace, he'd worried about her reaction to his kiss. Then, when she blew it off as part of his husbandly guise, he wasn't sure whether to be relieved that she had misinterpreted his intention, or disappointed because she thought so little of it. It was the same thing with her remarks as he practiced. Were they sincere compliments or snide references to his lack of fighting skills?

Damn! He slammed a hand on the table. Why was it so hard to sort out his feelings for this woman?

He'd told her he wouldn't wait up, yet here he sat. He wanted to tell her he couldn't keep up a dispassionate relationship, but if she walked in the door and asked him for a casual romp to help her sleep—no emotions allowed—he'd be in bed with her two minutes later. Dee couldn't help himself; when Mya beckoned, he jumped.

Dee literally jumped when the bolt clacked and Mya burst into the apartment. Before he could ask how the meeting went, he saw the blood on her hands, the holes in her clothing, and leapt from his chair. "Mya! What—"

"We've got a problem." She slammed the door and started unbuttoning her shirt as she strode for the bathroom. "Hoseph destroyed the blood contracts."

"He…" Dee swallowed against a sudden lump in his throat as he followed. "You're *sure?*"

She stripped off her shirt and tossed it at him. "A journeyman Enforcer just shot me in the back with a crossbow. I'm pretty sure."

Dee examined the shirt. There was a hole in the back and another in the front, both barely halfway down and dead center. His skin went cold, his knees suddenly shaky as he followed her into the bathroom.

"Mya, this was *very* close to your heart!" *Pierce my heart or take off my head*, Mya had told him once in one of their languid moments, when both were sated and on the edge of sleep, *everything else will heal.*

"Tell me about it!" Mya kicked off her boots, then shucked out of her pants and tossed them to him as well. "Bastard shot me in the leg, too, before I killed him." She started unwinding her blood-soaked wrappings. "I *liked* those pants!"

"You could have been *killed!*"

Mya stopped, eyebrows raised and a sarcastic sneer on her face. "*Really?* You *think* so?" She resumed unwrapping, her beautiful tattoos smeared with blood. "Stop staring at me and stating the obvious. Put the shirt to soak in cold water. I don't know what you can do with the pants, since they're suede. I'll put the wrappings to soak in here after I bathe."

"Okay." He whirled and went to the kitchen.

Water began splashing into the tub in the bathroom as he put the shirt to soak in a pot of cold, soapy water. Dee inspected the pants; only one hole, but it was ragged; he'd have to stitch in a new swatch to mend them properly. First he'd have to clean them, but for that he had to pick up the right supplies. For now, he hung them over a chair and went back to the bathroom.

Mya sat in the tub, scrubbing at her skin with a brush. The water must have been cold; she was shivering. She looked up as Dee came in, and her expression unnerved him. Mya always presented an unassailable front—cocky, confident, in charge. Never before had he seen such fear in her eyes.

Raising one hand from the blood-tinged water, she presented the obsidian and gold band on her finger. "It's useless, Dee. Instead of protecting me, it makes me a target. And I still can't take it off." She tugged at the Grandmaster's ring. "It's fucking *useless*!"

Dee was speechless. He had no idea how to deal with this unfamiliar, uncertain Mya. No idea what to say. He stared at her as she stared at the ring.

Gradually, Mya's fearful expression hardened and her eyes narrowed. She slammed a fist down on the edge of the tub.

"I will *not* let Hoseph take this guild from me!"

That's the Mya I know! Dee thought with relief as he sagged against the doorjamb. "You know that *all* the contracts were destroyed? Not just the contract for this one person?

Mya nodded and started brushing the blood from under her fingernails. "Clemson ordered two of her people to hit her. They did it with no problem. We've got to assume the worst."

"And you know it was Hoseph who destroyed the contracts?"

"It only makes sense. How else could he use the guild against me? But he obviously didn't consider the ramifications to the guild." She snorted a laugh. "I don't know if he's mad, desperate, or just ignorant."

"The guild will fall apart," Dee concluded. "Without the blood contracts, people will flee right and left, abandon their posts."

"Maybe." Mya rested her hands on the sides of the tub and cocked her head. Dee could almost hear the wheels of her mind turning. "And maybe not."

"Why *wouldn't* they run away?"

She looked at him. "Are *you* leaving?"

"No! Of course not."

"Why not, if there's no blood contract keeping you here?"

Dee hesitated. "Because..." *I'm falling in love with you!* Of course, he couldn't say that. Besides, it ran deeper than that. "Because I believe in *loyalty*. I take *pride* in what I do."

"Exactly."

Mya dunked her head underwater and scrubbed at her hair, came up sputtering. Rising, she climbed from the bath, picked up her bloody wrappings, and dumped them in. The blood-tinged water turned deep red.

Dee tried to ignore the way the water sheened her rune-etched skin, and held out a towel.

"Thanks." Mya took it and toweled dry as she spoke. "I did a lot of thinking on the way back from Clemson's and I don't think the guild will fall apart entirely. There'll be some dissent, some abandonment, and maybe even some revenge violence, but I think most assassins have the same kind of core loyalty you have."

"Maybe, but there had to have been *some* reason for the protection clauses in the blood contracts and the protection spells on the rings. We are assassins, after all, and the quickest way to advancement is by killing your superior."

"Oh, absolutely." Mya toweled her hair, leaving it a spiky tangle. "There'll always be those who want a quick way to power, but I think most people take pride in their jobs. Even us assassins." She winked at him as she dropped the towel and walked past him toward the bedroom.

Dee mused on her assessment and nodded his agreement. "Respect instills more loyalty than fear. That certainly worked for you in Twailin. Your Hunters were fiercely loyal. And when Lad took over, the rank and file assassins of *all* the factions seemed to respect their new masters more than they feared them."

"They feared *Lad*..." Mya grabbed her robe and flung it on. "We all did."

Chris A. Jackson and Anne L. McMillen-Jackson

"But that was an…unusual situation. He didn't *like* using fear as a motivator. Living with him during the time he was guildmaster, it was obvious."

"He didn't like much of anything during those weeks, including himself." She looked sad for a moment, then shook her head hard, tiny droplets of water flying from her hair. "What about here? I know you haven't spent much time with the Blades and Enforcers yet, but what's your opinion? Do you think they'll rebel against Clemson and Noncey or leave?"

"Some might leave, but not everyone. Those who stay out of loyalty…" He blinked as he thought about it. "…might be better assassins than those who stayed simply out of fear."

"Exactly!" Mya punctuated her agreement by jabbing his shoulder with a finger as she strode past again, this time toward the kitchen. "If the guild survives this war, it'll end up stronger than it was. Fear's a crappy motivator. The old Grandmaster learned that the hard way when he picked a fight with Lad."

As Dee followed her, realization struck him like a thunderbolt. "The attack at the orphanage!"

"Was undoubtedly guild." Mya smiled ruefully as she pulled a bottle and two cups down from the cabinet. "We were lucky to survive."

Dee's stomach flipped queasily as he considered how close he'd come to dying. He fingered the scab where the assassin's crossbow bolt had creased his side. "Lucky indeed."

Mya wrenched the cork from the bottle and poured spiced rum into one of the cups. Despite her bravado, her hand trembled. Quaffing half, she topped off her cup, then held out the bottle. "Want some?"

"Sure." Dee sat at the table, and she brought over the bottle and the other cup.

Mya sat across from him, poured a hefty shot into his cup and pushed it toward him, then gulped from her own.

"So…" Dee sipped the rum—sweet, spicy, and strong—watching as Mya finished hers then poured more. "Do you want me to draft letters to the guildmasters throughout the empire? Warn them that Hoseph has destroyed the blood contracts? That alone will show them how crazy he is."

126

"Excellent idea!" She downed another big swallow and smiled at him. "What would I do without you, Dee?"

Mya's smile warmed his heart, but he silently wondered if it was the drink talking. He had never known her to drink much, but she was now pouring her third cup of rum.

"You're planning to get roaring drunk tonight, aren't you?"

"Damn right." Mya quaffed half her cup and hiccupped, then held up finger and thumb about an inch apart. "This is how close I came to dying tonight, Dee. I deserve to get drunk."

"Okay." He pushed his cup away. "I'll put you to bed when you pass out."

"Oh no, you don't." She pushed the cup back toward him. "I hate to drink alone."

"You always drank alone at the *Golden Cockerel*."

"Which is why I never drank much." Mya downed her cup, then blinked as if to clear her eyes.

"Mya!" Dee reached for the bottle, but she was faster by far. "It was a close call, but you've had them before. You're okay."

"I know." She poured another shot into her cup and put the bottle down on the table a bit too hard. "I don't know why I'm so rattled. I guess I'm just feeling vulnerable. I can't rely on the protection of the ring anymore," she wiggled her finger, "and I don't have Lad watching my back." She drank some and hiccupped again.

Dee's stomach clenched like he'd been kicked in the gut. *And all you've got is me.*

Mya nudged his cup toward him. "Drink."

"Sure." Dee sipped minutely.

Mya didn't even notice, but just sat and watched her cup. When she drained it, he refilled it for her.

Not an hour later, when Mya's head lolled onto her shoulder and her eyes seemed too bright in the lamplight, Dee guided her to bed and tucked her in. Back in the kitchen, he finished cleaning her bloody clothes, feeling a strange kinship to the crimson wastewater as it swirled down the drain.

CHAPTER X

Sleep… Relax… Don't think…

Mya stared at the ceiling, her eyes tracing the hypnotic swirls in the stucco. The technique worked sometimes…but not tonight. Some malign portion of her mind transformed the patterns in the plaster into the winding streets of Tsing. No wonder, really; for days she'd been studying city maps with Clemson and Noncey. Clemson had one that covered an entire wall, each street named, a pin inserted for each of the dozens of known businesses, abodes, hideouts, and fortifications of all the Assassins Guild factions. Somewhere out there, three young boys were being held captive, and Mya had promised the emperor she'd get them back. Her Enforcers and Blades had been searching and watching for any hint of where the Tessifus boys were being held. So far, they'd come up empty.

Needle in a haystack… Can't search everywhere… Can't follow everyone…

The only good news had been how little the destruction of the blood contracts had affected the guild. There had been a few squabbles, mostly old animosities flaring up between senior and junior journeymen. All had been dealt with quickly and decisively. The most notable had been when one of Noncey's Blades had tried to put a dagger in the master's back. The man had died by his own weapon, and his peers just shook their heads. Mya thought at first that the man might be another assassin wooed by the opposing guild factions, but the consensus was no. He'd simply been a foolish malcontent.

To Mya's delight, few Enforcers or Blades had fled the guild. She had no way to know how many may have left the other three factions. If she was lucky, Mya would have a stronger and *intact* guild when she finally resolved this mess. Of course, for that to happen, she had to rescue the boys, kill Hoseph, reconcile the warring factions…

Sleep… Relax… Don't think…

It still wasn't working.

She thought about Lad's dance of death. He'd used the exercises to overcome his insomnia; perhaps they would help her sleep, too. But here in Tsing, she had no privacy, and the dance was an intensely private ritual. *Besides, it would only remind me of Lad.*

Distant thunder rumbled. *Another one?* She hadn't thought it possible, but the weather turned even hotter as summer deepened, the air still and sultry with daily torrential rains. *The urchins will be out in this, getting soaked.* Maybe she should send them home. Maybe she should send all the Blades and Enforcers home, too. It wasn't like their efforts had done any good. *Maybe…maybe…*

Stop obsessing!

It was still early, not even midnight, and she should be asleep. She'd been out every night, checking the surveillance, watching for spies, and visiting the distillery to consult with her two masters. She tried to sleep during the day, but she'd never been able to sleep in a lit room, and it was too stuffy with the curtains drawn. She caught a few hours of sleep in the evenings and early mornings, often after Dee relaxed her as only he could. He'd performed admirably only an hour ago, but still, her mind refused to settle down.

Dee snorted in his sleep, and she turned on her side, propping her head on her hand to watch him. He slept deeply, his chest rising and falling, eyes moving beneath his lids. He lay with only a sheet draped over one leg, a light sheen of sweat glistening on his skin.

Poor, exhausted Dee… she mused, recalling their recent tumble with a wry smile. She was afraid she might hurt him, but he never complained.

So why can't I sleep?

Mya considered waking him, coaxing him into taking her mind off of her troubles again. He would, of course. He was always willing, though the last few days he'd been rather subdued. *The heat,* she assumed. She reached toward him, but stopped before her fingers brushed his skin. He was resting so peacefully, she hated to disturb him. There was only one other thing to do with her excess energy.

129

I need to hunt.

She slipped out of bed slowly and carefully so as not to wake Dee. With one more glance at his sweat-glistened body, she suppressed a tingle of carnal desire, grabbed her wrappings and clothes, and tiptoed out to the living room. Maybe she would wake him when she got back.

Dressing silently in shirt, trousers, and a dark stocking cap to hide her lightened hair, Mya tucked her daggers into belt and boot sheaths. She looked longingly at the blackbrew pot on the stove, but rattling around in the kitchen would surely wake Dee.

Maneuvering carefully past the wind chime they'd hung on the door as an alarm, she turned the bolt and eased the handle down. She opened the door gingerly and slipped through, then relocked it. She descended the stairs, avoiding the squeaky ones, and stopped at the bottom to listen. Hearing nothing but faint city night noises and another distant rumble of thunder, she leaned out to scan the street, windows, and rooftops.

All quiet.

Starting up the street, Mya kept to the shadows, as silent and invisible as she could be. Since the discovery of the destroyed blood contracts, she'd been walking on eggs, and with good reason.

They can touch me… Any assassin in Tsing can put a blade in my heart.

After a few blocks, the tense muscles of her neck and shoulders eased. The familiar rhythm of the night worked almost as well as Dee for easing her stress. These streets were now fairly familiar; she was finally learning Tsing well enough that it felt like home.

It was still early enough that a few eateries and taverns were open. Even the blue-bloods of the Heights District enjoyed a night on the town, though the establishments were less bawdy than those in Midtown and the Wharf District.

The familiar clank and stomp of an approaching patrol of constables stopped Mya in her tracks. She suppressed the urge to confront them and introduce herself as Moirin just to see their response. *Bad idea…* She didn't need their notice or their recognition. She was more comfortable in the shadows. Besides, after Sergeant Benjamin's advice to Dee and the masters' warning that Lakshmi had informants in the constabulary, she couldn't safely expose herself to their scrutiny. Slipping into an alley, she rounded the block to let them pass before continuing on her way.

A flash of lightning cast razor-edged shadows, followed seconds later by a rumble of thunder. Mya smelled rain.

Damn... A hiss like bacon on a skillet heralded the coming deluge, a curtain of water racing down the hill toward her. Mya ducked under an awning and backed into a shadowed corner as it hit.

In Twailin, spring was the rainy season, with gray skies and showers that lasted for days. Here in Tsing, summer squalls raked the city on a daily basis. Moving fast and passing quickly, they dumped enormous amounts of rain in a short time. This one promised to be a real frog-drowner, as Pax called them.

Garrote weather. That was what assassins called it. Rain dulled the senses. masking noise, washing away scents, obscuring vision... A skilled killer could sneak close enough to an intended victim to use a garrote or dagger without detection. Even Mya's enhanced senses couldn't penetrate the driving rain as it pounded on the awning overhead and cascaded off the edge in a curtain before her. Lad used to complain about the rain when he was her bodyguard, and about Mya's disregard for his concerns. Now that she had no one guarding her back, she had to be doubly cautious.

As if calling attention to her vulnerability, a man ran by, cloak held over his head in a futile effort to stay dry, passing within arm's reach of Mya's refuge.

He didn't see me, she assured herself, but shivered because she hadn't even heard him coming.

She tried to relax, watching the torrent of water and trash as the filth of the city flowed downhill. *No wonder the rich live on high ground,* Mya thought with a curled lip. The locals, at least those who didn't inhabit the lowest-lying neighborhoods, welcomed the summer storms. The city smelled better after the rain, cisterns filled, the aqueducts that supplied the wells ran clear, and the river flowed stronger and cleaner.

Finally the storm passed, and the water lapping at the toes of Mya's boots receded to a trickle in the gutter. Mya listened cautiously and peered into the shadows that edged the night-bound city street, consoled by the thought that the weather would also hamper any would-be follower. Deeming it safe, she continued on her way.

Mya neared the elaborate Heights District bathhouse where she had first met the Master Inquisitor. Though Lakshmi had abandoned it as her headquarters, the business was too profitable to close down despite a guild war. It was also Mya's greatest hope of tracking down the master.

"Follow the money," had been Clemson's suggestion.

Someone would have to deliver a percentage of the earnings to the Master Inquisitor. Unfortunately, Mya's people had yet to pinpoint that someone. The watchers—both urchin and assassin— now knew every bath attendant, masseuse, host, and cleaning worker who came and went from the establishment. Each had been followed and confirmed as a bona fide employee. Wealthy men and women indulged themselves daily in the services offered, and most of these had also been vetted. Mya considered that a wealthy noble or aristocrat *might* be working for the guild—Hoseph had used a noble in Twailin, after all—picking up payments during their appointments. Some of Noncey's hired bodyguards worked for regular patrons, but none had heard anything suggesting guild connections.

Mya first checked to see if anyone was watching her watchers, slowly circling the block twice in narrowing circles. Spying no one, she edged around to the alley behind the building. During the day, both front and back doors were watched, but no one used the front door after the bathhouse closed, so she set watches on only the back door at night. Flitting through the shadows, she ducked into the shrubberies several doors down from the bathhouse, squatting beside the child huddled there. "Hey, Kit. Anything new?"

"No, Miss Mya. The same folks left after they closed up, the last one just a little while ago. No sign of anyone since."

"Okay." Mya noticed Kit shivering and put a hand on the girl's cold, skinny arm. Though the rain had stopped, fat drops hung from the shrubbery leaves. "You're soaked, Kit, and shivering. Go home and get someone to take over."

"I'm okay, Miss Mya." The girl wiped her nose with a grimy sleeve. "I still got more time on my shift."

"I wasn't asking." If the urchins had a fault, it was with following orders. "Go."

"Yes, ma'am." Kit wiggled out from under the shrub, a scowl on her face. "But I'm not that cold."

"Yes, you are. Don't dawdle, and don't let anyone see you."

Kit skulked off, looking like any one of the hundreds of urchins that roamed the streets of Tsing. They were resourceful and they knew how to avoid trouble. Any who couldn't, didn't survive long.

Mya slipped between two buildings across the alley from the bathhouse. The close was narrow enough for her to touch the walls of both buildings at the same time. Fingers and toes finding easy purchase on the bricks of the opposing walls, she ascended with little difficulty. At the top, she grabbed the eaves and hoisted herself onto the low, sloped roof, then crouched and listened: dripping water, distant echoing thunder, and the faint scuff of leather on tile as someone shifted their weight.

Inching up to the crest and peering over, she spotted the black-clad Blade prone at the roof edge, positioned to see the back door of the bathhouse without being observed by someone looking up from the street.

"Whetstone," Mya whispered, just loud enough for the assassin to hear.

The figure twitched and its head turned slowly. Dark eyes stared through a slit in the cloth that wrapped the person's face. "Razor," a woman's voice replied.

Mya inched closer, noted that the Blade's eyes were wide. *Fear? Excitement?* "Anything new?"

"Maybe."

Mya thrilled with anticipation. "What?"

"The last of the regular workers just left, but something was…different. One of them was carrying a load of dirty towels under his arm."

Mya's anticipation waned. "Dirty *towels?*"

The woman's dark eyes blinked quickly. "Yes. But the laundry's closed this late at night, and when I took over, I was told that the towels had *already* been taken out."

"Maybe there's a bin at the laundry to put them in after hours?"

"Maybe, but he was carrying them bundled in his arms instead of over his shoulder in a sack. The towels are *always* in a sack, and we've never seen two deliveries to the laundry in one day."

Mya sighed. It was probably nothing, but any anomaly bore looking into. Since the watcher couldn't abandon her post to follow the man, it was up to Mya. "When did he leave?"

"Only about five minutes ago, right after the rains quit. He went downhill. The laundry is that way, but so is the man's flat."

"Where does he live and what does he look like?"

The Blade rolled onto her side and withdrew a tiny notebook from a waxed leather pouch at her belt. From beneath her collar, she pulled out a garnet hung on a chain around her neck. Closing her fist around the gem, she whispered "Light!" Red light glowed from between her fingers, bright enough to read by, but dim enough not to be noticed from afar or ruin her night vision. "His name's Hanz Brolly, and he lives at twenty-one Greenhollow Street, Midtown, second floor. The laundry's four more blocks down the hill on the same street. He's tall, wide shoulders, long blond hair pulled back in a queue, very good-looking. I imagine he's pretty popular with the rich old ladies who come here for a massage."

Mya smiled at the young woman's commentary and patted her on the shoulder. "Good work. I'll check it out."

"Thanks."

Mya worked her way back over the crest of the roof and down to the street, then down the hill into Midtown, moving quickly. If Brolly had gone straight home, he'd be there by now, but if he had gone to the laundry, he probably wouldn't be back yet.

Twenty-one Greenhollow Street was an unremarkable building, well-built but not fancy. That he lived in the Heights suggested that massaging rich old ladies was profitable.

Or Hanz is making extra gold on the side. Perhaps this wouldn't be just another wild goose chase.

Mya tucked into a shadowed spot across the street and inspected the building. Shops occupied the street level with apartments above. Wooden staircases climbed each end of the structure, punctuated by landings with doors to several apartments. A light illuminated a second-story window. He'd either come straight home or lived with someone.

The click of a door latch and the creak of a hinge drew her attention. A wedge of light swept the second-story landing, silhouetting a figure for just a moment before the door closed. Feet thumped on the stairs, and a man emerged onto the street. Above, the light in the window went out. Either Brolly did indeed have a roommate, or this wasn't him.

Mya peered more closely at the man as he stepped onto the street. He wasn't particularly tall or broad-shouldered, and he certainly wasn't blonde or what she—or anyone with two eyes and reasonably good taste—would consider good looking. Though he wore no weapon that Mya could see, his left hand hovered about his waist, and his jacket was bulky enough to hide just about anything short of a broadsword. Casually sweeping his eyes left and right, he crossed with a quick, confident stride to the shadowed side of the street, avoiding street lamps as he approached the next intersection, crossed, and faded into shadow again.

If he's not an assassin, then I'll eat my cap. Time to hunt.

Mya followed, staying quiet and hidden. Stalking prey was one of a Hunter's first lessons, and Mya excelled at her trade. She followed the man back uphill into the Heights, keeping him barely in sight, listening to his steady steps, freezing in shadow whenever he turned to look around.

After about eight blocks, he ducked into the alley and disappeared from view. Mya had just reached the alley when the click of his boots on the cobbles suddenly stopped, and knuckles rapped a distinct tattoo against wood. Peering around the corner, she glimpsed the man at the back door of a shop. The door opened, and dim light illuminated him.

"You're late," said a feminine voice.

"The rain," replied the man as he slipped inside and the door closed.

Mya dashed forward, low and quiet, her footfalls a faint *pat-pat* on the wet cobbles. She crouched near the door he'd entered and cocked her head to listen. The voices were muffled, but when she pressed her ear to the wood, they became clear.

"Here, I'll take that. The bathhouse, right?"

"Yeah. A week's payment. Hey, I'm soaked. How about a whiskey before I go?"

Mya smiled. *Follow the money...* She didn't recall seeing a pin in this block on Clemson's map, so this must be a new money drop. One more link in the chain that would lead them to the Master Inquisitor.

Glass clinked within the building.

"Thanks, that's good. Damn rain. Nothing ever dries out this time of year."

"At least you get some fresh air. I've been stuck in here for days."

The man chuckled. "At least you're *dry*. Why don't *you* slog through the rain running collections and *I'll* babysit?"

"No, thanks."

"How is the brat, anyway?"

Mya's ears perked up.

"A pain in the ass. Nobles…"

They're keeping one of the boys here!

"Why not just drug him senseless?"

"Because I'm not stupid. Orders are to keep him drugged enough to be happy, but not out."

The man laughed low and something clicked, then thumped. "Thanks for the drink. I better go." The voice came louder. A door had opened inside.

"Watch your back."

"Always." The voice was right on the other side of the door now.

Mya skittered back and crouched behind a bin full of trash just as the door latch clicked. The man emerged and started up the alley. She'd let him go; he was just a collection runner. No doubt he'd have information on Lakshmi's businesses, but snatching him would only alert the Inquisitors that they'd been found out. She considered kicking in the door and staging a rescue, but blundering in could get her, the kid, or both of them killed. If they didn't know that they'd been discovered, then they probably wouldn't move him. She had time to plan.

As the man walked past her, he brought along muddled scents, sweet and heavy, stronger even than the trash. Not until he passed around the corner did the pungent scent fade into the sultry air.

Odd that I didn't smell that while I was following him.

Mya frowned as she looked up and down the alley at the row of identical doors. She had to know exactly which shop front around the other side of the block matched this door. Unfortunately, without seeing through walls, that seemed impossible. She edged forward again and put a hand on the door handle. It was locked, of course. She might be able to pick it, but...

That muddle of aromas tickled her nose again. Leaning down to the keyhole, Mya inhaled deeply. Flowers, musk, fruit, and myriad other pleasant odors vied for attention. *Perfume?*

She left the door and rounded the block, crossing the street again to stay in shadow as she examined the store fronts. The *Scent of Beauty* perfumery was situated in the center of a block of high-end shops. Mya memorized the address. Someone would have to scout out the business, determine the layout inside, before they mounted a rescue.

And I know just the person.

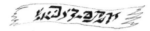

I'm going to kill Mya, Dee vowed as he adjusted the frothy lace cravat at his throat.

Dee flounced up to the perfumery door, dabbing a lace handkerchief to the sweat on his forehead and heaving a gusty sigh as he entered. "It's simply *unbearable* outside!" he declared to no one in particular, fluttering the handkerchief to cool himself.

Two elderly ladies garbed in finery and wide-brimmed hats glanced at him with little interest, then looked back at the shelves of bottles. The primly dressed woman waiting on them smiled at him.

I'll be with you in a moment, sir. Please feel free to look around."

"*Thank* you, dear." He waved his lace handkerchief again and set about perusing the shelves of bottled scents.

Dee suspected that Mya took great delight in dressing him up as a dandy for this reconnaissance mission. She'd shown far too much amusement as she plucked his eyebrows and dabbed rouge on his cheeks.

"You're perfect for this," she had insisted. "I can't do it with every assassin is looking for me, and I don't trust a Blade or Enforcer to do a Hunter's job. It's got to be *you*, Dee."

So here he was, sampling one perfume after another until the air was chokingly thick with the scents of flowers, musk, and spices. The two older ladies chatted amongst themselves and ignored the sales woman who hovered behind them. Finally, the proprietress caught Dee's eye, flashed a smile, and skillfully disengaged herself from the women to attend this new, flamboyantly dressed customer who looked like he might actually buy something.

"Can I help you, sir?"

"I certainly hope so." Dee dabbed his forehead with his handkerchief again. "I've been all over the *city* looking for just the right scent for a dear friend of mine, and simply can't find the right one! I'm at my wit's end, not to mention simply dying from the heat!"

The last part was true; the heavy brocade jacket and frilled shirt were stifling, and his state of nervousness didn't help. He'd had little opportunity to wear disguises and assume identities, let alone seriously case a target. Now, lives—Mya's, the captive boy's, and his own—depended on him getting this right.

"Would you like a glass of cool water?"

"Oh, you are a *dream*, my dear! I'd *love* something cool!" He smiled at her and fanned his face.

Following the woman—the shop's real proprietress or an assassin, he wasn't sure—to the counter, Dee looked casually around. The broad front windows on either side of the entrance were framed by drapes gracefully tied back to display the wares and entice passersby into the shop. The afternoon sun glittered on the vials of all sizes, shapes, and hues artfully arrayed on the shelves that lined the walls. On the back wall behind the counter was another door, unfortunately closed. What lay beyond that door was what interested Dee.

The woman filled a crystal goblet from a pewter pitcher, twisted a wedge of lemon into the water, and pressed the cool glass into his hand. "Here you are, sir."

"*Thank* you, my dear!" Holding the glass daintily, he sipped and sighed in unfeigned bliss. "Oh, that's *lovely*."

"So, what type of scent are you looking for?"

"Well, that's part of the problem, I'm afraid. I don't exactly know." Dee looked around at the shelves as if bewildered. "My friend is very particular. He's quite a slave to fashion, but in a, dare I say, *sensual* sort of way, so nothing too flowery or overpowering, I think."

The proprietress pursed her lips in thought, then said, "Perhaps something spicy. Why don't you come over here with me."

Dee sniffed the vials that she proffered, dabbing a few to his wrists at her insistence, while keeping an inconspicuous eye on the front door. When he felt like he might gag if he had to smell one more scent, the door opened. *Finally!*

Three young ladies entered. Brazenly dressed in low-cut frocks, giggling and fanning their plump décolletages with frilly hand fans, they looked more than a little out of place in such a high-end establishment. The welcoming expression on the saleswoman's face as she looked toward the new customers promptly fell. Painting a smile on her lips, she turned her attention back to Dee, but kept one eye on the newcomers.

"Oh, try *this* one!" A stark redhead with a smattering of freckles encouraged her friends to sniff as they passed around a vial. Tipping some onto her finger, she dabbed the fragrance behind each ear and between her breasts while the other two grabbed tiny bottles of their own from shelves and popped the corks, sniffing and exclaiming.

"Ewww, what is *this* made of? Pig's wallow?" exclaimed another. Putting the vial back on the shelf, she knocked over several others. Braying a laugh, she fumbled to put them upright.

The two older ladies looked aghast and started for the door. The redhead made a rude comment as they passed.

"Now see here, you…" One of the elderly women gripped her parasol like a weapon.

"These scents here are muskier." The proprietress looked distraught, as if trying to decide which was more important, attending to the customer at hand or heading off an incipient altercation. A vulgar gesture from one of the blondes decided the situation. "If you'll excuse me for a moment."

"Of course." As the woman turned away, Dee held up his empty glass. "Might I pour myself another?"

"Oh, please do. I'm afraid I'm rather…"

"Best put that up, Granny!" the redhead said, pointing at the parasol. "I'll stick it somewhere you won't like and *open* it."

"You!" The older woman took a step back, her face flushed. Her companion hurried out the door, but the parasol wielder refused to back down. "You *harlot*!"

"Please, ladies!" The proprietress rushed forward.

Dee quickly slipped behind the counter, taking full advantage of the distraction. The three "ladies" were Midtown trollops hired to make a scene. They hadn't been told to start a fight, but it was working beautifully. He reached for the handle of the back door.

"You can't make me get out!" complained a blonde loudly. "The emperor's given us rights, he has!"

"Fenly!" the proprietress shouted.

Dee heard a thump from behind the door and jerked back his hand back, turning away just as the latch clicked and a man stepped through. Thinking quickly, Dee started and whirled, dropping his water goblet. It hit the floor and shattered. Stepping back, he pressed his handkerchief to his mouth. "Oh! You *scared* me!"

"Sorry, sir." The man stopped short and eyed him, one eyebrow raised.

"I'm sorry about the glass, but—" Dee gestured to the pitcher and the broken glass.

"Fenly!" the proprietress snapped, struggling to keep the warring factions separated.

Fenly eyes turned and apparently recognized the trouble. "Excuse me." He shoved the door closed as he hurried forward to aid the proprietress.

Dee stuck out his foot and stopped the door from closing. Glancing back at the scuffle, he noted the proprietress flailing uselessly to keep the women at bay—*Definitely* not *an assassin*—while Fenly snatched two wrists with ease and twisted, immobilizing the women instantly—*but he is*. The parasol-wielding patron seemed intent on smacking anyone within reach and connected with poor Fenly's head. He gave her a disgusted look and frogmarched two of the combatants toward the front door. The distraction was working better than Dee could have hoped.

Dee slipped through the door and pulled it not-quite-shut behind him.

A corridor extended to the back of the building, ending with a door sporting a number of bolts that undoubtedly opened onto the alley. Three closed doors lined the right-hand wall. To the left, about a third of the way down, was an opening with a chair standing beside it, and beyond that, an open door. The hallway reeked of a thousand competing scents.

Dee hurried down the hall. The opening turned out to be a landing. The seat of the chair was warm. *Fenly was sitting here.* The stair descended into a basement, switching back after a half-dozen steps, so Dee couldn't see anything at the bottom. He crept down a few steps and peered over the balustrade. Leaning against the wall across from the bottom step stood a bored-looking man, arms crossed, a loaded crossbow dangling from one hip.

Guard! Dee ducked back and continued exploring the upper hall. The first door on the right opened readily into a storage room. The second door was locked, and he didn't have time to pick it. In the open room to the left, two women and a man worked at benches, grinding ingredients for perfumes if the overwhelming confusion of aromas was any indication. Dee slipped past unseen. The last door yielded as he turned the handle. It was an office.

The woman seated behind the lone desk blinked in surprise at Dee. "Who are you?"

"Oh! Well...just a concerned customer!" Dee fluttered his handkerchief in the direction of the front shop, thinking fast. "There's a frightful disturbance. I thought I should get help."

"Disturbance?" The woman, handsome and older in an expensive but plain dress, stood and rounded the desk, hurrying to the door. "What disturbance?"

"Some rather, shall we say, *unsavory* women are making quite a scene in the shop." Dee glanced around the room, a typical office like any shop owner might have, with no visible guards or weapons.

"What in the name of... Follow me!" The woman hurried down the corridor.

Dee watched her walk. *Maybe an assassin, maybe not.*

With the added reinforcement, the scuffle was quashed in short order. Dee took refuge behind the counter until the last trollop was ejected and the rampant elderly woman with the parasol was comforted and assured that she would receive a discount on any purchases in recompense for her inconvenience. By the time she was ushered out and the three employees turned back to him, Dee stood calmly sipping water from a new goblet.

"I'm *so* sorry I dropped the glass," he apologized, sweeping some of the shards into a little pile with a toe. "Your man scared me when he burst through the door like that."

"I'm sorry, sir. At Ursila's shout, I thought...well, I *certainly* didn't mean to startle you so." Fenly squeezed Dee's arm gently and gave him a tentative smile. "Are you all right?"

Oh, bother... The last thing he needed was any unintended entanglements here. Dee patted the man's hand and returned the smile. "Oh, I'm fine. You're such a dear."

"It's no matter." The older woman from the office dismissed the incident with a wave and shot Fenly a hard glance, causing the man to release Dee's arm and step back. "You were quite right to fetch me. In fact, you probably prevented some breakage. Ursila, please give Mister..."

"Donnely," Dee said with a smile. "Terrence Donnely."

"Mister Donnely his choice of one fragrance for his assistance."

"Why, *thank* you!" Dee gushed, pressing a hand to his chest and beaming in delight.

"My pleasure." She flashed him a smile and went back though the door, motioning for Fenly to follow. The guard cast Dee a longing glance before closing the door firmly behind him.

Dee breathed easier.

"Now then, you said your friend didn't care for floral scents..." The proprietress guided Dee toward a row of shelves. "Let's see which of these you like."

A quarter of an hour later, Dee left the shop reeking of a dozen different perfumes, a tiny bottle of sultry musk tucked in his pocket. Unhurriedly, he worked his way back to the apartment, stopping twice in different shops to make sure he wasn't being followed.

"Good gods!" Mya exclaimed as he came in, waving her hand in front of her face. "Did you *bathe* in perfume?"

"I had to sample some." Dee removed his coat and hung it gently on a chair back, brushing out the wrinkles. He pulled the bottle of fragrance from the pocket and handed it over. "For my fussy friend. A gentleman searching for just the right fragrance is bound to try them out. A scent in the bottle is nothing like a scent on the skin."

142

"Yeah, well, you're going right into the tub and wash that stink off. Wait!" Mya snatched up a piece of parchment and a pencil, "first sketch the layout of the shop and whatever you saw while it's still fresh in your mind. I'll draw you a bath."

Once Dee was done with the drawing, he went to the bathroom, stripped off his uncomfortable clothing, and sunk gratefully into the cool water. Mya kicked the reeking clothes into a pile and sat tub-side, sketch in hand, and started peppering him with questions.

"Only one salesperson?"

"Yes, the shop's not very large."

"The drapes were closed when I was there. Are there shutters?"

"No, just the drapes. But the windows were barred. Fancy wrought-iron painted white."

"Did the guard downstairs have a chair?"

"He was standing."

"But did he have a *chair*?"

"Uh, I didn't see one, but then, I only had a quick glance."

It always fascinated Dee to watch her mind at work. No detail was too minor for her to consider. No wonder she was such a great Hunter. And the more she asked, the more he realized just how much he had actually observed.

Finally she lurched up from the chair and began pacing the small room, her gaze distant. After several minutes of contemplative silence, she stopped and nodded. "Okay, I've got a plan. We'll go see Clemson and Noncey once it's dark."

"We?" So far, it seemed like Mya had been avoiding being seen with Dee. They'd each visited the masters separately, but not yet together. He brightened at the thought that maybe, just maybe, she wasn't ashamed of him.

"Yes, 'we'. We'll take a few Enforcers and Blades with us to the perfumery, of course, but the core of this operation will be you and me."

"*Me?*" Dee's mood plummeted. *She can't be serious.* "You'll want more than just *me*."

"No, I won't." Mya tapped his drawing. "You said the stairs were narrow. That means tight quarters, probably with narrow halls and small rooms below. More will just get in our way. We'll use

Blades or Enforcers for backup, keeping the workers quiet, and keeping watch."

Why me? Dee grasped at straws. "Clemson and Noncey won't like you going. You're *Grandmaster.*"

"And that means I get to make the rules. I'm faster and stronger than anyone else, so why not use that to our advantage? Besides, why should the journeymen have all the fun?"

"But, Mya—"

"No, Dee, two is perfect. I'll take point and you watch my back. You know how I work and you've gotten pretty good with those little crossbows of yours."

Dee swept his fingers through his bath and watched the water swirl. It had been years since he participated in any kind of raid—Hoseph's unexpected attacks didn't count—and Mya had dozens of Blades and Enforcers at her beck and call. It didn't make sense for her to want him at her back.

He looked her in the eye. "Really Mya, tell me the truth. Why me?"

Mya looked at him sidelong and fingered the mended hole in her shirt. "Who *else* can I trust to watch my back and not put a dagger or crossbow bolt into it?"

"Ah." *It figures...* She didn't want him watching her back because he was a good assassin, but because he wasn't likely to betray her. It was probably the only reason he was sharing her bed, too.

CHAPTER XI

Mya gripped Dee's arm and tried to walk properly. *Swing, but not too much. More bounce in the legs, less in the chest. More rotation of the shoulders...* This was one disguise she'd never done before. Ladies and prostitutes, boys and bargemen, maids and beggars, yes, but never a dandy.

"Don't overdo it," Dee whispered as they neared the perfumery.

"Too much?"

"Just a little. Less 'I'm for sale' and more 'I'm just so pretty I can't *stand* myself.'"

She smirked, but knew what he meant and altered her gait. "Better?"

He smiled at her and patted her hand on his arm. "*Fabulous*, dear."

He does that just a bit too well. She couldn't complain about the disguise he'd put together, however. The frilly shirt and waistcoat fit beautifully over her tightly bound breasts, and the deep-purple jacket with lavender brocade broadened her shoulders, with plenty of room for daggers. Mya could have done with less padding in the codpiece, however; it felt like she had a coconut in her crotch. Lace cuffs dangled gracefully from her sleeves, long enough to cover her smaller hands...and the Grandmaster's ring. He'd even styled her hair in a swoopy confusion of short curls that bounced when she walked. The assassins were looking for Mya, the woman, not an affluent young fop out strolling with his gentleman friend. Also, she could move more freely in this outfit than in a dress. She had no doubt there would be a fight before the day was done.

The lowering afternoon sun lit the last shoppers of the day in rosy hues. Picking up their final purchases before the stores closed, they were already discussing where to dine or what to wear to the theater. Half a block ahead, she spotted the hulking Jolee and two more solid Enforcers. Uniformed in the livery of Noncey's private security firm, they didn't seem at all out of place in this swanky neighborhood, just a few more bodyguards loitering outside while their employers shopped. The Blades, assigned to watch the perfumery and prevent Inquisitors from escaping, she didn't spot at all, which was either very good or very bad. *Stop being paranoid, Mya. They are there!* Once betrayed, it was hard to dispel the pervasive sense of doubt.

"Here we go," whispered Dee as he opened the perfumery door and ushered her through. More loudly, he said, "After you, dear!"

"You're so *sweet.*" The lilting masculine intonation came easier than the walk. Mya swept the shop with a glance and beamed. They'd gotten lucky. There were no customers, just a woman behind a counter jotting a note in a ledger. "What a *lovely* little shop!"

The proprietress looked up. "May I help you, si—" Her professional smile widened in genuine pleasure at the sight of Dee. "Mister Donnely! *Lovely* to see you again!" She hurried forward. Taking Dee's hand, she smiled slyly as she looked at Mya. "And is this the friend you spoke of?"

"Yes it is!" Dee shook her hand daintily and waved his handkerchief at Mya. "Ursila, let me introduce you to Maurice."

"Wonderful to meet you." Ursila smiled and shook Mya's hand.

"Delighted!" Mya shook the woman's hand carefully to ensure that the fluffy lace cuff of her shirt adequately hid the ring on her finger. They'd painted the Grandmaster's ring gold to disguise it. Ursila might not be an assassin, but there was no sense in taking chances. "Thank you *so* much for helping Terrence pick out my gift. I *love* the fragrance."

Ursila leaned forward and sniffed in the vicinity of Mya's neck. "It's *perfect* for you."

Mya tensed, but managed to keep from killing the woman. "Oh, *thank* you, dear. Terry, you're *so* right; she *is* sweet!"

"Maurice insisted that we come right back here so he could pick out a gift for *me.*" Dee batted his eyes at Mya and squeezed her arm. "He spoils me something *terrible!*"

"I'm sure we can find something you both like." Ursila turned to peruse the shelves. "Maybe something—"

Mya brought the edge of her hand down at the juncture of the woman's neck and shoulder, hard enough to send Ursila reeling into unconsciousness, but not hard enough to snap her neck. Dee caught her before she hit the floor.

"Take care of her. I'll get the drapes," Mya said.

"Right."

As Dee dragged the comatose woman behind the counter, Mya strode to the windows. Flipping loose the ties restricting the curtains, she pulled them shut. The lamps had already been lit, so she turned down the ones near the door so light wouldn't blaze out from around the curtains. A soft knock sounded, and she opened the door to admit the Enforcers led by Jolee. A quick glance up and down the street before she closed the door confirmed few people were about. Nobody seemed to take notice that the perfumery was closing a bit early.

"Get the rest of the lamps," she ordered in a whisper, securing the door with the heavy dead bolt.

By the time she turned around, the lamps in the shop had all been turned low, lending a inappropriately romantic atmosphere to the situation.

"Ready?" Mya asked Dee as she joined him at the door to the back. He had shucked off his brocade jacket and donned the long black jacket that Jolee had brought for him.

"I'm ready." Dee nodded firmly, but his voice quavered just a bit. "Stay out of sight. If Fenly's on guard, he should recognize me and I'll be able to get close for a shot. If not, I may need help."

Mya nodded. This was the tricky part of the plan. If the guard at the top of the stairs shouted a warning, they'd have a pitched fight on their hands against a ready foe. If they could take him out quietly, they might be able to pull this off without casualties. *At least, casualties on our side.*

Dee drew one of his crossbows and checked the bolt, then held it back beside one leg so it was hidden by the folds of the long jacket. Mya had watched Dee practice for days, and Noncey had assured her that the anesthetic toxin on the bolts would drop a victim quickly, but relying on another's prowess came hard to her. Lad had been the only person whose skills she'd never questioned.

She drew a dagger and shifted nervously. "Don't miss."

"I won't *miss*, Mya." Dee stood with his left hand on the door latch and took a deep breath. He exhaled, assumed a friendly grin, opened the door, and flounced forth. "Fenly! Ursila said you were on duty."

"Mister Donnely!" The voice lilted with surprise and pleasure, not alarm.

"She's just closing up, but said I could pop back here to say hello. Actually, if I'm not being too bold, I wondered if you'd be interested in coming out with me for a—"

Crack!

Mya lunged through the door, dagger at the ready, but the guard was already reeling, a dart jutting from his thigh. Dee tried to catch him, but Fenly outweighed him by a lot. He did manage to cushion the man's fall so he slipped quietly to the floor.

"…little drink. No?" Dee motioned the others forward while Mya helped move Fenly out of the way. "Well, perhaps another time then. Ta ta!"

Jolee dashed past them, surprisingly light on her feet, despite her bulk. She pulled the door to the workroom closed and secured it by jamming a spike into the lintel and tying a stout cord from it to the handle. By the time muffled voices called out in surprise, she had already spiked the office door and secured it. Pressing her shoulder to the back door, she pushed until something crunched and it gave way. Opening the door a crack, Jolee glanced out into the alley, then stuck her thick thumb in the air. Their exit route was clear.

The second Enforcer joined Mya and Dee at the stairs. He would hold the stairs while Mya and Dee went down. Clemson had assured Mya that this man was one of her most trustworthy.

A quick glance down the stairs confirmed one guard standing against the far wall at the bottom, corridors branching left and right. Mya raised an eyebrows at Dee, who nodded and drew his other crossbow. Her heart pounding in anticipation, she lifted her fingers one at a time: one…two…*three*!

Mya hopped over the balustrade and landed three feet in front of the guard. His eyes widened, his mouth opened, and he raised the crossbow, but she reached him before he could shout or fire. Cracking the pommel of her dagger into the side of his head hard enough to spin him around like a top, she grabbed both the crossbow and his body before they crashed to the floor.

"Hey!"

To Mya's left, perhaps twenty feet away, a man stood in front of the door that terminated the corridor. He was already raising his crossbow.

Shit! Mya threw her dagger at the same moment he fired.

The bolt and dagger passed each other as they hurtled toward their targets. Mya twisted sideways, and the bolt zipped harmlessly by. The guard was not so quick. Her dagger plunged into his stomach and he folded over with a loud cry.

"Damn!" So much for the element of surprise. Mya looked left and right. Two doors; the guarded one would lead to the Tessifus boy.

Just then, both doors opened, assassins in each. As Dee pelted down the stairs behind her, they raised crossbows, fixed Mya in their sights, and fired.

Mya flung out a hand to stop Dee's descent as she flipped up and back. She evaded one bolt, but the other transfixed her calf. As she landed, the assassin who had shot her yelped in pain. The bolt she'd evaded had struck him in the arm. The wounded man stumbled into the room behind him and slammed the door closed.

"Watch right!" she shouted to Dee, dashing down the left-hand hall.

Dee's crossbows cracked in quick succession.

I hope he hit something, she thought as she smashed into the door at full speed.

The iron-banded oak proved solid enough to stay in one piece, but the latch and hinges gave way. The door crashed into the wounded assassin, sending him sprawling. He skidded to a stop and lay still, dead or unconscious. There were two more in the tidy little room, a woman pointing a crossbow at Mya, and a man lunging toward a bed with a dagger. Upon the bed lay a groggy-looking boy.

Decisions, decisions...

The dagger descended toward the boy.

Mya threw her own dagger into the man's back and dodged, but too late. The crossbow bolt caught her in the arm. She looked at the shaft transfixing her bicep, the blood already staining the silk brocade, and cursed. Jerking the bolt free, she advanced on the woman. "You ruined my jacket!"

The assassin dropped the crossbow and reached for a dagger, but Mya reached her first. Her kick smashed into the woman's chest hard enough to send her crashing into a cabinet. She crumpled to the floor and lay still. From down the corridor came a cry and a thump. Mya tensed, but the voice hadn't been Dee's, so she recovered her daggers and dragged the dead assassin off the bed.

"Who…" The boy blinked at her with glazed eyes.

Drugged.

Another shout, but it still wasn't Dee, so Mya ignored it. The boy's wrist was secured to the bed frame by a steel manacle. She didn't have time to pick the lock, so she grasped the manacle, braced her foot against the bed frame, and pulled. The thin metal hasp bent, then the fragile lock gave way with a crack.

"Who…are…" The boy stared at her in vague surprise. Barely a boy, really, almost a young man.

"Can you walk?"

"I…" He tried to sit up and failed.

"I guess that's a no." Mya jerked him up off the bed and tossed him over her shoulder, ignoring his yelp of surprise. Striding for the door, she halted abruptly as a crossbow bolt zipped through the opening and stuck in the far wall. "Dee? You okay?"

"Oh, just *peachy*!" He sounded more angry than hurt, which was good.

Mya peeked around the door jamb. Three figures lay slumped in a pile in the far doorway, and a fourth leaned around the sill, taking aim. Dee leaned out from the stairwell and fired at the woman, jerking back as her shot careened off the corner of the wall near his head. Dee's bolt quivered in the door frame, and the woman ducked back into the room.

"How many left?" Mya asked, gauging the distance. She could easily make the stairs in the time it would take a single assassin to reload. But if there was someone waiting with a ready weapon…

"How am I supposed to know?" Dee complained as he reloaded.

At least two, Mya reckoned as a man leaned out to shoot. Before he could fire, the assassin dropped with a tiny bolt in his shoulder. Dee flashed Mya a grin as he ducked back to reload.

The female assassin leaned out again, her crossbow braced on the door frame, waiting for Dee to reappear. Then she saw Mya peering from around the other doorway, changed her aim, and fired.

Mya ducked back and the bolt shot past where her eye had been.

Another look revealed no one visible in the far doorway. Chancing that meant that only one opponent left was busy reloading, she dashed for the stairs, the boy's limbs flailing against her. Dee saw her coming and leaned out with his crossbows to provide cover. She ducked into the stairwell just as the assassin leaned out for another shot. Dee fired, but she didn't see if he hit anything or not.

"Come on!" She started up the stairs two at a time, grateful to see the Enforcer still on station at the top. She shouted, "Go!"

They went.

Jolee flung open the back door, looked around, and waved them through. Mya hurried down the corridor, Dee still at her back, the Enforcer from the front room pounding after them. A carriage waited in the alley. By the time Mya got to it, Jolee had the door open.

"Thanks!" She hoisted the boy through the narrow doorway and climbed aboard. Dee followed her in. Jolee slammed the door shut, and the carriage lurched into motion before he even sat down.

Mya lifted the boy onto the seat where he curled up and promptly started snoring softly.

"Well! That went just about as well as it could have, don't you think?"

"You're still bleeding." Dee pointed at the crossbow bolt sticking through her calf.

"I'd forgotten about that. Thanks." Mya snapped the bolt off and jerked it out. The wound closed in moments. Remembering the second bolt she took, she inspected the bloody hole in in her jacket. "I wish I hadn't ruined this jacket. I kind of like it."

"I wish you weren't so reckless." Dee's scowl vied with relief on his face.

"Good thing I was." She gestured to the sleeping boy. "They were going to kill him. Five more seconds and we'd be bringing his corpse to the palace."

"I guess you're right." Dee breathed deep, clenching and unclenching his hands to still their trembling.

Nerves. Mya smiled and nudged his knee. "You did well, Dee. The practice paid off."

He snorted a short laugh. "Nice to know I'm useful *somewhere* besides between the sheets!" He clenched his hands again.

Dee's sharp tone caught Mya off guard. She examined him, partly concerned, partly confused. *Nerves…it's just nerves.* "You're useful *lots* of places, Dee. Just relax. It's over."

"No, it's not." Dee flung a hand toward the boy. "He was the *easy* one. They'll be ready for us next time, and we don't even know where to look."

Mya leaned back, trying to relax and keep her attention focused while her pounding heart slowed. "True, but one is better than none."

Chapter XII

A frantic knock on the library door snapped Arbuckle's attention from his work. The insightful phrase he'd been crafting scattered like ashes on a breeze.

"Damn it, Tennison. I thought we were not to be disturbed!" He threw himself back in his chair and gazed sullenly at his beleaguered secretary. Dozens of books and hundreds of sheets of parchment littered the table between them, testimony to their efforts to craft the perfect document, his nascent New Accords.

"I'm sorry, Majesty." Tennison frowned at the door and put down the book he'd been reading. "I told the guards to allow no interruptions unless there was an emergency."

"An emergency…" Arbuckle looked to the door, a thousand scenarios of disaster trundling through his mind.

Another knock, even more insistent, and the two imperial guards stationed there looked uncertain. They would not open the door without permission, of course, but they knew, as Arbuckle did, that the guards outside would not have allowed anyone to knock if it wasn't a matter of dire import.

Arbuckle swallowed his trepidation and waved a hand. "See what it is."

Truth be told, the interruption was not wholly unwelcome. He and Tennison had been working nearly without stop for days, postponing appointments, audiences, and social events alike. They'd made good progress, but the deeper they delved into matters of law, the more the emperor wished he had been born a commoner. Arbuckle's eyes felt like they'd been rolled in sand, and his back ached from sitting hunched over pen and parchment for untold hours.

The guards opened the door to admit a harried Captain Ithross, his face sheened with sweat.

"Your Majesty!" The captain bowed low, heaving breath. "Forgive the interruption, but a…uh…your hunting expedition has bagged a prize."

"My *hunting* expedition?" Arbuckle's mind stumbled, still befuddled with a thousand details of imperial law. "What are you…"

"Yes, Majesty!" Ithross glanced significantly over his shoulder at the guards. "The young *miss* you contracted has arrived with…something you need to see."

The "young miss" could only mean Miss Moirin.

"She recovered…" Arbuckle caught himself, realizing why Ithross was being cagy. The guards assigned to the door were not of the trusted few privy to the details of the kidnappings. "…what We wished her to find?"

"One of them, Majesty. The…um…quarry is out of sorts, but undamaged."

"Well, We should like to see this!" Arbuckle stood stiffly. Tennison lurched to his feet, but the emperor raised a forestalling hand. "Stay here, Tennison. We've got many more hours of work yet tonight. You needn't come along."

"Thank you, Majesty." The secretary sat down and picked up the tome he had been reading.

"Lead on, Captain!" The emperor strode toward the door, his guards closing in to surround him and the captain in a protective cocoon of steel. "Ithross, have you notified the…other concerned person of this development?"

"I sent a horse messenger the moment the parcel arrived." In response to Arbuckle's raised eyebrows—an imperial horse messenger clattering through the Heights District to Duke Tessifus' mansion would not go unnoticed—the captain smiled reassuringly. "A *trusted* messenger, Majesty."

"Very good, Captain." He had to trust Ithross to be discreet. If anyone in the palace was more paranoid than Arbuckle, it was the captain. "And the young miss? Is she here as well? We would very much like to thank her."

"Yes, Majesty. I thought it prudent to keep her under guard for now, at least until we confirm the…authenticity of the catch."

Arbuckle raised his eyebrows in admiration. He hadn't considered that the boy Moirin recovered might not be the right one.

For all they knew, this could be some elaborate ruse to get an infiltrator into the palace. There was, after all, a conspiracy to assassinate him.

They wound through several corridors to a little-used audience chamber. Half a dozen guards stiffened to attention as the imperial entourage came into sight, shifting to clear the way to the door. Ithross paused and knocked.

A guard lieutenant answered, glancing over her shoulder before stepping out and closing the door behind her. "All is secure, sir. All of the...delivery persons have been searched and sequestered in the adjoining chamber under guard. Master Corvecosi is attending the package."

"Good. You, you, and you," Ithross pointed at several of the emperor's guards, ones who were not privy to the operation to recover the Tessifus boys, "back to the barracks."

"Sir!" The squad hurried off without question. They had to know something secret was afoot, but they were well trained and followed their orders without question or comment.

"I'll await the package's owner at the gate, Majesty, just to make sure he's brought in quietly."

"Good thinking, Captain." Ithross was definitely on top of the situation. "Carry on."

As Ithross bowed and hurried off, the lieutenant gestured to the door. "Please follow me, Majesty." She opened the door and ushered him through.

Subdued lamplight and tightly drawn curtains seemed incongruous for this late hour of the day, but Arbuckle took it as another sign of the captain's attention to security. Though the room was on the second floor, Ithross was taking no chance that a passing gardener or footman might glimpse what was happening through the windows.

Master Corvecosi knelt beside a cot. Atop the white linen sheet a boy lay still...too still. Arbuckle's heart quickened as he hurried over, his guards close around him. "How is he, Master Corvecosi?"

"Alive, reasonably well, and drugged senseless, Majesty." The healer placed a hand briefly on the boy's sweaty brow, then stood and bowed to his liege. "He'll wake in time, probably with an addiction to opium."

"Opium? Why would anyone give opium to a child?"

Corvecosi shook his head, his dark features cast in an unusual scowl of disapproval. "Apparently to keep him quiet, Majesty."

"Well, he's alive anyway. Do whatever you can for him."

"Of course, Majesty."

"Well..." Arbuckle stepped back and sought out the guard lieutenant, a taut young woman with short-cropped hair and piercing eyes. "We'll have to wait for the duke to arrive, so We might as well have a chat with—"

A knock at the door interrupted him. At Arbuckle's nod, the lieutenant opened it.

Ithross stepped in. "Duke Tessifus, Majesty." He stepped aside to avoid being bowled over by the distraught duke hot on his heels.

The duke rushed across the chamber, a hoarse cry tearing from his throat. The guards tensed, but stood down at Arbuckle's gesture. Tessifus ignored everyone except the boy lying on the cot.

"Wexford!" He fell to his knees beside the cot and clutched his son's limp hand. "Wex! Speak, lad. It's your father."

"We suppose that confirms the boy's identity," Arbuckle whispered wryly to Ithross. "How in all creation did he get here so quickly?"

"The duke dragged my messenger bodily from the saddle and stole his horse, Majesty." Ithross grinned ruefully. "He about got shot from the saddle when he refused to stop at the gate, but the guards recognized both him and the horse in time."

"Well!" Arbuckle looked to the duke with new respect.

"What's wrong? Why is he—" Tessifus looked around for the first time, his eyes focusing on Master Corvecosi.

"He's been drugged, milord, but he'll be fine." Corvecosi's customary smile and soft manner reassured the distraught lord. "Time and love will bring him back."

"Oh, thank the gods!" The duke turned back to his son, but Arbuckle took the moment to interject.

"Milord Duke, We must speak with you for just a moment. Your son is well, and this can't wait."

"Majesty!" Tessifus lurched to his feet and bowed deeply. "Forgive me. How...who managed to rescue my boy? What about my other two sons?"

"We can't divulge anything yet, cousin, but rest assured that We have exquisitely competent people on this. Now, we've discussed this situation with Captain Ithross and decided that, for safety reasons, you and your entire family will move into the palace."

"But, Majesty," the duke spoke hesitantly, "we *have* bodyguards and security, and—"

"Not good enough, apparently." Arbuckle swept the objection away with an imperial wave. "Captain Ithross, please explain the issue to the duke."

"Yes, Majesty. Duke Tessifus, you must understand that, though one of your sons is now safe, knowledge of his rescue could actually imperil the lives of his brothers. If word of the rescue gets out, the perpetrators may suspect that we know who they are, and they might do away with the...evidence."

"Do away with..." Tessifus swallowed and glanced nervously at his son.

Arbuckle nodded. "Therefore, to keep this matter *utterly* secret, you and your family will move into the palace. You'll stay until your two other sons have been rescued and the guilty brought to justice."

"But, Majesty, I—"

"The issue is decided, cousin. Like it or not, *you* are the next in line for the throne. It will give Us peace of mind to know that you're safe from undue influence should...something happen to Us."

"But the rumors..."

"Leave that to Us." Arbuckle grinned deviously, pleased with the scheme he had concocted. "Word will be leaked that We have tired of your relentless opposition to Our New Accords and decided to consult with you in their creation. Being an impatient man, We want you readily available, insisting that you and your family move into the palace. Let them spread rumors that We're pressuring you into compliance. As long as the truth doesn't get out, your sons have a chance of survival."

Tessifus looked aghast. "Majesty, you've done so much for me already. How can I..."

"Cousin," Arbuckle said quietly, placing a hand on Tessifus' arm, "this isn't about you or even *me*. It's about the future of the empire." He gestured to the unconscious boy. "If we both die, *he* will take the throne. It's the empire that must survive. Right now that means you and your family must remain safe. That means *here* where We can protect you."

Finally Tessifus smiled—a weary, overwrought smile, but a smile nonetheless. "As you wish, Majesty. I'll send a message to have our household moved to the palace. I daresay the duchess will be beside herself, at least until she sees Wex. I don't know how to thank you."

"Thank Us by keeping this a *secret*, cousin." Arbuckle fixed him with a level stare. "More lives than ours depend on it."

"I will, Majesty."

Tessifus bowed and turned back to his son. Arbuckle nodded to Corvecosi, confident that the healer would take care of the boy. He turned to Ithross and clapped the man on the shoulder, enjoying the startlement on the captain's face.

"Well done, Captain!"

"I did little, Majesty," he deferred, gesturing to the chamber's other door. "Shall we thank the people who did?"

"By all means." Arbuckle strode for the door, eager to congratulate Miss Moirin on her success. When the captain opened the door and ushered him through, however, he stopped in puzzlement.

Several imperial guards stood around two young men dressed in frilly finery. One of the men was tall and dark, his pants and lacy shirt bright and finely tailored, though he wore no jacket. The second young man was shorter and fair, his blonde hair intricately curled. Blood stained the sleeve of his brocade jacket and one pant leg.

"Majesty," the smaller man said, elbowing his companion.

The taller fellow bowed stiffly, but the blond fellow curtsied with feminine grace.

The emperor started in sudden recognition. "Miss Moirin! We didn't recognize you."

She smiled briefly. "Pardon the disguise; a necessary affectation to secure the young lord's safety and my anonymity." She gestured to her companion. "This is my assistant, Dee. He helped me recover the boy."

"You have Our gratitude. Both of you." Arbuckle approached and extended a hand, aware of Ithross shifting nervously at his shoulder. He shook Moirin's hand with a smile, then her companion's. The fellow looked discomforted by the emperor's familiarity. "The duke has been reunited with his son, but young Wexford is still all but unconscious. We daresay that's a boon, for he won't be able to give a description of his rescuers, will he?"

"*Wexford?*" Dee whispered to Moirin, just too loudly to be covert.

Moirin smiled thinly and elbowed him to silence. "Yes, Majesty, that *is* a stroke of luck."

Arbuckle ignored the man's comment. "Have you any notion of where the other two boys are being held?"

"I know *who's* holding them, but not where." She looked grim. "Finding them and recovering them will be doubly difficult now that they know we're onto their plot."

"If they don't just cut and run," Dee added, drawing a thumb across his throat. He endured a glare from Moirin.

"Yes, We've been worried about that risk, but We don't think they'll resort to such a drastic measure." Arbuckle had been thinking about that a lot lately. "As long as they hold the boys, they still hold power over Duke Tessifus. And he is still the heir to the throne if they manage to kill Us. They won't destroy their only advantage."

"I agree," Moirin said.

"So, you say you know who is behind this plot, besides Hoseph, of course?" Arbuckle considered the conspirators listed in the anonymous note. *Are they truly guilty?*

"Yes, but I can't say, I'm afraid."

"We understand. We'll trust you to proceed, then. Let Us reiterate, if there's *anything* you need to help find the boys—money, manpower, whatever We might be able to provide—you need but ask."

"Well, now that you—" A sharp elbow silenced Dee.

She shook her head. "Thank you, Majesty, but we have everything we need for now. I'll accept payment when the job is done and all three boys are returned."

"Of course." Arbuckle hadn't thought that his admiration for this young woman could increase, but her obvious commitment to rescuing the boys warmed his heart. The emperor gestured to her bloody sleeve. "At least let Our Imperial Healer tend to the wounds you received in the course of your service to the empire."

Unease flashed across Moirin's features before she bent in

another curtsy. "I'm fine, Majesty, thank you, but I'm afraid we must be off. The longer we stay here, the more likely it is that someone will recognize me and suspect something. It'll be even more difficult to recover the other boys with the culprit aware that an effort is being made to rescue them. If someone starts spreading rumors that *I'm* involved, it'll be near impossible."

"We understand." Arbuckle waved Ithross forward. "Captain, please see Miss Moirin and Master Dee out of the palace with as much discretion as can be managed."

"Yes, Majesty. This way, Miss Moirin."

"Your Majesty." Moirin curtsied again.

"You have Our best wishes for your health and success, Miss Moirin. Don't hesitate to contact Us at need."

"We *won't*," Dee said, despite the glare Moirin shot him.

They followed Ithross out, surrounded by guards, and the door closed behind them. Arbuckle had no illusions that rescuing the remaining boys would go as well as this one had, but Moirin seemed undaunted. She continued to impress him with her cool professionalism.

What a shame she refused to be Our bodyguard, he mused as he followed his escort up the stairs. Such a capable woman watching over him would give him peace of mind. Eventually, he would take an empress and sire his own heirs, but before that happened, he would have to make sure he, and they, would be safe. *But how?*

A remembrance of Miss Moirin in his arms as they danced during the coronation reception flashed into Arbuckle's mind. She'd been a little unpracticed in the social graces, or perhaps nervous enough to make her seem so, but she'd been a more amiable partner than any of the nobles' flighty daughters who'd been forced on him. What he truly needed was a woman like Moirin for his empress: capable, forthright, and dauntless. And woe to anyone who even considered harming her children.

Arbuckle paused at the top of the stairs as the thought struck him. *What an empress she would make!* He smiled at the notion. She was, of course, a commoner, and the nobility would throw a fit, but it wasn't unheard of for a commoner to be bequeathed noble status for service to the empire. If Moirin recovered all of Tessifus' sons, a title might be an apt reward. *Then...*

Arbuckle found himself thinking happily on that prospect all the way back to the library.

"I can't *believe* you turned down money!" Dee shut and bolted the apartment door behind them, glad to be home. Walking into the constabulary had made him nervous; at the palace he'd felt like a cockroach on a ballroom floor.

Mya kicked off her shoes and started stripping off her bloody clothing and tossing it in a pile on the floor. "We're not in this for the money, Dee."

"Really? The guild's not out to turn a profit?"

"Of course it is, but consider how much *more* of a profit we can turn if we have the emperor's good will! I'm thinking long-term here. You can't buy that kind of influence." Clad only in her wrappings, she scooped up her clothes and strode to the kitchen. "Why are you bringing this up now?"

"We couldn't discuss it in the carriage. Assistants don't question the Grandmaster's decisions. I didn't want the driver taking stories back to Blade headquarters." Dee doffed his jacket and draped it across the table, then fetched his case of extra bolts from a cupboard. He needed to cultivate the habit of replenishing his ammunition immediately. Living with the Grandmaster in the midst of a guild war, one never knew when the next attack might come.

"Good point." Mya dumped her clothes in the pot and drenched them with water to soak out the blood. "No one needs to know that you're anything more than my dutiful assistant."

Dee flinched at the offhand remark. *That's right, Dee's the ever-obedient assistant blindly following his mistress' every order.* More violently than he intended, he flung open the jacket to expose the holstered crossbows and bolts, then stopped.

What in the Nine Hells...

The jacket had two rows of long, thin pockets in the lining, one on each side, to safely hold and separate the anesthetic bolts from the lethal ones. The right side was full, and only four remained on the left, just the opposite of what should have been. Dee dropped into the chair as all the strength left his legs, his mind spinning.

"Oh, no," he whispered hoarsely. "Oh, *gods*."

Mya froze. "What's wrong?"

He pointed at the empty bolt slots. "I used the wrong bolts when I reloaded. I... I *killed* them, Mya."

"You..." Mya came to the table and looked at the array of tiny bolts, unmindful of the bloody water dripping from her hands onto the floor. "Are you *sure*?"

"Yes, I'm *sure*!" Dee pulled a white-capped vial from a little pocket on the right side, and a black-capped vial from the left. "White is anesthetic. Black is deadly."

"How many?" Was that disappointment in her voice?

It should be. I failed her again. Dee forced himself to look up at her. "Four, at least. Mya, I'm sorry."

Mya sighed, and he wondered what thoughts raced through her mind... *Repercussions? Cost?*

She shrugged. "Well, there's nothing for it now. What's done is done. They were trying to kill *us*, after all. I think I killed at least one."

"I screwed up, Mya. And it's not the first time. I shouldn't even have gone into that basement. I'm no good at—"

"Forget it, Dee! They're dead, and we're alive. End of story. I need a bath." Mya headed for the bathroom, unwinding her wrappings as she went.

"But..." Dee's mind stumbled in confusion. She was letting him off the hook...but why?

Mya stopped at the bathroom door and looked back over her shoulder at him. "Join me?"

Realization hit him like a hammer blow to the chest. *Because I'm sleeping with her. Because sex is the only thing I'm good for...*

Suddenly, Dee knew he had to get out of the flat, get away from her before he did or said something foolish. He shot up out of the chair and strode to the bedroom. Plucking his dark clothes from the clothes press, he dumped them on the bed and pulled off his gaudy attire. As he was redressing, Mya leaned through the door.

"You going somewhere?"

Dee averted his gaze so she couldn't read the lie in his eyes. "I need to touch base with the Blades and Enforcers, see if anything happened after we left the perfumery. Lakshmi's going to know you took the kid, and she might make a move."

"You need to relax, Dee. I understand that today was...stressful, but it was a mistake! You can't beat yourself up for killing someone who would have had no problem killing you. You're too keyed up to go out now. It would be dangerous."

"They're hunting you, not me." Dee cinched his trousers and stomped his feet into his soft boots.

Mya continued unrelenting. "It's also unnecessary. Clemson and Noncey know their jobs. By morning they'll have made their observations, followed up on leads, and have the details all ready for us."

Dee stepped past, keeping his eyes off her enticing rune-etched skin, taut muscles, and delicious curves. *No! Not now.* He picked up his jacket and turned toward the door. "Relaxing isn't something I think I can do right now."

"Then *I'll* help you relax." Mya stepped into his way and reached for the collar of his shirt, stroking it before trailing her fingers onto his chest. "You help me relax all the time. It's only fair that I return the favor occasionally."

Dee jerked back involuntarily, as if her touch burned his flesh. For the first time, he found Mya's eagerness off-putting rather than enticing. "No, Mya. I'm sorry, but...I need to go out."

Mya's face flushed as she spun on her heel. "Fine. But remember, they might be hunting me, but they saw you, too." She stopped at the bathroom door and looked back again. "Be *careful.*"

"Don't worry. I'm a *Hunter*, remember." The words tasted bitter on his tongue.

"I know that, Dee."

Without another word, Dee hurried down the stairs to the street, his spirit sinking lower with every step. It felt like when Hoseph's spell had dredged up every bad memory of his life, but worse, because he'd brought this on himself with his ineptitude. He'd become more of a liability to Mya than an asset.

Why did I come to Tsing at all?

Much more of his help, and Mya would end up dead.

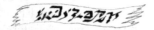

Following the resonance of the summoning chime, Hoseph shifted from the Sphere of Shadow into the physical world, his nerves as taut as a bow string. He had instructed Lakshmi to summon him only an emergency, so he materialized with the invocation of soul searching on his lips and his hand glowing with the pearly essence of Demia's power. He whipped around in a quick circle, his head lurching in pain with the sudden motion, then stopped.

"What's going on?"

Three master assassins looked at him with varying miens, none of them panicked or even particularly urgent. In fact, the greatest distress seemed to be Master Hunter Embree's trepidation as he halted in mid-pace at Hoseph's arrival. Kittal shifted uncomfortably in his chair, fingering a vial of black liquid worn around his neck on a chain, his eyes quickly averting from Hoseph's. The Master Inquisitor reclined unperturbed upon her divan, the chime dangling from her fingertips as if she had just rung to summon tea, not a high priest of Demia.

"What's wrong?" Hoseph banished his invocations and blinked back the blinding pain throbbing behind his eyes. He'd been resting, so the single transition hadn't incapacitated him, but he knew the fatigue and pain would be a long time ebbing. "I told you to use that only in dire need!"

"No, you didn't." With pursed lips, she dismissed his concerns with a casual flick of her hand. "You said if the event of something important, and this is important. We've experienced a setback and need your assistance."

"What *kind* of setback?" Lakshmi's calm bothered Hoseph more than the others' apprehension. The Master Inquisitor was a mistress of dissemblance.

"One of the Tessifus boys was taken from us."

"*What?*" A nauseating roil of rage in Hoseph's stomach exacerbated the pain and fatigue of the transition. "Taken *how?* You told me they were safe! Who could have…"

164

"Who do you think took him? Mya." Lakshmi inspected a fingernail, still seemingly unconcerned.

Sweet shadows of death, why am I plagued by this woman? "I thought you had a plan to *kill* Mya!"

Lakshmi shrugged. "We did. It didn't work out."

Hoseph fought to keep control as his pounding head goaded his temper. "How did she find out where you were keeping the boy?"

"She's a Master *Hunter*, Hoseph. Finding people is what they do!" She shot him a cold look. "We don't know how she found him, and we don't know where she took him, but six of my assassins were killed and three more were injured."

"It doesn't matter *where* she took him, what *matters* is that she did!" Hoseph jabbed a rigid finger as if he could stab her with it. "*You* said you'd kill Mya. You failed. You also said the boys were *safe*. They *weren't*. I can't believe a master could be so—"

"Oh, shut up!" The Master Inquisitor waved her hand as if dismissing a bothersome child.

"How *dare* you!" Seething, Hoseph flicked the silver skull into his palm. All he need do was grab hold of Lakshmi as he uttered the invocation...then release her once they were in the Sphere of Shadow. But...he knew he couldn't.

And so did Lakshmi.

While Kittal and Embree shrank away from the enraged priest, Lakshmi just gave him a look of bored indignation. "How *dare* I? You're not even a member of the guild, yet you sow discord in our ranks by killing our guildmaster, destroying the blood contracts, murdering our Master Hunter in a fit of pique, and now ranting and raging that *I* have failed! Don't think to threaten me, priest. We've lost nothing but a minor bargaining chip, a pawn. We still hold the one piece that truly matters."

"Where are the other two boys?" Hoseph demanded through clenched teeth.

"You know I'm not going to tell you, so don't ask again. *We*," her encompassing wave included Kittal and Embree, "are the Assassins Guild, Hoseph, not you. You don't appoint guildmasters, or even successors to masters, for that matter."

"*I* hold the guildmaster's ring! It's mine to bestow on the one who—"

"It is *NOT!*" The Master Inquisitor shot up from the divan, her carefully cultivated poise finally dispelled. "You dangle that ring like a carrot before a recalcitrant mule, but it's not yours to bestow! When we hand you Mya, which we will, eventually, you'll hand over the ring, and the masters of this guild will chose Tara's successor."

Hoseph glared at her, then at the other two masters. "You agreed to this?"

"Yes," Kittal said without hesitation, apparently emboldened by Lakshmi's speech. "The rules of succession are quite clear. The masters choose their own guildmaster. Only in cases of irreconcilable differences does the Grandmaster appoint a guildmaster. If you were an assassin, you'd know that."

"And you, Embree?" Hoseph glared at the new Master Hunter. "I was the one who put that ring on your finger. Are you saying that I was wrong? That perhaps you shouldn't be a master at all?"

Embree's face gleamed with sweat, but his expression remained steadfast. "The position of master was my right. A master's ring goes to the senior journeyman of that faction. But they're right." He nodded to Kittal and Lakshmi. "*We* decide who succeeds Lady T, not you."

"And tell me," Hoseph said dangerously, "who will succeed *you* when your soul is sent to the afterlife?"

Embree blanched, but held his ground. "My senior journeyman, of course!"

"Don't threaten us, Hoseph." Lakshmi had recovered her poise. "We'll consult you as an advisor and utilize your unique skills and influence, but you wield no power in this guild. In fact, we summoned you to see if your contact can find out if Mya took the boy to Duke Tessifus. If she's not working for someone, then why not just kill him and be done with it? That would be enough to disrupt our plan."

Hoseph seethed as he glared at the three masters. They were treating him like some kind of menial. Together, they stood unified against him, a bulwark against any threat or bribe he might use to coerce them into doing his bidding. But when each was alone...

Abruptly, Hoseph changed tactics. "I'll see what I can find out. See to the safety of your charges, Master Inquisitor. The future of the guild rests upon the success of our plan."

Lakshmi wrinkled her nose in a poisoned smile. "Goodbye, Hoseph. If you discover anything important, please drop by."

Without taking his hard stare from her face, Hoseph faded into mist.

CHAPTER XIII

Dee trudged down the stairs into the heart of Clemson's hideout. Noncey's people were still out doing their jobs, and he'd been assured that they'd have a detailed report ready in the morning. The last thing he wanted was to go back to the apartment and tell Mya that she'd been right, so he'd decided to stop at the distillery to pick up the fancy jacket that Jolee had taken for him at the perfumery.

"Good work today, Dee!" The guard at the bottom of the stairs smiled and jerked his head in the direction of the journeymen quarters. "You might still catch them before they all pass out."

"Thanks." *Good work?* Of course, none of them knew his mistake, his failure. Dee followed the sound of laughter and carousing. Maybe he could just grab his jacket unnoticed.

"Dee!" Jolee stood with a grin as he peered into the room. Silence fell, and every head swiveled toward him.

So much for being inconspicuous. "I just need to—"

"Have a drink with us!" Jolee dragged him into the room, poured amber liquid into a cup, and handed it to him. She raised her cup to the others. "Here's to Dee, the Grandmaster's assistant and wily bastard extraordinaire!"

"To Dee!" The Enforcers and Blades raised their cups and drank.

"Wily bastard?" A hot flush crept up his neck. Were they mocking him?

"You were the one who reconned this mission, and it went off like clockwork; no one seriously hurt or killed, on our side anyway." She shoved him into a chair. "That's no mean feat. I mean, I can bash a head better than anyone, but when it comes to sneaking around and intelligence gathering? I leave that to you Hunters."

They don't know I screwed up... How strange it seemed to Dee, this camaraderie, the laughs and appreciative comments on his performance. He'd never known anything like it in Twailin. He'd been the butt of jokes there, the assassin who couldn't throw a knife. *There*, they knew of his failures. But here... He sipped from his cup, the scalding sweetness of spiced rum burning a lump from his throat.

"And I saw the bodies they dragged out of there," said a Blade who had been on watch outside the perfumery. "Two of you go into the basement and come out alive *with* the kid, and a half dozen of them come out dead. The Grandmaster had her hands full with the boy, so I'm guessing it was you who racked up the count."

"Actually, I—"

"Don't be modest, Dee!" Jolee grinned and nudged Dee's shoulder, nearly knocking him off his chair. "You covered the Grandmaster's backside pretty good."

"Bet he covers her *front* pretty good, too!" another joked, earning a round of laughter. "Lucky bastard!"

Dee choked on his rum, spilling some down his shirt. He hadn't told anyone he and Mya were sleeping together, and she sure as *hell* had avoided saying anything that might have suggested intimacy between them. "Who told you *that*?"

Jolee chucked him on the shoulder hard enough to bruise. "Come on, Dee! Just gotta see the way you look at her to know. She's lucky to have someone. Can't be easy being Grandmaster in the middle of a guild war."

"Can't be easy being Grandmaster at all," another Enforcer added.

"Couldn't pay me enough," a third agreed.

"Don't worry. We won't tell anyone you're warmin' Mya's bed, though *I'd* certainly claim braggin' rights," another journeyman declared. "Noncey and Clemson are doin' it like two rabbits in a hutch, but it don't make no difference."

"She took *you* into that basement with her, so he's got the best of both worlds!" An Enforcer raised his glass to Dee. "A kick-ass Hunter to watch her ass in a fight, and someone she trusts in her bed."

"Aye, everybody needs somebody." Jolee shrugged her massive shoulders.

Dee tried—and failed—to imagine who Jolee's someone might be, but wasn't about to ask. He sipped his rum and sat back, the turmoil of his earlier disposition somehow tempered. They respected him for the job he'd done. They also knew about his relationship with Mya and actually approved. Not one had suggested that he was garnering favor by sleeping with her. Warmth suffused his body, from the alcohol or their esteem, he didn't know or care. *I'll stay here tonight*, he decided. Maybe a drunken night with friends would give him the fortitude to face Mya tomorrow.

Friends… Dee had never had many of those.

Jolee leaned in close, her breath redolent of rum. "We ever get in a tight spot, you can watch my back any time."

"Thanks, Jolee. Likewise."

"I'll be happy to watch *your* back, or something a bit lower," she laughed as she reached around to pinch him.

Raucous laughter burst out all around, but everyone fell silent as an Enforcer barged into the room, out of breath and sweaty.

"Jolee! We got a message for Master Clemson!"

"This time of night?" Jolee looked dubious. "Who's it from?"

"Don't know, but it came to Clemson's chandlery. The foreman sent it through the rounds to make sure no one could trace it here, so it just arrived." He pulled a message tube from under his jacket and held it out. It gleamed red in the lamplight.

They all looked at one another. Colored message tubes had particular significance given the ongoing guild war: red meant negotiation, white signified surrender.

"Take it to Clemson," Jolee ordered.

"*I'm* not wakin' her up." He shoved the tube toward the huge Enforcer.

With a roll of her eyes, Jolee snatched it from his hands. "I'll take it. I'm the senior journeyman here, anyway. Besides," she swept her gaze around the crowd, "the rest of you are drunk. Stick around, Dee. I'd bet my best cudgel Clemson'll have a message for Mya."

"I'm not going anywhere." Dee wiped his suddenly damp palms on his jacket, hoping against hope.

If one of the other masters wanted to negotiate, this could mean a quick end to the conflict and constantly looking over their shoulders. It might even mean Hoseph's head on a platter. *What might the emperor give Mya as a reward for bringing Hoseph to justice?* , he mused. *A title, maybe?* Would she be the next Lady T, living in a fancy house, wearing expensive clothes, attending court functions, dancing with barons and dukes?

The notion both thrilled and terrified him. *Where would that leave me?*

It seemed like forever before Jolee stuck her head in the door. "Come with me, Dee. Clemson wants to see you."

"Of course." Dee got up and followed Jolee out of the room, glad that he'd had only one drink. "What was the message?"

"They didn't tell me. I didn't ask." The cheerful off-duty Jolee had vanished, replaced by the deadly serious Journeyman Enforcer Jolee.

At Clemson's office, Jolee knocked, opened the door, and ushered Dee in.

"Dee! Excellent! Damn lucky you were here." Clemson sat at her desk clad in a red silk robe. Behind her paced Noncey in a black robe of the same design. The Master Enforcer scrawled her name on a note and pressed her guild ring to the page, impressing it with a faintly magical seal to ensure its authenticity. She then rolled it, stuffed it in a scroll tube, capped it, and pressed her ring briefly to the end of the tube, sealing it for the intended recipient. Standing, she handed it over the desk. "For the Grandmaster's hand only."

"Right away." Dee took the tube and turned to go. He'd be facing Mya a lot sooner than expected...whether he wanted to or not. The walk home would give him time to think about what he needed to say to her.

Mya sprawled on the sweat-dampened sheets, letting her gaze wander over the patterns on the ceiling and begging for sleep. She wasn't having much luck. She'd been tossing and turning for hours, sweating in the torrid air because her wrappings were still wet from washing. No breeze cooled her despite the open window; the night air was as still as death.

After such a stress-filled day, she should have dropped off in minutes. She didn't know if her insomnia was due to the temperature or Dee. She'd known he was upset about the unintentional killings, but she'd absolved him of responsibility.

What more does he expect from me?

She closed her eyes again, then snapped them open when the stairs outside creaked. She listened hard: footfalls, breathing, and *there*...a single heartbeat just on the other side of the apartment door. Mya tensed. She had four daggers in easy reach. The rustle of cloth, then the distinctive *click-clack* of a key in the lock reached her. Unless someone had followed Dee home, killed him and taken his key, it was him. The door opened slowly enough that the wind chimes didn't jingle, then closed again with a near-silent thump. The lock clicked back in place.

It's Dee. It has to be. A burglar or assassin wouldn't lock their escape route.

Cloth rustled, and a chair moved on the kitchen floor; Dee hanging up his jacket. Mya breathed easy as his soft footfalls whisked across the floor toward the bedroom. She closed her eyes and slowed her breathing, pretending to be asleep. He didn't need to know that she'd lain awake worrying about him.

The footsteps came into the bedroom, paused, then approached the bed. "I know you're awake, Mya," he said.

Her bluff called, Mya opened her eyes. "How…"

"Your breathing's different when you're sleeping." He unbuttoned his shirt and she caught a whiff of rum.

"Are you drunk?"

"No." He turned up the lamp beside the bed and pulled a scroll case out of his shirt. "I went to the distillery to pick up my jacket. While I was there, a messenger came with a scroll for Clemson. Red case. She drafted this message for you."

"Someone wants to negotiate?" She sat up, crossed her legs tailor fashion, and took the case. "Who was it from?"

"I don't know." He stepped back and leaned against the door jam. "Not my place to ask."

Mya pressed her ring to the tube to banish the magical seal, then popped the end free and pulled out the message. She read Clemson's note with rising excitement. "Wow!"

Dee waited quietly.

"Twist Umberlin is dead," she said.

"The Master Hunter?"

"Yep. Hoseph killed him for screwing up the attack on the orphanage. The new Master Hunter's name is Embree. He wants to meet with me tomorrow night and is willing to trade information for switching sides. He doesn't want anything to do with Hoseph."

"Sounds like a trap." Dee frowned. "Where?"

"Our choice. Clemson suggests her chandlery." Mya thought about it. "It makes sense. That's Clemson's home turf, so it'd be near impossible for the other factions to set up an ambush. And even if Lakshmi's people watched it after Clemson's defection, nothing's happened there, so she probably gave up and focused her people elsewhere."

"Are you going?"

"Yes, I want to hear what he has to say. Maybe he knows where Lakshmi's holding the other two boys." Mya's heart hammered as she considered the implications of the news. "This could be the tipping point, Dee! If Embree can tell us where Lakshmi and Kittal's hideouts are, and if we can strike quickly enough, this war could be over. Hoseph's nothing without the other factions."

Dee stood quiet for a moment, then said, "Do you want me to run a reply back to Clemson?"

"No. Morning is soon enough." She looked up at Dee's blank expression, his face half lit by the lamp light, half in shadow. There were lines there, and dark smudges under his eyes that she hadn't seen before. She patted the sheets beside her. "You look exhausted. Come to bed."

"I..." His eyes flicked over her, then he licked his lips and swallowed hard. "I have something to tell you first."

Finally! Maybe now we'll get to the bottom of this. "Okay, tell me."

"It's rumored among the Blades and Enforcers that we...sleep together."

"Damn! You didn't—"

"I didn't say anything. They figured it out on their own. I just thought I should let you know before you heard it from someone else. But...it's not just that." He stopped speaking and looked down at the floor, at the clothes press, back into the living room, everywhere but at Mya.

"What?" she said. "This is me, Dee. You can tell me anything."

Clenching his fists as if strengthening his resolve, Dee said, "I...think I should go, Mya."

What the hell? "Go where?"

"Leave Tsing...go back to Twailin."

"*What?*" A cold ball of dread formed in Mya's stomach. "You can't leave!"

"I've got to! I screw up. I'm a liability."

"No, you're not."

"Then tell me why you were awake when I came in instead of sleeping."

"What? It's hot and airless in here, and I was uncomfortable without my wrappings."

"Bullshit."

"*What?*" Dee wouldn't have dared use that tone when she was Master Hunter.

"You can't even admit it to yourself that you were awake worrying about me, worrying that the inept Hunter would get himself killed or let someone follow him back here."

"That's not what I was thinking." It sounded like a lie even to her own ears.

"Bullshit again."

Mya's temper flared. "So, you can read *minds* now?"

"I don't *have* to read your mind, Mya. I was your assistant for five years. I know how you think."

"And you think I'd be better off without you?"

"Yes." His gaze fell to the floor between them. "I think we'd both be better off."

"Bullshit." She took some cold satisfaction at throwing the epithet right back at him.

"What?"

"Now you're just being an idiot. You're not inept; you're a valuable assistant."

"And that's all."

"What the hell are you talking about?"

"That's all I am to you, just an assistant you sleep with when you need tension relief. I can't be...just that anymore."

"*Just* that?" Snippets of memories whirled through her mind,

174

lined up, and snapped together. Dee's excessive concern when she went out alone. His insecurities. The passion with which he took her in his arms and fulfilled her every carnal wish. The kiss... She raised her fingers to her lips. *So* that's *what this is about!* "Damn it, Dee, I told you..."

"I *know* what you told me. I'm not asking anything from you. I can't change the way I feel about you, and it's driving me crazy. If you were killed because I screwed up..."

Mya stared at him, the heat of her initial frustration chilling to fear. "Damn it, Dee, I can't *do* this without you."

"Come on, Mya! There are a dozen Blades who would have been better than me in that basement today. I screwed up, and you only let me off the hook because you want me in your bed, but you're ashamed of that, too.

Mya fell back against the headboard in shock. "*Ashamed?* Is *that* what you think?"

"You sure as hell wanted to keep it a secret! What am I *supposed* to think?"

Mya ran her fingers through her sweaty hair and shook her head slowly. "I was trying to *protect* you!"

Confusion furrowed Dee's brow. "Protect me?"

"Of course. Just look at what Hoseph's done to pressure Tessifus; he kidnapped his sons. The same thing happened in Twailin when the masters took Lad's daughter. That's how they get to you, by taking the people you care about."

"You...care about me?"

"We've worked together for years, Dee. How could I not? Yes, you run errands and keep me organized and put up with my moods, but that's such a small part of it. I trusted you with my *life* this afternoon, didn't I? I value your friendship, enjoy your company, and I like the way you think. And you..." Mya heaved a deep breath, "You remind me that I'm human."

Dee cocked his head at her, an unasked question in his eyes.

Mya extended one arm and ran a finger up her tattooed flesh, turning it back and forth as the runes writhed on her skin. "I got these to make myself safe, but instead they made me feel like a monster." She swallowed hard as she remembered the self-hate that had nearly destroyed her. "Then you said they were beautiful. You saw *me* through the ink, not just the magic or the power or the Grandmaster. You saw me, and you touched me, and you gave me back my humanity. *Every time* you touch me, you make me feel human. If I didn't have that," she shrugged, "I don't know where I'd be now."

Silence reigned for a long moment as Mya chose her next words carefully. "But I can't say that I'll love you, Dee. Love is a weakness I can't afford."

Mya closed her eyes, but even the darkness couldn't block the pain. She'd loved only two people in her life—her mother and Lad—but they'd only given her anguish in return.

"*Bullshit!*"

Mya jumped at Dee's vehemence. His eyes were wide now, intense in a way she couldn't pin down.

"Do you think Paxal rode a thousand miles to Tsing just because he wanted a *jaunt?* No, he did it because he *loves* you. And what about those kids you saved by taking them off the street? You think they're just in this for a free meal? You've given them pride, something to do with their lives, and they love you for it. You think that's a *weakness?* You think you could have survived here without them? And you're lying if you tell me that you don't love them."

Mya blinked to clear her suddenly blurry vision.

When he spoke again, Dee's voice sounded wistful. "If all you can do is love me like that, not romantically, but as someone you can trust, someone you rely on...I'll take it. I've hoped for more, but I can live with that much."

Mya felt a strange pain in her chest that no rune magic could ever block. "You're not leaving?"

"No."

"Thank you, Dee." Relief like nothing she'd ever known flooded through her. Maybe love wasn't like a lock that was only either open or closed. Maybe there was more to it than that.

Dee doffed his shirt and kicked his boots into the corner. The sweat on his long, lean body glistened in the lamplight, but to Mya it now seemed like forbidden fruit, despite her ache of desire. After all this, how could she blithely ask for sex?

Dee's head bowed as he turned away and unbuckled his pants. "Can I ask you a favor?"

"Of course." She tried to keep her mind on what he was saying as he stepped out of the pants and turned to face her. It was difficult.

"If I ever ask you for a letter of reference, would you please leave out any mention of my skills between the sheets?"

"Now who's ashamed?"

"Ashamed? You know I'm not!" Dee tossed his pants onto a chair and dropped onto the bed. He turned to her with the first smile she'd seen tonight. "One of the Enforcers was even envious. Called me a lucky bastard."

Mya's jaw dropped. "He...he what?"

"He said I was lucky. That we were both lucky to have someone we could trust."

"Well, I can't argue with that." Mya had never had anyone she trusted enough to both watch her back *and* share her bed. "I *am* lucky."

"I like the sound of that." He cocked an eyebrow and his eyes drifted down along her body. "Are you feeling lucky *tonight*, then?"

Mya knew that look, and the fire in her stomach blazed. "You can never have too much luck."

"Good." Dee grabbed her and pulled her down next to him. "I was hoping you'd say that."

Chapter XIV

Mya sat at Clemson's desk and gave the room one final glance to make sure everything was ready. Noncey and Clemson stood behind her, one at each shoulder. Dee and a half dozen Blades and Enforcers, all armed to the teeth, formed a gauntlet between the door and the desk. Her own hand rested beside a dagger strapped under the desk, out of sight of her pending guest. She was taking no chances that this defection might be a veiled assassination attempt.

Satisfied, she nodded. "Bring him in."

Dee opened the door, and Master Hunter Embree entered the room. Mya recognized the smooth, stealthy stride of a Hunter, the quick shifting of eyes that took in the room at a glance, noting the people and their positions, assessing the situation. Embree might be new to his position, but he was well-trained. He stopped in front of the desk and nodded to her. A sweat-beaded brow belied his calm. He knew certain death awaited him if he made a false move.

"Have a seat." Mya indicated the chair across from her. Pouring hefty measures of spiced rum from a crystal decanter into two tumblers, she pushed one across the desk. "Drink?"

The Master Hunter sat, looked at the liquor, then met Mya's level stare. "Thank you." A drop of sweat trickled down his temple as he picked up the glass and downed half.

Mya lifted her own glass and tilted it toward him as a salute, then sipped the rum, pleased. The rum might have been poisoned, yet Embree drank first. He trusted her to a certain degree. She hoped the rest of the interview went as well.

"Master Hunter Embree, I'm glad to know that your distrust of Hoseph matches mine." Mya swirled the liquor in her glass, her eyes never leaving his. "Tell me how you came to this conclusion."

His answer was firm and immediate. "He has no loyalty to the guild. One failed mission was no reason to kill Twist, and it deprived us of an excellent Master Hunter."

"Despite you being the beneficiary?"

Embree rolled his eyes. "I'd rather be out on the street doing my job than taking care of schedules and accounts…or dealing with Hoseph."

Mya couldn't disagree with him on that count. "Is that all it took to make you want to side with me rather than Hoseph?"

"No. Yesterday he ordered me to assign Hunters to watch Lakshmi and her people. He said it was because she wouldn't share information, but I think it was because she told him off."

"She told him *off*?" Mya's estimation of Lakshmi went up a notch. The Master Inquisitor had seemed little more than a sweet old lady when they'd met. Of course, Mya knew Inquisitors hid their true personas deep, but facing down Hoseph bespoke uncommon nerve. "Why?"

"She accused him of driving a wedge between the factions, turning us against one another. And she wasn't talking about the…uh…guild war, but those who are presumably on his side. She's right. She also told him that he wasn't guild and had no right to presume any authority."

Oh ho! Mya wished she had seen that confrontation. "And he didn't kill her like he did Twist?"

Embree smiled grimly and sipped his rum before answering. "He can't. Lakshmi's got him over a barrel with these kids she's holding. She won't tell him where they are, and he doesn't like that one bit." He sipped again and cleared his throat. "That's why he told me to set my Hunters on Lakshmi's people, to find out where the kids are. I decided that I don't want anything to do with him and wrote to you."

Mya's pulse quickened. "Do you know where Lakshmi's keeping the boys?"

"No. I did the reconnaissance of the Tessifus estate for Noncey," he nodded to the Master Blade, "but haven't seen them since. If you don't mind my asking, why are *you* interested in them?"

Mya rested her hand on her dagger hilt. The interview had gone well so far, but if she thought for a moment he was only here to weasel information out of her, she'd kill him where he sat. *He is new,* she considered, *and they may not have taken him completely into their confidence yet.* Better to keep her answer vague until she was sure of him.

"I'm interested in them because Hoseph is using them for some plot." She cocked an eyebrow. "Do you know what that plot entails?"

The Master Hunter shrugged. "It's not hard to figure out. Duke Tessifus is next in line for the throne. If the guild has his kids, the guild controls the emperor."

"Just as I suspected." Mya sipped her rum with a smile. It all fit perfectly. "So they still plan to assassinate the current emperor?"

"Yes, but I don't' know how." Embree narrowed his eyes at her. "So, you weren't sure what they were planning, but you took the boy just to screw up Hoseph's plans?"

"That's exactly correct." Mya hardened her tone a trifle. "Hoseph wants to control the guild from behind the scenes. I won't have that. I want to keep the guild intact and lead us in a direction that will be good for everyone. Hoseph only wants to regain the power he lost when the Grandmaster died. His plot depends on these kids. If I take them away, Kittal and Lakshmi will come over to my side."

"Not as long as he holds the guildmaster's ring."

"Then we'll kill him and take it back. Either way, if Hoseph loses, I win."

Embree seemed to consider for a moment, then nodded. "Lakshmi's made it clear that Hoseph doesn't control the guild, but that he *is* important to her picture of the guild's future. Without him, that future crumbles. She and Kittal won't have any choice but to agree to your terms. What do you need from me to make this work?"

"The locations of Lakshmi and Kittal's new headquarters. My rescuing the first Tessifus boy will leave her cautious about the remaining two. My guess is that she'll keep them close by and under heavy guard, which probably means at her headquarters. Maybe one at Kitall's to keep them separated. What do you think?"

Embree assumed a thoughtful look, most of his nervousness gone. "She'll definitely keep them separated. When we last met at Lakshmi's headquarters, Kittal brought her a couple of small boxes, vials of opium. They might be drugging the boys to keep them quiet."

That supposition certainly meshed with Mya's observations of the groggy Wexford. "And where are their headquarters?"

"Lakshmi's is behind a soap shop in the Heights on Fetterly Avenue. Kittal's set up in the basement of a glassblower's workshop on Flatiron Street where it breaches the wall between Midtown and the Wharf District."

"Do you know where else Lakshmi or Kittal's people hole up?"

"A few, but not all of them, just like they don't know all of mine."

"Before we make a move, I'll want locations for as many of their hideouts as you can give me. We can't hit them all simultaneously, but we can have people watching to see how they react. Have you moved your headquarters yet?"

"No. I wanted your answer first. I don't want my people to suffer for my miscalculation if you…don't want us."

Mya considered the meeting. Embree seemed to be telling her the truth, as far as she could tell. *If only I could wave a feather like Keyfur to discern the truth…* He also seemed to care for his people. She liked that. Mya stood and extended a hand. "We want you. Welcome aboard."

The relief on the Master Hunter's face shone clearly as he shook her hand. "Thank you, Grandmaster."

Mya held his hand, squeezed it just hard enough to let him know her strength. *No sense in being too trusting.* "I don't have to tell you what will happen to you if this turns out to be a trap, do I?" She released her grip and sat back down.

"No, you don't." Embree flexed his hand.

The tension in the room eased. Clemson and Noncey came around and perched on the corners of the desk, ready to participate in the planning.

"So, how soon can you be ready to move your headquarters?"

Embree frowned, obviously considering all the details. "Tomorrow maybe, but the next day would be better. Getting ready to move is easy, doing it without anyone noticing will be harder. If they catch wind that something's up, I'll be floating face down in the harbor."

"Right. Have people ready to move your headquarters when we start the operation. So, now, what time of day do we do this?"

"I say during the day, like the last time." Noncey looked from face to face. "The shops will be open, so it won't be suspicious for people to be entering either business."

"Maybe, but after the perfumery attack, Lakshmi's likely to be ready any time of day, and I don't want to involve a bunch of innocent bystanders." Mya considered how to change their tactics. "Early morning, I think, when the night shift is tired and thinks everything's gone quiet. Say…an hour before dawn, day after tomorrow."

Embree nodded. "I can do that."

"We'll need some reconnaissance."

Embree grinned. "I can give you sketches of the buildings, the number of guards, where they're posted, and a bit on the fortifications and surprises they have."

Every head turned toward him with expressions ranging from skeptical to curious.

Mya raised an eyebrow. "You picked all that up?"

"I'm a *Hunter*, Grandmaster. It's my job to observe."

Mya returned his grin. This just might work.

Dee hunched with Mya in the shadows of a doorway, scanning the street in front of the soap shop.

All clear…so far.

Mya tapped his arm and pointed up. Scanning the rooftops across the way, he caught a flicker of motion. Blades were supposed to be taking out the watchers Embree had told them about.

But if this is a setup… He dismissed the thought. He had to trust Mya's assessment of the Master Hunter. Embree's offer to accompany them had bolstered Dee's confidence, but Mya had insisted that the Hunters stay out of this. They had enough to do moving their headquarters, and she'd gotten reconnaissance from Embree himself.

"That's it," Mya whispered, tugging his sleeve. "We're on."

"Are you *sure* you want me to come with you?"

"Who better to watch my ass?" She grinned and slipped away.

"And it's such a nice ass, too…" Dee drew his crossbows and followed.

Flicking from shadow to shadow, they stole down the street. Halfway to the shop they were joined by another shadow, a Blade particularly skilled at picking locks. Across town, a similar group would be advancing on Kittal's headquarters on Flatiron Street.

When they reached the shop's front door, Mya and Dee put their backs to the wall to either side while the Blade got her tools ready. Drapes were drawn over barred windows, and no light leaked from around the edges, but that didn't mean it was safe. Embree had told them there were always two guards in the shop at night, and perhaps trip wires on the front door.

Here's where things get dicey…

While the Blade knelt to examine the door's lock, Mya leaned near the window to listen for any hint that they'd been detected. Dee stood ready, watching for any trouble. He knew that Enforcers and Blades lurked in the shadows, but couldn't see any. All was still.

The Blade pulled a thin steel feeler tool from a pocket and slipped it under the door. She slid it slowly and gently from left to right, then up the latch side, stopping about three inches up.

"One wire," she whispered, withdrawing the feeler, then reinserting it above the spot. She paused again at the latch, then again halfway across the top of the door. "Two."

She finished the circumference and put the feeler tool away. Pulling out two thin picks, she slid them into the lock and teased the tumblers, a look of intense concentration wrinkling her brow. The faintest of clicks brought a smile to her face and she nodded. She rotated the picks until the bolt released and the door moved minutely.

Dee licked the sweat from his upper lip and tensed as Mya and the Blade traded places. If Kittal had lent his expertise to Lakshmi's security measures, pulling either of those two wires could release all Nine Hells. If that happened, Mya would be far more likely to survive or deal with whatever mayhem ensued.

Mya wrapped the fingers of one hand around the latch, drew a thin pair of snippers with the other, and gingerly pushed the door open the tiniest crack. Slipping the snippers through, she clipped the bottom wire.

Twang!

"What the—" muttered a startled voice inside the shop.

Mya moved like lighting, reaching up to clip the top wire, then bursting into the shop. Dee pivoted into the doorway and raised his weapons, flinching as a crossbow bolt embedded itself in the doorjamb. Across the room, Mya had already knocked one Inquisitor flat with the pommel of her dagger. The other was reaching for a pull rope. Dee took aim, but motion above his head caught his attention. A melon-sized glass sphere tumbled from a niche above the door.

"Shit!" Dropping his crossbows, Dee reached for the orb. Slick and surprisingly heavy, it slipped from his grasp. Desperately, he stuck out a foot to break its fall. The sphere didn't rupture, but rolled across the floor to shatter against the far wall. Liquid spattered the nearby shelves, and smoke billowed as wood and the carefully stacked soaps smoldered and blackened.

A crash drew his attention from the hissing acid. Mya's kick had sent the other Inquisitor slamming into the wall, but not before his fingers closed around the pull rope.

An alarm bell rang deeper inside the building.

"Damn!" Mya noticed the mess and cringed. "What the— Never mind that! Come on!"

Dee snatched up his crossbows hurried across the shop to take up position beside Mya. Blades and Enforcers flooded through the front door. Jolee and another burly Enforcer picked up a heavy table laden with soaps and bath oils, hefting it like a battering ram. At the drop of Mya's hand, they slammed it into the inner door.

Dee cringed. *Gods, I hope that one's not wired.*

Wood splintered under the onslaught, but held, and nothing exploded. Tossing the table aside, Jolee kicked the door hard, and it came off the hinges. Then she staggered back, a crossbow bolt sticking out of her upper chest.

In the horrified moment that Dee stared at Jolee, Mya took off down the hallway. *The gauntlet*, Embree had called it, for doors lined the walls on both sides, and it was a safe bet the rooms behind them didn't hold just boxes of soap. Dee raced after Mya.

At the far door—Lakshmi's office—stood two assassins. One was already falling to the floor with one of Mya's daggers in his thigh. The other fired a crossbow at the charging Grandmaster, but

Mya batted the bolt out of the air. Dee raised a crossbow to take aim, but Mya was faster. Before he could pull the trigger, the Inquisitor went down, clutching his crotch from Mya's kick.

Can't be that easy, Dee thought.

As if to confirm his dread, three of the six doors along the hallway opened, and Dee had no shortage of targets. Two assassins fell unconscious with Dee's bolts in their flesh, but a half dozen more took their places...between him and Mya.

Dee flattened himself against a wall to make room for the Enforcers and Blades charging into the hallway. To his surprise, Jolee led the onslaught despite a bloody crossbow bolt sticking out of her shoulder. She and her equally huge partner wielded cudgels the size of small trees, smashing people aside with gleeful abandon. Reloading quickly, Dee dropped two more assassins, then struggled to fight his way through to Mya.

If she isn't dead already...

But the Inquisitors apparently considered two massive Enforcers with clubs and Blades with crossbows and daggers a greater threat than a single woman, because they paid no attention to Mya. Accordingly, Mya paid no attention to them. Instead, she attacked the door to Lakshmi's office, but she didn't appear to be having much luck. The heavily reinforced oak held its own under her frantic onslaught, already spattered with blood from her fists.

"Dear Gods of Light, is the woman *trying* to kill herself?"

A high-pitched tone reverberated within Hoseph's mind, rousing him from a deep sleep. He blinked in the darkness, momentarily disoriented and unsure of the time. Instinct told him it was still night. *But that sound...* He looked around for the source in the glow of Demia's summoned magic, then realized it was coming from inside his head.

The chime I gave to Lakshmi!

He lurched up from his blankets, worry banishing the last vestiges of sleep. Flipping his talisman into his hand, he whispered, "Shahallariva," and Demia's power dissolved his flesh to mist.

Even in the Sphere of Shadow, the tone resounded in his mind like a beacon. That was the true value of the chime; he needn't be familiar with the location to arrive at the summoner's side. Bracing himself for the pain he knew would come, he concentrated on the source of the tone and invoked the talisman again.

Pain pierced him like a knife thrust between his eyes. Hoseph gritted his teeth and blinked, swallowing the nausea that threatened to empty his stomach. Through a fog of agony, he saw flickering light, heard curses, shouting, and a loud bell.

"Hoseph!" Lakshmi's voice cut through the haze, and his surroundings resolved into the opulent confines of her office. The Master Inquisitor stood in an uncharacteristic state of dishevelment, her hair mussed, a red silk robe hastily tied over bright yellow night clothes. She twitched her head in a quick, birdlike gesture, as if wincing in pain. "We're in trouble."

A heavy impact punctuated the alarm bell. Hoseph realized there were others in the room. Four of them were pressing a heavy table against the door. It rattled with another impact, and the Inquisitors looked to their master with panic in their eyes.

Lakshmi ignored them as she clutched Hoseph's sleeve. "We're under attack and all the exits are blocked. You need to get me out of here!"

Hoseph's thoughts cleared as if he'd been dashed with cold water. It could only be Mya, and she could only be here for one reason. "Mya's come for the boys. You're keeping them *here*, aren't you?"

She narrowed her eyes at him. "Only one, the eldest, but he doesn't matter. Now get me out of here!"

"He *does* matter!" The agony in his head pounded in time with the clanging alarm bell. He was in no mood for Lakshmi's defiance. "Take me to him or I'll leave you here for Mya to dismember."

"You *wouldn't*." Lakshmi's eyes flashed with trepidation before she clenched her jaw stubbornly. "Besides, she wouldn't waste my talents the way you wasted Twist's."

Hoseph smiled grimly. "Would you bet your life on that?" He folded his arms, fingering the talisman. "Take me to the boy and I'll take you *both* to safety."

Lakshmi glared, but another sharp thump against the office door galvanized her into action. She pointed a bony finger at an Inquisitor. "Sarin! Hold that door. You've got to give us at least a few moments to get out of here. Once we're gone, surrender. Mya won't slaughter guild members if she doesn't have to." She sneered at Hoseph. "She's not stupid."

"Yes, Mistress!" The assassins gathered more furniture, wedging it into place as another strike shivered the door in its frame.

Lakshmi turned to a broad credenza and pressed three ornate bits of filigree in sequence, her long fingernails clicking against the polished wood. The massive piece of furniture slid silently aside, exposing a recess in the wall. Reaching inside, she flipped something, then pushed. A section of the wall swung up and inward to reveal a secret passage with stairs leading down into the dark.

Something crashed against the outer door again, and this time wood splintered.

A fist had punched through both the door and table, slim and bloody, a woman's hand. *Mya!* Unfortunately, one of the Inquisitors holding the table had been in the fist's path. The man flew back to land on the floor, clutching his chest.

A quick-thinking assassin stabbed a dagger through the hand, but it just twisted, grasped the assassin's wrist, and yanked. The man was jerked forward, his arm disappearing through the hole until his face smashed into the wood. His surprised cry devolved into a scream, then he was flung back, his arm twisted at an impossible angle.

"Good Gods of Light!" Lakshmi gasped.

Hoseph knew better than to think that a mere stab wound in the hand would stop Mya. The Grandmaster had buried a dagger in her stomach and a blademaster had skewered her with a sword, yet still she had fought on. He stared at the bloody hand scrabbling through the hole in the door, trying to find the latch. *If I can just get hold of her for a moment, I can send her soul to Demia, and my troubles will be over.* He took a step toward the door, but stumbled as fingers like talons grasped his robes and yanked him back.

"Don't be a fool!" Lakshmi hissed. "We've got to get out of here!"

The hand disappeared back through the door, his opportunity lost. Another impact splintered the door further, and the table flew back, landing atop the two assassins still struggling to keep it in place.

"Justi, Verna, seal this behind us! Lock it from the inside!" Lakshmi hurried into the secret passage, light blossoming around her as she descended the stair.

The door splintered under another impact.

With a surge of panic, Hoseph followed her down, the two assassins crowding in behind to seal the portal. Mya might spare the assassins who opposed her, but he held no illusions of mercy for himself if he was still here when she broke through.

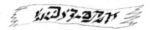

Bones in Mya's shoulder crunched as she rammed into Lakshmi's office door once again. *It will heal,* she reminded herself. Her shattered fists and the stab wound were already healed. Though she felt no pain, it still nauseated her to think too closely about the damage she was inflicting on her body. The bones knitted as she switched tactics and slammed a kick into the door near the latch.

Finally, the door gave way completely. Charging through, she assessed the situation at a glance. Four assassins littered the floor, a couple beneath a broken table, two more groaning or unconscious. None of them were Lakshmi. Movement caught her eye, and she whipped around to see a heavy credenza sliding unaided along the wall. She launched herself at it, gripping the edge with bloody fingers to wrench it aside.

Lakshmi must have a bolt hole... The thought of a secret room felt right. *What better place to keep a kidnapping victim?* But there was nothing behind the credenza save a small niche in the wall.

Footfalls behind drew her glance; Dee and several others charged into the room. "They went this way, Dee. Come on! Keep up!"

"I was *busy!*"

Digging her hand into the nook exposed by the cast-off credenza, she found a hidden lever and tried to move it. It seemed stuck, and her bloody hand slipped on the metal. Taking a two-handed grip, she wrenched it. Metal screeched in protest, but nothing else happened.

Mya kicked the wall in frustration and it moved. The locking mechanism was broken, but something was holding it shut. She slammed into it with all her weight, and the false wall swung in and upward. She heard a truncated yelp and glimpsed a figure tumbling down a staircase, arms and legs flailing. Closer at hand stood a second assassin, face contorted in a muddle of rage and fear, a dagger readied.

"Stop!" he yelled. "I don't—"

"I *do*!" Mya grabbed the front of his jacket and heaved him into the room behind her.

"Hey!" Dee yelped indignantly as the Inquisitor nearly bowled him over.

Mya bid him a quick "Sorry!" and flew down the steps. "Come on!"

"Slow down!" he snapped.

"Speed up!" She wasn't about to wait for him. If Lakshmi had the boy below, she might kill him rather than let him be taken.

Glow crystals lit her way down the long, steep stair, the walls progressing from quarried stone to seamless native rock. She leapt over the fallen assassin, a tangle of twisted arms and legs that still moved weakly. Far below, she could hear labored breathing and the sound of metal rasping metal—a key in a lock. A door scraped open ahead as she reached the bottom of the stair. Two figures stood in the opening, Lakshmi and...

"Hoseph!"

The priest started at her shout and glanced back. He looked different, short hair and unkempt facial stubble making him look like a beggar rather than a priest. Rage, fear, and indecision flicked over his face.

"Come on!" Lakshmi howled, dragging him into the room beyond.

Mya charged the door.

Crack! A tiny projectile shot past, but Dee's bolt stuck into the door as it slammed shut.

"Not this time!" Mya vowed, sprinting full speed and leading with her shoulder as she heard the lock click home.

Impact… Splintering wood… Darkness… No pain, but overwhelming dizziness.

Cool stone pressed against Mya's cheek. Brilliant stars shot through her blurry field of vision, coalescing into a single bright light that grew in her sight. Blinking rapidly, her heart skipped a beat as she finally distinguished a pearly glow and a leering face.

Hoseph…and his glowing hand of death.

I've waited so long for this! Hoseph gloated as he approached Mya's sprawled figure.

Though the impact had stunned her, the bloody contusion on her temple was already healing, her eyes clearing. He had to be quick. Invoking Demia's blessing, divine light flared in his palm. Only a moment to release Mya's soul from her body, and he would be free of her…

"Hoseph!" Lakshmi struggled to free a young man manacled to a small cot.

Hoseph ignored her. Once he'd killed Mya, there would be no need to flee. *Just one touch…*

Pain blossomed in Hoseph's left buttock.

He jerked, stumbling, his head suddenly reeling. His legs folded. Catching himself on hands and knees, he wondered what had happened to him. It didn't matter. Mya lay only steps away… He tried to crawl forward. *I have to kill her.*

Hoseph's arm buckled, twisting him away from Mya. In the doorway stood a dark-haired man in a long coat, a small crossbow in each hand.

I've been shot, Hoseph realized, *poisoned.*

The world began to fade to gray, as if a fog oozed out of the corners of the room. *Demia, give me strength!* His waning consciousness steadied for a moment, so his plea must have found a sympathetic ear. He turned to look at Mya. Already she was struggling to her feet, murder in her eyes.

Flee… Get away… But to where? He was poisoned. Without an antidote, he would likely die. But if he stayed here, death was certain.

The word of invocation leapt into his mind and onto his numbing lips. "Shahallariva."

"Hoseph!"

Lakshmi's cry cut through the fog that shrouded Hoseph's mind. The Master Inquisitor struggled to pull the Tessifus boy toward him, her frail old frame straining, her free hand reaching out for him. Horror chilled her eyes as the shadows started to consume him. She lunged forward, her bony hand grasping his as the mists took him.

The Sphere of Shadow swept the fog from his mind as a gale sweeps away an ocean mist. Here, with no corporeal body to be affected by poison, Hoseph's thoughts cleared. He could feel Lakshmi with him, but... His rage flared.

Where is the boy?

The foolish old woman must have left the boy to save herself. He considered letting her go, leaving the Master Inquisitor to drift here as punishment for her failure, but reconsidered. As much as he hated to admit it, he needed her. Only she knew where the last Tessifus boy—the most important boy—was being held. Also, she was the foremost Inquisitor in Tsing, the only one fit to train the next Grandmaster. He couldn't kill her. In fact, he wasn't even sure he could save himself.

First things first. He'd die if he didn't get an antidote to the poison, and there was only one place he knew he could get one. *Kittal.* With a prayer to Demia, he pictured the Master Alchemist's headquarters and invoked the talisman once again.

Pain and nausea, screams, and the concussive roar of an explosion ushered Hoseph back into the physical world. His mind swirled through the oppressive fog, but the shouts, the mayhem... They were under attack. Had Demia forsaken him, dropped him back into the secret room beneath Lakshmi's headquarters?

It doesn't matter... Nothing matters anymore.

Hoseph no longer had the strength or the will to save himself. The fog enveloped his mind until there was nothing left at all.

Dee slapped a new bolt into place and raised his crossbow, but it was too late. Hoseph was gone.

Mya's foot lashed through the dissipating cloud of black mist. Stumbling with the wasted effort, she glared around the room, her bloody hands clenching and unclenching spastically.

"*Damn* it!" Her flinty gaze settled on Dee. "Tell me that the shot you put in his ass was poisoned."

"Sorry. You said you didn't want to kill anyone if it wasn't necessary."

"Stupid me." She shifted her glare to the two Inquisitors cowering near the Tessifus boy's bed. "Cover them."

Dee redirected his crossbows and steadied his hammering heart with a deep, calming breath. Mya's close and almost lethal encounter with Hoseph had disturbed him even more than her reckless charge through the Inquisitor's stronghold. If he hadn't been right behind her… He shuddered at the thought.

Blades and Enforcers poured into the small room to take control of the Inquisitors. They surrendered without a struggle, perhaps in response to their mistress' sudden departure.

The room looked like a disused wine cellar, cool and dry, lit by glow crystals. The only furnishings were a table and chairs, some cabinets and cupboards, and a narrow bed.

Mya knelt beside the groggy young man manacled to the bedpost, peering into his glassy eyes. "He's alive, anyway. This one must be the oldest, the heir. I hope Noncey finds the last boy."

"You've got blood on your face."

She wiped at the blood with her sleeve and grinned at Dee. "And you made it through without a scratch."

"You didn't leave anyone left to scratch me."

"I couldn't have done better myself," said an admiring voice behind them.

They turned to see Jolee examining the shattered door. She had a bloody hole in her shoulder, but the bolt had been removed.

Flexing one enormous bicep, she nodded at Mya. "Grandmaster, we've got everything under control upstairs."

"Good. I wish I could say the same about down here, but we missed Hoseph and Lakshmi." Mya hefted the boy over her shoulder like a sack of grain. "Is the carriage ready?"

"Ready and waiting."

"Good. Get this place cleaned up, Jolee, all the prisoners to Clemson's. Dee, you're with me."

Dee ignored Jolee's crooked grin and knowing wink as he followed Mya through the door and up the stairs.

At the top, Mya said, "I want you to take the brat to the palace. I need to find out what happened at Kittal's."

"*Me?*" Dee couldn't believe it. "You want me to go to the palace *alone?*"

"Why not? They know you, and I don't think they'll complain about *who* brings the kid back, as long as they get him in good shape."

"Sure." Dee didn't know if the Imperial Guard would be as welcoming of him as they would be of the heroic Miss Moirin, but he couldn't argue with her. She was Grandmaster and she was right.

Lakshmi's office was crowded with Enforcers securing the dazed and beaten Inquisitors. Dee almost laughed at the awe in their eyes when they looked at Mya, but it really wasn't funny. Though he understood their reaction, he didn't share it. Watching Mya throw herself headlong into danger felt like a dagger in his gut. On the bright side, the rumors about her would certainly grow after this, which might lure some Inquisitors and Alchemists over to their side.

He followed her out the soap shop's back door, where a nondescript carriage waited, an Enforcer holding open the door. The driver, the same one who had taken them to the palace with Wexford, tipped his hat from the driver's seat. Mya dumped the unconscious boy inside the carriage, then stepped aside to let Dee board.

He hesitated. "You should probably clean up before heading to Kittal's, Mya." Dee nodded to the brightening sky. "It'll be dawn soon."

"Right. Thanks." She grimaced at the blood on her hands, her own, though her flesh was smooth and unmarred. "Plenty of soap inside. You better get going."

"Sure." He climbed aboard and reached for the door handle, but Mya already had it.

"And thanks again for watching my back. You did good, Dee." She grinned at him.

For once, Dee didn't doubt her sincerity, but his own assessment wasn't so forgiving. "Except for Hoseph."

"No, *especially* with Hoseph." Her face turned serious. "If he'd gotten a hand on me…"

Dee swallowed hard and opened his mouth to speak, but there were no words to express what he was feeling right now. Nothing he could say aloud, at least.

"Anyway, thanks for that." Another smile flicked across her lips. "I'll see you back at the flat."

"Right."

The door closed and the carriage lurched into motion. Dee checked the unconscious boy's breathing, then settled back for the ride, struggling to calm his jangling nerves as he looked out the window. Hoseph as still out there, and that was the second time Dee had put a crossbow bolt in his ass. He was going to wake up very pissed off indeed.

Chapter XV

Glass crunched beneath Mya's boots as she rounded the corner onto Flatiron Street. She let out a low whistle. An explosion had blasted out windows from the glassblower's shop halfway down the block. Acrid smoke still wafted through the still air, reminiscent of the explosions that had rocked the orphanage. She wondered that the entire neighborhood hadn't burned to the ground.

Pulling her cap down over her brow and stuffing her hands into the pockets of the loose jacket she had borrowed, Mya joined the crowd of gawkers. The neighbors—some still in their night clothes—chattered excitedly, regaling each other with stories of their rude awakening and speculating on what mishap had befallen the poor glassmakers.

Mya shifted her attention to where a squad of constables picked through the debris. Though the sun wasn't yet fully above the buildings, she had no trouble seeing that several bodies had been dragged out to the curb. She recognized no Blades or Enforcers. *Thanks to Embree's reconnaissance.* She thanked her lucky stars for the Master Hunter's defection.

"Ah, dearie, such a one as you shouldn't be wastin' time lookin' where there's nothin' to see. You should be off to your work!"

Mya flicked a scornful glance at the interfering old woman passing by. A wink of the crone's wrinkled eye caught her off guard, but a covert flick of gnarled fingers explained all; the woman was one of Noncey's Blades.

Ducking her head like a contrite youth caught dawdling, Mya mumbled, "Yes, ma'am."

Mya followed the old woman at a discreet distance as she toddled down Flatiron Street and around the corner. A block farther along, she approached an tenement house, waved irritably at the drunken sailor lolling on the stairs to get out of the way, then opened the door and stepped inside. Mya followed suit, sidestepping the drunk as she mounted the steps. She recognized him as one of Clemson's senior journeymen. The reek of whiskey on his clothes didn't quite mask the scent of smoke.

"Just upstairs and left," he whispered as she passed.

Through the door and up a narrow stairwell she went. At the first landing, Mya spied the old woman at one of the doors along the left passage, fiddling with the latch. As Mya approached, the woman opened the door and entered. Mya ducked in right behind her, and the Blade closed the door behind them.

The small flat was empty of furniture, but crowded with Blades and Enforcers, some lying injured, others tending to the wounded. Four blanket-draped shapes were stretched out in the far corner. The scent of scorched meat, hair, and leather wrinkled Mya's nose.

Noncey stood from where he knelt beside a badly burned man. "Grandmaster."

"I went by Kittal's place. It looked like you walked into a mess." She looked around at the injured and dead. "Is this all the damage?"

"No. These are just the worst off. We lost six in all, and there were maybe ten more injuries. I've called for a healer who works for me on occasion to come here and tend to the wounded."

"Did you get anything?" Mya asked hopefully.

Noncey shook his head, his eyes heavy with regret. "We captured a few of Kittal's people, took them to Clemson's headquarters, but we found no boy."

"Lakshmi had a secret room where she was hiding the Tessifus boy. Might Kittal have had one, too?"

"Possible, I suppose. I can't give a definite answer. Everyone in the building was either killed or captured, but there wasn't time to search the place thoroughly enough to find a secret room. The explosion drew constables like shit draws flies." He grimaced helplessly. "I'm sorry, Grandmaster."

Mya waved off his apology. "If I hadn't actually seen the secret passage at Lakshmi's closing, we might not have found it either. What about Kittal?"

Another shake of the head. "Close, but no luck." The Master Blade gestured for her to follow him to a big man seated with his back against the wall, a swatch of cloth pressed against his face.

"Bratt, tell the Grandmaster what you told me."

The man started to stand, but sank back as Mya crouched down and motioned him to remain seated. Removing the cloth to speak, he exposed red, blistered skin that was already beginning to slough off.

"I busted into the room that Embree told us was Kittal's office. I was by myself because my partners," he frowned as he jerked a thumb toward the blanket-shrouded bodies, "went down to a bomb hidden in the hallway. Kittal was there, and Lakshmi, and...Hoseph."

"Lakshmi and Hoseph were there?" Rage burned Mya's cheeks and she gritted her teeth. How many times would this priest slip through their fingers? "And I supposed he spirited the masters away, dissolved into that godsdamned mist of his!"

"Well, yes and no, Grandmaster." Bratt swallowed, his voice thick and his eyes wide as he watched her with alarm. "He and the masters vanished, but it was Kittal who did it. He swallowed some potion that was hanging on a chain around his neck, grabbed the other two, and they all puffed into smoke right there in front of me."

Mya rocked back on her heels in shock. "Kittal can travel magically?"

Noncey shrugged. "I've never heard of him doing it, but who knows what kind of concoctions he brews."

"And you're sure it wasn't Hoseph," she asked, "disappearing as a black mist?"

The assassin set his ruined features firmly. "No, it was a whitish smoke, and it was definitely Kittal. Hoseph was on the ground, looking...well, he looked *dead*."

"He was drugged," Mya explained. "Dee shot him, but it was only anesthetic. He got away with Lakshmi before I could kill him."

Bratt frowned, wincing as the gesture tugged his burned face.

"Don't worry, Bratt. You did fine." She stood, trying to calm her temper. Despite her frustration, she couldn't fault Bratt for not killing Hoseph, considering her own failure. "It's hard to catch smoke with your bare hands."

"That it is." Noncey patted Bratt's shoulder and turned to her. "Orders?"

"Regroup. Take care of your people, get things settled, and I'll visit you at Clemson's this evening. I want to talk to the prisoners."

"Yes, Grandmaster. I'm sorry we failed to retrieve that last boy."

Mya shrugged and smiled reassuringly. "He's safe for now. They're not likely to hurt their only remaining hostage. We'll just have to find where they're keeping him. And now that we've got Hunters on our side, we've got a definite advantage. We'll talk tonight."

"Yes, Grandmaster."

Mya left the flat and strode quickly toward home. It had been a hell of a day, and she hadn't even had breakfast yet.

Pain clawed at Hoseph's sanity like razors shredding a thin tapestry.

Demia, take me! he pleaded, but the Keeper of the Slain either deigned not to listen, or had other plans for her priest. Regardless, the agony confirmed one important fact: *I'm alive.*

Hoseph rose unwillingly into full consciousness. The chill of cool stone pressed against his back. The sour taste of vomit and an overlying astringent tang coated his tongue. Blinking open his eyes, he peered through dim lamplight into the spectacled and disgruntled visage of Master Alchemist Kittal.

"He's back." Kittal wrinkled his nose and stood.

"What..." Hoseph struggled to recall where he was. *Chime, noise, panic, pain, darkness...* "I was poisoned."

"As a matter of fact, you were *drugged.* Luckily for you, I have an antidote." Kittal wiggled an empty vial between his fingers. "If it had been poison, one of *my* poisons, you'd be dead."

Swallowing the bile that threatened to rise in his throat, Hoseph assessed his condition. Kittal was right; the weakness and disorientation of the poison were gone. His nausea and pain were simply the familiar aftermath of using his talisman.

"Why drug me? Why not use a *real* poison?"

"I *told* you Mya wouldn't slaughter guild members unnecessarily. You were just lucky; if the shooter had realized it was you, it probably *would* have been poison." Lakshmi's shrewish tone pounded like a hammer on his headache. She sat on a stool in one corner, her wizened features once again calm.

Hoseph glanced around. He was lying on the floor of a workshop or storage chamber. Bottles, jars, vials, and urns competed for space upon shelves that lined the walls. This didn't look anything like the Alchemist's office. He levered himself up to a sitting position, wincing at the pain in his backside. He felt the wound, but the bolt had been removed.

"One of Mya's assassins shot you with a dart. I didn't recognize him."

Hoseph had—*Dee*—but everything after that was a blur. "What happened? How did we get away?"

"You brought us to Kittal's, then Kittal brought us here." Lakshmi nodded respectfully to the Master Alchemist. "He saved our lives."

Kittal frowned at the empty vial hanging on a chain around his neck. "Don't expect that trick again any time soon. This potion is expensive, onerous to prepare, and loses potency over time. I make it only when necessary and save it for emergencies."

"Where are we?" Hoseph massaged his temples and tried to concentrate.

"One of my repositories." Kittal squinted at Hoseph. "And you're *welcome* for the rescue and antidote."

Offering gratitude for an action that was clearly as much self-centered as altruistic struck Hoseph as ludicrous. "I won't try to flatter you with false sentimentality. Just as I saved Lakshmi's life because I need her to fulfill the goals we've set, you saved mine for the same reason."

Hoseph tried to rise, only to have the pain behind the orbs redouble. He gasped, quickly regretting the lapse as Kittal leveled sharp eyes at him.

"You're in pain?"

Hoseph tried to wave it off; he'd be damned if he'd let these two know how incapacitating it was for him to use his talisman. His ability to travel instantaneously anywhere the empire was his unique contribution to the guild. Without that...well, they might choose to practice their deadly profession on him.

"Just a headache I had before this all started. The drug or the smoke made it worse, not to mention getting *shot*."

Kittal selected a non-descript brown bottle off a shelf and handed it to Hoseph. "Put a drop—only a drop, mind you—on your tongue."

Hoseph examined the lettering on the white paper label. Whether it was some strange arcane script or a code particular to alchemists, he had no idea, but he couldn't read it. He wondered briefly if Kittal would poison him for his lack of gratitude. *No, that would be absurd.* Why save him only to kill him? He unscrewed the top and opened it. Attached to the bottom of the cap was a small glass tube filled with a greenish liquid. He touched the tube to his tongue. A minty, fruity flavor suffused his mouth, banishing his pain as quickly as it dispelled the vile taste of vomit.

"That's amazing!" His headache was gone, his nausea, even the pain in his backside. It was all just…gone. He stood easily and without dizziness, silently berating himself for his innate aversion to asking for help. He should have known to ask an Alchemist for a cure to his affliction. "A healing elixir?"

"Healing *and* restorative. A formulation of my own. You're *welcome.*" Though Kittal's words were sharp, his features expressed satisfaction at Hoseph's reaction. The Alchemist plucked the bottle from Hoseph's fingers, capped it, and placed it back on the shelf. "Now that we're all conscious, we need to consider what happened. Lakshmi and I were attacked at precisely the same moment, a concerted effort by Blades and Enforcers led by Mya."

"It seems obvious that we were betrayed," Lakshmi said. "The force was too overwhelming and too knowledgeable not to have inside information. I would wager that Master Embree has shifted his loyalties." Her eyes slid sideways to focus on Hoseph. "It's not difficult to understand his motivation."

Hoseph felt too good to put up with any of the Master Inquisitor's sly accusations. "If you're implying that Embree's treason is somehow *my* fault, I—"

"Treason depends on your point of view," Kittal interrupted. "Hoseph, you murdered our guildmaster for acknowledging Mya as Grandmaster. Mya, of course, murdered the previous Grandmaster to usurp his position. Who is right and who is wrong is irrelevant!"

He shifted his gaze to Lakshmi. "As is pointing fingers and laying blame."

"Point taken." Lakshmi nodded contritely.

Hoseph glanced first at Lakshmi, then Kittal. *Well, well, well, the cat is declawed.*

It occurred to him that he had only ever seen Lakshmi in her own headquarters, among her own people, where she reigned supreme. *Maybe that's why she always arranges for meetings at her place, so she holds the upper hand.* He tucked this valuable insight away for future consideration.

"The formula is simple, each side has their own goals," the Alchemist explained. "We desire an imperial Grandmaster, whereas Mya wants the Grandmaster's position for herself. Barring Mya's ascension to the throne—an impossibility due to her low birth, among other things—these two goals are mutually exclusive. The key to winning this war is not in arguing over who is a traitor and who is not, but in foiling the other side. Mya has tipped the scales in her favor by recruiting Embree and rescuing two of our three hostages."

"But not the most important one," Lakshmi insisted. "I'll step up his training so that we can institute control sooner rather than later, but it'll still be *years*, at least."

Hoseph threw back his head in frustration, muttering a silent prayer at the ceiling. "We'll never be able to institute control with Mya around. As I've said from the beginning, we need to *kill* her!"

Lakshmi slid off her stool and spread her hands wide. "How, Hoseph? She's resisted every effort to kill her—yours *and* ours—and after today, I see how." She turned to the Master Alchemist, wide-eyed. "You should have *seen* her, Kittal. She punched through a solid oak door like it was parchment, shrugged off injuries instantly, flew down the stairs as if she had wings! I'd heard rumors about her abilities, but didn't truly believe them."

"Believe them," Hoseph warned. "I saw her fight the emperor's blademasters. She took wounds that should have killed her, yet her attacks never waned. She moves like lightning, and fights like..." *Like Lad did*, he realized.

Kittal turned to Hoseph. "There's certainly magic of some sort behind her abilities. Do you know its origin? Performance-enhancing potions, perhaps?"

"I don't know for certain, but for a time she wielded Saliez's human weapon. He was crafted by a master runemage. Mya may have sought to copy that enchantment somehow." A thought occurred to Hoseph as he mind ran unhindered by pain or fatigue for the first time in recent memory. "You obviously deal with magic to some degree, Kittal. Can you counteract rune magic?"

"Without knowing the precise spells employed, I would have no way of designing a specific counter-potion." His eyes flicked to the many bowls, vials, jars, and bottles lining the shelves. "But I doubt she's invulnerable."

"Perhaps if we captured her," Lakshmi mused, "we could study her, unravel her mysteries. If we could duplicate her abilities... The world's greatest army couldn't stand in the way of a host of superhuman assassins."

"Out of the question," Hoseph said. "Trying to capture Mya is too dangerous. We have to kill her and be done with it. But to kill her, we have to catch her unaware, which means finding where she sleeps. Lakshmi, how far have your people gotten with that constable in charge of investigating Lady T's murder?"

"Sergeant Benjamin?" The Master Inquisitor shrugged. "According to my sources, he's uncouth and unbribable. He lives alone and likes the ladies, but all his liaisons are aboveboard at reputable brothels. He has few real friends. He drinks, but not to excess. and knows the city like the back of his hand, both north and south of the river."

Hoseph waited a moment, but no more information was forthcoming. Irritated, he asked, "Where does he go? Who does he see? My source tells me that he's meeting with Mya's assistant on a regular basis."

Lakshmi's eyebrow cocked sharply. "How should I know? Inquisitors specialize in questioning people, reading between the lines, teasing information from presumably innocent conversations. We don't stalk the streets tracking constables. That's a job for Hunters."

"And if your theory about today's attacks is correct, then we no longer *have* Hunters."

"And whose fault is *that*?"

Kittal stepped between Hoseph and Lakshmi, his eyes narrowed behind his glasses. "Stop it! Arguing gets us nowhere."

"If you want my Inquisitors to—"

"Forget it!" Hoseph spat. *Blessed shadow of death, soothe me...* "I'll do it myself." He glanced at the brown bottle perched upon the shelf. With Kittal's potion to remedy his pain, there was no longer any barrier to Hoseph's travel through the Sphere of Shadow. Besides, he could identify Mya's assistant more easily than anyone. *I owe you, Dee...* "You do at least know where Sergeant Benjamin lives, don't you?"

"Yes. He has a flat above a brothel on the corner of Greenleaf and Southshore in the Dreggars Quarter."

"I'll find him and follow him, then. He'll lead me to Mya's assistant, and then I'll follow *him* to Mya. Done!"

"Very well." Kittal looked from one to the other. "If you can learn where Mya lives, then Lakshmi and I will work on a plan to bring her down."

"Frontal assaults don't work," Hoseph reminded him.

"Nooo..." Lakshmi tapped her lips with one long nail, "but a *trap* might. We have something Mya wants, and she won't stop until she gets it. We can lure her in."

"No!" Hoseph stabbed a finger at the Inquisitor. "You *won't* use the last Tessifus boy as bait. He's crucial to our plan."

"I *know* he's crucial, Hoseph!" Lakshmi regarded him with narrowed eyes. "Do you have a better idea?"

Despite his best efforts, Hoseph did not.

"A trap is worth a try." Kittal nodded absently. "We can minimize the risk. Rest assured, Hoseph, if Mya walks into a trap of *my* construction, she won't be walking out again."

Hoseph considered Kittal. Perhaps the pragmatic Alchemist was the one he should be dealing with, not the egomaniacal Inquisitor. "Fine. I'll find Mya. You two think up a plan to kill her." He flicked the silver skull into his hand. "Summon me if something important occurs."

Hoseph muttered the word of invocation and felt his corporeal body begin to fade. He swirled his cloaks dramatically, mist spreading wide around him. A tendril of darkness drifted over the shelf of bottles and vials. When it dissipated, the brown bottle containing the elixir was gone.

Arbuckle girded his impatience as the footman finally poured his blackbrew, his mouth watering in anticipation of that first euphoric sip. He snatched up the cup before the servant could stir in the cream and downed a careless gulp. *Bliss…*

"May all the Gods of Light bless whoever first discovered *blackbrew!*" He downed another swallow and put the cup down as a second footman placed his breakfast before him. He'd been working on far too few hours of sleep lately, but a peaceful and refreshing breakfast would set him to rights. The heavenly aroma of eggs, bacon, toasted bread, and pastries rumbled his stomach. *Even an emperor has to eat.* His fork was halfway to his mouth when a knock at his chamber door interrupted.

"Please continue, Majesty," Barris insisted. "The guards will see who it is."

Before the guards stationed there could even reach the door, a second knock sounded, harder and more insistent than the first. When the guard turned the latch, Captain Ithross burst through.

"Your Majesty." The captain bowed quickly. "Forgive the early intrusion, but we've received another…um…special delivery from your coronation acquaintance." His eyes flicked to the footmen waiting unobtrusively near the table.

"Really?" Arbuckle put down his fork. His faith in Miss Moirin had been proven yet again, despite Ithross' concerns. He rose and dropped his napkin onto his chair. "Take Us to them."

"Majesty!" Baris looked aghast at the untouched food. "Your *breakfast…*"

"Baris, We're sure there are enough eggs and bacon in the kitchens to make another breakfast after I deal with this…issue." Arbuckle downed the remainder of his cup of blackbrew and turned to Ithross. "Lead on!"

"Yes, Majesty." Ithross nodded and they stepped into the hallway, surrounded by imperial guards. "I've sent for Master Corvecosi, but still haven't informed…the other interested party."

"See to that, Captain. We assume the package is being examined in the same chamber as the previous one?"

"Yes, Majesty, and we kept it quiet."

"Good. On your way then. We're adequately escorted." He gestured to the grim guards.

"Very well." Ithross bowed and hurried off.

On his way through the palace, Arbuckle considered that he probably could have finished his breakfast before attending to the matter. His presence wasn't required at all, but he wanted to personally congratulate Miss Moirin on another stunning success. He'd been thinking about her a lot lately.

The guards stationed at the door to the receiving chamber snapped to attention as the emperor approached.

"Is Master Corvecosi in there?" he asked.

"Yes, Majesty." The sergeant in charge reached for the door latch.

Arbuckle held up a hand. "We don't want to disturb them. We're sure Captain Ithross would have mentioned if there was a problem. We'll see the others." He strode toward the second door. More bows, and the guards ushered him inside.

Arbuckle glanced around in surprise. Four imperial guards watched over only one person, Miss Moirin's assistant, Dee. "Where's Miss Moirin?"

"Your Majesty." The young man bowed stiffly. He wore common attire this time, simple trousers and shirt instead of the flamboyant garb of before. "Miss Moirin regrets that she's unable to come in person. Another matter required her attention."

Arbuckle smiled to cover his disappointment. "Master *Dee*, isn't it? We're very glad to see you well. We trust your mistress is likewise."

"She was when I last saw her, Majesty."

"When you last saw her?" Arbuckle didn't like the man's choice of words. "Meaning that she might not be well now?"

"May I," Dee glanced pointedly at the attending guards, "speak plainly, Majesty?"

"Please do. All here are privy to the mission that's been entrusted to Miss Moirin."

The young man's gaze hardened and his tone became accusative. "Miss Moirin takes terrible risks at *your* behest with little heed for her own safety. She thinks she can't back down from an imperial request!"

The guards stiffened at the perceived insult to their sovereign, but Arbuckle waved them down. "You think We've put her in danger by asking her to rescue these boys?"

"An imperial request is all but a command to a commoner, Majesty." Dee took a breath and let it out slowly. "But Miss Moirin makes her *own* decisions on which jobs she'll take on."

Dee hadn't answered the question, but his tone made his opinion on the matter clear. An awkward silence weighted the air while Arbuckle considered the younger man. Tall and good looking, with an air of quiet competence, Dee's gaze was unsettling.

Arbuckle finally broke the silence. "And yet the task seems to be progressing well."

"Well, we *have* recovered another of the Tessifus boys. Miss Moirin's gone to see if perhaps the third boy was also recovered by…some of our colleagues. I don't know how likely that is, but she was hopeful."

"As are We, Master Dee. With luck, We'll soon be thanking her personally."

"If she *survives*, Majesty."

Arbuckle saw it then, the emotion in Dee's eyes. The young man seemed to care more deeply for Miss Moirin than a purely professional relationship would warrant. His manner bespoke a subtle challenge, as if he regarded Arbuckle as…what? A meddler? An interloper? A rival?

Am I? Arbuckle caught himself, unsure of his own feelings. He *had* been thinking about Miss Moirin in a different light lately, impressed with her abilities and her poise, grateful to her for not only saving his life, but also for accepting responsibility for the Tessifus boys' rescue. But was it more than that? That was a question that bore consideration.

"Tell your mistress that We wish her every bit of luck the gods can send, Master Dee. We await her report." He turned and walked out without waiting for a reply.

Chapter XVI

Mya took a deep breath and nodded. "Bring them in."

Jolee opened the door and jerked a thumb. She still wore the bloody shirt from the raid, though her shoulder had been bandaged. The captured Alchemists and Inquisitors filed in, escorted by glowering Blades and Enforcers. There were too many people to fit in Clemson's office, so they were using one of the larger training rooms. The prisoners lined up in the center of the room. Most looked at the floor, the walls, anywhere but at Mya. Only a few glared defiantly.

Many sported injuries from the fights, but their wounds had been tended, and none bore signs of beating. Mya had forbidden any mistreatment. Instead, she had ordered that they be left alone, crowded into one room with ample opportunity to talk amongst themselves. Inquisitors were trained in torture and the manipulation of minds, and Mya knew they would dream up a much worse interrogation scenario than she had planned for them. In fact, she was counting on it.

I hope this works.

Mya strolled forward, stopped a few steps away from the line of prisoners, and crossed her arms. "You have no idea how lucky you are. In fact, you're the luckiest members of this guild, right now."

Eyes focused on her, surprise etched on their faces.

"Don't think so?" She counted off on her fingers. "You're out of the fight until the war's over. You're going to be fed and kept healthy. You won't be faced with the decision of whether or not to kill someone who was an associate only weeks ago. All you've got to do is consider one question: what kind of future do you want for the guild?"

The expressions on the prisoners' faces ranged from quizzical to confused to worried and, in at least one case, suspicious. They didn't understand, but she was about to explain.

"Do any of you even know why we're fighting each other?"

"You murdered the Grandmaster," said a grim-faced woman with the sly look of an Inquisitor.

"Actually, I didn't, though I *was* there when he died. The story your masters told you is that I came up from Twailin to kill the Grandmaster and usurp his position. That story is wrong. I arrived as a loyal assassin—a Master Hunter like Embree here—and ended up fighting for my life because I *disagreed* with the Grandmaster."

Mya began to pace slowly, never averting her gaze from the prisoners. "By now, you know that our former Grandmaster was the emperor. You all grew up under his rule. I imagine that many of you knew people who ended up in the Imperial Plaza, hung, whipped, or pilloried for no reason other than trying to survive. Maybe you joined the Guild to escape that, but he ran the guild exactly the same way! Even if you did a good job, achieved the goals he set for you, you might *still* end up in his dungeon. He'd flay the flesh your bones just because he *enjoyed* it."

A vision of Kiesha's bloody, mutilated body rose unbidden, and Mya had to force her mind back to the job at hand.

"His entire rule was about exerting control for the betterment of himself and his nobles. And the guild"—Mya stopped pacing and waved an inclusive hand—"*all* of us, were his means of doing that.

"That's the kind of guild that Lakshmi and Kittal are working to keep, but they're not the real problem here. The problem is *Hoseph*. He had power under the previous Grandmaster, and he'll do anything to get that power back. He wants the guild to remain a tool of the nobility. He doesn't care about the guild itself, because *he's not guild*!"

A few of the prisoners shifted nervously.

"I want a guild run *by* assassins, for the *benefit* of assassins. I want do away with the unnecessary violence, expand our operations, and do things we haven't done before."

"You want an Assassins Guild that doesn't *assassinate* anyone?" The disgruntled Inquisitor sneered in derision.

Mya raised an amused eyebrow. "Did I say we wouldn't assassinate anyone? I don't *remember* saying that. If we never killed anyone, we wouldn't be much of an Assassins Guild, would we?"

Blades, Enforcers, and Hunters, as well as a few of the prisoners, chuckled at the furious Inquisitor's expense.

Mya looked straight into the woman's eyes. "Do you know what percentage of guild income is generated from assassination?"

The woman shook her head with a frown.

"About ten percent. You're an Inquisitor. You deal in information, not death. We run dozens of different kinds of operations that have nothing to do with killing. We've even started hiring out Enforcers and Blades to protect rich nobles. They *pay* us to put spies in their homes! Beating up poor shopkeepers for a few crowns a month only makes people hate us." Lad had taught her that. *Damn him anyway.* She fingered the ring. *He's the reason I'm in this mess.* "Yes, we'll take contracts, but there are so many other ways to fill our coffers. We've done it in Twailin. We can do it here in Tsing and elsewhere."

"And you want to do away with torture?" goaded the annoying Inquisitor. "You won't let us practice our art?"

Mya narrowed her eyes. "Having been on the receiving end of it, I *abhor* torture. It's also ineffective. It gives false information and breeds ill will."

The woman snorted a laugh. "An assassin squeamish about torture?"

In two strides, Mya stood in the woman's face. The surrounding prisoners stepped back, but the Inquisitor held her ground. Mya pulled one of her daggers from its sheath, regretting that she had to make an example of someone.

"*Squeamish* isn't a word that's *ever* been used to describe me." She raised a hand between their faces and drew the razor-edged steel across her palm. *No pain...* The wound bled, but healed instantly right before the woman's eyes. "Don't mistake my dislike of violence for weakness." She wiped the blood on the woman's cheek and turned away.

"You've probably heard rumors about my...abilities." Mya turned back and showed them all her unmarked palm. "As I said, I'm *very* hard to kill. Hoseph burned the blood contracts because he thought it would help him kill me. How many assassins' lives has he spent trying to kill me? How many more will die trying? That's one more reason to end this guild war as quickly as we can."

She started pacing again.

"So, you each have a decision to make. Help me end this war, or don't." She paused. "It *will* end. I *will* see this guild whole again. I don't want to kill Lakshmi or Kittal; I want them to come over to my side, just as Embree did." She waved a hand at the Master Hunter.

Embree nodded solemnly in acknowledgement.

"Some of you," she flashed a glance at the belligerent Inquisitor, "don't seem to share my philosophy. That's fine. I'll keep you confined until this matter is settled, then you're free to go. There's nothing to prevent you from leaving, and I don't want anyone in my guild who isn't dedicated and loyal."

"But...we tried to *kill* you," said one Alchemist, clearly mystified.

"You were following orders. I don't kill people for following orders." Mya regarded them again, pleased to see a few more introspective looks. "I'm going to ask some questions. I'd like your cooperation. If you refuse, you won't be harmed, but when this war's over, you also will no longer be part of the guild."

Shock registered on many faces. Mya didn't want to lose good assassins, but she didn't have any other way to pressure them.

A wide-eyed young Alchemist spoke up. "What about everyone still working for Kittal and Lakshmi? You going to kick them out of the guild, too?"

"This isn't about them, it's about you. Right here, right now." Mya raked them all with a cold stare. "I won't kill you and I won't torture you, but if you don't help me, you're out of the guild. Anyone who wants out, go now." She pointed to the door.

"Crazy bitch," the belligerent Inquisitor muttered, starting for the door.

The rest looked at one another dubiously. One shook his head and followed the Inquisitor, then another. The rest didn't move. The Inquisitor glared back at the group and opened her mouth to say something, but Mya wouldn't let her intimidate any others.

"Jolee, get them out of here. Put them in a separate cell."

"Yes, Grandmaster." The Enforcer herded the three malcontents out.

"The rest of you, give me everything you can." Mya gave them her most beseeching look. "The key to Hoseph's plan for regaining his power is control of the emperor, which is why he had the sons of Duke Tessifus kidnapped. Kill the present emperor, put Tessifus on the throne, and control him from the sidelines by threatening his children. Now, we've already taken back two of the kids. The last boy is the linchpin. Without the boy, there *is* no plan. No plan, no guild war. So, who can tell me where he's being kept?"

Silence and blank stares were all that met her request. *Come on,* she pleaded silently. Frankly, if this appeal didn't work, she wasn't sure where to go next.

"Only Lakshmi know where he's being kept," volunteered a young man.

Yes! Mya rejoiced.

"A few others do," another piped in. "Lakshmi sequestered him someplace and assigned a squad to attend him. Every few days, one of them shows up to replenish their supplies of food and drugs."

Mya nodded, remembering the groggy Wexford and his brother. "Opium."

"No," said a small woman with the stained fingers of an Alchemist. "I made up the opium doses, but only for two boys, the larger ones. The dose depends on the person's size, you know."

"So the youngest boy *wasn't* being drugged?" Perhaps he was small enough to manhandle and didn't need sedating.

"Oh, he was," the Alchemist insisted, "but with something special. I don't know what it was. Kittal prepared those doses himself."

"Special?" That was strange. What plans did they have for the youngest Tessifus boy other than to use him as a hostage to pressure the duke? "Does anyone know why he's being treated differently from his brothers?"

They all shook their heads.

The helpful Inquisitor offered, "Lakshmi holds her cards close, only tells us what we need to know to do our jobs."

Well, I got some information, but not enough. Mya bridled her frustration and decided to try another tack. "What about Hoseph? Does anyone know where he stays, any of his habits or weaknesses? Are there any patterns to his movements?" She recalled Dee's theory that Hoseph could only travel magically to locations he'd already been. "When your masters moved headquarters, he probably arrived on foot the first time. Did anyone notice what direction he came from?"

The prisoners looked at one another. One man shrugged. "He comes and goes on foot *most* of the time that I've noticed, but not from any particular direction."

"He does?" That was strange. Why would Hoseph walk the city streets with the entire constabulary looking for him when he could travel effortlessly and anonymously with magic? *Unless it's not effortless.* She'd have to keep that in mind.

"Have any of you seen him use magic to travel recently?"

"Yes." The speaker was one of the Inquisitors from Lakshmi's office. "Just before you broke through Master Lakshmi's door. She rang a little chime, and he popped in. That's why Lakshmi summoned him, to use his magic to get her out of there."

A few others nodded.

"All right. That's valuable information." She'd wondered how Lakshmi, and Lady T before her, had contacted Hoseph. "So why doesn't he pop in like that all the time?"

Blank stares and shrugs were all she got.

"All right…" Mya hadn't really expected any of them to know much about Hoseph. "Anything else you can tell me about the Tessifus boy or Hoseph?"

They all shook their heads.

"You'll be held here under guard until this is over, but you'll be treated well. If anyone has information for me, just tell one of the masters. Any information could help, so they'll be asking questions about hideouts and movements."

Mya stood there until the prisoners had all been herded out and only the masters remained. Her shoulders slumped as fatigue settled on her like a leaden blanket. She rubbed her eyes, trying to think past the desire for a soft bed and a warm pillow. It had been a very long day.

"That went remarkably well, Grandmaster," Clemson said.

"Did it?" She looked from face to face. "I suppose it could have been worse."

"It could have been a *lot* worse," Embree added. "Did you mean all that about changing the guild?"

"Every word." She sighed, trying to think of anything she might have forgotten. "Question them each separately about the whereabouts of any of Lakshmi or Kittal's hideouts. I doubt we'll get anything useful, but send people out to keep an eye on any likely places. I'll have Dee come by tomorrow to pick up the addresses so I can have some of my urchins keep watch, too. Oh, and those new sketches of Hoseph. Have the artist make as many as she can. I want to get some to the constabulary." It was no wonder they couldn't find him the way he'd changed his looks.

"Where *is* Dee?" asked Clemson, exchanging a glance with Noncey. "I expected to see him here with you."

"He took the boy to the palace." Mya sighed again. *Does everyone know about me and Dee?* "If you learn anything new, give it to him in the morning. Get some rest and start hunting."

"Yes, Grandmaster."

Mya set off for home. She needed a bath and food right now more than she needed Hoseph's head on a platter.

"Tennison." Arbuckle leaned back in his chair and rubbed his eyes. He'd been reading the same passage for an hour and making no progress. His mind kept straying. "I need...*We* need to ask you something."

"Yes, Majesty?" The secretary looked up from the parchment he was scribbling on. His eyes were red, his hair disheveled, and he had a small soup stain on his doublet. Long hours of work on the New Accords, day after day, were taking their toll on the poor man.

Arbuckle felt responsible for Tennison's misery, but there was nothing to be done about it. "We...are considering elevating someone of common birth to noble status. We know the *procedure*, but there are bound to be repercussions. How do you think the nobility would react?"

"Majesty?" Tennison looked confused at the non sequitur question. "Is this to be part of the Accords?"

"No, no, it's just a question." At Tennison's puzzled look, he waved dismissively at the chaos of papers and books littering the table. "Sit back and take a break. We're both tired. We insist. Consider this a...thought exercise."

Tennison put down his pen and looked thoughtful. "It would depend on many factors, Majesty. People of financial means purchase titles as a matter of elevating themselves with little repercussion, though, from what I understand, some of inherited nobility have a dim view those with purchased titles. That prejudice, however, doesn't affect the benefits of being entitled."

"What about bestowing a title to a commoner for...a particular service performed for the empire."

"Squires are bestowed knighthood for services on the field of battle, valor, or merely tenure of loyalty, so there's certainly a precedent. It was rare during your father's reign, however."

"We don't doubt *that*." His father had reviled the common folk. "What about someone of low birth with no connection to the crown or the military. Someone...like a servant, who performed a valued service to the empire."

Tennison's eyebrows arched. "What type of service do you mean, Majesty?"

"Something monumental. Something...heroic, that ensures the security of the very throne."

"A commoner who..." His eyes widened. "Do you mean...Miss Moirin?"

"Yes, We mean Miss Moirin." Arbuckle chuckled at his futile attempt to be vague. He could never fool Tennison. "She *did* save my life, and she's rescued two of Duke Tessifus' sons so far."

"You rewarded her with a very fine necklace for saving your life, Majesty," Tennison reminded him.

"Yes, but We think she may deserve more."

"I doubt the nobles will appreciate it. Perhaps if it was a minor title..."

"Yes, a minor title. We would like to show her our appreciation. And perhaps invite her to dine occasionally." *Or more than occasionally...*

Tennison paled, but nodded. "I...see, Majesty. I would suggest caution. Jealousy is a very sharp sword."

"Yes..." Arbuckle looked back to his work, invigorated by the thought of Miss Moirin—*Lady Moirin*—attending a private dinner, perhaps in the garden. "Yes, We will have to be careful."

For the first time since learning that his responsibility to the empire included providing an heir to the throne, the thought of choosing a woman to join him in that task sent a thrill of anticipation through Arbuckle.

Chapter XVII

Dee stepped into the tidy little pub and doffed his broad-brimmed hat. This was a workman's pub, as were most of Sergeant Benjamin's haunts. Hitching his suspenders, he shoved his hands into his pockets and sauntered toward the back. Though he had put together several simple disguises to help him fit in, his lack of callouses would be a dead giveaway. He scanned the afternoon crowd for the sergeant's unshaven face.

Benj sat at a back-corner table. A buxom woman in a tight corset leaned provocatively over him, one finger playing with the laces of his shirt. The sergeant spotted Dee and waved him over, then said something to the woman and slipped her a coin. With a pout, she tucked the coin into her impressive cleavage and turned away, squealing with mock indignation as Benj swatted her backside. Catching sight of Dee as he passed her, she stepped into his path.

"Well, *hello* there, handsome." The trollop eyed Dee from head to toe and smiled seductively. "Lookin' for company?"

"Not tonight, love." He nodded politely and stepped around her. "My wife's the jealous sort."

"Wives usually are," she said with a wink before continuing toward the bar, "but I won't tell her."

Dee sat down at the table. He would prefer having his back to the wall, but the sergeant had already claimed that seat. He wasn't really worried; if Benj saw anything suspicious, he'd warn Dee.

How strange it seemed to trust a constable to watch his back, but he and Benj had developed a rapport over the course of their regular meetings. The sergeant was crude and blunt, but his mind was as sharp as the sword at his hip. Unfortunately, they never had much information to exchange—the caps had no leads on Hoseph, and Dee wasn't about to divulge Mya's affairs, since the constabulary wasn't privy to the hunt for the Tessifus boys. Tonight, though, Dee had something he could share.

Benj gestured to the barman. "I need another drink. Talkin' to priests gives me a hangover without the pleasure of first gettin' drunk."

Dee sat up straight. "Priests?"

"Don't get excited. It wasn't…him. Word came down from on high that we should question the priests at the temple of Demia again."

A barmaid delivered two tankards of ale. Dee held out a coin without looking at her and waited until she'd hurried away to ask, "About what?"

"Just rattlin' their cages." Benj reduced the volume of his tankard by half. "The emperor asked for help from their high muckety muck and apparently got told to stuff it up his arse. I guess the high priest didn't know that you never piss on a noble's shoes. All it gets you is pain, and I'm the needle."

"They deny knowing anything about Hoseph?" Dee sipped his ale. Not bad. He would have preferred wine, but workmen drank ale.

"Yeah. I ask, and they claim ignorance. They're probably tellin' the truth, but you don't get any fruit without shakin' the tree."

"Speaking of fruit…" Dee produced a roll of fine parchment from his tool satchel and handed it over. "One of our people spotted *him* in Midtown. He's changed his appearance."

"Really?" Benj unrolled the sheaf of paper and looked at the top page. The sketch of Hoseph stared up from the parchment. "Don't look much like a priest anymore, does he?"

"More like a vagabond."

"This might help, but he could be stayin' in any one of a thousand inns or flop-houses. The way he pops around, nobody would see him come or go. I'll spread these around." He downed his ale and wiped his sleeve across his mouth. "Anything else?"

"Nothing."

"Don't suppose Miss Moirin had anything to do with an explosion that took out a glassblower's shop on Flatiron Street?" Benj raked dirty nails over his stubbled chin, the sound like coarse sand under a boot.

"An *explosion*?" Dee snorted in distaste. "Not her style."

217

"No, I suppose it's not. It was strange, though. Six dead, but no injured, like someone cleaned up the scene before we got there." Benj pointed to Dee's nearly full tankard. "You gonna drink that?"

"Um…no." He pushed the tankard across the table. "Doesn't sound like Hoseph's style either. Explosions aren't very subtle."

"No, they're not. Thought I'd ask."

"It's like looking for a twig in a forest," Dee confessed. It was the truth.

"I'll keep askin' around." Benj patted the rolled parchment. "Thanks for these."

"I hope they help. Where do you want to meet next?"

"There's a place halfway up the hill on Greenbriar called the One-Eyed Tom. Day after tomorrow?"

Dee nodded and got up to leave.

"Sure you don't want some company, love?" The trollop at the bar downed a cup and gave Dee a lascivious grin. "A knee trembler in the alley. Yer wife'll never know."

"Oh, she'll know." Dee smiled and walked past. "She always knows."

"Suit yerself then."

Dee donned his hat and left the pub, glancing up and down the street and longing for the day when they wouldn't have to be so paranoid. It was growing dark already, and foot traffic was sparse. No one gave him a second look. Nonetheless, he chose a random, circuitous route as he headed for home. There was no such thing as being too careful.

Hoseph waited patiently on the rooftop across from the pub Sergeant Benjamin had entered. He breathed in the cool evening air, and released it in a sigh of satisfaction. His untold hours flicking around the city following the disgusting constable, enduring the pain, nausea, and fatigue of using the talisman, had finally paid off. Only minutes ago, he'd recognized the distinctive soul of Mya's assistant, Dee, as he entered the pub. Where a guild of assassins had failed, Hoseph was about to succeed. All he had to do was follow Dee to

Mya.

And there he is.

Dee emerged from the pub, pulled his broad-brimmed hat low, and glanced left and right, but not up. Apparently satisfied, the assassin started down the street, turning left at the next corner.

Smiling, Hoseph clutched his talisman, checked to make sure the pilfered bottle of Kittal's elixir still resided in his pocket, and pictured his destination. With a word, he faded away and appeared on the distant rooftop. He staggered with the usual wave of pain and dizziness, but Hoseph didn't fear the pain anymore; it wouldn't last long.

Crouching to conceal himself from anyone passing by or looking out a nearby window, he reached a trembling hand into the pocket, uncapped the bottle, and placed a drop of elixir onto his tongue. Relief washed over him. The pain ebbed, dizziness vanished, and his limbs stopped trembling, but...a twinge lingered behind his eyes, a dull, persistent ache. He'd been traversing the Sphere of Shadow frequently of late, and the cumulative effect must have overwhelmed the elixir's curative capacity. Well, he needn't be so frugal, there was plenty in the bottle, and, despite the Alchemist's warning, he was feeling no ill effects from multiple doses. Hoseph placed another drop of elixir on his tongue, and the last hint of pain vanished.

Tucking the bottle away, Hoseph peered over the edge of the roof and watched Dee stroll down the street, surreptitiously checking over his shoulder at every turn. No doubt he would lead Hoseph on a merry chase, but there was no way he could evade the priest. He could disguise himself as he liked, but he couldn't disguise his soul. Eventually, Dee would lead the priest to his quarry.

I'm coming for you, Mya.

The sound of shattering glass brought Mya bounding up out of bed like a startled cat. The room resolved around her into a slow-motion nightmare, shards of glass glittering like shooting stars, sprinkling her hair and embedding in her wrappings. A metallic sphere trailed smoke across the room from the shattered window.

Her sleep-addled mind screamed, *Catch it!* She flung out a hand and watched the sphere pass just beyond her fingertips to rebound off the wall. When her feet touched the floor, she grabbed the frame of the bed and heaved.

"Wha—?"

Dee's shout of alarm was cut short as Mya jerked the bed out from under him and flung it onto the smoking sphere. Snatching Dee up like a ragdoll, she pulled him into a hard embrace and turned her back to the bed.

The explosion slammed them against the wall. Shards of metal and splinters pierced her back, and goose-down bedding filled the air like snow. Mya's ears rang, and she couldn't see for the feathers. She blinked and shook her head.

"What the hell?" Dee looked around with dazed eyes. The mattress had a huge scorched hole in it and the room was a shambles, the walls riddled with gouges. At least there was no fire.

"They've found us!" Mya cast about the room and found her daggers beside the splintered nightstand. Broken glass crunched under her bare feet as she recovered them. "Arm yourself!"

Dee gaped at her for a moment before reaching for his pants. "We have to get out! There'll be—"

Glass shattered in the front room.

"Down!" Mya dragged Dee to the floor and covered him. The concussion of the second explosion was muffled, but the thin walls didn't stop the shrapnel.

Dee shoved her off. "How did they find us?"

"Doesn't matter how!" Mya vaulted up and dragged Dee to his feet. While he frantically pulled on pants and a shirt, she crept across the room, ignoring the bloody footprints she left on the floor. She didn't have time to worry about a few cuts. Mya leaned out the bedroom door to check the hall. Dee pushed his feet into his boots, slung on his long coat, and crept up behind her. The click of his crossbows comforted her; he had her back covered.

Other than a few startled shouts from the apartment upstairs, everything was quiet...too quiet. "Watch the window. I'll check the front. They're waiting for us to move."

"Right." Dee turned to face the bedroom window.

As Mya stepped cautiously into the shattered front room—*The landlord's going to be livid*—ominous noises sounded from the bedroom.

Crack! Crack! Crack! Crack!

Dee cursed, then she heard a cry and a thud.

Mya started to go back and help when the front door burst open in a shower of splinters. Several figures moved in the shadows on the landing outside. She heard Dee curse again, reconsidered—*He's alive. Got to trust him*—and stepped into the front room.

A man leaned through the front door and hurled a disturbingly familiar glass cylinder at her. He gaped in surprise when she caught the missile and flung it right back at him, but ducked out of the way. The cylinder tumbled over his head onto the landing. Shouted curses and the pounding of feet fleeing down the stairs were drowned out by the explosion. Flames blasted through the doorway, flinging the assassin into the apartment.

Her back to the wall, Mya readied a dagger for throwing, but the assassin lay sprawled on the floor, unmoving, his cloak and hair burning. *Damn!* She took a step forward. He moaned, struggling weakly. *At least he's alive.*

Unfortunately, the stairwell was fully involved in flames. They had to find another way out, but to leave him to burn to death wouldn't do.

Mya jerked the cloth off their table and smothered his smoldering clothing. He moaned again. *Good enough... Someone will get him out.* She backed up to the bedroom door. Dee stood there with both crossbows aimed at the window. Another assassin lay half in, half out of the window, one of Dee's darts in her neck.

"Dead or drugged?" she asked.

"Drugged." Dee pointed at the ceiling above the window, riddled with crossbow bolts. "They shoot every time I get near the window, so going that way is probably not smart."

She pulled him toward the bathroom. "The bath is the—"

The small bathroom window shattered. Mya threw a dagger as Dee whirled and fired. With a scream, the darkly clad assassin tumbled backward out the window, his face contorted in pain and horror.

That face! I know him! He was one of Kittal's senior journeymen. They were sending in the guild's best to take her down. She heard a crash from the alley below.

Four long strides took Mya to the window, and she glanced out quickly, wary of crossbowmen waiting below. She caught a glimpse of movement, but nobody shot her. The alley was barely ten feet wide, the opposite wall sturdy brick.

Easy as pie... "We'll go out this way. Wait for my whistle, then follow."

"Mya, you can't be *serious!*"

"Got a better idea?" She jerked a thumb at the burning staircase.

Dee's face contorted. "Don't die, please."

"That's the goal." Mya stepped back for a running start.

Dashing forward, she dove through the window and tucked, meeting the brick wall across the alleyway feet first. Bending her knees, she launched off on a new trajectory. Crossbows cracked from below. Two bolts whizzed past, ricocheting off the wall, and she batted aside a third. When Mya landed, the assassins were already running away. She let them go. Listening hard and peering into the darkness, she scanned the alley and the rooftops for more snipers. The man who had fallen lay in a pile of refuse bins, unconscious, but still breathing. Putting her back to the wall to make sure Hoseph didn't pop in behind her, Mya whistled.

Dee crawled through the window, lowered himself until he hung from the sill, then dropped the rest of the distance to the cobbles. Drawing his crossbows, he whispered, "Where to? There's going to be a dozen constables here in two minutes, and you're not dressed for an interview."

"We'll be gone in thirty seconds." She retrieved her dagger from the fallen man and started away, then stopped. *Kittal's senior journeyman...* "Wait."

"What?"

"This is one of Kittal's senior people. He was there when I met Kittal that first time."

"So?" Dee's voice hummed with impatience.

"So, he may know something important." Mya bent down and hoisted the assassin up onto her shoulder. "I want to ask him some questions."

"You're kidding me."

"Nope. We'll take him to Clemson's. Where can I hunker while you grab a carriage?"

"Fine." Dee pointed down the alley. "This way. There's a bakery around the corner. It should be empty at this time of night. We can slip in the back."

"Perfect." Mya shoved him forward with a grin. "I'm starving."

Mya paced before the bound prisoner, flexing her hands open and closed, straining to keep them from around the Alchemist's neck. After an hour of Dee digging bits of metal, glass, and wood out of her back and feet, and Clemson's people treating the prisoner's injuries, the anesthetic drug from Dee's bolt had worn off, and she had started asking questions. The next hour had been an exercise in frustration.

Salish was his name, but she'd gotten that from Noncey. From Salish, she'd gotten nothing, not a word, not a single syllable. She'd pled her case as with the other prisoners, but this time it had yielded nothing but sullen silence. He just stared at her, his mouth firmly closed.

One more try…

"Do you *like* the idea of working for a power-mad priest, Salish?"

Nothing.

"Wouldn't you rather work for a real assassin?"

No response.

She didn't understand.

"Fine! Jolee, keep our guest company." She leaned down until their faces were nearly touching, and poked Salish in the chest with a rigid finger. "I'm not through with you."

She swept out the door, Dee and the masters on her heels all the way down the hallway to Clemson's office. She sighed and started to pace the floor.

"I don't get it?" Mya vented. "It worked on the others. Granted, I didn't get much of use, but at least they cooperated. It's like he

223

wants the guild war to continue!"

"Salish is one of Kittal's highest ranking aides." Clemson plopped into the chair behind her desk. "He has more to lose than the others if Hoseph's side wins and he's called out for treason. Even if *you* win, and Kittal comes over to your side, he'll never trust Salish again if he thinks that he betrayed him."

Noncey cleared his throat. "Are you *sure* you don't want me to send in a couple Blades to rough him up? You could come in later and play the good guy, chew me out for letting it happen."

"No." The memory of the emperor's torture chamber turned her stomach. "No. It'll make me no better than our last Grandmaster. If word gets out that I'm abusing prisoners, assassins will flee the guild in droves. But the longer this war drags on, the worse it is for everyone. We've had no better chance than this." She started pacing again. "Salish knows something. I can see it in his eyes! I need what's in his *head*!"

"Too bad we can't just peek inside and see what he's thinking," Dee muttered.

Mya whirled on her assistant. "That's it! Dee, you're *brilliant*!"

"I am?" He smiled uncertainly.

"What is it?" Clemson asked.

The other two masters looked just as bewildered.

"Look into his head! With *magic*!" Mya snapped her fingers in triumph.

"But we don't have a wizard who can—"

"Yes, we do! At least, we can borrow one." Mya grinned in satisfaction. "Keyfur!"

"Oh, no." Clemson stood. "Grandmaster, you can't take a senior member of the guild into the palace to be questioned under magical compulsion! They could discover—"

"They won't discover anything I don't want them to. I'll insist that I conduct the questioning personally. I'm the one who knows what to ask, after all!" Pieces of her plan began clicking into place. "I need a carriage and some clothes for me and Dee. Nicer ones than these."

"It's two in the *morning*, Mya." Dee looked horrified. "You're talking about waking up the emperor!"

"No. All we need is his wizard."

The masters all stared at her.

"Um…clothing, carriage, escort… Now would be good."

"I'll get some clothes." Clemson hurried out.

Embree strode out the door right behind her. "I'll get a carriage and driver."

Noncey frowned and shook his head. "I wish you luck. You've got bigger balls than me."

"You have no idea," Dee muttered

Salish rode on the floor of the carriage between Mya and Dee's feet, bound, gagged, and hooded. His eyes had flashed alarm as they prepared him for the trip, but he hadn't uttered a word. Dee looked out the window at the dark buildings as the carriage rumbled up the hill toward the palace, as silent as their prisoner. Mya tried to shut out the voice in the back of her mind screaming, *Are you crazy?*

"Miss Moirin to see Master Keyfur," she told the imperial guard who stopped them at the first gate. He sent a runner off before assigning a squad of guards to escort the carriage inside.

A sleepy but excited Captain Ithross met them by the small side door where they'd been admitted before, wearing his sword and imperial tabard over nightclothes.

"The third Tessifus boy?" he asked, glancing at the figure on the floor of the carriage as Mya stepped out.

"No, but hopefully someone who can tell me where he is. I have to see Master Keyfur right away."

The captain's smile dropped, and his thick eyebrows shot up. "You *have* to?"

Mya sighed. Ithross had always regarded her with suspicion; she'd overheard his protests to the emperor against the access she'd been granted. *I don't have time for this*, she thought as she donned her sweetest smile.

"Captain, I understand that it's late, but this man," she hooked a thumb at Salish, "might be able to tell me where the boy is. If I don't learn it soon, they may move him. I *know* Master Keyfur can help me. It shouldn't take long. You can be present while I question him, if you like."

The captain's stubborn expression wavered.

"And there's no need to disturb the emperor," she assured him. "He promised any help he could provide, but I don't want to take advantage of his generosity by intruding on his rest...if I don't have to."

The subtle threat seemed to make up the captain's mind. "Lieutenant, take them to the west waiting room. I'll get Master Keyfur."

Keyfur appeared with the captain at his side not too long after they got Salish settled. Though a bit disheveled at being woken, the wizard still dressed in a rainbow of flowing robes, the characteristic long feather bouncing on its perch behind his ear.

"Miss Moirin!" His weary countenance brightened, then sobered when he saw the bound and hooded man in the chair. "What can I do for you?"

"Master Keyfur, thank you for seeing us. This is my assistant, Dee, and this," she indicated Salish, "is someone who may know the location of our person of interest. I'd like to find that out, but he's not cooperating. When you...um...cast that spell to see if my vow to the emperor was truthful, you mentioned—"

"Compelling someone to speak the truth." Keyfur twisted his mouth in indecision, then nodded. "It's not something I do often—it's rather intrusive, you know—but under the circumstances, I think it's apt."

"Thank you!" Mya avoided the anxious look in Dee's eyes. She'd purposefully neglected to tell him that she'd been ensorcelled during her previous visit.

As the mage plucked the feather from behind his ear, Mya stepped back, tugging Dee with her. She had no idea how the magic worked, but she didn't want to get caught up in it. Ithross was suspicious enough of her. If she was compelled to answer *his* questions...well, she'd already seen enough of the palace dungeons to last her a lifetime.

Keyfur flourished the feather. Waving it in a slow circle around the prisoner's hooded head, he muttered a few airy words. Multihued motes of light—matching the rainbow of the wizard's robes—trailed the feather. Finally, the wizard stepped back, his shimmering feather fading. "The spell is cast. Ask away."

Mya approached Salish, wishing she could see his eyes through the hood, but reluctant to reveal his face to the imperial guards. She'd been racking her brains trying to figure out what questions she could ask the Alchemist without giving away the guild. All she really needed were a few pertinent details. She reached under the hood and loosened his gag.

"Do you know where the kidnapped Tessifus boy is being held?"

"Y…y…yes." The word sounded torn from Salish's mouth through clenched teeth, but was clear and audible.

"Where?"

"Someplace secret."

Gods damn it! "Someplace secret" was a perfectly truthful answer. This wasn't going to be as easy as she'd thought.

"Where *precisely* is the boy is being kept?"

"B…b…beneath a brick factory on Dunworthy Street in Midtown, in…in a cellar that used to be a smuggler's stash."

Mya's heart raced. "Okay. How can I access this cellar?"

Salish's voice lost its resistance as he realized he had no choice but to answer. "Through the factory, or through a tunnel from the river."

"Are there guards?"

"Yes."

"Are there guards with the boy?" she asked more specifically.

"Yes."

"Are there guards in the factory?"

"Yes."

"Are there guards in the river tunnel?"

"No."

"Why not?"

"It's been abandoned for years. Some rocks fell in. It's nearly impassable."

Nearly… Mya winked at Dee. This was useful. "Where on the river is the tunnel's mouth?"

"In Midtown."

Mya sighed. "Where *precisely* in Midtown?"

"I don't know."

"All right! I can work with this." Mya secured his gag and turned to the wizard. "Thank you Master Keyfur, Captain."

Ithross stepped forward. "I'll take custody of the—"

"No!" Mya cringed at the authoritative tone of her voice. "No, Captain, you can't do that."

"I most certainly can!" Ithross snapped his fingers, and imperial guards closed in around them.

Dee reached beneath his jacket.

"Let me rephrase that, Captain." Mya put a restraining hand on Dee's arm. "I can't allow you to take custody of this prisoner. I may need this man in the future, and I can't waste time coming to visit him in the palace dungeons. I also have to ask you to refrain from doing *anything* with the information you heard him give me." Mya had horrific visions of Ithross mobilizing the constabulary and storming the brick factory. "The emperor entrusted *me* with this mission. So far I have been successful. Two boys returned *alive*. I have my own team and my own methods. We'll take care of this."

The captain narrowed his eyes, but finally nodded. "Very well, Miss Moirin, but I'll be telling the emperor every word you've told me in the morning.'"

"I'd expect no less."

"The spell will fade if he's taken from my presence," Keyfur warned. "You won't be able to ask any more questions of him and be assured of a truthful answer."

"That's all right. I've got everything I need for now. Thank you, Master Keyfur. We've got to go. We'll be in touch as soon as we've recovered the boy." Waving Dee over to Salish, they each grabbed one of the man's arms and shuffled him toward the door. "Thank you again, Master Keyfur! You're indispensable!"

"My pleasure!" The mage waved his feather at her and grinned.

Not until the carriage exited the outer palace gates and started downhill did Mya finally breathe a sigh of relief. "That was close." She felt more assured of success than she had in weeks. "And we're close, Dee. Close to the end of this guild war."

"I hope so." He leaned back and rubbed his weary face. "I can't take much more of this."

Chapter XVIII

"Dear Gods of Light!" Dee gazed in disgust at the filthy water lapping against the quay wall. "I can't believe you expect us to wade in that!"

The river flowed dark and sluggish through the heart of Tsing. In the silence of the night, the waterway might have been the black River Oblivion sweeping damned souls down into the Nine Hells.

"Afraid of the water, Dee?" Mya asked as they strode along Riverway Avenue.

A sudden roil of motion caught Dee's eye as something large— probably one of the giant catfish rumored to ply the dark waters— molested a bloated carcass floating by. A vital tributary for commerce, the river was also a reeking repository for the waste of a quarter million people.

He shuddered. "No, I'm afraid of what's *in* the water."

They walked on, the silence invaded only by their soft footsteps and the creak and groan of barges tied to the stone riverwall. Unlike the Wharf District, the Midtown waterfront was relatively quiet at night. A pool of darkness loomed just ahead, three consecutive unlit streetlamps courtesy of a lamplighter willing to shirk his duty for a few coins.

"You *sure* we can't go in through the brick factory?" Dee asked again.

"I'm sure." Mya sounded amused. "Noncey and Clemson's people attack the brick factory as a diversion while we sneak in through the tunnel. We'll be out with the kid before they even know we're there."

"But—"

"Trust me, Dee; it's the best way in." Mya grabbed his arm. "Ready?"

"No."

"Too bad." After a glance up and down the avenue to check for witnesses, Mya steered them hard to the left, and they stepped off the quay wall.

Dee's stomach lurched, but it was only a short drop to the top of the waiting barge. They hunkered down with the several other figures already concealed there, invisible in the shadows.

"Welcome to your floating staging area, Grandmaster."

Dee could barely see the speaker, but recognized the woman's voice. Damn, but it was nice to have Embree's Hunters on their side. With some discreet inquiries and a lot of leg-work, they had located an old woman with knowledge of the smugglers' tunnel leading to the brick factory. She'd been a smuggler herself until she was caught and lost a hand as punishment. She was more than willing to tell them all she knew for a pint of ale and a few crowns.

"Good work, Taelish." Mya released Dee's arm. "Did you have any trouble getting set up?"

"No. We rented a barge and bribed our way to this mooring." She pointed to the riverwall.

Squinting as his eyes adjusted to the darkness, Dee could just make out a low arch of stonework in the face of the quay wall, one of the many sewer outlets that flushed the city's waste into the river. The tunnel's top was barely two feet above the surface of the water.

Dee cringed at the thought of getting into that dark water. "So much for my best pair of boots…"

Mya ignored him. "What about reconnaissance?"

"I've been in," Taelish said. "You'll have to duck a little, Dee. There's a ledge inside so you can wade. It shallows quickly, but it's wet all the way to the blockage. We didn't touch that, but you can feel air flow, so you should be able to move a few rocks to wiggle through."

"Great work, Taelish. Jondy, Folk, you ready?"

"Yes, Grandmaster." The two Blades assigned to accompany them shuffled to the ladder rigged over the side of the barge.

Mya pulled out a pocket watch and looked at the face. "We've only got an hour until the diversion starts, so let's move."

Reluctantly, Dee shed his long coat, rolled it carefully around his crossbows, and tied it high on his shoulders to keep it the weapons and bolts dry.

Mya turned to Taelish. "Keep watch. We'll come back this way unless something changes or an exit out of the brick factory looks better. If we're not out in two hours, leave the barge and head home."

"Will do." The Hunter's pearly teeth flashed in the shadows. "Good luck."

"Thanks." Mya squeezed Dee's arm. "Let's go!"

Dee followed Mya down the ladder. Water as warm as piss filled his boots, rose up his shins, thighs, finally stopping at his waist. With one foot on the bottom rung, he reached out with his other and found the ledge, slick and uneven. It was as black as pitch inside the tunnel.

"I can't see you, Mya," he whispered.

"Just walk forward. Watch your footing."

His boot slipped alarmingly. "No shit." He ducked and moved inside.

"Actually, I think there's quite a *lot* of shit in here," she muttered, her voice brimming with revulsion.

"You don't like this any better than I do."

"No, but I can't let everyone know that. Morale, you know."

"What about *my* morale?"

"I'll work on *your* morale later."

Dee jumped as something grabbed his crotch, visions of hungry catfish lurching through his mind, until he realized it was Mya's questing hand.

"Stop it!"

Mya snickered quietly, then led the way through the darkness, the two Blades sloshing along behind them. Dee bit back a yelp as something brushed past leg. This time it *wasn't* Mya, but he *really* didn't want to know what it was.

Thankfully, the level of water fell steadily. Within minutes, it barely reached his boot tops. Moving quietly became harder. They were deep into the tunnel now, and one of the Blades ignited a dim glow crystal. Dee wasn't sure whether to thank him or curse him. Actually *seeing* what he was wading through didn't make it any better. He unwrapped and donned his coat, but didn't pull his weapons yet. They still had the barrier to get past.

The rockfall loomed out of the murk ahead, slime-covered

boulders and masonry from the collapsed basement of a building above. Long since shored up and reworked overhead, the tunnel seemed otherwise solid. Dee understood why Kittal considered this way blocked; the barrier looked impenetrable.

Mya clambered up the obstruction and paused. "Taelish was right. I can feel air moving through here. I don't hear anything, but we'd better be quiet at this."

She pulled some of the smaller rocks away from the blockage and passed them back to Dee, who passed them along to the Blades to be deposited carefully behind them. They worked quickly, only the occasional click of a falling pebble, quiet grunts, and whispers punctuating the silence. Then Mya stopped.

"Problem," she whispered. "There's one big rock in the way, and I don't know if it might be supporting others. I've got to lift it, but it might make noise. If it does, we're going to have to move fast up the rest of the tunnel."

They all signified their readiness. Dee checked his crossbows, but didn't draw them. If Mya needed help lifting, he wanted his hands empty.

Mya clutched the boulder—fully two feet across—braced her legs, and lifted. Amazingly, it moved. Dee would have sworn that they'd have to use a crowbar and lifting tackle.

"Holy Father of All," muttered Folk as Mya pivoted slowly with the rock in her arms.

Dee gaped and backed away. He knew Mya was strong, but had never realized just *how* strong. The rock must have weighed four hundred pounds. He could see her straining, but it looked like she was working harder to keep her footing than to keep the rock aloft. She took a step down the rough incline and wobbled, steadied, and took another.

Free of the rockfall, Mya bent her knees and put the rock down as gently as lowering a babe into a crib. She rose and shrugged her shoulders, wiping her grimy hands on her equally grimy shirt. She noticed the three men's amazement and made a face.

"Stop staring. Come on, we can get through now."

She clambered up the incline and wiggled through the hole. Dee followed, his mind awhirl as he pictured her in the throes of passion. *It's a wonder she didn't break me in half.*

Mya paused beyond the rockfall to empty the water from her boots. The floor here was dry, and squishing along in water-filled boots might give them away. The others joined her with only minor noise. So far, they seemed to have made it without discovery.

Don't get cocky now, Mya, her conscience warned. She heeded the advice and took point, advancing slowly. That this passage was unguarded didn't mean it wasn't trapped. Kittal's alchemical explosives would make a potent defense if rigged to a trip wire or pressure plate. She scanned the darkness ahead, scrutinizing the ground before she placed every step, her Hunter's skills and enhanced senses working together to detect the faintest hint of anything wrong.

On and on she prowled. *Nothing...* The absence of any defense piqued Mya's chronic paranoia.

Suddenly, she froze and raised one hand to stop the others. Jondy doused his light.

A dim illumination shone far ahead. This far back, she and her companions remained hidden in darkness. The tunnel was straight as an arrow, but the grade flattened ahead.

"Forward slow," she whispered over her shoulder. Hand signals would be safer, but it was too dark for her companions to see her clearly. "Quiet as you can."

They started forward, the soft squelch of soggy socks in wet boots barely audible above their pounding hearts. Mya's eyes pierced the gloom, scanning for danger.

There! Mya froze, and Dee bumped into her, but she dare not even whisper to her companions now.

Ahead, the tunnel changed from hewn rock to a corridor of worked stone set with intermittent glow crystals. Just before an opening to the right—*The stairs up to the brick factory*—a faint shimmer near the floor caught her eye. What might have been strands of spider silk—nigh invisible—stretched from wall to wall. *Trip wires,* she determined, *set at odd angles, intervals, and heights. Nice.* Well beyond the stairs, the corridor ended at a door flanked by two guards, crossbows at the ready.

Well, shit!

The distance from where they would be lit by the glow crystals to the stairs was a kill zone. Once in the light, they'd be within the crossbowmen's range. Barreling straight down the corridor almost guaranteed that you'd set off the trip wires, but slowing to maneuver over the wires would allow the guards to get off at least two shots before you reached them.

Mya analyzed the corridor carefully, then waved her people back and retreated with them until they were well out of sight of the guards.

"Bad news. Six trip wires just before the stairs, two guards at the far end with crossbows."

"How far?" Jondy asked, holding up one the short blowguns the Blades had brought.

"You'd be able to get a shot from the trip wires, but you'd be a target until you got there. It's a long way to run while under fire. Suggestions?"

"Wait for the diversion," Dee said, looking up as if he could see through solid rock. "The guards might be drawn up the stairs."

"Maybe…" Mya considered what orders she would give guards stationed to protect her most valuable asset. "Or they could retreat and seal that door behind them, set off another alarm, or even collapse the entire tunnel." She bit her lip. "No, we should go just before all Nine Hells break loose upstairs." She checked her watch. "That's in six minutes. Any other ideas?"

"Could be someone on the stairs, too."

"Good point. What else?"

Dee and the Blades shook their heads.

Mya sighed. *Up to me, then.*

"I'll go first and draw their fire. Dee, stick as close to me as you can and take the first shot you can get, but make sure you stop before the trip wires until the guards are down. Got it?"

"Sure." Dee swallowed hard and nodded. "I can do that."

"Good. Jondy and Folk, you follow behind Dee as backup, but once you're past the wires, I want you to stop at the stairwell and cover that. Anyone comes down, you take them out."

"Yes, Grandmaster."

"Okay. Ready?"

Three nods. Mya looked at her watch again. "We go in two minutes."

When it was time, Mya glanced at her people and jerked her head toward the light.

"Be safe," Dee whispered.

She smiled and nodded, then turned and jogged down the tunnel as quietly as she could. The squelching footfalls behind her sounded like thunder to her sensitive ears, but she doubted the guards would hear. As she hove into the light, she lunged forward, sprinting flat out. She was almost to the first trip wire before the guards spotted her.

As their eyes widened and they raised their bows, Mya dodged right, bounded off the wall to give herself momentum, then ran in a spiral up the left wall, across the arched ceiling, and down the right, evading all six wires.

The guards fired, and the bolts streaked toward her, their tips glinting green in the light.

That can't be good.

Snatching one bolt out of the air, she noted its crystal tip. She tried to catch the second one, but her fingers only batted it aside. *Please don't explode...* The bolt struck the wall and spattered an acrid green liquid that smoked and sizzled.

Kittal and his damn chemicals!

Mya sprinted on toward the door. One of the guards frantically reloaded as she bore down on them, but the other dropped her crossbow and started to reach for a small lever set into the wall. *An alarm or a trap?* Mya could only take out one of the two before one shot or the other pulled the lever. *But which one?* Her dilemma was solved as a tiny dart shot past her to imbed in the crossbowman's chest. The man fumbled his weapon, reeled, and dropped.

Good shot, Dee!

As Mya slammed into the door, she snatched the other assassin's wrist. The woman screamed as she was jerked away from the lever. Metal squealed as the door tore free and they tumbled into the room beyond. Mya flung the woman aside as she rolled to her feet, and surveyed her opponents.

The woman from outside lay sprawled with her arm bent at an impossible angle and a nasty contusion on her head. *One down.* The

235

three other assassins in residence were caught off-guard, and luckily none of them were near the canopied bed near the back of the chamber where a boy lay. One looked up startled from his book. A second, stretched out on a divan, blinked sleepily as she raised her head from a pillow. Only the third was already on his feet and reaching for a weapon.

You first.

Mya was moving before any of the assassins could bring a weapon to bear. Her foot caught the standing assassin in the gut. Air whooshed from this throat as he doubled over. Pulling a dagger, she flung it through the book-reader's hand before he could grasp his crossbow, then kicked him in the temple with just enough force to knock him out.

The sleepy assassin, now wide awake, rolled from the couch and plucked a vial from her pocket. She flung it at Mya and dashed for the canopied bed and the boy.

Damn it! Though the boy was their last hostage, Mya wouldn't put it past Lakshmi to have ordered him murdered instead of allowing him to be rescued. Unfortunately, the glittering crystal vial arcing toward her seemed a more immediate threat. Mya caught it gingerly and lunged after the woman. They reached the bed at the same moment.

"Oh, no, you don't!" Mya grabbed the assassin by the hair and jerked her away from the boy.

The woman yelped in protest. Clutching at another crystal vial dangling on a chain around her neck, she thumbed out the stopper and raised the vial to her lips.

Mya snatched the woman's wrist before she could quaff the contents, and squeezed. "Drop it, or I break your arm."

With a cry of pain, the woman dropped the vial, the dark liquid spilling onto the rug.

Dee raced into the room, clattering over the fallen door. His low whistle caught Mya's attention and she looked around, really seeing the room for the first time.

What the hell?

Unlike the austere quarters that the other two boys had been held in, this room was lavish. Tapestries draped the walls and were suspended from above, giving the illusion of a cozy, low-ceilinged room. Soft rugs cushioned the floor. The furniture was finely crafted from gleaming wood and upholstered with silk. Shelves along one wall were stacked with all manner of toys and trinkets.

"What's going on here?" she asked the assassin in her grip.

The woman looked at Mya through a veil of disheveled hair, her eyes panicked. "Please don't take him! Lakshmi will *kill* me." She grabbed for the boy.

"I don't have time for this. Dee, shoot her."

"Sure." Dee's shot lodged into the woman's leg, and she folded.

Mya slung the assassin over her shoulder. She hadn't planned to take a captive, but there was something going on here that wasn't quite right. She'd take the woman and ask questions later.

"Dee, get the boy. We're out of here." Mya glanced around as Dee hurried past her to the bed, her paranoia rising. *Too many places in here for assassins to hide.* "Hurry."

He folded his crossbows and jammed them into their pockets. "Give me a second! He's not going anywhere. He's out cold."

Out cold? That didn't make sense. One of the captive Alchemists had said that they weren't drugging this boy, at least not with opium. Mya scanned the room, but nothing moved. Still her paranoia screamed danger. "We have to get out of here. Now!"

With a grunt, Dee lifted the boy from the bed.

Click!

The sound embodied Mya's worst fears and kicked her instincts into motion.

"Trap!" Dropping the unconscious assassin, she lunged for Dee. Overhead, she heard the sound of ripping cloth. She grasped Dee by the arm and flung him toward the door.

Dee yelped, but kept hold of the kid as they tumbled across the room.

Something pelted down on Mya like hail. It fell in a dark cloud, so thick that she momentarily lost sight of Dee at the doorway, thousands of tiny black ovals no bigger than pumpkin seeds.

They didn't hurt and they didn't explode, but they stuck to whatever they touched—the floor, the furniture, and her—so tenaciously that she couldn't wipe them off. Wherever they landed, rootlets sprouted and the seeds split open, birthing tendrils that quickly lengthened and thickened into writhing, woody vines.

"Shit!" She took a step for the door, but fell to her knees. The vines had already bound her feet to the floor.

"Mya?"

She looked up at Dee standing beside the door, the boy limp in his arms. Ripping away vines just to stand up, she tried again to take a step, but couldn't. "Gods damn it!"

Mya wrenched one foot free and took a step, but where she put it down, more vines entwined her. She tore her other foot free, leaving behind the sole of her boot, and struggled to take a step. She could barely move. Panic surged up in her.

"Mya!"

Mya ignored Dee's anguished cry in her frenzy to free herself. Tendrils wriggled through her hair and across her face. Vines wound up her limbs and around her torso. She ripped off dozens, hundreds, kicking and thrashing to keep her legs free as she fought toward the door. Drawing her daggers, she slashed desperately at the growths, heedless of the damage the blades did to her flesh. She would heal, if she could only escape. She slashed at her boots and lunged, but the springy vines dragged her down.

"Mya!" Dee's shout now verged on panic.

She looked up at him. He'd dropped the unconscious boy and drawn a dagger, was looking frantically at the thrashing foliage.

"Stay away, Dee!" Mya lurched forward, managing another step, but more vines entangled her instantly.

"Mya! The hangings!" Dee pointed over her head.

Stout ropes hung from eyebolts in the rock ceiling, the supports for the tapestries. Mya's blood quickened. If only she could reach one, she could swing above the clinging vines to the door. But to do that, she had to break free.

Slashing wildly at the tendrils that bound her to the floor, Mya dropped one dagger, crouched, then leapt with every vestige of strength she possessed. Arm stretched, she reached for the rope, but only managed to grasp the edge of a tapestry. She slashed at the vines that curled up and around her dangling legs, but the blade fared poorly against the woody growths. The tapestry tore, and Mya fell.

She landed in an eerily springy bed of vegetation. Grasping tendrils instantly enveloped her. She struggled to get up, but only managed to twist. Not far away, the assassin she had flung aside lay entwined in vines, unconscious and oblivious, yet seemingly unharmed.

"Mya!"

Wrenching her neck around, she could just see the doorway. Jondy was there, his eyes as wide as saucers. Dee clutched the door frame, a dagger in his hand and desperation in his eyes. As if she could read his mind, Mya knew that he was going to try to try to cut her free.

"Don't, Dee!" she screamed. "You'll just get caught!"

"Mya, I—"

"Dee, listen to me! These godsdamned things aren't hurting me but I can't...move! Get the boy out and come back with...*something* to cut or...burn it!"

"Right!" Dee turned away and began snapping orders to the Blades.

Mya listened to their footsteps recede into the distance. She was alone.

With no hope of breaking free, Mya stopped struggling and took deep breaths to calm herself. The vines seemed to have lessened their writhing, but hadn't eased their grip on her. It was unnerving to be so tightly bound...helpless. Memories of being strapped down on the Grandfather's table rose unbidden. *Dee will be back soon,* she hastily assured herself. *He'll bring help, get me out.* The vines covered every surface of the room except for the ceiling, but had stopped growing. *Gods, what a pretty trap, and I walked right into it.*

A soft grinding of stone on stone perked her ears and set her heart racing. Mya couldn't turn her head to see, but felt the vines stir. A wet-dog odor touched her nostrils and she heard the murmur of voices from the back of the room.

But there's no door there, and Dee would come from the other *direction...*

More wet-dog smell, and the vines shifted again. She could discern heartbeats, quiet footfalls, and a strange, intermittent hissing. Someone was coming. Muscles straining, she managed to turn her head. Kittal and several Alchemists waded into the wriggling foliage. Each brandished a perfume atomizer, spraying a fine mist before them. Where the mist settled, the vines retreated.

The female assassin tumbled from a receding clump of vines. Kittal knelt and checked her. "She's been drugged. See to the others,

I'll get Mya myself." The Master Alchemist rose and started working his way toward her, spraying the atomizer carefully. The vines withdrew before him.

He knelt barely an arm's reach away. "So, how do you like my little pets?"

"I'll rip your arms off, you sonofa—" Mya tried to wrench a hand free to reach him.

"An idle threat." The Master Alchemist flicked a hand dismissively. "Dragons' bane vines are strong enough to bind great wyrms, let alone humans, however enchanted you might be. Winter-cap mushroom tea"—he held up the atomizer—"is the only way to make them loosen their grasp. Renders them powerless, you could say. But I've got something different to render *you* powerless."

Withdrawing a bottle from his coat, he uncorked then upended it into a kerchief. When the cloth was wet, he shook it out and draped it gently over Mya's face.

"What the…" Mya tossed her head in an attempt to throw off the soaked kerchief, but the vines tightened with her movement. A caustic vapor filled her nostrils, seemed to fill her entire head. The world went fuzzy around the edges. She coughed and tried to break free one more time, but she couldn't feel her hands and feet any longer.

"Just let it happen…" Kittal's voice floated melodic and calming through a fog. "Just relax and drift with it."

Mya drifted into darkness.

Dee's legs burned as he struggled up the long stair with the Tessifus boy heavy over his shoulder, and guilt heavier on his mind. If Mya hadn't pulled him away from the trap, she could have gotten out. *That should be me down there!*

Two steps ahead, Jondy stopped before a closely fitted wooden door. "It's shouldn't be locked," he whispered back, "but our people might not have gotten this far yet."

"Listen," Dee said as Folk slipped past him, loading a dart into his blowgun. Dee shifted the boy to his left shoulder and pulled one of his crossbows. For all they knew, the room beyond—an office if their Hunters' reconnaissance was accurate—could be filled with bomb-wielding Alchemists.

Jondy pressed an ear to the door, then looked back and shook his head. "Nothing."

"Nothing at all?" Frustration flared along Dee's already frazzled nerves. *Mya!* He fought down the panic. "There should be—"

A muffled thud and faint shouts from far beyond the door interrupted him.

"They're breaking in now! Go! We'll take them from behind! Now!"

Jondy nodded, loaded his blowgun, and put a hand on the latch. "One…two…three!"

The Blades burst through, and Dee followed. Two Alchemists were already crumpling to the floor when he stepped into the cluttered office. Dee shot a woman with a long metal rod in her hand, and she fell before she could bring whatever it was to bear. Jondy and Folk both threw daggers at the only remaining Alchemist. The man fell clutching one blade in his throat and another in his gut.

An impact shivered the heavily barred door.

"Open it! But be careful!"

"Right." Jondy hammered on the door with a dagger hilt until the pounding stopped. He shouted the code phrase that announced him as an ally, threw the bolt, and pulled open the door.

Jolee's wide, tusked face poked through the gap, followed by her raised cudgel and several more Enforcers.

"Dee!" she exclaimed. Her triumphant smile faded as she scanned the room. "Where's the Grandmaster?"

"Trapped! Some kind of enchanted plants. No time to explain." Dee shoved his way past the Blades. "We need torches, axes, anything to get her free and every available assassin to help, but I need to get this kid to Clemson first!"

"I'll get the masters." Jolee barked orders, and Enforcers scattered. She turned back and wrinkled her nose. "You three stink!"

"We waded through a sewer, what's your excuse?" Jondy snapped, nearly receiving a ham-sized fist in his face for his flippancy.

"We don't have time for this!" Dee tried to get past Jolee, but she put a hand on his shoulder.

"Don't, Dee. The place is a mess; Kittal's Alchemists had traps set. Don't worry, they'll be here in a shake."

"But I've got to—"

Clemson rounded the corner and strode toward the office, Embree on her heels, followed by Enforcers carrying shovels, rakes, canvas, and oil lamps.

"What happened?" the Master Enforcer demanded.

"There was a trap. We got the boy, but Mya's caught. Some kind of animated plant or something. We've got to get her free, but she told me to get the kid out first." Dee thrust the boy into Clemson's grasp. "Can you get him out of here? I've got to see to Mya!"

Clemson opened her mouth, then nodded. "We'll take him to my place. You four, go with Dee."

"I'll go, too," Embree said, waving a couple of Hunters forward. "Plants and snares I can deal with."

"Thank you!" Dee flew down the stairs three at a time, feet thundering behind him. Skidding around the corner toward the chamber, he froze.

The unconscious guard who lay by the door only minutes ago was gone.

"What the—" Dee drew his crossbows.

"What's wrong?" Embree asked, pulling a pair of kukri from his belt.

"There was a guard unconscious right there. I hit him square and he went down, drugged. He *couldn't* have gotten up.'" He pointed to the door still wreathed with entangling vines, then peered down the dark tunnel to the river.

"Folk, Jondy, you know that tunnel. Trace it back and see if you can find the guard." Embree pointed to the door. "The rest of us will get Mya."

The two Blades high-stepped over the trip wires and jogged off down the tunnel, their glow crystal bobbing away into the darkness. Dee led the others to the door, the Enforcers and Hunters already fashioning torches out of shovel handles, canvas, and oil.

"Mya, hang on! We're coming!" he called as someone thrust a burning brand into his hand.

No answer. That didn't bode well. The plants seemed quiescent now, no longer twitching and writhing as if questing for something to strangle. Hopefully, they hadn't strangled Mya. At the door he thrust the make-shift torch at the vines. They recoiled from the flames, rustling back a full foot.

"It's working! Come on. She's about thirty feet from the door, straight in!"

"Carefully!" Embree barked, a torch in one hand and a kukri in the other. "Form up and keep your eyes open!"

They formed a vee with Dee at the apex and moved slowly forward, waving their torches at the foliage. The vines recoiled from the flames and receded, leaving tattered carpet and bare stone behind. Hunters dribbled oil on the floor and ignited it to keep the vines from closing in behind them.

"Mya?" Dee peered ahead. There should have been a lump where Mya lay, but the vines before him formed a perfectly flat carpet about a foot thick. "Mya! Answer!"

No one answered and nothing moved.

If she had died here, alone... *Stop it!*

Foot by foot they advanced, and the vines retreated, but they found nothing. Dee stopped and checked the distance to the door. Forty feet at least.

"She was right there!" He pointed to a spot on the floor, trying not to sound panicked. "There were four Alchemists in this room, too!"

"Did the damn plants eat them?" asked a Blade.

"No, I don't believe that." Dee's denial sounded more like desperation than conviction, even to his own ears. He had no idea what these obviously enchanted plants could do. He swung his torch against the vines, advancing recklessly. "She's *got* to be here!"

They cleared the center of the room all the way to the canopied bed, but found nothing.

"Where the hell could they have gone?" Embree muttered.

Jolee shrugged her heavy shoulders. "Maybe someone took them away."

"How, with these damn things all over?" An annoyed Enforcer thrust his torch deep into the foliage. The plants writhed and thrashed to get away from the flames.

"We can't discount anything," Dee declared. "There's got to be some sign of what happened! Look!"

The Hunters, far more skilled at looking for traces, searched the spot where she lay, but found nothing.

"Search back to the walls," Embree ordered. "Burn the vines if you have to!"

They searched every crevice, every niche, every inch of the threadbare carpet. They found blood where Mya's dagger had pierced one assassin's hand, and even found Mya's dagger and Dee's spent bolts, but no trace of any of the assassins. They searched the walls and tore down the shelves, even looking under the canopied bed.

Jondy and Folk came huffing into the room. "Taelish hasn't seen anyone come out of the tunnel."

How could she just have disappeared into thin air? Dee knew the answer to that question—*Hoseph!*—and prayed that he was wrong.

"Blood!" Embree barked, pointing at a smudge on the back wall. "There! A hand print!"

Dee's heart caught in his throat as he vaulted up and dashed to the wall. "There was nobody here! There shouldn't be blood here!" He examined the wall, spied another drop. "Here!"

"And here!" Embree touched a smudge about four feet up the wall. Running his hand over the wall, the Master Hunter suddenly stopped and ran his fingernail slowly up a tiny slit. "There's a door here!"

"A door?" Dee stared, but couldn't see it. He was a Hunter, but not of Embree's skill. "Can you open it?"

"Step aside." Jolee's order brooked no argument. Even Embree stepped back.

The massive Enforcer launched herself at the wall, leading with her shoulder. The room shook, and the fissure that had been only a hair's breadth before, now widened to that of a fingernail.

"Again!" Embree ordered.

Jolee complied, taking several steps back and flinging herself at the wall. The crack widened.

"Here!" Folk held out a crowbar.

Embree jammed it into the fissure and pried. Several more assassins grabbed on and they all heaved on the bar. Jolee finally wedged her thick fingers in the crack and roared with effort as she wrenched open the hidden door. Beyond yawned a straight, clean tunnel of quarried stone.

"Bloody good thing it wasn't trapped," Embree said with chagrin.

"What now?" a Blade asked, peering into the dark tunnel.

"We follow it!" Dee's spirits soared. *We're coming for you, Mya!* He stepped forward, but someone dragged him back.

"Not you, Dee." Embree's expression might have been worn by an executioner for all the emotion there.

"What?" Dee's knuckles whitened on the hilt of the dagger in his hand. "Oh, I'm going along!"

"No, you're not." Jolee's hand closed around his in an unbreakable grip.

Dee glared at her. "What?"

"The *boy*, Dee," Embree stepped up to him, his cold eyes inches away. "That's the objective. You're the only one who can deliver him to the palace. *We'll* follow this tunnel. I'm a better Hunter than you'll ever be, so tuck your dick back in your pants and grow a brain. You're an *assassin*. Start acting like one, not a smitten school boy."

"But…" Dee knew he was thinking with his heart, not his head, but his heart was the more persistent of the two by far. "The boy's safe!"

"But you're not!" Embree waved Jolee back and gripped Dee's sewage-mired shirt. "You've got a job to do; a job the Grandmaster *ordered* you to do! Do it."

Dee's heart raged to use the dagger in his hand, to chase down the dark corridor after Mya, but his brain knew Embree was right. *Don't be a fool…* "R…right. Make sure—"

"I've *got* it!" Embree snapped, shoving him toward the door. "I'm a *Hunter*. Let me hunt! Jondy, Folk, go with him. And for the sake of all the gods, change your clothes before you go to the palace! You stink like a sewer!"

Dee's heart hammered with something between fury and despair as he strode out of the room and up the stairs. Silently, he damned himself for not being the one captured in the trap, and damned Mya for insisting they try to rescue these noble brats. They should have devoted their time and energy to finding and killing Hoseph, not chasing down kidnapped children.

It's not the boy's fault, his conscience chided.

Deep down, Dee knew that was true. The boy was an innocent. The only person he could rightfully blame was the one who had manipulated Mya into accepting this mission in the first place.

Emperor Tynean Tsing III...

Chapter XIX

Wake him! I have news he'll want to hear!"

"He just got to sleep, and I'll not have you disturb him!"

Arbuckle tried to shut out the voices from beyond his bedchamber door and drift back to sleep.

"It's not your place to decide, nor to give *me* orders!"

"The emperor's well-being is my responsibility! He's sleeping, and he's gotten precious little of it lately!"

"The security of this palace is *my* responsibility! If I have to beat on that door myself, I'll damn well wake him if I deem it necessary!"

Why would Baris and Ithross be fighting? Arbuckle's curiosity woke him fully despite his fatigue, and he threw off his blankets. Both men were dedicated and stubborn, and Arbuckle wanted to defuse the situation before it devolved to violence. The emperor grabbed a robe from the stand and hurried to the door.

"Baris, Captain Ithross, what's going on?" Arbuckle blinked in the bright lamplight at Baris facing off with the captain. The scene would have been a comical—the valet in nightshirt and cap, Ithross in chainmail and tabard—if they hadn't been ready to kill each other.

"Majesty, I'm sorry!" Baris bowed and glared at the guard captain. "The captain *insists* upon seeing you immediately. I couldn't forestall him."

Ithross bowed low. "I'm truly sorry for waking you, Majesty, but you said you wanted to be notified as soon as the final of the three lost packages was returned."

Lost packages? Arbuckle's sleep-addled mind stumbled before he decoded the captain's cryptic statement. *The last Tessifus boy!*

"He's here?" *Moirin!* Arbuckle tied his robe tight. "Baris, get Us a pair of slippers!"

"Yes, Majesty." The valet glared again at Ithross, but dashed into the bedchamber.

"That woman never ceases to amaze me!" Arbuckle said. "By the Gods of Light We *will* give her a title for this! How is she, by the way? Well enough, if she can deliver..." He fell silent as Ithross shook his head.

"Miss Moirin's not actually here, Majesty," the captain whispered conspiratorially.

"What? Who..."

"The situation is difficult to explain *here*, Majesty. Perhaps while we *walk*." The captain cast a meaningful nod toward the bedroom door.

"Of course." Arbuckle allowed Baris to put the slippers on his feet and fuss over his appearance for a moment before waving the valet off. "That's good enough, Baris. I'm sure this won't take long."

"Yes, Majesty." Baris bowed and backed away.

"Lead on, Captain."

Outside the royal chambers, a squad of guards started to close in around them, but Ithross waved them back. "Follow at ten paces," he ordered.

They started out, walking a discrete distance behind the two guards bearing lanterns to illuminate their path through the dark halls of the palace.

Ithross spoke quietly. "As the last time, the boy was delivered by Master Dee alone, Majesty. I'm afraid he's quite agitated."

"About what?"

"He wouldn't say, but he...demanded to see you."

"*Demanded?*" Few commoners had the temerity to demand anything within the walls of the palace, let alone to wake the emperor in the middle of the night. "Does it have to do with Miss Moirin?"

"He won't say. He just insists that he needs to speak with you."

"And the boy? How is he?"

"Unconscious, but alive, like the others. I've sent for Master Corvecosi and the duke."

"Good."

Ithross led them to a familiar corridor with two guarded doors and stopped in front of the first.

"Would Your Majesty like to see the boy?"

"Not necessary. We'll give the duke privacy to be with his son."

Ithross turned to one of the door guards. "Has the duke arrived yet?"

"No, sir. Only Master Corvecosi."

"All right. We'll be in the adjoining room."

The guards in front of the second door opened it and bowed the emperor inside.

"Master Dee, We—" Arbuckle stopped short. Moirin's assistant stood surrounded by four guards, one sleeve of his shirt torn and a bruise darkening his left cheek, obviously livid. "What happened?"

"He was rather too emphatic in *demanding* to talk with you, Majesty," Ithross explained. "He had to be...restrained."

If looks could kill, Dee would have made a fine executioner.

"Very well." Arbuckle stepped closer, but kept well out of reach. "Master Dee, where is Miss Moirin?"

Muscles bunched at the young man's jaw. "She's *gone*."

"Gone?"

"Gone, taken, kidnapped. She might even be *dead* by now, because she was working on *your* mission!" Dee stabbed a finger toward Arbuckle and took a half step forward, but the burly guards interceded, hands closing on his arms.

"You'll settle down this instant or I'll have you in chains," Ithross warned.

Kidnapped! Arbuckle's stomach clenched. "What happened? Who took her?"

"Who do you *think* took her? The same people who took the boys. Moirin was caught saving him...saving *me*." The man's face flushed, his voice cracking.

He blames himself, Arbuckle realized, *and me. Maybe he should.* "Master Dee, We want to help. How can—"

Rapid-fire knocking rattled the door, and Ithross gestured to a guard to open it.

Duke Tessifus strode in, his nightclothes askew and hair disheveled. Sketching a hasty bow to the emperor, he turned to Ithross. "Captain, where's my son? I was told he was here!"

"In the next room, milord. Master Corvecosi is checking him..." The captain's voice trailed off as the duke shook his head.

"No!" The duke's face flushed. "I've *been* in there. That's *not* my son!"

Arbuckle's jaw slacked. "Not your son?"

Ithross whirled on Dee. "What in the name of—"

"Not your *son*?" The young man's face blanched to the hue of fine parchment. "It was a *trap*! A trap for My...Moirin."

Arbuckle saw the pain and guilt writ clear on Dee's face, and understood. *My Moirin...* His hunch had been right; there was more than just a working relationship between the two. A sudden, sharp stab of jealousy rose in his breast, shaming him. To think only of himself when Moirin is lost... *No! She's not lost yet!*

"Master Dee, what can We do to help recover her? We'll have every constable in the city searching if you just tell Us who took her and where. We want to help. *Please*."

Dee looked at him, mistrust and hope battling in his eyes. Then he shook his head. "There's nothing you can do. It's best to leave it up to us."

Now Arbuckle was confounded. "Us?"

"Who *is* this?" Duke Tessifus stared at Dee in confusion. "And what does he know about my son?"

"Ah...milord, if you'll come this way." Ithross gestured respectfully toward the door, his anxious expression a reminder that the details of the mission to save the duke's sons had been kept secret even from Tessifus himself.

The duke balked. "I want an explanation!"

Arbuckle sighed. "It's all right, Captain. He deserves to know what's going on. Milord Duke, this is one of the people tasked with the rescue of your sons. Apparently, the miscreants who kidnapped your sons have used this decoy"—Arbuckle gestured toward the next room—"to lure and capture his mistress."

The duke's face darkened. "But why is all the talk of saving *her*? What about my *son*?"

"Without *her*, your other two sons would still be missing!" Dee snapped.

"Gentlemen!" Arbuckle interceded. "Emotions are running high. We must all keep our heads. Duke Tessifus, please wait in your quarters. We promise to send what news we can." He turned to Dee as the duke stormed from the room. "Master Dee, are you *sure* that there's nothing We can do to help?"

The young man glared daggers. "No, Your *Majesty*. You've done quite enough already."

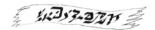

Mya shivered as her mind slowly rose into wakefulness. *Cold...why am I cold? Dee's always warm.* She reached out to pull him close, but couldn't move her arm.

The vines! Now she remembered: sneaking up the tunnel, breaking into the cellar room, becoming caught up in the godsdamned enchanted vines so tightly she couldn't move. There was more, but...she couldn't quite remember. Her eyelids weighed tons, but she forced them open.

Even in the dim light, she could see that there were no vines.

Then what's holding me? Mya tried to move, felt metal scrape against her wrists and ankles, arms and thighs, and her neck. She yanked on the restraints, to no avail. Chill stone pressed against her back, and she realized why she was so cold; her wrappings had been removed. She was strapped naked to a stone slab.

Her heart hammered in her chest. *Oh, gods, where am I?*

Mya blinked away the blurry vision and turned her head as far as she could to survey her surroundings. Stone walls lined with shelves supporting innumerable bottles, jugs, and alchemical paraphernalia stretched as far as she could see. Obviously one of Kittal's hideouts.

Kittal... Now the memory returned, his calm, confident voice as he parted the clinging vines and draped the cloth over her face, a chemical stink...gagging...darkness. She strained against the bonds until something in her wrist popped. No pain, but she relented. Her flesh was weaker than whatever bound her.

Calm down, Mya. Think!

The cool air and earthy scent beneath the chemical odors told her she was underground. Her apartment in Twailin had been constructed in the disused wine cellar beneath the *Golden Cockerel*. Its subterranean secrecy made her feel snug and safe. This place felt more like a tomb. *My tomb.* Panic swelled in her like a rising tide, banishing the last cobwebs of her drug-induced sleep.

Think, Mya! Think like an assassin. Why am I alive? She heaved deep, measured breaths, forcing her heart to slow, remembering the peaceful meditations with Lad after their exercises. *No fear...*

251

First things first. Mya assessed her situation. She wasn't hurt, of course; her runes would have healed any injury. But something felt...wrong.

Well, I'm naked. That her carefully kept secret had been exposed bothered her more than the thought of someone stripping off her wrappings. Dee was the only person who had ever seen her runes in their entirety. Vonlith, the runemage who inscribed the tattoos, was dead, so he really didn't count.

But no, it was more than just her nudity. Starting with the top of her head, Mya concentrated on how everything felt. She could turn her head. Her breathing was fine, though her throat felt thick with mucus. She was hungry and thirsty. She shifted her arms and legs, wiggled her toes and...fingers. She came up one short on her left hand. The finger with the Grandmaster's ring was gone.

Well, shit, doesn't that just figure! Once again panic threatened, and once again Mya forced it down, this time with anger. She should have expected them to take it. It didn't really matter anyway. With the blood contracts destroyed, all the ring protected her from was direct harm by the masters.

Except now Lakshmi has free rein, gloated her conscience. *You may not feel pain, Mya, but a Master Inquisitor can surely work around that.*

Dee's fears redoubled during the long carriage ride from the palace to Clemson's headquarters. *A trap!* his conscience screamed. *And it only worked because she saved me!*

At the distillery, Dee leapt from the carriage before it even came to a full stop. The first predawn glow had barely lit the sky, but the yard was a bustle of activity. Instead of workers grinding cane, carrying jugs of juice, and stirring the vats, however, assassins hurried about carrying boxes and bags, loading wagons.

Packing up? That concern seemed trivial compared to the news he had to bring to the masters. Nobody interfered with his progress to Clemson's office, and the Enforcer guarding the door opened it without pause.

"Dee..." The stern visages of the masters stopped him short.

His heart skipped a beat. "She's not—"

"We haven't found her yet." Clemson sat at her desk, Noncey and Embree on either side. The desktop was strewn with maps, diagrams, and parchment held down by mugs of thick, white porcelain. "We're searching but—"

Dee strode forth and slapped his palms down on the desk. "It was a trap! The boy was a ruse. This whole godsdamned operation was a setup to capture Mya!"

The three exchanged hard looks. Embree nodded and sighed. "We thought it might have been. It was too clean, too precise. Someone was waiting behind that concealed door ready to take her."

Rage boiled Dee's blood. "Where did it go? What did you find? Why aren't you still looking? You're sitting here drinking *blackbrew!*"

"Dee, calm down, right now." Noncey's voice was a hard and as sharp as one of his blades. "We *are* looking, but everyone's exhausted."

Dee gritted his teeth, but nodded. Getting angry wouldn't help. "Where did the tunnel lead?"

"To a laundry." Embree poked a finger at a spot on one of the maps. "Quite a distance away in the Wharf District. We lost the trail there, in the basement. I left Jolee and her crew to lock down the place. Nobody's getting in or out, and we've started questioning everyone. Several of the workers live above the place, but so far, no one saw anything and no one heard anything."

"What about people outside on the street? Someone must have seen *something.*"

Embree shook his head. "We're asking, but we're not getting any answers. At that time of night in that part of town, everyone's minding their own business. Even if they saw someone being carried down the street, they'd just think it was someone too drunk to walk."

"Hoseph or Kittal could have whisked her away magically." Noncey got up, poured a cup of blackbrew, and thrust it into Dee's hands. "They'll have planned this carefully. They won't have left any witnesses."

"It's my fault," Dee confessed as he sank into a chair. "Mya could have gotten out of that room, avoided the trap, but she tossed me and the kid out instead."

"*Your* fault?" Clemson's almond-shaped eyes softened as she glanced toward Noncey, then back to Dee. "No, Dee. The Grandmaster rescued the last two boys, so it's only natural that they expected her to do the same here. They set the trap and bagged their target."

"But *why*?" Dee's hand trembled, sloshing blackbrew over the rim of the cup onto his fingers. The pain felt strangely appropriate. "Why take her? Why not just kill her?" *Please, they can't have killed her!*

"Lakshmi's not one to let information pass her by. The opportunity to interrogate the Grandmaster might keep Lakshmi from killing her…for now."

Dee put the cup aside before he spilled all the blackbrew. "Torture won't work very well on Mya."

"Perhaps not," Clemson admitted, "but we're taking precautions anyway."

Dee nodded. The assassins packing up the distillery made sense now. They were moving their headquarters because Mya knew where it was. "But aside from the locations of your bases, what could Mya tell them? Lakshmi and Kittal know more about the Tsing guild than Mya does."

Clemson pursed her lips. "Consider what you told us about how the interim Twailin guildmaster—"

"Sereth," Dee added automatically.

The Master Enforcer nodded. "—Sereth, defied Hoseph's orders. Hoseph won't take that lightly. I've no doubt that, once things are settled here in Tsing, he intends to send a contingent of our people down to convince the Twailin assassins to cooperate."

"Or kill them."

"Or kill them," she agreed. "Regardless, it would be a bloody battle, but now they have the Grandmaster. And who knows more about the Twailin guild than her? Who else could give them the information to usurp or destroy that guild?"

Dee swallowed hard. "I do. I was the guildmaster's assistant. They could have been trying for me, too."

"That's right!" Embree snapped his fingers. "You *both* were in on the previous rescue operations. They could have been hoping to get both of you."

"But like you said, torture won't work very well on Mya. They'll have to figure out some other means of getting what they want from her. That gives us some time."

Clemson's pragmatic analysis of Mya being tortured made Dee want to scream, but she was right. "We've got to get word to Sereth."

"We'll send a courier."

"How long do you think," Embree asked uneasily, "before Mya breaks?"

Dee shuddered to consider it. "I don't know. Her body will heal, as you've seen, but..." *But her mind...*

Dee knew from Paxal that Mya's life had been driven by fear. He had seen the result of it himself, that beautiful web of magic etched into her skin, designed to keep the fear at bay. But now, that magic could work against her. *What could be more frightening than a body that refuses to die?*

"We have to find her quickly." Dee's voice cracked, but his own fear stiffened his determination.

"We've got assassins out there looking," Clemson assured him.

"But Tsing is a *huge* city." Noncey sighed softly, then turned to Embree. "How about magic? Don't you Hunters use..."

Both Dee and Embree were already shaking their heads.

"It *can* be done," Embree said. "If we had her blood contract it would be simple, but... Otherwise, we need a body part or something very personal. Hunters know this, so we generally don't get attached to things. You don't have any keepsake of Mya's, do you, Dee?"

"No. Mya kept no personal items that I know of."

They sat silent for a time.

"Well, we've got the best Hunters in the guild on her trail," Embree finally said. "They'll find something."

"Not the best..." The words were out of Dee's mouth even before the thought gelled in his mind.

"What are you talking about?" Embree asked.

Lad could find her—but he clamped his lips shut. The entire guild thought Lad was dead, a lie to allow the former guildmaster to live his life in peace with his family.

But he could be Mya's only chance. What's more important, Lad's peace or Mya's life?

In Dee's mind, there was no question. *Lad put her in this position by putting the Grandmaster's ring on her finger, so he damned well should help get her out!* And maybe, just maybe, Dee could figure out a way to keep Lad's secret, keep him anonymous. After all, no one in Tsing knew what he looked like. *Except Hoseph...*

Dee resolved that he could make this work. *It's the only chance...* "I know someone in the Twailin guild who can find her. They call him The Bloodhound." The pseudonym had come to him like a gift from the gods. *Yes, this could work...*

"Maybe, but it'll take *weeks* to get him here." Embree sounded slightly affronted, bud Dee didn't care.

Unfortunately, Embree was also right. Weeks would pass in getting Lad to Tsing. *If Lad will even come.* It would take some convincing. Dee clenched his fists in frustration. If only he could pop down to Twailin like Hoseph had. Unfortunately, he lacked the magic...

Dee caught his breath. *He* didn't have magic, but he knew someone who did.

If I haven't burnt that bridge.

Well, there was only one way to find out. Picking up his cup, Dee downed the scalding blackbrew in one long draught, stood, and headed for the door. "I've got to go."

"Where?"

"Back to the palace," he said, "to eat crow and beg for a favor."

CHAPTER XX

Hoseph contemplated death.

Not his own death, nor even Mya's. Rather, he contemplated the nature of death itself. Many feared death—the loss of worldly possessions, the final judgment with the possibility of endless torment for mortal transgressions. Hoseph knew better. Death was a release from the burdens of life, an end of sickness, decrepitude, anxiety and anguish—a blessing from Demia.

Death, he had learned, was also a powerful tool, though that wasn't one of the tenets of his faith. Years ago, the temple elders had frowned upon the young acolyte who dared suggest using Demia's gifts to broaden and strengthen the cult. Hoseph paid them no mind, and his perseverance had earned him a seat at the emperor's right hand. And though the elders may not have condoned his unorthodox use of Demia's gifts, they didn't complain about the benefits conferred upon the temple as a result of his new-found influence. He'd lost that influence with the emperor's death, but he would soon regain that and more. With a young, malleable boy on the throne, Tsing would be Hoseph's to mold as he saw fit.

The sweet tone of a bell drew Hoseph from his deep meditation. Urgency pulsed along his nerves. The signal from Lakshmi could mean success...or disaster.

Hoseph rose and straightened his drab robes. Clutching the silver skull in one hand and the bottle of Kittal's wondrous elixir in the other, he invoked the talisman and followed the tone of the chime.

"Well met, Hoseph."

The unusual lilt in the Master Inquisitor's voice and the bright expression on her face reassured Hoseph. *Success, then. Mya is dead...* His fleeting elation vanished as the twinge behind his eyes swelled into a fierce throb. Feigning a cough, he turned aside and surreptitiously dashed several drops of elixir into his mouth. As the pain vanished, he covertly tucked the bottle away in a pocket of his robe.

"Are you all right?"

"I'm fine," he lied, straightening and considering his surroundings. Hoseph recognized the hidden repository where Kittal had delivered them from the attack on the Master Alchemist's headquarters. "The reek of chemicals in this place irritates my throat. Why have you summoned me here?"

"Because it's convenient and private."

Or because you don't want me to know where you're staying, he surmised.

"I have a gift for you, Hoseph." With a smile that only emphasized the maze of wrinkles on her face, Lakshmi held out a closed hand.

"A gift?" Hoseph held out his hand, and she dropped something into his palm. Lamplight glinted on a small circlet of gold and obsidian. He knew it well. "The Grandmaster's ring!"

"You look surprised."

"I am." Even her smug expression couldn't quell his delight. *Mya's dead!* "Both with your success and that you would hand this over so readily. I suppose you want the guildmaster's ring in exchange."

"Keep it for now." She waved a wizened hand as if unconcerned. "I'll take it when I give you Mya. Then our bargain will be complete."

"Give me Mya?" His mind stumbled—*Why would I want a dead body?*—before realization struck. "She's not dead?"

"In due time."

"Kill her!" The glow of victory burst into an inferno of rage. "*Now!*"

Lakshmi's smiled again, but now it looked stiff and unnatural, and her eyes narrowed warily. "Not yet. I'm not done with her."

"Done with her? There's nothing to *do* with her except *kill* her!" He couldn't believe the woman would be so foolish as to keep their most deadly enemy alive.

"And we will, don't worry. In fact, we'll let *you* do the deed when the time comes."

"Where is she?" Hoseph fixed Lakshmi with a cold stare.

"Secure." Lakshmi tapped her long fingernails on the counter. "I gave you that ring as a good faith token, Hoseph. Both the Tessifus boy and Mya are safe. Once I'm finished with her, I'll hand her over to you in exchange for the guildmaster's ring. The Tsing guild will unify under my guidance, and we'll put *that* ring"—she pointed to the band in Hoseph's hand—"on the finger of our imperial-Grandmaster-to-be."

"You're playing with fire." Hoseph clenched his fist around the ring, remembering Lakshmi's fascination with Mya's abilities. "You think you can study Mya and learn her secrets? She's *beyond* dangerous! She cut through the Blademasters of Koss like they were paper, and you want to make *more* like her? Don't be a fool! Kill her now, and I'll give you the guildmaster's ring."

"No." Lakshmi's face was implacable. "I'm quite aware that Mya is dangerous, but she is *secure*. What's *foolish* is throwing away the opportunity to *use* her. If my experiment succeeds, the guild will reap untold benefits."

"What experiment?"

"That's not your concern. You aren't *in* the guild!" She slapped the counter in an uncharacteristic gesture of annoyance. "We're done here! I'll call on you, Hoseph, when we're finished with her."

Hoseph seethed, but he had no recourse. He needed Lakshmi to finish the conditioning of the Tessifus boy, and he didn't know where either the boy or Mya were being kept. He flicked his talisman into this palm. She might hold the upper hand now, but the moment the crown was placed on that boy's head, Hoseph would be in charge once more. The thought made him smile, and he enjoyed the flash of worry in the Master Inquisitor's eyes as he misted away.

A scent drew Mya from the depths of darkness. Spicy and distinct through the miasma of chemical odors, it triggered a curious physical reaction. Unlike the mouthwatering aromas of a kitchen or bakery, however, this spicy scent made her skin crawl. Mya took a deep breath and wracked her brain for the association.

Lakshmi.

The scent wasn't strong, but it persisted. Then she heard the scuff of shoes against stone, a quiet cough, the trip of a heartbeat, close, but not in the room. Craning her neck, Mya could just make out the edge of a door. Lakshmi must be outside.

Dread wormed through her gut. *What is she waiting for?*

Mya strained against her bonds yet again, cursing silently. After what seemed like hours of girding her fear and analyzing her environment, she had succumbed to exhaustion, losing precious time in figuring out a plan. The approaching tread of several more people stopped her struggles. Her fate approached.

"What took you so long?" Lakshmi sounded annoyed. "I've been waiting half an hour."

"I was asleep." Kittal sounded no less irritated. "I've been sitting in a dark tunnel for days, Lakshmi. I needed rest."

"Very well. You're rested. Now, let's get to this."

Dissension? Perhaps the two masters weren't as close as they were rumored to be. *Maybe I can figure out how to play one against the other.*

Metal clicked against metal, and a key clattered in a lock. Mya closed her eyes, unsure what advantage she might gain by feigning sleep, but desperate for any edge she could get. The door squeaked open, and several people entered. Mya mimicked sleep as she gauged how many, where they were, and what they were doing.

"You can stop pretending to sleep, Mya. I know how long my concoctions last, and you've been awake for some time."

Mya opened her eyes and glared at Kittal. He stood beside her table, spectacles perched low on his nose, his eyes roving over her from head to foot as if analyzing or reading her runes. Behind him, Alchemists carrying large jugs of liquid and trays of equipment set their burdens on a nearby table.

The scent of spice doubled, and Mya shifted her gaze to Lakshmi as she approached the opposite side of the table. The Master Inquisitor's expression was unreadable, her smile thin, sharp, and precisely painted.

"What do you want from me? You already took my ring." Mya clenched her hand, acutely aware of the absence of both ring and finger. "I guess *you're* Grandmaster now."

Lakshmi laughed with delight. "Oh, no, my dear. I'm not going to be Grandmaster, but you *do* have something I want."

She's an Inquisitor, Mya reminded herself. *She wants information. She'll interrogate me.* "So what now? If you intend to torture me to see what I know, you'll be disappointed." She barked a dry laugh, forced, but enough to quell Lakshmi's mirth. "You may as well turn me over to Hoseph in exchange for the guildmaster's ring." At least death at the hands of the priest would be painless. In Lakshmi's hands...who knew?

"Not yet. I need something from you first." Lakshmi raised one wizened hand and turned it this way and that, peering at the wrinkled flesh as thin as parchment, brown age spots, bony knuckles. "I'm old, Mya, much older than I look. Thanks to Kittal's potions"—she gave the Master Alchemist a fond glance—"I've staved off the infirmities and frailty of old age."

Mya thought of Neela, the Twailin Master Alchemist of unknown years who had downed potions like fine wine to keep herself alive.

The Master Inquisitor's voice turned hard as she continued. "But potions can only do so much for so long. My mind is as sharp as ever, but my body is failing. I do *not* intend to let that happen."

"Sorry, but I don't have anything to make you young again."

"Oh, but you do." Lakshmi trailed one long nail across Mya's bare skin, raising goosebumps. "I was told that it's your runes that give you your remarkable abilities. They *are* truly magnificent. Such magic might not make me young, but it would negate the ravages of age, grant me many more years of strength and vigor."

"Yeah, well, good luck finding a runemage. They're hard to come by."

Lakshmi traced her fingernail down Mya's leg. "I don't need a runemage, my dear. *Your* runes will do nicely, thank you. Kittal is going to give them to me."

"What the hell are you talking about?" Chills even colder than the stone slab upon which she lay raced down Mya's spine.

Lakshmi smiled with the sweet expression of a loving grandmother. "Kittal's going to remove your runes and graft them onto me."

"Remove my..." Mya' stomach heaved, but she managed to swallow the bile. The room suddenly closed in around her.

"It's not going to be that easy, Lakshmi." Kittal's voice sounded distant, but she felt his rough touch on her skin. "The runemage who inscribed these was a genius. When she's cut"—Mya felt pressure upon her belly, smelled blood—"the runes simply move out of the way, then move back as the tissue heals."

"If the runes move, how can you collect them?"

"I designed *this*."

The pride in the Alchemist's voice drew Mya from the depths of her horror. Kittal held something out for Lakshmi to see. The device sported two sets of steel blades and a spiked drum. When he turned the hand-crank, the tiny blades scythed back and forth like miniature shears, and the spiked drum rotated.

"It simultaneously cuts two parallel lines, capturing the runes between them and separating the dermis from the underlying muscle. As I crank, it rolls up the strip of skin."

Mya finally found her voice again. "Touch me with that thing, and I'll stick it up your ass and turn the crank."

Neither master even spared her a glance.

"Once the skin is detached," Kittal continued, "we'll treat it with a special concoction that I've devised before we transplant it onto you. We'll have to test the procedure on a limited scale to start."

"Can we test it now?" Lakshmi asked.

"Yes. I've had supplies brought in."

Mya felt pressure as the Master Alchemist pressed his machine to her thigh. A memory of Kiesha's bloody, skinless body rose in her mind, and bile burned her throat. She jerked as hard as she could against the restraints. Suddenly, another recollection flashed—the Grandfather and her former master, Targus, standing over Lad similarly bound on a slab. *Lad fought back!*

Mya jerked up her shoulder, wrenching her right hand through the iron restraint. Bones cracked and blood flooded over her fingers, but her hand came free. She snatched Kittal's wrist clumsily with a disjointed thumb and squeezed hard. Beneath her fingers, a bone snapped.

Kittal screamed, and the skin-peeling device clattered to the floor.

Lakshmi stumbled back as Mya wrenched her other hand free. Jerking Kittal closer, she strained to reach his throat with her left hand, but an iron band still pinned her upper arm to the slab. Her bloody fingers only stretched far enough to grasp the lapel of his coat. She yanked it hard.

"Dose her! Now!" Kittal screeched, flailing at her as Alchemists scrambled to their master's aid.

Releasing Kittal's wrist, Mya reached for his throat. Her thumb popped back into joint, giving her a proper grip. A damp cloth came down on her face, but she held her breath. She grabbed onto something and squeezed. Bone crunched under her fingers, but Kittal's scream told her it wasn't his neck. She released her grip and reached again.

Something punched into Mya's leg, and her senses reeled. She gasped, inhaling the acrid fumes of the cloth over her face. Mya fought to stay conscious as her grip turned to water. Feebly she flailed, trying to reach Kittal, anything to keep him from using that vile device to strip away her skin.

The shouts and screams faded as the drugs overwhelmed her and darkness engulfed her mind. Mya wondered if she would ever wake again, and thought that perhaps it would be better if she didn't.

The imperial guards at the palace gates were surprised to see Dee again so soon, but ushered his carriage on to the inner courtyard nonetheless.

So far, so good.

The driver steered around the outer court to the small postern door where he and Mya had previously been admitted. Dee stepped out and found himself facing a scowling lieutenant he recognized from his previous visit. Ithross had taken Dee's rudeness as an affront to the crown, and apparently his officers shared that opinion.

"You'll have to wait for the captain." Her voice wasn't exactly belligerent, but it wasn't friendly either.

"It's urgent," Dee said, but he could see by her expression that his urgency didn't equate to theirs.

"The captain's been summoned."

Dee nodded and stood as still as he could. Showing impatience would only make this harder. Finally Ithross arrived, flanked by a brace of guards. The captain's hard expression made the lieutenant's seem welcoming.

Time to eat crow, Dee.

Dee bowed respectfully. "Captain Ithross, I—"

"What do you want?"

Dee swallowed hard. "Other than to apologize for my previous outburst, sir, I've come to request the emperor's help in finding Miss Moirin."

"Really?" The captain's eyebrows shot up. "I thought we'd done enough already."

Dee took a deep breath and let it out slowly. "I'm afraid I was overwrought earlier. You must understand that Miss Moirin is very important to me, as I believe she is to the emperor."

"The *emperor* is busy. You can't expect the sovereign of Tsing to jump every time you have a request."

"I don't. In fact, there's no need to disturb His Majesty at all. I need to speak with Master Keyfur. May I…please?"

For a long moment, Dee wondered if Ithross would refuse out of hand, but the man's professionalism finally won out over his temper. "Come ahead then. I'll see if Master Keyfur's available and if he'll see you. You'll have to wait."

"Thank you, Captain. Please tell Master Keyfur that Miss Moirin's life hangs in the balance."

Ithross deposited Dee in a small waiting room, stationed two guards to watch him, and stalked off.

Dee waited, worrying and cursing his previous behavior. One didn't spout off to an emperor without repercussions.

The door opened and Keyfur strode in, robes swirling, feather bobbing behind his ear, a worried expression on his face.

"Master Dee! The captain said it was urgent, that something's happened to Miss Moirin." His frown deepened as he extended a hand. "I hope nothing dire."

Dee shook the hand. "I'm afraid so, sir. She's been kidnapped. I need your help to—"

"Please, Master Dee." Keyfur glanced at the guards. "Let's discuss this in the privacy of my quarters."

"Oh. Of course."

Dee followed Keyfur through the palace on a long and winding path, escorted by imperial guards. Ithross hadn't reappeared, but he had no doubt that the captain would be summoned—and furious—if Dee stepped one inch out of line.

Keyfur finally stopped before a door like any one of the hundreds they'd already passed and pressed a hand to its center, ignoring the latch. The door opened without even a click.

"Please, please, come in." Keyfur ushering Dee through, then held up a hand to the guards. "Wait here."

At first glance, the large chamber resembled the parlor of a rich, eccentric packrat. Attractive paintings adorning the walls, an ornately woven carpet underfoot, a plush chair near a low table, and myriad shelves and bookcases crowded with all kinds of tombs and knickknacks. Then he took a step forward, and it all went...weird.

Dee caught movement from the corner of his eye. A chair that had been in the corner now stood at the table alongside the other one. A nearby painting of a colorful garden of flowers changed to a seascape before his eyes. The door seemed much farther away than it should be, and he had the strangest dread that it would vanish entirely. He took another step, and the intricate pattern on the carpet writhed and shifted.

Just like Mya's tattoos.

"What *is* all this stuff?"

Keyfur gazed around the apartment. "Aside from my own things, I'm not sure. I recently inherited all kinds of enchanted doo-dads from my late colleagues—wizards do love their toys—but I haven't had a chance to figure them out yet. I've been too busy learning to do all the work that used to be split up amongst all the members of the Imperial Retinue. But come, have a seat and a cup of blackbrew. You look positively done in, and we can't have you fainting dead away."

Dee crept over to the proffered seat carefully, afraid that he might sink into the carpet and disappear. Sitting, he nearly leapt up as the chair adjusted to accommodate the contours of his backside.

The wizard sat opposite him and poured a cup of blackbrew from a silver service that Dee would have sworn had not been on the table a moment ago. He passed a fine porcelain cup over.

"Thank you." He sipped the blackbrew. It was delicious. "It's been a long night."

"So I understand." Keyfur waved to a silver plate of sugared dainties. "Pastry?"

Mya loved pastries... Dee's stomach clenched as he realized that he'd thought of her in the past tense—*She* loves *pastries!* He shook his head. "No, thank you."

"Well then, what can I do to help you find Miss Moirin?"

Dee decided to be straightforward. "The only person I know capable of tracking her down is in Twailin. Can you magically transport me to Twailin, then bring us both back?"

Keyfur looked bewildered. "No, I can't. Why would you think I could?"

"W...w...why *not?*" Dee felt like he'd been punched in the gut. "You're the emperor's wizard! Hoseph can travel magically. I've seen him do it! I've even heard of an *alchemist* who can do it by drinking a potion."

"Really? A potion? Let me make a note to look into that." Keyfur twiddled his finger in the air as if writing, and a pen across the room scratched on a sheet of parchment. "Unfortunately, High Priest Hoseph's abilities are divine in origin, while mine are arcane. *Very* different magics. The former archmage, Master Duveau, could travel instantly by passing through stone, and I've heard of others who can do so through living wood, and even a few who can create a rift in... But never mind. Suffice to say that I haven't that skill. Wizards tend to be specialized. My specialty is the manipulation of air, light, color, and, to a lesser extent, charms over the human mind."

"Damn it!" Dee resisted the impulse to throw his cup of blackbrew against the wall, and carefully put it down on the table. "If we don't find Moirin soon, they'll *kill* her. We need this man to help us, but we can't wait the month it would take to send a message and get him back here. Isn't there *anything* you can do?"

"Wait a minute." Keyfur snapped his fingers. "Twailin...Twailin...Woefler!"

"Woefler?"

"Master Woefler, Duke Mir's wizard. *He* can travel magically."

Dee heart leapt into this throat, then just as quickly sank back into this stomach. "But it would still take at least a week to get word to him."

"Oh, no, *that's* easy!" Keyfur bounced to his feet and strode to a golden lectern set with a scroll mounted vertically on two spindles. Pulling a quill pen from the inkwell beside the scroll, he waved it at Dee. "This is highly secret, Master Dee. You won't remember my use of it once you've left here."

"I won't?"

"No, you won't."

"You're going to cast a spell on me?" Dee jumped up from his chair.

"I already have." Keyfur shrugged. "Don't worry, it's very limited in scope, but absolutely necessary."

It's for Mya... "All right." Dee joined the wizard at the lectern, studiously averting his eyes from the writhing carpet.

"With this, I can send a message to Master Woefler instantly." Keyfur turned back to the scroll. "Just give me the name and address of this person you need, and Woefler can fetch him for us."

"Ah, that might be a problem." Woefler showing up at the Tap and Kettle and demanding that Lad come with him sounded like a great way to kill a wizard.

"Why?" Keyfur looked perplexed. "I'm sure Duke Mir will give his full cooperation. If he sends his royal guards to..."

Dee shook his head; guards would be even worse. *This isn't working out the way I expected.* "This man is very particular about his privacy. I have to meet with him personally. Do you think Master Woefler could travel here to bring me to Twailin?"

"We can ask." Keyfur began writing on the scroll. Though he dipped the quill in the pot as if to capture ink, no words appeared on the parchment. This lack didn't seem to perturb the wizard, and he kept writing. "I'll simply tell Woefler that a service for the emperor requires him to come here immediately. When he arrives, we can discuss your needs."

"Thank you, Master Keyfur." Dee watched as Keyfur finished the message and turned the spindles on the podium. "Now what?"

"Now we wait. My message will appear on Woefler's scroll, and his return message will appear right here."

The two men stood and watched the scroll.

Dee peered closely at the parchment, but it stayed blank. "It's instantaneous, you say?"

"Yes. As soon as the words were written here, they appeared on his scroll."

They watched some more.

"Of course," Keyfur shifted uncomfortably, "if Woefler isn't there to get the message…"

Dee groaned in frustration.

"Not to worry!" Keyfur said brightly. "I know he's in the palace; I conversed with him just yesterday. I'll send you a note as soon as I receive his reply. Where can I reach you?"

Dee was as likely to provide the location of Clemson's new headquarters as he was Lad's address. "Send a message to the *Little Ditty Bakeshop* on Wester Street in the Dreggars Quarter. They'll make sure I get it. Anytime, day or night. I'll come immediately."

"Consider it done." Keyfur waved Dee to the door. "Anything else?"

"Nothing I can think of right now."

"Well, don't hesitate to ask." The door opened of its own accord, and the wizard ushered Dee out. "We'll do our best to help you, Master Dee. We owe Miss Moirin so very much."

"Thank you."

En route to Clemson's headquarters, Dee tried closing his eyes, but could find no peace. Images of Mya struggling against the tangling vines plagued him.

I've got to do something!

Dee wondered how long he'd have to wait for Keyfur's summons. He blinked and shook his head against a little wave of dizziness. Strange, but he couldn't remember how Keyfur was contacting Mir's wizard. Well, it didn't really matter *how* he did it, as long as Woefler got here soon.

Dee laid his head back and closed his eyes again. His mind now whirled with visions of the carpet in Keyfur's quarters, how it writhed with magic.

If only it was a flying carpet, he thought as he fell toward sleep, *I could fly off to Twailin to fetch Lad myself.*

CHAPTER XXI

*B*_{*lood.*}

Of all the odors in the world, that was not the one Mya wanted to wake to. She wondered if she'd dreamed it, some dark nightmare... Then she opened her eyes and reality made her nightmares pale in comparison.

My blood.

Kittal stood beside her slab with the skin-peeling device in hand. Blood dripped from the blades, and a roll of excised skin spiraled around the spiked spindle.

My skin. Nausea swelled in her throat.

"Perfect!" Kittal smiled. "Berta, bring the jar."

"Yes, Master." Berta—an older woman with a somber expression and hair bound in a severe braid—held a fluid-filled jar with a wide neck beneath the raw skin. A drop of blood plopped into the clear solution, tinting it the palest pink.

"Steady now." Kittal unwound the crank, unraveling the strip of flesh.

Without warning, the dangling skin twitched. Berta gasped, sloshing the liquid in the jar.

"Careful!" Kittal snapped. "Kelsey, bring tongs!"

Another Alchemist used a pair of long-handled tongs to guide the wriggling skin into the liquid. As it immersed, the runes glowed the color of hot embers.

"A positive reaction to the concoction. Excellent!" Kittal lay the peeling device aside. "The runes remain potent."

The Alchemists gathered around the table to see. Mya had the best view, whether she wanted it or not.

The skin had taken on a life of its own, writhing like an eel in the fluid-filled jar. The runic tattoos had always shifted and moved. Now they seemed to be straining to escape their prison of disembodied flesh.

Trying to come back to me... Mya swallowed hard and dismissed the fanciful thought. They weren't alive, couldn't think.

"Now we see if the graft will take." Kittal turned toward another long table. "Tieg, keep an eye on her breathing and pulse. If either quickens, apply the cloth for a single breath. Kelsey, you take the jar, and *don't drop it*! Berta, you've got the steadiest hands; you'll assist with the sutures. Now, let's get to it."

Before the Alchemists closed in around the other table, Mya glimpsed Lakshmi laying there, her eyes closed in what must have been a drug-induced sleep. She was covered in a sheet except for her left leg, which had been relieved of a strip of flesh along the thigh.

Kittal hunched over the Master Inquisitor. "Kelsey, the graft."

The young man reached into the jar with the forceps. It took him several tries to grasp one end of the squirming ribbon of flesh, but he eventually got a grip and lifted it out. Mya couldn't see the operation, but she could hear readily enough.

"Ah, lay it right here. Clamp it down there. Good. Now, pass me the catgut."

"Did you know they would *move* like this?" Berta asked, her voice uneasy.

"No," Kittal admitted. "Their motility is astonishing, isn't it?"

With her head turned as far as she could, Mya watched the Alchemists work, her thoughts deep and dark. *My skin... My runes...*

She had once thought to forgive Lakshmi and Kittal's transgressions in favor of guild unity, but now... Though she might forgive an assassin for trying to kill her on the orders of their superior, these two were working of their own accord, and their actions were beyond redemption. They'd crossed the line. This wasn't war any longer; it was personal. She'd kill them for violating her like this.

But first I've got to get free.

Mya tested her bonds once again, but while she was asleep, her captors had moved the wrist band up to her forearm, so there would be no more pulling free. If she couldn't rely on sheer strength, she'd have to devise an alternative plan. No matter how hard she considered, however, she came up blank.

"There! That's the last stitch. Unguent, Felan."

The junior Alchemist uncapped a large jar and passed it to Kittal. A moment later, a musky reek touched Mya's nostrils. Along with the scents of blood and antiseptic, it made her want to retch.

Kittal called for bandages and pins next, and they wrapped Lakshmi's leg. Finally he sighed and stepped back from the table.

"Berta, clean up. Felan, Tieg, take Lakshmi to her quarters. She's to stay abed until morning. I'll check to see how the graft is healing then. Stay with her until she comes around, then bring her a meal; she'll need the energy."

"Yes, Master." The two young men transferred the Master Inquisitor to a stretcher and carried her from the room.

"What is it with you and Lakshmi?" Mya had talked her way in and out of situations for years before she had the physical enhancements granted by her tattoos. Now, she had nothing to lose by trying.

The Master Alchemist glanced over at Mya, pushing the glasses up on his nose with a bloody finger. "You wouldn't understand."

Dismissal wasn't about to stop Mya. "Try me."

Ignoring her, he began laving his hands in a shallow basin.

"What kind of hold does she have on you to make you betray your guild?"

Kittal dried his hands in silence, then turned his back on her to fiddle with something on another table.

"Okay, let me put it another way. What do *you* get out of this? You're doing all the work just so she can take the guildmaster's ring and become your master. Why do you help her?"

"Lakshmi and I have been close associates for a very long time."

At least he's listening.

The soft whisk of steel on a whetstone reached Mya's ear. She shivered and tried to keep her voice steady. "You'd be better off earning the good will of the Grandmaster than helping the Master Inquisitor become guildmaster. I can offer you more than she can."

"No, you can't." He peered over his shoulder at her, his face set in hard lines. "And you're not Grandmaster." He went back to work.

"Do you really buy into this plan of Hoseph's? You think you can control the next emperor with only one of his three sons, and not even the eldest?"

"You know nothing of our plans."

"I know that Hoseph's using the guild to do his dirty work for him." Mya let that hang for a moment, but Kittal didn't answer. "Are you so used to following orders without question that you'll follow *anyone's* orders, even if they're not an assassin...not guild?"

"What goes on in the upper echelons of the guild doesn't concern me. Truly, I don't care."

"Really?" Mya injected disbelief into her tone. "Wouldn't you rather work for someone who allows you to develop your expertise as you see fit rather than just telling you exactly what to do?"

Kittal ceased his sharpening for a second, but it was enough for Mya to know that her words had struck true. She dared to hope...

"You don't understand, and I'm not going to explain it to you." Kittal turned to her, and Mya saw what he'd been working on—the skinning device, gleaming, spotless, and newly sharpened. "Now be quiet or I'll have Berta gag you."

Berta moved over and started washing the dried blood from Mya's wound. In a voice tinged with awe, she said, "The previous excision is completely gone, Master."

Kittal came over to look at Mya's leg, brushing his fingers over her renewed skin. Mya suppressed a shudder.

"Yes...and the remaining runes have migrated to fill the void. This will present a problem as we progress. Each graft will yield fewer runes as they're thinned out. We'll have to work much more quickly toward the end. I just hope she can withstand having such extensive surgery over a short period of time."

"Well, if the magic heals her so rapidly, she should—"

"Not *her!*" Kittal gestured dismissively toward Mya. "I meant Lakshmi. She's...fragile. The unguent you developed will promote growth of the grafts, but there's trauma to consider. If we're lucky, the runes we've already transferred will further enhance healing."

"Do you think she will survive to the end?" Berta indicated Mya with a nod.

"We'll make sure she does. If she dies, her skin dies. We have no way of knowing what the removal of the runes will do to her, so we'll have to keep a close eye on her condition."

Mya did *not* like where this conversation was going, but she knew better than to voice any impotent objection. Knowledge, however unpleasant, was power, and right now, she needed anything she could get.

Kittal turned back to the instruments and chemicals. Berta continued to scrub Mya and the table. Their eyes met for a brief moment, but the woman quickly looked away.

After a while, Kittal opened the door, stopping halfway through. "Get plenty of rest tonight, Berta. If the graft is a success, we'll be busy tomorrow."

"Yes, Master."

The door closed, and the two of them were alone. Mya watched Berta work. Her hands were deft and not ungentle. She'd made no progress speaking to Kittal, but...

"He treats you like a slave, doesn't he?" Mya asked.

Berta didn't answer, didn't even look at her. She hurriedly toweled Mya dry and whirled away, dimming the glow crystals and tucking away a few more items before she left the room. The lock clicked home, and her footsteps receded down the corridor.

"Well, that didn't work."

Mya lay alone in the chill gloom—bound and betrayed—with nothing but her own morbid thoughts. She closed her eyes against the welling despair, desperately clinging to her one thin shred of hope.

They're looking for me. Hurry, Dee... I don't have long...

Dee steeled himself as his carriage pulled up in front of Tawny's Maritime Victuals. Telling Paxal about Mya's capture wouldn't be easy.

If he doesn't just kill me.

Tossing a coin to the driver, he strode to the building. The air above the chimneys wavered with heat, and when Dee passed through the open double doors, the torrid air seemed to suck all his energy away. Breathing hurt, and his head swam for a moment.

"Help ya, sir?" A red-faced woman hurried forward, wiping her hands on her flour-dusted apron.

Dee supposed this was Tawny. He'd only been here a couple of times, and only at night, so he'd never met the woman. "Pardon, ma'am, but I need to speak to Paxal."

She tossed her head toward the rickety stairway. "Upstairs."

Dee started for the stairs, but stopped as a shout rang out.

"Master Dee!" Nestor grinned at him from behind a low table piled high with biscuits. Twigs, Nails, and Gimp were there, too, packing the biscuits firmly into barrels. Digger emerged from a back room carrying a sack of flour, and little Kit looked up from where she was placing rounds of dough onto a baking sheet. They all dropped what they were doing and ran out to greet him.

The baker's face turned even redder. "Here now, you can't just be runnin' off to—"

"Stay here," Dee said, waving them back to their work. "I've just got to talk to Pax."

"What's wrong, Master Dee?" Digger's eyes searched his face anxiously.

Dee realized that his grim expression must have given him away. "You'll learn everything soon enough." He climbed the stairs, fatigue and dread dragging at his legs, and rapped on the door to the loft.

"Knock knock?" Knock opened the door, and her broad flat face broke into a tusky grin. "Knock!"

"Hello, Knock. I need to—"

Paxal crossed to the door, stopping short as he spied Dee's face. "Dee? What's wrong?"

"It's Mya." Dee stepped into the room and closed the door behind him. "She's been taken."

"*Taken?*" Paxal stared at him, the veins in his neck throbbing faster. "What do you mean, taken?"

"The people opposing her took her, Pax. That's all I know right now. She's not dead, as far as we know, so there's a—"

Paxal's gnarled old hands clenched into fists. "This is the *second* time you've come to me with bad news about Mya."

"And I wish it was her bringing you news they'd taken me, Pax, but I can't change what happened. I need help if I'm going to get her back."

"You mean if *we're* going to get her back," the old innkeeper growled.

"Yes, we."

"Knock!" The squat girl's eyes flicked fretfully between Dee and Paxal.

"Yes, Knock, that includes you all." He looked back to Paxal imploringly. "I need the kids. I know they're working, but—"

"To *hell* with the work!" The fire in Paxal's eyes rivaled the ovens downstairs. "Knock, start packin' up!"

"Knock!" The girl scuttled off and began gathering their sparse belongings.

Paxal flung open the door and yelled down, "Kids, get up here!"

"Wh— What? Get back to work, you!" Tawny's shrill commands hurt Dee's ears. "What are you thinkin', old man? We contracted—"

"We're *leaving*!" Pax bellowed. "No arguments!"

Feet pounded up the steps amid the woman's curses. The urchins swarmed into the room.

"What's up?" Digger asked, his eyes wide with worry.

Dee sighed. "Mya's in trouble. I need you all to start asking your friends questions."

"Ain't got no *friends*, but there's kids enough on the streets. Just tell us where and what to ask." Digger pulled a pitted dagger from under his flour-dusted shirt. "And how bad you want answers."

"Money'll work better'n cuttin' 'em," Kit said, her tiny face pinched into a sour expression. "A few coppers here and there, and street kids'll sell you their *mothers*!"

"Good." Heaving a deep breath, Dee looked down into their expectant faces. "Here's what I need you to do…"

Hoseph prowled the archives beneath the temple of Demia. Over the years, he'd spent untold hours amidst these books and scrolls, reading, learning, sometimes just browsing. But over the last few weeks, he'd focused his search, looking for answers to one particular problem.

Does my pain derive from my talisman? He peered at the small silver skull. *Or perhaps from time spent in the Sphere of Shadow?*

Paging through yet another tome, he cringed at the theoretical drivel. The author obviously hadn't ever visited any of the alternate spheres of existence. Serious scholarly work was much rarer. One didn't travel to another sphere on a whim; some were hostile, requiring special protections just to survive.

"Another dead end." Disgusted, he placed the tome back on the shelf. Nowhere had he discovered any mention of symptoms such as his brought on by either sphere travel or use of a talisman. It was hopeless. He would have to endure.

At least enduring was much easier now.

Hoseph fished the bottle of elixir he'd stolen from Kittal from the pocket of his robe and examined it in the light. The meniscus wobbled halfway down the brown glass. He used it sparingly, but there would be many tasks ahead that would require travel through the Sphere of Shadow. He inspected the script on the label, but the characters meant nothing to him. Hoseph was a scholar of Demia, not alchemy.

"May the Mistress of Death take them and their secrets to the afterlife!"

He couldn't ask Kittal for more without revealing his weakness, not to mention the theft of the first bottle, but to run out would be a catastrophe. There was only one thing to do. Sighing, Hoseph flipped out the silver skull and invoked Demia's grace, passed through the Sphere of Shadow and on to Kittal's secret hideaway.

Hoseph materialized in the dark, staggered with the blinding pain, and brought the vial of elixir to his lips. One dash, a few drops, and the pain faded to only a memory. Calling forth a glow from his palm, he inspected the bottles and vials on the shelves, comparing their labels to the one in his hand. The search took time, but he had time and, more importantly, need.

Here! Hoseph picked a similar bottle off a shelf and compared the labels. *Not quite the same.* He put it back and picked another. *Yes…yes!* A perfect match. Unfortunately, it was the only one like it remaining. If he took the last bottle, Kittal would know something had gone missing.

Easy enough to remedy… Hoseph pulled the stopper from the full bottle and transferred half its volume to his own, then put the half-empty bottle back on the shelf. Nobody would be the wiser.

Chapter XXII

Mya lay utterly still on the slab. Not out of choice, but under the chemical compulsion of the Master Alchemist. With the scent of blood and antiseptic filling her head, she would have been thrashing and fighting every second, but Kittal had preempted her struggles with the application of a paralytic oil that rendered her muscles inert. She could breathe, speak, and scream, which she had done aplenty, but she couldn't move. She stared at the ceiling and tried to ignore what Kittal and his Alchemists were doing.

No pain... Mya felt only a tugging sensation and the warmth of blood oozing down her thigh.

Eight strips of rune-etched skin had been taken from her so far. They now writhed and squirmed, each in their own jar of fluid. Two more jars waited.

Dee's looking for me...

Though heartening at first, the mantra was becoming less comforting.

In an effort to ignore the peculiar tugging of the peeling device, the scent of blood, and her own helplessness, Mya had been running one rescue scenario after another through her mind. As a Hunter, she knew that their chance of finding her decreased with every passing moment. The trail grew colder by the minute. Finding someone deliberately hidden was hard enough, especially in a city the size of Tsing...

And Dee doesn't know Tsing... The thought plunged her into despair until she forced it down with the reassurance that Embree and his people *did* know the city. They'd find her. After all, they'd found and rescued the two Tessifus boys, hadn't they?

Actually, I did most of the finding and rescuing... Despair threatened again.

Something splashed, bringing her back to the horrific moment. Another strip of rune-etched flesh writhed in a jar of liquid. *My runes...*

"One more," Kittal said, turning back to the table, that evil peeling device in hand. "There, before the wound heals completely."

It hasn't healed yet? Minor wounds like these usually healed instantly.

A sudden twinge—a flash of both hot and cold together—snapped Mya's attention from her musing. The pressure of the peeling device against her leg evolved into an ache that escalated to a throb and climaxed with a sharp sting.

Pain...

Mya had forgotten the sensation. The last physical pain she'd experienced was the prick of Vonlith's needles as the runemage tattooed her. Their removal would undoubtedly be far more painful.

Mya bit her lip, and the muscles of her leg twitched involuntarily.

"She's moving!" Kittal snapped. "More oil, or this graft will be ruined! Hurry!"

An assistant dampened a cloth with the sweet-smelling oil and rubbed it along Mya's leg. Her twitch died, but the sting remained. A cool hand touched her wrist.

"Master, I think she's in pain. Her breathing's fast, and her heart's racing." Berta picked a bottle off a shelf and popped the cork, a cloth in her other hand. The scent of the doping drug leached into the air. "Shall I—"

"No, Berta." Kittal glanced at Mya, his eyes narrow and hard. "We're almost done. Besides, she broke my arm and dislocated my shoulder yesterday. Payback only seems fair."

The oil may have paralyzed Mya's body, but it didn't affect her speech. "You want payback? How about I wind your intestines around a stake in a pit of hungry rats?"

"Brave words for someone in your position." Kittal tapped her restraints. "Brave, or foolish."

"I'm going to kill you for this, you know. You're committing atrocities against your own guild, and you'll die for it."

"Ignore her," he instructed, redirecting his efforts to the device in his hands. The crank turned, and skin parted from flesh with the sound of tearing silk.

Mya clenched her teeth as he worked. The pain intensified, luring unwelcome memories out from the dark corners of her mind. Pain induced fear, and Mya had spent a lifetime running from fear.

And now I can't even run.

Mya was panting by the time Kittal finished and the immediate pain vanished. Turning her head, she stared at the ten jars, watched her severed runes glow and dance. She'd once thought that the runes made her a monster. If so, should she thank Kittal for giving her back her humanity?

No, Dee *made me feel human again.* Losing her runes merely made her vulnerable.

"Berta," Kittal was drying his hands, "clean up here and get a bite to eat. You two, decant preservative solution into ten more jars. I want everyone back here in two hours. We'll transplant what we have onto Lakshmi, then take more grafts." Kittal left, followed by the two younger Alchemists.

Ten more... Mya's heart raced. She couldn't take ten more...

Berta drew two buckets of water and placed them beside Mya's table. Rolling up her sleeves, she proceeded to wash Mya and the table both, scrubbing up the dried blood with a rough sponge and warm, soapy water. As she worked, the paralyzing oil was washed away.

Mya clenched and relaxed her hands, envisioning them around Kittal's throat.

Berta stumbled back from her, eyes wide on Mya's flexing hands, fear clear on her face.

"I won't hurt you," Mya said.

The woman turned away and emptied her bucket without answering.

Mya tried a different tack. "You're Berta, right?"

Berta returned with a towel and began drying Mya, her lips pressed tightly together.

Mya watched her work for a moment, efficient and thorough. The Alchemist had noticed when Mya was in pain during the procedure, recognized the symptoms, and had started to use the anesthetic before Kittal stopped her. *Maybe...*

"I'm going to die here. I'd at least like to know who's killing me."

The woman snapped her eyes to Mya's, her mouth a drawn in a defiant frown. "I'm not killing you. I'm just following orders." She went back to her work.

"Orders..." Mya considered the woman carefully. "Kittal said that you developed the unguent you're using on Lakshmi."

The woman's eyes flicked to hers, then away.

"You're obviously skilled in the healing arts. What I'd like to know is why someone like *you* is doing *this*."

Berta stopped for a moment, then continued with renewed vigor, but it was enough to tell Mya that her comment had struck a nerve. If she could make Berta feel guilty about what was happening to her, maybe she could coerce her into helping.

"How long..." Mya cleared her throat, unsure if she wanted an answer to this, but hoping to at least provoke sympathy. "I mean...how many more times will it take?"

"I don't know." Berta looked up and down Mya's body. "Kittal's taken maybe a tenth of your runes, but the yield will diminish as we progress."

"A tenth..." Mya shivered and bit down against the sob that wanted to escape her throat. That meant at least a *ninety* more times Kittal's device would cut into her, ninety more strips of skin would squiggle in the jars. And the pain, she knew, would get worse. Today she'd been able to bear it, but when the pain-blocking runes were finally all gone, and her healing runes as well...

I'll lie here begging for death, just like Kiesha, driven made by the agony.

Despair rose in her like a dark tide. Hope of rescue, slim at best, seemed a dim beacon in that darkness. But what else was there? There was only one other future that she could hope for, and maybe she'd found someone to help her.

"Kill me, Berta. Please." Mya struggled to keep her voice from shaking. She'd never been one to beg, even when it meant enduring pain, but death seemed her only hope for a painless end to this.

The woman looked startled. "I *can't*."

"You *can*. There have got to be poisons in this room. You're an *Alchemist*, not a torturer! You can tell Kittal that you found me dead. He'll never know." Mya hated herself for pleading like this, but she saw no other option.

"He'd know." Berta dropped her towel into a bucket. "And then *I'd* be strapped to a table, but it'd be Lakshmi holding the blade."

"Then kill me and run away! There are no more blood contracts."

Berta stopped and looked Mya in the eye. "Where would I go? What would I do? The guild is my life."

"The guild was *my* life, too. And now it seems it will be my death."

The Alchemist tore her gaze away and returned to her work.

"Please." Mya strained to reach the woman's robe, to grasp her, hold her there, to make her listen. "Don't let them *do* this to me."

"I can't stop it." Berta jerked away. She stood hunched over another table for a minute, then finally straightened, wiping her eyes with one sleeve. She picked up the two buckets and headed for the door, then stopped. She spoke without looking back. "I'll see about getting you some drugs while Kittal...operates. That's the best I can do."

Mya swallowed a hot retort. Berta's offer wasn't much, but it was more kindness she had reason to expect in this place. At least she might die sane and not screaming.

"Thank you, Berta."

The Alchemist looked back at Mya one more time before fumbling with the door latch and hurrying out.

"Here's the pastry you ordered, sir."

Dee's head snapped up and he blurrily regarded the cheerful serving woman beside his table. Gods, he was tired! He must have fallen asleep over his blackbrew.

"I didn't order another pastry."

"I'm sorry this one was stale." The young woman swept aside the plate with his half-eaten sweet roll and replaced it with the new one. "I hope you'll find this more to your liking."

Dee shook his head. He was tired, but he wasn't senile. He'd have remembered ordering another pastry.

"I didn't—"

Then he saw it, the edge of an envelope tucked beneath the plate. *Finally!* Picking up the new pastry, he bit into it and nodded. "Delicious. Thank you."

"Of course, sir." The waitress nodded with a smile and hurried off.

Dee didn't know if she actually worked for the guild or if Embree just paid her to deliver messages, but he appreciated her discretion. He probably shouldn't have come here, but waiting at Clemson's new hideout only reminded him of how little had been accomplished in the search for Mya. After an entire night pouring over maps, lists, reports, and the scant evidence, they'd finally told him to get out, get some sleep, eat something, and stop bothering them.

Sleep... It had been a nice thought, but every time he closed his eyes he saw Mya struggling in the vines, telling him to run, to save himself. So he'd come to the *Little Ditty* to wait for Keyfur's message.

Sliding the envelope out from under the plate, he spied the inscription—Master Dee—written in an unfamiliar, ornate script. He broke the wax seal and pulled out the message.

Dear Master Dee,

Please attend me at my residence as soon as you get this message. We have an appointment to keep.

K

Well, it seemed Master Keyfur also understood discretion. Even if someone intercepted the message, they wouldn't have understood it. Dee dropped a few coins on the table and strode from the bakeshop.

He dozed off during the carriage ride to the palace despite his attempt to be vigilant, the shuddering stop of the heavy wheels on the cobblestones jolting him awake. The imperial guard who peered in the carriage window looked familiar.

The woman smiled. "Master Dee, we're seeing a lot of you lately."

"I have an appointment with Master Keyfur."

"Drive on!" she called to the driver. "Outer court, postern door to the right."

When his carriage pulled to a stop beside the postern door, Dee dismounted and started to doff his long coat, as usual, but one of the guards held up his hand.

"No need for that, sir. You're to wait here for Master Keyfur." He ushered Dee into a tiny room just inside the door.

Dee thanked the guard and rubbed his face to wake up. He would have paced, but the room was so small it wasn't worth the effort. He remained standing, afraid that if he sat down he might fall asleep again.

"Ah, Master Dee. Good news." Keyfur entered in a flourish of colorful robes, his stride jaunty and his face beaming with pleasure. "Master Woefler awaits us at *The Hyacinth*, a lovely little café just a few blocks from the palace gate."

Dee fell in beside the wizard as he strode out the door to the palace courtyard. "Why didn't he come straight here?"

"The palace is protected from entry using magical means." Keyfur leaned in and lowered his voice. "Else we'd be much more concerned about High Priest Hoseph popping in unannounced, wouldn't we?"

They stepped into the courtyard to find an ornate carriage waiting, an imperial guard holding the door open for them. Dee cocked an eyebrow. "Did you know that Hoseph can use his magic to pop into a moving carriage?"

"Yes. The death of Baroness Monjhi taught us all that lesson, but rest assured, *nobody* can arrive magically in a carriage that I'm riding in." Keyfur mounted the step and dropped onto a well-cushioned seat. "You're safe with me, Master Dee."

Dee settled into the plush cushions and found himself nodding before they even emerged from the palace gates. He leaned back, closed his eyes just for a moment...and started awake when a hand lightly touched his knee.

"We've arrived, Master Dee." Keyfur looked worried. "You seem exhausted."

"I'm fine." Dee blinked himself fully awake, embarrassed that he'd fallen asleep.

They exited the carriage in front of an elaborately decorated café. The building was painted pale blue and the door a cheery yellow. Large windows trimmed in white sported colorful sashes. Flowers and vines overflowed from window boxes and large pots beside the door.

Two liveried doormen snapped to attention. "Master Keyfur, good to see you again."

Obviously, this was a frequent haunt of the wizard's. While one doorman opened the door and bowed Keyfur in, the other discreetly inspected Dee from head to foot, his gaze lingering on his boots and the drape of his long jacket.

Probably meant to keep riffraff like me out of the place. But being accompanied by Master Keyfur was apparently sufficient endorsement of his character, and the doormen didn't impede his progress.

"Master Keyfur! How *delightful* to see you!" The hostess, a stunning creature in a dress that would have ransomed a prince, took the wizard's hands in hers and kissed him on the cheek. "Your friend awaits you in the Blue Room." She gestured with one hand, and an escort appeared as if by magic.

"Thank you, Laila." Keyfur followed the waiter through the busy café.

Dee fell in behind the wizard, returning the hostess' smile with a nod. He surveyed his surroundings, noting potential hiding spots and exits. Richly dressed patrons lunched at about half of the tables. Dee ignored the contemptuous glances cast his way.

The Blue Room was, true to its name, painted a deep sapphire blue, the ceiling overhead the palest azure. It made Dee feel as if he was under the sea. The tablecloth, too, was blue, set off by pure white porcelain settings and intricately cut crystal goblets. Platters of food crowded the table.

A youngish-looking man stood from his chair, smiling as they came in. "Master Keyfur!" He rounded the table with a hand extended. "Good to see you looking well."

"And you, Master Woefler." The two wizards shook hands amiably and Keyfur gestured to Dee. "This is Master Dee, assistant to Miss Moirin, that wonderful young woman you met at the coronation."

"Indeed!" Woefler extended a hand to Dee. "Well met, sir. You have a remarkable mistress."

"Thank you, Master Woefler. She's the reason I need your help."

Woefler arched his eyebrows as he looked to Keyfur. "Your message said that the *emperor* required my presence?"

"In a matter of speaking," Keyfur assured him. "He's ordered help for Master Dee from any and all of us."

"Well, I'm at your service, then." Woefler gestured to the table. "Let's sit and discuss this while we eat. I took the liberty of ordering us a meal. I *always* eat at *The Hyacinth* when I'm in Tsing, Master Dee. The food here is amazing."

Dee had to admit that the food looked and smelled delicious, but his stomach clenched, an unfortunate result of too much blackbrew, sweet rolls, and nerves. The thought of food made him wince.

"Let me first ensure that our conversation remains private." Keyfur drew a slim glass rod from his robes and proceeded to touch each of the walls, muttering all the while under his breath.

Woefler's eyes lit up. "Oh, so it's a *secret* kind of mission, eh? I *love* secrets!"

Dee clenched his teeth at the flippant remark. "My pardon, Master Woefler, but we don't have time for lunch. Miss Moirin has been kidnapped. Master Keyfur said you could travel magically. I need you to take me to Twailin, then bring me and a colleague back to Tsing."

"My goodness!" Woefler's eyes widened. "Well, I certainly understand your desire for haste, sir, but you must also understand that traveling by magic isn't without cost. I must eat, rest, and prepare."

"Master Dee, please sit and eat." Keyfur gestured to a chair. "Miss Moirin won't benefit if you collapse from malnutrition and exhaustion."

Dee clenched his fists. "I'm not hungry. I'll just wait for—"

"Master Dee." Woefler stood with his hands on his hips. "With or without you, I'm going to have a nice meal, relax for a time, and prepare for the arduous task of whisking you a thousand miles through the ether to Twailin. I'll make you a deal. You sit down and share this meal with us, and I'll give you something that will alleviate your exhaustion. Trust me; the time we spend here is *not* wasted."

Dee glanced at the table and his mouth watered at the sight and scent of the luscious fare. He felt his resolve weakening as reason battled with impatience. He nodded to the wizard. "I know nothing of magic, Master Woefler, but I need your help, so I'm in your hands. How soon we can travel?"

"This evening, perhaps earlier." Woefler poured pale wine into three glasses, and Keyfur began serving. "Taking others on such a journey is more taxing than traveling alone. I'll need a full night's rest before returning here with you and your associate."

Dee's frustration flared again. "Is there no way to hurry this up? Is there some other wizard in Twailin I might contract to return us sooner?"

"No one else in Twailin is capable of this spell." Woefler sounded slightly affronted by the idea of being upstaged by another wizard. "This isn't like conjuring pixies from a dandelion, my good man."

"Sorry." Dee reluctantly sat. If he wanted anything from these wizards, he'd have to cooperate. "As I said, I don't know anything about magic."

"Then you'll have to trust in our expertise," Keyfur said with his usual radiant smile. "Now eat something before you collapse."

"And here." Woefler reached across the table and poured a tiny vial of white powder into Dee's wine. "Drink this and you'll feel like a newly minted gold crown."

Dee looked suspiciously at the wine, but relented. If he trusted the man to take him a thousand miles through some kind of magical passage, he may as well trust him to banish his fatigue with a potion. Sighing in contrition, he sampled the wine. It tasted perfectly normal, with a slightly tannic finish. Suddenly he was ravenous. He sampled a delicate breast of roast fowl, the flavors exploding in his mouth, and soon found himself eating with relish.

The wizards chatted amiably for a time, and Dee found his fatigue slowly ebbing away. Finally, Woefler turned to him with a question.

"Did Miss Moirin ever tell you how she saved the emperor's life?"

Dee swallowed before answering. "Yes. She killed Archmage Duveau."

"Oh, there's more to the story than that!" Woefler grinned and raised a glass.

"She's amazing, isn't she?" Keyfur's eyes sparkled. "She saved my life as well."

"Her abilities are obviously augmented by magic. I suspected those black wrappings she wore under her dress, but I couldn't very well ask her, could I?" Woefler looked at Dee expectantly.

"No, you couldn't." Dee didn't want to be rude, but he'd burn in the Nine Hells before he revealed Mya's secrets. "She's very guarded about that. You have to understand that if everyone knew what she could do, her livelihood would be at risk, if not her…life." Dee's throat closed on a bite of food and he swallowed hard. "Pardon me, but I'm not easy speaking of her…abilities like this."

"Oh, of course. Just professional curiosity, you understand." Woefler waved it off without concern.

They passed on to other subjects having nothing to do with Dee, Mya, or anything else pertinent to their plight. Dee finished his meal and his wine, but refused a second glass. Though the potion had banished his fatigue, it had fueled his impatience. He sipped water and fidgeted, but the wizards seemed insensible of his distress. He couldn't rush them, couldn't calm his jangling nerves, and couldn't stop thinking about Mya in the hands of the Master Inquisitor.

"And…*done!*" Arbuckle flourished his pen like a rapier and stabbed it into the inkwell.

"Congratulations, Majesty!" Tennison grinned in shared triumph. "The New Accords are a fine set of laws. If I may be so bold, I believe your father would thoroughly disapprove."

The emperor laughed with a lighter heart than he'd felt for months. With assassins, murderous priests, kidnapped children, and Miss Moirin's recent abduction, he'd had little to laugh about. "That, Tennison, is the highest praise We could ask for. We need to celebrate!" He waved to a waiting footman. "Fetch Us a bottle of sparkling wine and two goblets!"

"Would you like me to summon Duke Tessifus, Majesty?" Tennison stood and took a step toward the door.

"No, We would *not*!" Arbuckle stared at his secretary in surprise. "*You'll* share this achievement with Us! By the Gods of Light, we've *both* put our life's blood into this document! The good duke may have offered some suggestions, but *we* did the work!"

"Majesty, I..." Tennison looked shocked. "I don't think it's appropriate that I—"

"Sit down and quit protesting! We deserve this! *We* earned it!" Arbuckle clapped his ink-stained hand on the stack of parchment before him. "These accords will transfigure the empire and usher in a new era of justice, and you put as much work into them as We did. You have Our undying thanks."

"You did the lion's share, Majesty," the secretary said, looking embarrassed. "Your knowledge of history found precedents for the framework. Without that, we would have been lost."

Arbuckle sat back in his chair in contentment. "It *is* nice to know that Our years of being a bookworm weren't wasted."

The footman hustled back through the door carrying a silver bucket sweating condensation, a dark bottle resting within. A second footman bearing two crystal goblets on a silver tray followed. The first extracted the bottle from the ice and expertly drew the cork. The *pop!* echoed off the library walls, drawing another laugh from the emperor's throat. Gods, it had been so long since he'd laughed...

The footman expertly filled the two glasses, not spilling a drop, then proffered the tray first to Arbuckle, then to Tennison, who looked a little unsure about drinking with an emperor.

"To Our New Accords." Arbuckle raised his glass, and Tennison's chimed sweetly against it.

Arbuckle closed his eyes as he sipped, relishing the delicate flavor of the wine and the satisfaction of his long toil completed. For a moment, he purged his mind of worries. He'd been looking forward to this day for too long not to savor it.

"So, We send it off to the archivists for a fair copy and enact it into law!"

"I should review the document one more time for errors or omissions before we send it off, Majesty, but yes. The archivists will make it a work of art worthy of the laws within."

"How long do you think that will take?" Arbuckle turned to the imperial scribe seated in the corner. "Verul, what do you think?"

Verul eyed the pile of parchment. "A month or so, I would say, Majesty."

"A *month*?" The emperor drummed his fingers on the table. "We can't institute the laws for a month?"

"Majesty, the laws can be instituted *immediately*," Tennison explained. "Copies can be sent to the provincial dukes in a matter of days and posted on notice throughout the city. You should also make a formal announcement, but you needn't wait for the archival copy to be completed."

"Well, then, We'll read them out. Set a time and place, Tennison, and have announcements posted throughout the city. We think the Imperial Plaza would be appropriate."

"You'll read them out in *public*, Majesty?" The secretary looked horrified. "Personally?"

"Of course! Why not?"

Tennison swallowed and put his glass down. "*Because*, Majesty, there's still a certain…faction at large trying to *assassinate* you. They could take the opportunity of a public appearance to do so."

"We won't cower in the palace, Tennison!" Arbuckle frowned and drained his glass. He might not have blademasters to protect him or, sadly, Miss Moirin to save his life with her amazing prowess, but he still had a knighthood, an Imperial Guard, and a constabulary to keep him safe. "I'll read the New Accords out in public to the common people of Tsing. They *deserve* it! Set up a date as soon as may be."

"Yes, Majesty." Tennison scratched a note in his ledger, still looking dubious.

"And pick up your glass, man! We're celebrating!" Arbuckle waved the footman forward with the bottle.

"Yes, Majesty." Tennison picked up his glass, and the footman topped them off. However, as crystal chimed in toast to their accomplishment, Arbuckle saw more worry than victory in his secretary's eyes.

Chapter XXIII

Approaching voices woke Mya from her troubled doze, a welcome disruption of the snippet dreams filled with sharpened steel and blood. She couldn't escape this horror even in sleep.

"Yes, yes, we took ten, but I don't know how many we should graft on."

Kittal's voice…close…

"Why not all of them?"

Lakshmi now…

Metal clicked, and the door opened. Kittal, Lakshmi, and the assisting Alchemists entered the chamber.

"Because the trauma is dangerous for you," Kittal said.

Berta came in last and pointedly avoided Mya's gaze.

So much for sympathy… Mya had hoped for some compassion from the woman, but then, she could hardly expect a wink and a nod.

"Hello, Mya." Lakshmi's smile, so sweet and benign, turned Mya's stomach. The Master Inquisitor approached her captive. "I see you've recovered."

Mya glared at her in silence. Any response would only buy her more pain.

"Nothing to say? Well, I really must thank you for the runes you donated. The graft worked perfectly, and I feel stronger already."

"At this point that's probably wishful thinking, but we can certainly call our trial an unmitigated success." Kittal guided the Inquisitor to the other table, past the row of jars with their writhing strips of luminous skin. "Your grafts await, Lakshmi. Let's get started."

"Yes, let's." Lakshmi turned away without another glance at Mya.

"Prepare the anesthetic," Kittal instructed his assistants.

Lakshmi doffed her silk robe, comfortable in her nudity as she climbed up onto the table and lay back. The strip of Mya's flesh shone starkly against the Master Inquisitor's dark skin, circumscribed by a thin line of pink scar tissue. Curiously, the runes hadn't migrated beyond the borders, though they did writhe and dance within their confines. Mya had hoped the runes would lose their magic, but they seemed as animated as ever.

Traitors...

Berta draped a sheet over the Master Inquisitor's wizened body, leaving both legs exposed.

Kittal accepted a dampened white kerchief from Tieg and held it gingerly over his colleague's face. "Breathe deeply. Just sleep, Lakshmi. You'll wake up in no time."

A stifled cough ruffled the handkerchief, then a gasp, then slow breaths. Kittal drew away the cloth. "All right, let's get to work. We have a lot to do."

Mya watched in morbid fascination as they began grafting her flesh onto her enemy's body.

A knock on the door of the Blue Room stopped Dee's pacing. He glanced at the two wizards. Keyfur lounged at the table, sipping tea and scratching notes in a slim notebook. Woefler, seated away in the corner, was so engrossed in a book that he hadn't even noticed the knock.

"Go ahead and open it, Master Dee," Keyfur said. "It's probably just the staff asking if we want anything."

"No more gods-be-damned blackbrew..." Dee muttered as he turned to the door.

He opened it to find Laila, the hostess, her face animated. "Just thought I'd drop this by." She held out a single-page flier of the type usually tacked to posterboards all over the city. "The emperor's made an announcement! He's finished his New Accords!"

"Oh..." Dee took the paper without much interest. He didn't really give a damn about the emperor's new laws. "Um...thanks." He closed the door and resumed pacing, dropping the flier on the table as he passed.

Keyfur picked it up and looked it over, then grimaced. "Oh, bother! Another public appearance? What in the names of the Gods of Light is he thinking?"

"He's probably thinking someone like *Moirin* will keep him safe so he doesn't have to worry." *Even if they get killed in the process.*

"You don't think much of our emperor, do you, Master Dee?"

Dee shrugged. "Better than the last, I suppose."

"Yes, he is, quite a lot better, actually." Master Keyfur looked displeased, which struck Dee as uncharacteristic; the wizard always seemed so happy. "I risked my life to save his and I'd do so again. He's worthy of our respect."

I hope so." Dee continued pacing. "How much longer, do you think?"

"I don't know." Keyfur turned back to his notebook. "As long as it takes."

"Great," Dee muttered, resuming his back-and-forth course.

Finally, Woefler's book thumped closed, and the wizard looked up.

Dee froze in anticipation. *If he calls for more food, I'll…*

"Done!" Standing, Woefler stretched, working the muscles of his shoulders and neck. Looking around the room as if surprised by his surroundings, he saw Dee and smiled. "Sorry for the wait, but magic can't be hurried, Master Dee." He cracked his knuckles. "You do *not* want this spell to go awry."

"Awry?" Dee didn't know things like this *could* go awry. "What do you mean?"

"Oh, all kinds of horrible things can happen if a spell goes wrong. One mispronounced word or a distraction, and we could end up lost forever in the either! Ha!" He looked thoroughly amused at Dee's distress. "Don't' worry. I'm fresh as a daisy and have never erred in this incantation before."

"Let's hope this isn't the first time."

"Anything else before you go?" Keyfur tucked away his notebook and stood, his levity and brilliant smile again in place. "A cup of blackbrew, perhaps?" He winked at Dee, mischief twinkling in his eyes.

"No! We should go! I'll still need to talk with some people

before visiting my associate. It's going to take time, and time is what we're short of."

Woefler looked perturbed, but bowed to Keyfur. "I'll be in touch. If all goes well on Master Dee's part, we'll meet you here tomorrow morning."

"I'll make the reservations. Breakfast for four!" Keyfur smiled and laughed. "And apparently lunch is on me."

"Thanks. I'll pick up the bill for breakfast tomorrow." Woefler cocked an eyebrow at Dee. "Ready?"

Hours ago. Dee kept his mouth shut and nodded.

The wizard stuck his fingers into a pocket of his robe and withdrew them, raising his hand high. Murmuring softly, he snapped his fingers, and a cascade of iridescent motes drifted down. The air before him shimmered, then darkened to deepest black. Woefler held a hand out to Dee. "Now take my hand and don't let go. The transition can be disconcerting to the uninitiated."

Disconcerting? How about terrifying? Dee peered at the oval of darkness. It seemed impenetrable, annihilating the lamplight rather than being illuminated by it. Viewing the portal from the side, it appeared to be as thin as a sheet of paper. His skin prickled. *Nothing for it. Mya can't wait weeks...* Girding his nerves, Dee gripped the wizard's hand.

Woefler stepped forward and disappeared into the darkness as completely as if he'd been immersed in black oil. Only his hand, tugging Dee forward, protruded. Then it was gone, and Dee's own hand penetrated the black plane. An indescribable chill stung his hand and progressed up his arm as it was engulfed in the opaque portal. When the black void touched his face, his heart skipped a beat, his mind experiencing the strange sensation of being in two places at once. Then it was over, and he emerged into an unfamiliar room...and chaos.

"Who the *hell...*"

A man in uniform—gold braid at the collar—stood from behind a desk, a crossbow already half-raised. To one side, a huge beast growled and lunged, slavering jaws wide. Woefler thrust out his free hand, shouting words that shivered the air. A shimmer of light appeared before them. The beast—a massive dog—struck the barrier and rebounded with a snarl.

"Brutus! Down! Hold!" The man behind the desk lowered the crossbow and snapped his fingers twice. "Heel!"

To Dee's relief, the dog immediately turned and took station beside its master. It growled and glared, thick spittle dripping off its jowls onto the floor. The man's hand looked as small as a child's as he patted the dog's immense head.

"Master Woefler, you need to be more careful about when and where you pop in!"

Woefler let go of Dee's hand and heaved a deep breath. "*Must you keep that beast at your side every hour of the day, Captain?*"

Captain? Recognition came to Dee in a flash: the uniform, the braids on the man's collar. *Twailin Royal Guard? Betrayed!*

Dee plunged his hands into the pockets of his long coat and drew out his crossbows, pulling the first triggers as soon as they were clear. The bows snapped into place...and he froze. He had two shots, but three targets. *The captain and the dog? The wizard and the captain? The wizard and the dog?* Regardless of his choice, he would lose—there would be no time to reload before the third killed him.

The captain's eyes went wide and he raised his crossbow again. The dog growled and hunched its shoulders.

"Stop it, you two!" Woefler raised his hand again, and the air between them shimmered with light. "We're all *friends* here. Well, most of us, anyway." He cast a wary glance at the dog.

Dee hesitated. He had no choice but to trust Woefler. If he didn't, he'd never get help for Mya in time. He lowered his weapons and folded the bows. The sprigs clicked, and he returned the crossbows to their pockets. The captain placed his own crossbow on his desk before him.

"What's this about, Woefler, and who's *he?*" The captain pointed accusatively at Dee.

Woefler shook himself, banishing the barrier of light. Taking a step back from the dog, he held out a hand toward each of the two men. "Master Dee, this is Captain Norwood, commander of the Twailin Royal Guard. Captain, this is Master Dee. He's assistant to Miss Moirin, the young woman who saved the emperor's life at the coronation. You may remember I spoke of her."

"Well!" Norwood's whole countenance changed. Smiling broadly, he grabbed a cane, limped out from behind the desk, and stuck a beefy hand out to Dee. "Well, then, I'm sorry for the misunderstanding, and very pleased to meet you. Woefler has indeed told me of your mistress' actions at the coronation. She sounds like an amazing woman."

Dee swallowed a hard lump in his throat and shook the man's hand. "Yes…yes, she is."

"So…" Norwood looked back and forth between Dee and Woefler, "to what do I owe the honor of such an…uh…abrupt visit?"

"We're here on a matter of extreme urgency, Captain." Woefler's voice brimmed with excitement, which seemed to Dee a far cry from his subdued behavior at the restaurant. "And extreme *secrecy*!"

Norwood leaned back against his desk, rolling his eyes. "You and your *mysteries*, Woefler."

"Captain, I assure you, this is not *my* mystery!" the wizard insisted. "The emperor *himself* has commanded any assistance we can give Master Dee in…well, I'll let him tell you the details."

"Uh…" Dee wished Woefler had just dropped him on a street corner and let him get on with this on his own. "Miss Moirin's been captured. I need to talk with some people, then get back to Tsing with an associate, so I'm not sure why we're bothering the captain here."

Woefler shrugged. "Because nobody else in Twailin can get you what you need faster and with the least fuss!"

The captain nodded in acknowledgement. "I'll certainly do all I can, but some background would help. Who could possibly have captured Miss Moirin? By all accounts, she's damn near invulnerable."

There's no way around this if I'm ever going to get out of here, Dee decided, but that didn't mean he had to tell everything.

"Magic was used to trap her, Captain. Miss Moirin was assigned a mission by the emperor that involved retrieving…some stolen items from the same group responsible for the recent assassination attempts. They operate under orders from the former emperor's spiritual advisor, Hoseph."

"Hoseph?" Norwood surged to his feet.

"You know him?" Dee asked, startled.

"I've…encountered him. He tried to kill me, in fact." Norwood reached over and scratched behind the dog's ears. "That's the reason for Brutus, here, and my reaction when you two popped in."

Dee stared in shocked silence. *Hoseph tried to kill the captain of the Twailin Royal Guard? Why?*

"Ahhh…" Woefler nodded knowingly. "So that was who—"

"I'm not…at liberty…to discuss the details." Norwood stared down the wizard, then turned back to Dee. "Please continue."

"To make a long story short, Miss Moirin was kidnapped by the group Hoseph is working with, and we're trying to find her. That's why I need to contact my associates here."

"But why are you here in Twailin," Norwood asked, "if all this happened in Tsing?"

"Miss Moirin is from Twailin," Dee explained, wondering how best to weave a tapestry of truth and lies. "She…trained here and has many professional associates still here who may be able to help."

"I'm surprised you don't know her, actually," Woefler said to the captain. "A woman of her skills, in security…"

Norwood raised his eyebrows and considered the information for a moment before slowly shaking his head. "No, I've never heard of a young woman with such abilities, but then, I'm not well-acquainted with those in private security."

Dee flinched when both men turned inquiring eyes on him. "She…likes to keep a low profile."

"Well!" Norwood clapped his hands together. "If we're to save Miss Moirin from that motherless son of a—well, from Hoseph, then we'd best get to it!"

Finally! Dee stood. "Thank you, Captain. If you could just loan me a horse, I can send it back—"

"I can do better than that!" Norwood limped past them to his office door, opened it, and shouted. "Sergeant Flax! My carriage and a horse squad. Immediately!"

"Sir!" The sergeant dashed off.

"Brutus, heel!" Norwood snapped his fingers, and the huge dog trotted past them to the captain's side. "Let's go, Master Dee. Woefler, are you coming, too?"

"No, I've got my own things to do. Just contact me when you're ready, Master Dee. The Captain knows how."

Dee stared aghast at the captain. "You're going *with* me?"

"Of course! Nothing will stand in your way with me at your side." With that, the captain strode out of the office as fast as he could manage with his cane, his dog at his heel.

Woefler grinned at Dee. "See? Captain Norwood gets things done."

"So I've heard." Dee fell into step behind the captain. "I just didn't expect him to be so…enthusiastic."

Hoseph materialized in Otar's grimy little room and staggered. Grateful that the former Imperial Guard captain wasn't there to see his distress, he dosed himself with elixir. His headache, nausea, and fatigue faded away. Settling carefully onto the only chair in the room—though rickety and looking ready to collapse, it was a more appealing seat than the rumpled bed with its grubby sheets—he pulled a flier from his pocket and unfolded it. Reading it yet again, he smiled.

Soon enough, Arbuckle…soon enough.

Feminine laughter from the hallway drew closer, and shuffling steps stopped outside the door. A key rattled in the lock, and the door opened.

"Hey!" A woman in a low-cut bodice that looked several sizes too small for her ample figure stopped short in the doorway and stared at Hoseph. "Oatie, you didn't tell me there'd be two o' you. That'll cost extra, you know."

"What the—" Otar pushed pasted the woman and espied Hoseph, his eyes narrowing. "Go downstairs, Jacie. I'll be down in a minute."

"But who's this in yer room? I thought you said—"

"Not now! I'll be right down. Go!" Otar pushed the woman outside and closed the door, then whirled toward his unexpected guest. "What the hell are you doing here? I told you not to show up in the evening!"

"I have another assignment for you, Captain." Hoseph pulled a small pouch from his robes and bounced it on the palm of his hand so that the gold inside jingled enticingly.

Otar looked at the pouch and licked his lips. "What kind of assignment?"

Hoseph held up the flier he had snatched off a posterboard. "The emperor has finally finished his New Accords and intends to *personally* read them out to the public. I want you to find out from Chief Constable Dreyfus anything and everything you can about the security surrounding him at this event, and I mean *everything*."

The former captain grimaced. "Security for these things is extensive and hush hush."

"Yes, but you undoubtedly discussed security with the chief before. He trusts you."

"True."

"So he shouldn't have a problem talking with you about this."

"I don't know… It's a lot of work." Otar's gaze crept back to the pouch.

Hoseph flung the pouch onto the bed in disgust. Lust for wealth was a hallmark of the weak and venal. "You'll get more when the job is done…if it's done *well*."

"It'll be done well." The captain snatched up the pouch and hefted it.

"See that it is." Hoseph retrieved his talisman, his mind already beyond this squalid little room and its contemptable occupant. "I'll be in touch."

"Not in the evenings!" Otar snapped as mist devoured the priest.

In the swirling silence of the Sphere of Shadow, Hoseph assessed the status of his plan. The Tessifus boy was secure and in training. The guildmaster and Grandmaster's rings were in his possession, ready to be bestowed as he saw fit. Tynean Tsing III was unwittingly setting himself up for assassination, and with Mya out of action, there'd be no one to save the emperor this time.

Hoseph's fortunes had finally taken a turn for the better. With Demia's blessing, nothing would stop him now.

Chapter XXIV

Dusk faded into night as the Royal Guard carriage rumbled through the streets of Twailin, mounting the hill into Barleycorn Heights. Dee looked wistfully out the window at the familiar streets, the curbside cafés full of people enjoying a respite from the sweltering summer day. Had it only been a few months since he'd lived in the townhouse on Greensleeves Way, working as Lad's assistant? It seemed like years.

I'm homesick, he realized. *But home is where your heart is…and mine's in Tsing.*

The carriage slowed and stopped in front of a modest townhouse—Sereth's new home. Dee had only been here once, the night before he left for Tsing. The curtains were drawn, but light leaked around the edges. Hopefully, that meant the guildmaster was home.

"Here we are!" Captain Norwood grabbed the door latch and righted his cane.

"Please, Captain," Dee said before Norwood could open the door, "let me to speak with my associates alone. Those in the security business are very careful and private people, and…well…a squad of armed Royal Guards at the door might be misconstrued."

The guard captain frowned, but nodded. "If you think that best, I suppose. But let me know if they give you any trouble. The emperor's ordered cooperation with your mission; that goes for private citizens as well."

"Of course. Thank you, Captain."

Dee strode toward the townhouse door at a sedate pace. He had no doubt that assassins were watching him from both inside and outside the house and didn't want to give them any reason to feel threatened. A force of Royal Guards perched on the curb was threatening enough. With Hoseph on the prowl and the guild on alert, Sereth's nerves were undoubtedly already frayed thin.

And who knows what's happened since I've been gone. For all Dee knew, the priest had killed half of the Twailin guild, maybe even Sereth. He held his breath and knocked.

The door opened, and Dee breathed a sigh of relief at the sight of a familiar face—a journeyman Blade. Back in the shadows of the foyer, invisible from Captain Norwood's vantage, two more journeymen stood ready, crossbows aimed straight at Dee.

"What's going on, Dee?" the Blade asked, his eyes cold and tone hard.

"Don't overreact, Gerri!" Dee hissed between clenched teeth. "Everything's all right. Believe it or not, the guard's just here to watch out for me…but it's a long story. This is an emergency. I need to see Sereth."

"But that's—"

"—the captain of the Royal Guard. And if he thinks that you're not cooperating with me, then he and his men are going to come up here and make that sure that you do, and then we'll have all Nine Hells full of trouble. Just let me in and get Sereth."

"If this is some kind of trap…"

"Then I'll be the first to die! Now get Sereth before Captain Norwood gets suspicious!"

The Blade's eyes narrowed, but he nodded to one of the others. "Get him."

A moment later Sereth strode to the door, a broad smile on his face, obviously aware that he was in full sight of the Royal Guard. "Dee! How are you? Come on in!" He extended a friendly hand.

Dee clasped Sereth's hand and felt the inexorable pressure of the Blade's grip pulling him into the house.

"Wave goodbye to your new friends, Dee." Sereth's hissed whisper belied his pleasant expression.

Dee painted on a smile and waved to Captain Norwood, held up a single finger. "Back in a minute!"

Gerri shut the door, and assassins closed in around them. Even if Dee wanted to, he'd never get to his crossbows before being pierced by enough steel to arm a squad of knights.

"What the hell's going on? Why did you bring the Royal Guard to my home?" Sereth's voice was low and dangerous.

"It couldn't be helped, but don't worry about them. We've got bigger problems. Mya's been taken by Hoseph's people."

"Shit!" Sereth clenched his fists. "How the hell could they have done that? I've *seen* her fight, Dee. She's unstoppable."

Dee huffed a laugh. "You don't know the half of it."

"Apparently not. I do know that she's now my Grandmaster. Lad sent me a note with this." Sereth held up his hand, and the gold and obsidian ring on his finger glinted in the light.

At least Lad made it back safely. Dee breathed a sigh of relief.

"Master." Gerri was staring out the door's viewing glass. "The captain's gotten out of the carriage and is walking back and forth, and he's got a *huge* dog with him."

Sereth held his hand toward the door and turned to Dee. "Explain. Fast."

Dee took a deep breath. "Hoseph killed the Tsing guildmaster and the ranks split. The Blades, Enforcers, and Hunters are loyal to Mya, but the Inquisitors and Alchemists sided with Hoseph. They had some big plan to kill the crown prince and put their own puppet on the throne, but Mya thwarted the assassination attempt at the coronation, and—"

"That was *Mya*?" The guildmaster's eyes widened. "We'd heard vague stories, but..." He shook his head. "Go on."

"The emperor asked her to rescue some noble's kids that Hoseph had had kidnapped. When we were getting the last one...she...*we* walked into a trap. She got me out, but...not herself." Dee's voice petered out.

"Don't second-guess yourself, Dee." Sereth's tone was stern, but held none of the disgust that Dee had expected. "*Never* second-guess yourself, or you'll never get through your next assignment. So, they took Mya. Do you think she's still alive? It must have been a week or two ago that—"

"No, no! It was just last night. That's where the Royal Guard comes in. The emperor has pledged whatever help we need to get her back, so Duke Mir's wizard transported me here magically. Unfortunately," he threw a baleful glance toward the front of the house, "he brought me to Captain Norwood, thinking that the quickest way to get anything done was with an official escort, and the good captain is overly keen on fulfilling his duty. Turning him down would only make him suspicious."

"So, why did you come to Twailin?"

Dee proceeded carefully. "Since they didn't kill Mya, they might be interrogating her for information on the Twailin guild. I thought you should know."

Sereth nodded gravely. "The Hunters will be the most vulnerable. You were her assistant, maybe you can talk with—"

"No." Dee shook his head firmly. "Sorry, Sereth, but I can't take the time. I have to get back to Tsing, but I need your help with something first."

"Of course, but wait one second. Tomin!"

"Sir!" A young woman ran up.

"Send runners to all the other masters telling them to shore up defenses, move any headquarters that existed before Mya left for Tsing. I'll get more to them later."

"Right away, Master!" She took off toward the back of the house.

"So, Dee, what else?"

"I need you to come with me to the *Tap and Kettle*."

Sereth's eyes widened, then narrowed. "Lad's not guild anymore, Dee. He won't leave his family."

"He will. He *has* to!" Dee noted the subtle shifting of the journeymen Blades at his outburst and forced himself to calm down.

Sereth frowned and shook his head. "I have people watching the inn. He's barely left the place since he returned from Tsing. If you didn't know him, you'd think he'd been an innkeeper all his life. He's not going to like you giving him ultimatums."

"I know." Dee swallowed hard. He knew better than anyone Lad's desire for a quiet life with his family, the devastation Wiggen's death had wrought. *If there was any other way...but there's not.* "I don't really care if he likes it or not. He's the one who got Mya *into* this mess, and he's the only person who can get her out of it."

Sereth blinked at Dee in surprise. "Tsing has changed you, Dee. You wouldn't have even *considered* confronting Lad before. Why do you need me there?"

"Because you're going to tell him that you'll look after his family while he's gone, and because you're a guildmaster and I'm only an assistant. Also because he rescued your wife, so you and he have some...connection that I don't understand." Sereth opened his mouth, but Dee raised a forestalling hand. "I don't *need* to understand it, but if I can't convince Lad to do the right thing, maybe you can."

Sereth glanced toward the stairs that lead to the second story, licked his lips, and sighed. "I don't know how much good it will do, but I'll go. The convincing, however, I'll leave up to you."

"Thank you." Dee's hopes rose as he turned toward the door. "Oh, and Mya's known to the authorities as Moirin, a bodyguard from Twailin, recently moved to Tsing."

"I can work with that." Sereth opened the front door.

"You want company, Master?" Gerri asked, obviously not happy about Sereth taking a carriage ride with the Captain of the Royal Guard.

"No, that'd just cause trouble. Don't worry. Tell Jinny," his eyes flicked upstairs again, "that I'll be back soon."

Dee led the way down the walk to the carriage, glad to see that the royal guards seemed unconcerned by their wait, conversing quietly.

"Captain Norwood, I'd like to introduce Sereth VonBruce." He gestured to Sereth. "He's a long-time acquaintance of Miss Moirin, and has offered to help us."

"VonBruce." Norwood extended a hand. "I know that name... Oh! You're a dueling instructor, aren't you?"

"A swordmaster, yes, Captain." Sereth shook the captain's hand amiably. "Nice to know I have a reputation with the Royal Guard."

"And you run a security company, hiring out bodyguards. In fact, you used to *be* a bodyguard, didn't you?"

Sereth shot Dee a sharp look as he bowed his head in acknowledgement of the captain's question. "Yes, I did. I imagine your Sergeant Tamir told you that he interviewed me about my former employer, Horice DeVough?"

Dee admired Sereth's aplomb in the face of Norwood's subtle probing. He'd forgotten Sereth's report that the Royal Guard sergeant had come around asking questions after Horice's death.

The guildmaster's candor seemed to take the captain off guard. Norwood grimaced for an instant, then pasted a smile back on his face. "Yes, it was Tam who told me about you. Did Miss Moirin work for you as a bodyguard?"

Sereth smiled. "No, Captain, she didn't work for me, but she's a friend."

"Shall we go?" Dee gestured toward the carriage. They couldn't afford to waste time on pleasantries. "We can talk on the way."

"Of course." Norwood snapped his fingers, and the mastiff hopped back in the carriage, followed by the three men.

Dee and Sereth settled onto the seat across from the Royal Guard captain, shifting their feet to avoid the enormous bulk of the dog on the floor. As the driver flicked the reins and the carriage picked up speed, Norwood said, "Where are we off to next?"

"The *Tap and Kettle*. It's an inn in—"

"Eastmarket," Norwood finished.

"You know the place?" Dee asked.

"I do." Norwood shouted orders to the driver without taking his eyes off of Dee and Sereth. "They have wonderful ale and cookies."

The ensuing silence hung so thickly it felt smothering. As Dee turned to the window for air, he felt Sereth stiffen beside him, and looked back to see Captain Norwood staring at the guildmaster's hands...and the ring on his finger.

The captain looked up, his expression as clouded as a stormy day. As if sensing his master's unease, Brutus growled deep in his chest, the vibration thrumming through the carriage floor.

Shifting in his seat and adjusting his grip on his cane, Norwood said with a nonchalance that belied his clenched jaw, "Is the young man named Loren who works at the *Tap and Kettle* also an associate of Miss Moirin?"

"Um..." Dee glanced at Sereth, but the guildmaster's eyes remained on the captain. "He...uh...used to be. Loren's just an innkeeper now, but I hoped he'd be willing to help us find Miss Moirin." It wasn't exactly a lie.

"I see."

Sereth spoke up. "Can I ask how you know Loren, Captain?"

"You can ask, Master VonBruce, but I'm not going to tell you, just like your associate Master Dee hasn't told me everything that's going on here." He clenched his thick jaw, the muscles bunching like walnuts.

Silence shrouded the rest of the trip, each man tense and watching the others. Brutus was the only one with even a semblance of ease, panting and drooling all over the floor. Dee was relieved when they finally pulled into the courtyard of the *Tap and Kettle*. A confrontation with Lad couldn't be any tenser than this carriage ride had been.

"Thank you for the ride, Captain. We'll be out as soon as we can."

"Oh, no," Norwood said as he levered himself out the door with his cane and snapped for Brutus to heel. "I'm coming in with you."

Dee swallowed hard and looked to Sereth, but the guildmaster just shrugged. "Of course, Captain. No problem at all."

They strode toward the steps of the inn behind the captain.

Like three blind fools into the den of a dragon.

The Alchemists worked on Lakshmi with brutal efficiency, peeling off the old skin and stitching on the new. They swabbed and sliced, clamped, dosed, and bandaged with no conversation apart from Kittal's terse orders.

This time they woke Lakshmi before she left the table. The Master Inquisitor emerged from the anesthetic coughing and wheezing, grimacing as Kittal's assistants helped her sit up, her face twisted in pain.

Mya hoped it hurt a lot.

"Drink this." Kittal pressed a glass of clear liquid into the woman's shaking hands. "It'll blunt the pain and restore the blood you lost."

Lakshmi drank greedily and drew a ragged breath. Her grimace eased as the drug took hold. "Better."

"Now you sleep, Lakshmi." Kittal motioned to his assistants and they brought over a stretcher.

"Yes…" Lakshmi didn't struggle as they lifted her, but gripped Kittal's sleeve as they started to take her away. "I want…more, Kittal. As soon as we can."

"Of course." The Alchemist glanced at Mya. "We'll take more grafts while you rest. As soon as you're ready, we'll continue."

"Good." Lakshmi lay back and closed her eyes as they took her away.

When the door closed, Kittal took a deep breath and let it out slowly, fatigue etching his face. Mya studied him closely. He wasn't an old man—certainly nowhere near as old as Lakshmi—but he wasn't young either. *Maybe he'll drop dead*, she thought wistfully, but it seemed that the gods weren't on her side. After a stretch, he turned to Mya with a determined expression, surveying her like a carcass ready to be cut up into manageable pieces.

"Once you've got everything cleaned up here, Berta, we'll take more grafts."

Mya wanted to scream, to rage, to threaten, but refused to give the Master Alchemist the satisfaction of witnessing her desperation.

"Master." Berta had been collecting soiled linens and swabs. Dropping them into a bucket, she looked at Kittal. "I'm concerned about Mya's condition. She's lost a lot of blood, and her rate of healing will only decrease as we take more runes, especially with so little time between collections. In a weakened state, the pain could send her into shock, perhaps even kill her. As you said, she has to survive to the end."

Mya held her breath. She'd misjudged the woman. Berta had decided to help her, at least, as much as she could.

"Yes, that is a concern." Kittal tapped his lips with a finger, then shrugged. "I suppose you're right. Give her a restorative for blood loss and some opium for the pain."

Berta pulled jars from a shelf and began mixing powders into a cup of water. Carrying the glass of cloudy liquid to the table, she supported Mya's head and helped her drink.

Mya swallowed it down without a word, hoping that Berta would see the gratitude in her eyes. The woman didn't look at her, which wasn't surprising with Kittal watching. When the glass was empty, the Master Alchemist turned away. Already, Mya could feel the drugs at work. Like a cup of Paxal's mulled wine, its warmth radiated from her stomach, relaxing her, strengthening her resolve. Berta had given her more than relief from the pain, she'd given her hope.

I'm not going to die.

They had taken the Grandmaster's ring, and they would take her runes, but she'd survived before she had them, and she'd survive after. As long as she had breath, she would try to escape. And once she did…

Vengeance almost destroyed Lad, her conscience reminded her.

Lad is why I'm here in the first place! Mya recalled the moment he slipped the Grandmaster's ring onto her finger, how sweet it had been…until she realized what he'd done. His kiss wasn't love, as she'd hoped, it was betrayal.

And it wasn't the first time love had betrayed her.

Mother… She clenched her hands. The blood was still there, a stain she could never remove. She'd loved the guild, and it, too, had turned against her.

Love is a weakness…

Dee loves you, whispered the voice. *Dee will find you. Just wait…*

No! Mya shoved the voice into the deepest recesses of her mind. What if Dee failed? Should she take her last breath on this table while waiting for a lover who would never come? No, she couldn't depend on Dee to save her. She could only depend on herself.

Across the room, Kittal worked on his loathsome machine. Every soft rasp of file on steel as he sharpened the peeler fed Mya's anger, kindled her rage into a roaring hatred.

Hate…

Hate will keep me alive.

EPILOGUE

"I'll take these to be washed if you wipe down the tables." Josie hefted the loaded tray of empty dishes, balancing it on her shoulder as she made her way to the kitchen.

"Sure." The weight would have been nothing to Lad, but he wouldn't insult his mother-in-law by suggesting that he take it instead. Besides, Forbish was waiting in the kitchen for her so they could eat a late supper together.

The dinner rush was over, and only a few patrons still relaxed over their meals. The quiet was a nice break from the boisterous revelry of the laborers who came in for a quick ale after work. If he listened carefully, Lad could hear Lissa snoring sweetly in their bedroom.

The front door opened, and Lad looked up.

A beefy man in uniform limped in, leaning heavily on a cane, a massive dog at his side.

"Captain!" It hadn't been long since Norwood came to see him at the inn. The man's heartfelt thanks had touched Lad, and they'd parted friends. Though he hadn't been at all sure that the captain would actually come back, Lad had hoped he would. Smiling and waving toward a chair by the hearth, he asked, "An ale and some cookies?"

"Loren," the captain said, his voice grave and tinged with unease. "I've brought someone to see you."

Two men entered behind Norwood, and Lad froze.

Sereth? Dee?

Heat flushed through Lad's body, the runes tattooed upon his skin tingling as if ants trundled along his nerves. The mastiff at Norwood's hip flattened its ears and growled.

No wonder, I must stink of magic right now.

"Loren." Sereth nodded and flashed a covert hand signal—all clear, no immediate danger.

Dee strode forward, his gaze clear and direct. "We need your help."

Never had Lad thought to see these three men together. *Why...* He could think of only one possible reason.

"What kind of trouble is Mya in now?"

About the Author

From the sea to the stars, Chris A. Jackson's stories take you to the far reaches of the imagination. Raised on the back deck of a fishing boat and trained as a marine biologist, he became sidetracked by a career in biomedical research, but regained his heart and soul in 2009 when he and his wife Anne left the dock aboard the 45-foot sailboat *Mr Mac* to cruise the Caribbean and write fulltime.

With his nautical background, writing sea stories seemed inevitable for Chris. His acclaimed Scimitar Seas nautical fantasies won three consecutive Gold Medals in the *ForeWord Reviews* Book of the Year Awards. His Pathfinders Tales from Paizo Publishing combine high-seas combat and romance set in the award-winning world of the Pathfinder Roleplaying Game. Not to be outdone, Privateer Press released *Blood & Iron*, a swashbuckling novella set in the Iron Kingdoms.

Chris' repertoire also includes the award-winning and Kindle best-selling Weapon of Flesh Series, the contemporary urban fantasy *Dragon Dreams*, as well as additional fantasy novels, the humorous sci fi Cheese Runners trilogy of novellas, and numerous short stories.

To learn more, please visit jaxbooks.com.

Novels by Chris A. Jackson

From Jaxbooks
A Soul for Tsing
Deathmask

Weapon of Flesh Trilogy
Weapon of Flesh
Weapon of Blood
Weapon of Vengeance

Weapon of Flesh Trilogy II
(with Anne L. McMillen-Jackson)
Weapon of Fear
Weapon of Pain
Weapon of Mercy (summer 2017)

The Cornerstones Trilogy
(with Anne L. McMillen-Jackson)
Zellohar
Nekdukarr
Jundag

The Cheese Runners Trilogy
(novellas)
Cheese Runners
Cheese Rustlers
Cheese Lords

From Dragon Moon Press
Scimitar Moon
Scimitar Sun
Scimitar's Heir
Scimitar War

From Paizo Publishing
Pirate's Honor
Pirate's Promise
Pirate's Prophecy
Pirate's Curse (early 2017)

From Privateer Press
Blood & Iron (ebook novella)

From The Ed Greenwood Group
Hellmaw: Dragon Dreams

Check out these and more at

JAXBOOKS. COM

Want to get an email about my next book release?
Sign up at http://eepurl.com/xnrUL